The SURVIVALIST
(Freedom Lost)

Books by Dr. Arthur T. Bradley

෨ ෪

Handbook to Practical Disaster Preparedness for the Family

The Prepper's Instruction Manual

Disaster Preparedness for EMP Attacks and Solar Storms

Process of Elimination: A Thriller

The Survivalist (Frontier Justice)

The Survivalist (Anarchy Rising)

The Survivalist (Judgment Day)

The Survivalist (Madness Rules)

The Survivalist (Battle Lines)

The Survivalist (Finest Hour)

The Survivalist (Last Stand)

The Survivalist (Dark Days)

The Survivalist (Freedom Lost)

The Survivalist (National Treasure)

෨ ෪

Available in print, ebook, and audiobook at all major resellers or at:
http://disasterpreparer.com

The SURVIVALIST
(Freedom Lost)

Arthur T. Bradley, Ph.D.

The Survivalist
(Freedom Lost)

Author:	Arthur T. Bradley, Ph.D.
Email:	arthur@disasterpreparer.com
Website:	http://disasterpreparer.com

Illustrations used throughout the book are privately owned and copyright protected. Special thanks are extended to Siobhan Gallagher for editing, Marites Bautista for print layout, Park Myers and Vanessa McCutcheon for proofreading, and Nikola Nevenov for illustrations and cover design. Special thanks to John Avoli for graciously showing me around both the DeJarnette Center and the Frontier Culture Museum.

ISBN 10: 1540326667
ISBN 13: 978-1540326669

Printed in the United States of America

FOREWORD

The first African slaves arrived in Jamestown, Virginia, in 1619 to aid the colonists in farming tobacco and other lucrative crops. By the Revolutionary War, slavery had become a full-fledged institution, with slaves being recognized as a distinct societal class. Most slaves were brought over from West Africa and forced to endure the "Middle Passage." En route, they were chained together in the tight confines of the ship's hull and forced to ride as cargo on a horrific journey across the Atlantic. An estimated two million slaves died at sea, a full 15% of those bound for the New World. The number of fatalities was closer to four million, if loss of life due to capture, suicide, and other factors are considered. Surprisingly, only about 388,000 slaves were shipped directly to North America, with the vast majority transported to the Caribbean and South America.

The journey across the Atlantic varied from one to six months, depending on weather conditions. Slave ships typically contained several hundred slaves, with only a few dozen crew to manage them. The males were shackled at the ankles using iron bilboes and only infrequently allowed to exit the hold to breathe fresh air. At most, slaves were fed once a day, although such meals were always contingent on the crew eating first. Diseases were rampant throughout the slaves' meager living space and included smallpox, dysentery, measles, syphilis, and scurvy. The slave hold was often so foul that crew avoided entering the space, sometimes leaving slaves shackled to dead compatriots for days before finally disposing of the bodies overboard.

Shortly after the Revolutionary War, northern states began to abolish slavery. In 1807, Thomas Jefferson prohibited the importation of new slaves, although it did little to quell the interstate slave trade used to support cotton plantations across the Deep South. By the start of the Civil War in 1861, the slave population had reached four million. It wasn't until President Lincoln's signing of the Emancipation Proclamation in 1863 that slaves were legally declared free. Even with that proclamation, however, it took until the end of the war, in 1865, for their freedoms to be fully bestowed.

There is no scourge quite like slavery. It takes everything from a person—family, dignity, and free will. Slavery is a horror that displays mankind's darkest nature, the willingness to dehumanize another for personal gain. Freedom is a treasure we are fortunate enough to carry with us from our first breath to our last. It neither requires locking away for safekeeping nor shining like a gaudy trinket. Freedom enables us to dream of what is yet to come, to enjoy personal choices, and to experience lifelong exploration. If the very thought of liberty does not cloud your eyes with emotion, you have yet to fully understand it.

"Freedom is never given; it is won."

A. Philip Randolph
1889–1979

For the first time in his life, Deputy Marshal Mason Raines was a wanted man. Thanks to some clever maneuvering by The Farm's CEO Oliver Locke, his photo was likely being hung on the walls of law enforcement offices all across the New Colony. If Mason were lucky, their security forces would be of a mind to apprehend him. Given what he had done to Dix and the rest of his detail, however, he couldn't count on that kind of restraint. More likely, those sent after him would conclude that a little payback was in order, and would be all too happy to parade his lifeless body through the streets as a lesson to others.

Mason believed that his best chance at clearing his name was to reach out to General Carr, the New Colony's Chief of Security. With Norfolk situated at the tip of a peninsula, however, undetected entry would be extremely difficult. Thoroughfares in or out of Norfolk included the Chesapeake Bay Bridge-Tunnel, the Hampton Roads Bridge-Tunnel, the Monitor-Merrimac Bridge-Tunnel, and the much smaller Miller E. Goodwin Bridge that crossed over the Nansemond River. The bridge-tunnels were obvious pinch points, all but impossible to get through without being caught, and the Goodwin Bridge was heavily patrolled to ensure the unimpeded flow of goods between The Farm and the New Colony.

Going in by water was another option, but doing so without having General Carr in on the incursion was also likely doomed to fail. Mason's only chance was to contact Carr remotely to see if they could work out some way in which he could come in as anything less than a hostile combatant. To do that, he would need to gain access to a high-powered amateur radio system and electricity with which to operate it.

Only one idea came to mind, and it required reaching out to an old friend, Jack Atkins. Jack was a self-proclaimed prepper who had spoken with Mason numerous times over the airwaves. He had shared that his residence was in Gloucester, Virginia, a small community just northeast of Newport News, but for obvious reasons, had not broadcast his exact address.

Mason eyed the single-story, L-shaped motel directly before him. A red and white roadway sign read "Gloucester Inn Motel." While phonebooks were at one time ubiquitous in nearly every home, such was no longer the case with the advent of the internet. Motels, however, especially one as dated as the Gloucester Inn, were all but certain to have a phonebook in every bedside drawer.

Even the sight of the worn brick building gave Mason pause. On two previous occasions, he had witnessed the infected living out of motels. While he had no rational explanation for such, it seemed that they were drawn to motels as surely as zombies were to public bathrooms.

Bowie whimpered.

Mason looked down at the big wolfhound and smiled.

"You big baby. For all we know, the place is empty."

Bowie cut his eyes at him, clearly not buying it.

Mason reached down and gave him a little pat on the side.

"It is what it is."

He straightened and brought his M4 to the low-ready position and started toward the closest building. Bowie took a moment to consider his options before reluctantly falling in behind his master.

The manager's office sat to the front of the property. The door had been torn from its hinges and lay atop an abandoned police cruiser. Someone had used black spray paint on the motel's wall to write, "It's over. Why not party?"

Mason approached the open doorway and peered inside. The lobby looked like someone had gone after it with a sledge hammer. Fist-sized holes had been bashed through the walls, tile flooring obliterated into black and white shards, and light fixtures dangled from the ceiling by taut electrical wires. The check-in desk resembled something out of the Overlook Hotel, spatters of dried blood covering an old-time paper register. An open door revealed a small bedroom directly behind the counter, the remains of a decomposing corpse decorating the floor.

Mason stepped cautiously into the office and swept the room with his rifle.

Clear.

Whoever had played demolition derby was long gone.

He tiptoed behind the check-in desk, doing his best to avoid brushing against something brown and sticky smeared along its side. Other than the motel ledger, a small silver bell taped to the counter, and a photograph of an old Indian man and his wife, there wasn't much to see.

Bowie wandered past him and began sniffing the dead body. From the sarong wrapped around his waist, Mason assumed that it was the old man from the photo. His body had decomposed into little more than hair and bones, suggesting he had been dead for several months. A dark cadaver stain surrounded the corpse like a chalk outline at a murder scene. The man's skull had separated from his body and rolled sideways to face a small window, as if trying to enjoy the early morning sunlight.

Beyond the skeleton lay a small bedroom, fitted with a double mattress on the floor and a dresser that had been tipped over and rifled through. Clothes and empty food cans lay scattered about, as did a wicker basket piled high with brightly packaged condoms.

Mason reached down and pocketed a few, not because he was hoping to get lucky but because he knew that they could be used for a whole host of things, including storing water, keeping tinder dry, acting as fishing bobbers and sling shots, and even preventing crud from finding its way into the muzzle of his rifle.

Seeing nothing else of value, he turned and led Bowie back outside.

Together, they stared at a long row of crimson-colored doors. Bowie stood fast, not at all keen to lead the way.

"Think of it like we're contestants on *Let's Make a Deal*. If we pick the right door, there's a prize waiting for us. And if we don't..." He let the words trail off.

While Bowie clearly had no idea what Mason was talking about, the little pep talk was enough to get him moving down the narrow sidewalk. He stopped at the first door and sniffed along its bottom edge. A plastic "Do Not Disturb" placard hung from the doorknob.

Mason cupped his hands and tried to peer in through the window.

No good. The curtains were drawn tight, and even if they hadn't been, a layer of dirt covered the glass that would have required a scraper and a whole bottle of Windex to remove.

Moving to one side of the door, he reached over and gave it a good rap with his knuckles. While some might question the tactical soundness of announcing his presence, Mason thought it only polite to knock before kicking in a door. Who knows? A fellow survivor might be holed up and about to step into the bathtub. Such courtesies tended to keep misunderstandings to a minimum.

No one answered. Nor could Mason hear any movement coming from within.

He turned and heel-kicked just below the lock. The latch broke free, but a swing bar pulled taut, preventing the door from opening more than a few inches. Mason slipped his fingers inside and felt of the bar's construction.

The mechanism seemed to be fairly heavy duty, and while door chains could be knocked in easily enough, bar guards tended to be more resistant to brute force.

Bowie pressed his nose to the narrow gap, doing his best to discern what was inside.

"Hold on, boy. We'll be in soon enough."

Mason pulled the "Do Not Disturb" placard from the doorknob. Lining it up with the bar guard, he carefully eased the door back to the point of being almost closed. Then he pushed the placard forward, swiveling the bar off the guard's fixed lever arm. Once he could no longer feel any resistance with the placard, he gave the door a gentle push.

Voilà. It swung open.

Without waiting, Bowie pushed past him into the room. Two withered bodies lay on the bed, a thin white sheet draped over them. Like the innkeeper, they had died several months earlier and consisted of little more than bones, teeth, and clumps of hair. From the way their bodies were intertwined, it appeared that they had been holding one another to the very end.

The rest of the room was empty except for a nightstand, a television, and a bright green plastic chair that looked like it had been stolen from someone's backyard picnic. A doorway led into a small bathroom, the moldy shower stall visible within. What stood out most, however, was a four-foot-diameter hole in the motel room's wall.

Mason inched closer with his rifle pressed to his shoulder. A similar hole had been smashed through the adjacent room, and another in the room beyond that, forming a veritable tunnel that ran the entire length of the motel.

He stood for a count of thirty, listening.

Other than the gentle patter of Bowie's paws on the stained carpet, it was quiet. If someone or something were in the other rooms, they were either asleep or unwilling to challenge him.

He turned and motioned for Bowie to check the bathroom. The wolfhound immediately complied, and a few seconds later emerged with the fur around his mouth wet. When he saw his master staring at him, he licked the water from his nose as if to say, "What? I was thirsty."

"I'll take that as an all clear," Mason said, moving up to the bathroom door and giving the room a quick sweep. The commode had been torn from the floor, and a hole had been made that was just big enough for a man to squeeze through. "This place is like an ant farm."

Bowie moved closer and poked his head down into the wet hole.

"Leave it. I'm done sloshing through sewers."

Mason returned to the bedroom, sliding the M4 around to hang across his back. As he approached the bed, he noticed a small white box sitting atop the nightstand. The label read "Oral Transmucosal Fentanyl Citrate." Fentanyl—the residing king of opioids. He opened the box and found a dozen individually sealed packages inside. Curious, he popped one open, uncovering what was for all practical purposes a small lollipop. An orange label was wrapped around the base of the stick that read "1600 mcg." From his time in the army, Mason knew that doses of that magnitude were reserved for victims of extreme trauma.

He stuffed the remaining painkillers into a pouch on his backpack. Should he ever suffer a gunshot wound or other grave injury, something that softened the sting might make a trek out of harm's way that much more possible. Besides, medicines were easily traded, and a find as valuable as a box of high-potency opioids was not to be left behind.

Mason studied the bodies. Several spent Fentanyl lozenge sticks lay beside their pillows. He peeled the sheet down. They were naked, except for fuzzy green and red Christmas socks covering the woman's feet. It was hard to tell whether the two were husband and wife, boyfriend and girlfriend, or just two strangers who preferred not to die alone. All Mason could say for certain was that they had gone out together, and in a manner of their own choosing.

He covered them back up and turned his attention to the nightstand. Inside was a Bible with a wad of chewing gum stuck to the cover, a telephone book, and a pack of matches with the motel's name printed on its face. He stuffed the matches into his pack before turning his attention to the phonebook. Using the bed as a makeshift desk, he flipped through the white pages until he found what he was looking for: *Atkins, Jack and Peggy, 3736 Morris Farm Ln, Gloucester, VA*.

Bowie swung his head toward the bathroom, his ears perking up.

Mason became still and listened.

There was a wet sloshing sound, like feet mashing a vat of grapes.

He quickly tore the page from the phonebook, folded it, and stuffed it into his back pocket.

"This isn't our fight. Come on."

Bowie was already darting toward the exit, and Mason hurried after him, pulling the door behind them. As they high-stepped away from the building, a silver RV towing a flatbed trailer pulled into the parking lot. The

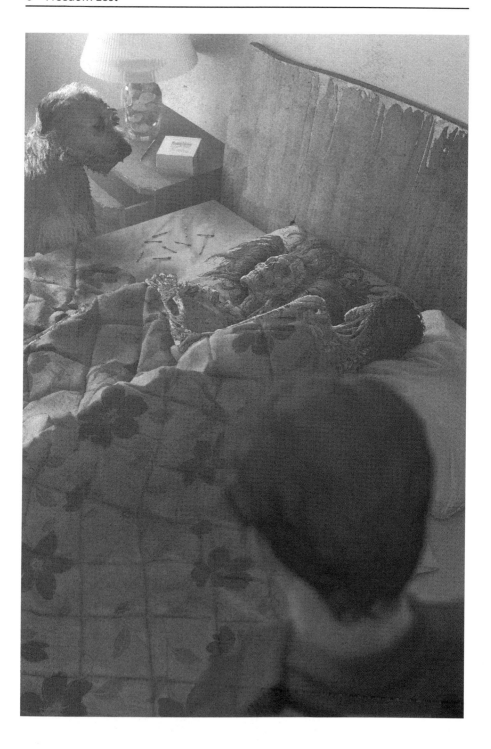

RV looked more like a camper than a bus, measuring twenty-two feet from bumper to bumper and built around a Mercedes dual rear-wheel wide-body chassis. The trailer behind it was a simple welded-steel frame that had likely been designed to haul lawn tractors. Now, however, it was piled high with so much miscellaneous junk that Mason wouldn't have been surprised to see a sign on the side that read "Sanford and Son Salvage."

He counted three men, all of them in the cab of the RV. The man riding shotgun spotted Mason and extended an open hand out the window. Mason reciprocated. A wave not only showed that one's hand was empty of weapons; it also suggested that someone was willing to act in a civilized manner.

By the looks of it, the men were *junkers*, people who made their way by collecting and reselling goods that had been left behind by the dead. Junkers dealt in everything from solar panels to boxes of tampons—anything of value to those trying to survive in the new world. Like all groups of people, there were good ones and bad, those willing to settle for what they could find and those ready to take what they wanted at another's expense.

The RV stopped, and all three men climbed out with short-barreled shotguns in hand. Two moved to stand beside the motel office's door while the third man went inside.

Bowie let out an uneasy growl.

"It's all right, boy. I don't think they mean us any harm." Mason eyed the RV. "Besides, if we play our cards right, maybe we can hitch a ride."

While abandoned vehicles remained easy enough to come by, finding one that had both a working battery and serviceable fuel in the tank was no easy matter. As such, they had been walking since crossing the James River Bridge earlier that morning, and Mason thought it might be nice to give his feet a much-needed rest.

He started toward the motel office, his pace slow and relaxed so as not to alarm the junkers.

As he approached, the two men standing guard visibly stiffened.

"Mister, if you're lookin' for trouble, you might wanna rethink it."

Mason offered an understanding nod. "I would say the same to you."

The man noticed the badge hanging on Mason's belt.

"You some kinda policeman?"

"Deputy Marshal." It was perhaps a bit misleading to identify himself as a lawman given his current circumstances, but Mason had found that it tended to let others know more about his intentions than words ever could.

The junker stepped forward and extended a gloved hand.

"Name's Bartley." He gestured toward the man beside him. "This here's my half-brother, Kyle."

Mason shook Bartley's hand and then Kyle's.

"Mason Raines."

Bartley studied Mason's badge, a silver circle surrounding a five-pointed star.

"I don't think I've ever met a marshal. You, Kyle?"

"Nope."

"Who knows," said Mason. "I may be the last."

Kyle said, "Sounds like a good title for one of them western shoot 'em ups." He briefly changed his voice to sound like that of a TV announcer. "The last marshal stands up to a band of dangerous outlaws." He turned to Mason. "Is that what you do, Marshal?"

Mason glanced back at the motel room that he and Bowie had just scurried away from, the term "lily-livered scaredy-cats" coming to mind.

"Only when I have to."

Bartley followed his gaze, surveying the rundown motel.

"You claimin' this spot?"

Mason knew that junkers were very territorial, often staking claim to buildings they considered ripe for the taking.

"Based on what I saw, there's all kinds of trouble waiting inside those rooms. But if you boys have a mind to, it's all yours. I got what I needed."

That last part seemed to interest both junkers, no doubt fearing that he had already removed "the good stuff." Hoping to put their minds at ease, Mason pulled the phonebook page from his back pocket and unfolded it.

"I was looking for an address." He held the page out to Bartley. "I don't suppose you know where I could find Morris Farm Lane?"

Bartley took a long look at the page, thinking. He glanced over at his brother.

"Morris Farm. That's up by Capahosic, ain't it?"

Kyle nodded. "Not much out that way though, 'cept for farms and such."

Mason nodded his thanks. "Any idea how far?"

"Ten, maybe fifteen miles." Bartley looked around the parking lot. There were a handful of cars, but none looked like they had been recently moved. "You needin' a ride?"

"If it wouldn't be too much trouble. I'd be happy to offer a trade, of course."

Before a deal could be reached, the third junker stepped out from the motel's office. He was big and smelled like sour mash—an odor that Mason had been unfortunate enough to experience firsthand thanks to an old moonshiner.

"And you are?" the junker said, revealing a mouth full of yellowed teeth.

"He's the last Marshal," Bartley said as if introducing a movie star.

Still hoping for that ride, Mason extended his hand.

"Mason Raines."

The big man stared at his hand, making no move to shake it. He turned to Bartley and Kyle.

"What'd you two tell him?"

Bartley's eyes tightened. "We didn't tell him nothin'."

"Good, 'cause you both got big mouths."

"Come on, Hoss," said Kyle. "He ain't out for nothin' of ours."

Hoss turned back and looked Mason up and down, his eyes occasionally flicking over to Bowie, who had developed a steady rumble in his chest.

"What are you doin' here, anyway?"

Before Mason could inform Hoss that where he went was no one's business but his own, Bartley said, "He's lookin' for a ride up to Morris Farm."

Hoss met Mason's eyes. "We ain't no taxi service."

"He said he'd pay us," Kyle added.

"Yeah? Pay us what?" Hoss leaned around to get a peek at Mason's pack. "Don't look like he has much."

"What is it you need?" asked Mason.

Hoss looked back at the trailer attached to the RV.

"It look like we need anything?"

"You must need something or you wouldn't be poking around this old dump."

The big man pressed his lips together, thinking.

"You got any candy?"

"I have a chocolate bar."

"A big one? Or one of them little pissy things?"

Mason lowered his pack to the ground and pulled out a large Hershey chocolate bar. On another occasion, it would have been worth more than a ride across town, but at the moment his feet were telling him otherwise.

"Will this one do?"

Hoss seemed more interested in Mason's pack.

"What are those? Perc-a-pops?"

Mason glanced down and saw that the fentanyl lozenges were visible. He quickly closed the flap. While he wasn't opposed to trading the medications, doing so with the likes of Hoss would have felt a bit too much like drug dealing.

"Those aren't for trade."

"Why the hell not?"

"It's why he's goin' to Morris Farm," Bartley blurted. "He's takin' them to a sick kid. Ain't that right, Marshal?" Clearly Bartley was trying to keep things from getting out of hand.

Mason held out the candy bar.

"You want this or not?"

Hoss seemed unable to let the fentanyl go.

"All right then," Mason said, tearing open the candy. He snapped off a piece and put it in his mouth. "Umm, that's good. Say what you want about those fancy brands. There's nothing quite like good old Hershey."

Everything stood still for a moment as Hoss let differing desires duke it out. Finally, he reached out and grabbed the candy bar.

"Quit eatin' my damn chocolate."

Bartley and Kyle both sighed with relief.

"We should go ahead and get a move on, right, Hoss? Ain't no reason to hang around this place. The marshal says monster freaks are all up inside it." While it wasn't exactly what Mason had said, Bartley's description was probably fairly accurate.

Hoss bit off a big chunk of the candy bar, and when he spoke, the chocolate was smeared across his front teeth.

"Your dog coming too?"

"Of course."

"Then you two are ridin' in the trailer. I don't want no mutt stinkin' up my camper."

Mason nodded, doing his best to hide a grin.

"We most definitely wouldn't want that."

Tanner and Samantha stood in front of the Raines' family cabin, the sun just beginning to light the trees around them. He hadn't said ten words since getting up, and she knew that it was because of his concern for Issa. Desperate to show the women of her colony that they could become pregnant, Issa had departed for Mount Weather some forty-eight hours earlier but had yet to return. That could only mean one thing.

Something had gone wrong.

Samantha tossed her pack into the bed of the Power Wagon as Tanner struggled to unfold a map and lay it across the hood. The sheet metal was cold and damp from the early morning dew, and she had to reach across to help smooth the bunched-up paper.

"Issa would have avoided the highway," she said. "That leaves out I-81."

Tanner grunted, studying the map.

"If she went east to Greensboro, she could have taken Highway 29 all the way up to Mount Weather."

He grunted again.

Samantha turned and looked up at him.

"Did you eat breakfast?"

"Huh?"

"Breakfast? Did you eat?"

"Of course."

"Did you have enough?"

He squinted. "What are you getting at?"

"It's just that you're snorting more than usual."

"I'll have you know that I ate fried potatoes, four eggs, and some of that stuff we pretend is bacon."

She shrugged. "A start, I guess."

Tanner growled and turned back to the map.

"Issa would have skipped Boone. She's never felt comfortable around those folks." He ran a finger up a small highway that cut north through the Blue Ridge Mountains. "I'm thinking she went straight up Highway 421 through Mountain City, and then turned east on Highway 11. That would get her almost all the way there."

"Highway 11…" she said, frowning. "Why's that sound familiar?"

"Haven't the foggiest."

Samantha began tracing the highway. "Wait a minute," she said, her voice rising. "That goes right by the Natural Bridge!"

"So?"

"So that's where we ran into that crazy army guy with the bow!"

"He's dead. You know that."

"Still, what if he had friends?"

"He didn't."

"How do you know?"

"He wasn't the friend-making kind of guy."

She mused on that for a moment.

"Fine. But we're not stopping there or anywhere else along the way. Agreed?"

"Okay by me." He folded up the map and took a moment to count the jerry cans in the back of the pickup. Four cans, each filled with five gallons of fuel. It should be enough, but just barely so.

"Why are we bringing those anyway? Can't we just siphon gas from cars along the way?"

"We're bringing them because most of the gas left in cars is about as useful as grape Kool-Aid."

"Now why'd you have to go and bring up Kool-Aid?" she said, licking her lips. "You know I miss that stuff."

"My point was that gas is degrading."

"Why's it doing that?"

"Because back in the early 2000s, the powers that be started mixing ethanol into fuel to make it burn cleaner."

"That's a good thing, right?"

"Well sure, but nothing's free. Ethanol-blended gas only lasts a few months before it starts to absorb water. Once that happens, it doesn't burn right. Not to mention that the water rusts out a car's fuel system."

Samantha furrowed her brow. "Is the gas in cars like that now? All watery?"

"If it's not there already, it's getting darn close."

"All of it?"

"Ninety, ninety-five percent. Darn near all of it."

A worried look came over her face.

"Does that mean the world's going to run out of gas? That we won't have enough for cars or generators? We'll be back to the horse and buggy days!"

"Nothing wrong with horses *or* buggies." When she started to protest further, he said, "But don't worry. I suspect there's plenty of gas without ethanol sitting at the refineries. Someone just has to go and get it."

"But not us."

He shook his head. "Not us. Not today, anyway."

She glanced over at a small gravity-fed fuel pump they had installed along the side of the cabin.

"What about our gas? Is it turning watery too?"

"It took some effort, but I managed to get nearly a hundred gallons of the good stuff. Unfortunately, thanks to our little trip over to the nuclear plant, we only have about half of it left."

She nodded toward the jerry cans.

"Are those enough to get to Mount Weather and back?"

"They are, as long as we don't get sidetracked."

"Then we're doomed for sure."

"What makes you say that?"

"When was the last time we didn't get sidetracked?" She waited for an answer, and when it didn't come, said, "Never, that's when."

"If we end up walking, so be it."

"Easy for you to say. You like walking." Samantha didn't complain about much, but walking long distances was on her short list of bellyaches.

"I'll have you know that some doctors say that putting one's feet in contact with the earth provides all kinds of health benefits. They call it *grounding*."

Samantha seemed surprised. "Really? Is that why you walk so much?"

"Of course not. I walk to get from one place to the other."

"But what about the doctors?"

"Nut jobs, every last one of them."

She rolled her eyes. "Has anyone ever told you that you make no sense whatsoever."

"Never."

Samantha scoffed. "Yeah, right."

He smiled, and they stared at each other for a moment. Another journey was about to begin, and they both felt the flutter of butterflies.

"You feed your chickens?"

"Of course. Did you leave a note for Issa in case she comes back while we're gone?"

"Of course," he said, mimicking her tone.

"Then I guess we're about as ready as we're going to get." Samantha swung open the driver's-side door and scrambled into the cab of the big truck. "Another day, another dollar."

"How's that?" he said, climbing in.

"My dad used to say that. It means that each day costs you a little something."

Tanner rarely corrected Samantha's misunderstandings of idioms. While it was probably not very parent-like to allow her to keep the misconceptions, he enjoyed hearing her humorous takes on such phrases.

"Sounds good to me," he said, starting the truck.

"What do you think today's going to cost *us?*" she said, staring down the long dusty driveway.

He popped the truck into gear. "Doesn't matter."

"Why not?"

"Because, darlin', we're going to pay it either way."

ও৵ ৵ও

They weren't even out of the driveway before life reminded them of the old adage about the best laid plans. A dark blue Impala barreled up the dirt road, bouncing over potholes as it narrowly avoided careening into the trees.

Tanner hit the brakes and reached for his sawed-off shotgun.

"It's Father Paul," Samantha said, laying her hand on his. Father Paul only infrequently came to visit, and never at such an early hour. "Something's wrong."

As the car drew closer, it came to an abrupt stop, sending a cloud of dust over the Power Wagon. Tanner and Samantha barely had time to open their doors before Father Paul climbed out and hurried toward them. He was a portly man, bald except for a white ring of hair that had always reminded Samantha of a fuzzy halo. Dressed in a dark blue union suit, it looked like he had just rolled out of bed. As he approached, they noticed there was a woman in his car, but with the reflection of the early morning sun, it was difficult to make out her face.

"Oh thank heavens," he breathed. "You're here."

Tanner nodded. "Father."

"Mr. Raines, I have a favor to ask."

Tanner shook his head. "Sorry, padre, not a good time."

"I wouldn't ask if it weren't terribly important."

"What is it?" said Samantha.

Father Paul offered a perfunctory smile but quickly turned back to Tanner.

"Please, sir."

"Not this time," he said, turning to get back into the truck.

"But bad men have done something awful."

Tanner pulled his door open. "Bad men are always doing something awful. That's why they're called bad men."

"What did they do?" said Samantha.

Father Paul looked back toward the Impala as if seeking the occupant's approval. Finally, he said, "It has to do with the nuns."

"There are nuns in Boone?" Samantha didn't remember seeing anyone that even vaguely resembled a nun. Perhaps they dressed differently now?

"No, no," he said, quickly shaking his head. "Their monastery is over in Crozet, Virginia."

Crozet? Samantha thought that the word sounded strange, like a cracker with cheesy stuff on top.

"Let's go, Sam," Tanner said, standing with his hand resting on the truck's door frame.

She was about to suggest that they at least hear Father Paul out when the passenger climbed from the Impala. A woman in her early sixties came forward, dressed in a white habit, black scapular and veil, and a thin red belt tied around her pudgy waist.

Samantha smiled, but it was met with a dispassionate stare.

The nun gently placed a hand on the back of Father Paul's shoulder.

"God will help us to find another."

"I'm sorry, Sister, but there are no others. The townspeople in Boone won't undertake something so far from home. For things like this," he said, and looked at Tanner, "we come to him or his son. There is simply no one else." Father Paul raised his hands, palms clasped together as if about to offer prayer. "You will help us, won't you?"

"It's like I said, Father—"

"We'll help," said Samantha. She turned to Tanner and repeated in a quieter voice, "We'll help."

"But Issa—"

"Issa would want us to help. You know that."

He sighed. "Detoured before we've even left the driveway."

"Which means that our journey hasn't technically yet begun." She turned back to Father Paul. "What is it you need us to do?"

"Allow me to introduce Sister Mary Margaret, the prioress of Our Lady of the Angels Monastery."

Samantha looked to Tanner. "Prioress?"

"Big cheese."

"Ah," she said, nodding.

"Please, Sister," said Father Paul, "tell them what you told me."

The nun stepped forward with a stiff stateliness.

"Yesterday afternoon, men came to the monastery. They took our four youngest nuns, Sister Mary Elizabeth, Sister Mary Josephine, Sister Mary Eunice, and Sister Mary Clare."

Samantha raised her hand.

"Yes, young lady."

"What's with everyone being named Mary?"

"The Blessed Virgin Mary gave birth to the Son of God through the Immaculate Conception. It's only right that we acknowledge her holy contribution." She cast a disapproving look in Tanner's direction. "Perhaps you and your father need to spend more time reading."

"Oh I read a lot. Don't I, Father Paul?" Before he could answer, she said, "Mostly I like books about animals. Kangaroos and rabbits are my favorites. I used to read a lot of vampire love stories, but honestly, just how many can you take? But you're right about Tanner. He says that books make him sleepy. Truthfully, I think his eyesight may be going, you know, given his age and all." She rattled the words off like she was playing catch-up with her oldest friend.

The nun stared at her with befuddlement, obviously not quite sure what to make of the twelve-year-old.

Hoping to get to the meat of things, Tanner said, "Do you know where the nuns were taken?"

"Yes. I'm afraid I do."

"Where?" Tanner knew what was coming next. The captors were no doubt holed up in some flea bag motel or trailer park, having improper relations with four of God's most faithful. It was just that kind of world nowadays.

"They've been taken to the DeJarnette Children's Asylum."

"Huh?"

"The DeJarnette Children's Asylum," she repeated.

"I heard you the first time. But why would they take them there?"

She shook her head. "That I don't know."

"What's an asylum?" asked Samantha.

"It's a place where the mentally ill are confined and treated," explained Sister Margaret.

"Confined? Like prisoners?"

She nodded. "The ones who can't be helped otherwise."

Samantha turned to Tanner. "They locked kids up?"

"Sounds like it."

"But why?"

"They were very sick," offered Sister Margaret.

"That's what hospitals are for," countered Samantha.

Sister Margaret argued the point no further.

"How do you know that's where they were taken?" asked Tanner.

"I overheard one of the men mention the facility."

"You're sure?"

"My ears work as well as most."

"How many kids are being held prisoner at the asylum?" Samantha was clearly having trouble believing that such a place even existed.

"I should have made myself clear," said Sister Margaret. "The DeJarnette Center has been boarded up for more than twenty years."

"Boarded up? As in closed?" said Tanner.

"That's right. There was talk at one time of converting it into a shopping mall, but that apparently fell through. For the past twenty years, it's been the den of drug users and would-be ghost hunters."

"There are ghosts?" Samantha said in an excited tone.

"Here we go," muttered Tanner.

"No, young lady. There are no such things as ghosts."

Samantha furrowed her brow. "But I thought Catholics believed in a Holy Ghost."

"We do, but that's different."

"How's it different?"

"It just is."

Samantha shrugged. "Okay, but I don't see how."

"Ghosts, monsters, and the like are all made up for late night storytelling. Our faith is most certainly not." The nun's tone was growing firmer.

"You don't believe in monsters?"

"Of course not."

Samantha nudged Tanner and cracked a smile.

"She doesn't believe in monsters."

"Not everyone can be as wise to the world as you are, darlin'."

Samantha nodded. "I am pretty wise."

Tanner turned to Sister Margaret. "Why would these men take a handful of nuns to an abandoned children's asylum?"

"As I said, that I don't know."

"You're sure the women had no connection to the place?"

Sister Margaret shook her head. "The nuns were barely old enough to walk when it was in service. Those of us who do remember the place were not taken. It's a real mystery."

Tanner said nothing, noting the woman's wrinkled skin and bulging midsection. The fact that men would take the younger, more nubile nuns wasn't quite the mystery she professed.

"All right," he said. "What is it you want from us?"

She looked to Father Paul to do the asking.

"We were hoping you could help to free the sisters," he said, shuffling his feet nervously.

"By going to this abandoned asylum?"

"That's right."

"And facing off with the men who took them?"

"I don't know that you would need to 'face off' with them, as you put it. But yes, I was hoping to have a firm hand at Sister Margaret's side."

"At her side?"

Sister Margaret met his stare. "I would, of course, be going with you. These women are in my charge, after all."

Tanner looked over at Samantha. "I'm liking this less and less."

Instead of trying to convince him, she retrieved the map and once again spread it across the hood of the Power Wagon.

"Can you show us where the asylum is?" she said.

Sister Margaret took a moment to find the city of Staunton, Virginia.

"There," she said, touching the map with her finger.

"There? You're sure?"

"Yes, dear. Is there a problem?"

Samantha turned to Tanner. "You do see where she's pointing."

"I see it."

"The asylum is directly in our path. We'll literally be seeing it out our windows."

"What's your point?"

"My point is that this was meant to be."

"Our stopping by an abandoned insane asylum to free some kidnapped nuns was meant to be?"

"Great," she said, folding up the map. "I'm glad we both agree."

It was a trick that Samantha had played on him a hundred times before, but Tanner didn't feel the need to contest the decision any further. Like it or not, they were taking a road trip with a cranky old nun.

CHAPTER 3

Issa awoke to the sound of women stirring on the floor around her. She didn't know when she had dozed off, certainly not before two in the morning. The antique rocking chair pressed against her back and hips, bruises already beginning to set in. Dolly, the old black southerner, had stayed up with her until just past midnight before finally curling up next to the other women on the floor.

Issa pushed up out of the chair. One of her legs tingled, and there was a painful crick in her lower back. Her cheek also ached from where one of the slavers had struck her. All in all, she'd had rosier mornings.

She brought her hands down to her stomach and gently caressed her unborn child.

"Time to get up, little one," she whispered.

The knob on the front door turned, and it began to swing open. Issa quickly bent down and snatched up the double-barrel rifle resting against the chair. Chambered in 470 Nitro Express, the Merkel 140-2 was designed for hunting big game and had proven itself more than capable of downing a man. She swung it toward the door, ready to unleash two loads of hell on any who sought to do harm.

A young redhead came into view. Her eyes grew wide at the sight of the gun.

"Issa," she said, her voice trembling, "it's me, Theresa."

Issa lowered the rifle. "What were you doing out there?"

"I had to pee. I didn't mean to startle you."

Issa motioned for her to come inside and close the door. As she did, the women on the floor began to sit up, yawning and stretching.

Dolly stood up and came over to stand beside Issa.

"You sleep okay, child?"

"Well enough."

"Gonna be a long day today." She looked around. "Be nice if we could find some food and water."

Issa thought of the supplies in the back of her car. They weren't enough to give everyone a bellyful, but they would at least take the edge off their morning hunger. Sacrificing the food would put her without supplies for the return from Mount Weather, but surely Mother or someone else in the colony would see that she didn't leave empty-handed.

"Have them search the tavern as well as the slavers' truck outside." She started toward the door.

"Where you goin'?" There was a worry in Dolly's voice. Clearly, she wondered if Issa might have changed her mind about helping to free their loved ones from the slavers.

"To fetch my car. I've got enough food and water to see us to Luray."

Dolly smiled and offered a friendly nod.

Issa left the historic Yates Tavern, wondering how she had gotten herself into such a predicament. Not only had she killed three men, she'd been roped into leading a band of ill-equipped women on a rescue mission that was arguably none of her business.

She hiked back across Highway 29's business route. The navy-blue Toyota Prius sat beside the road, where she had left it the day before. The doors remained locked, and nothing appeared to be disturbed. Issa opened the hatchback and rifled through her supplies, finally coming up with a rag, a bucket, and a jug of water. She stripped off her clothes, relieved herself in a small gully, and took a few minutes to clean herself up. By the time she was finished, the morning air had brought chill bumps to her skin. She hurriedly donned a fresh pair of pants and a long-sleeved sweater.

She closed the hatch and went around to the driver's side. Inside, she retrieved the wooden box of ammunition and carefully set it on the hood of the car. She opened the lid and began lifting out the remaining brass cartridges, stuffing them into a shoulder satchel that she had taken from one of the slavers. Each cartridge measured four inches in length and sported a 500-grain flat nose bullet. Combined with the two rounds in the Merkel and two already in her pocket, it gave her an even four dozen. She couldn't imagine needing more than that, let alone having time to use them. What the Merkel offered in raw power, it gave up in capacity and reloading speed.

Issa lowered the big gun onto the floorboard and climbed in. As she slid behind the steering wheel and pressed the Power button, she eyed the open highway. It would be so easy to leave Dolly and the other infected women behind, and she could hear Tanner telling her in no uncertain terms to do just that. He would point out that she had already done enough. If they wanted to go off on some fool rescue mission, that was up to them. She had a baby on the way and a loving family waiting for her at home.

Family. The word struck a chord that couldn't be quieted. Family was what it was all about. Hers. Dolly's. All of the women's. The men who had enslaved their loved ones had destroyed those families without the slightest twinge of shame or remorse. Perhaps one day those same men would come for her family too.

She took her foot off the brake and eased out onto the highway. A fight was coming, and it was better that she quit second-guessing her decisions. If she were lucky, perhaps the killing could be kept to a minimum.

Then again, perhaps it couldn't.

§ §

"Who can tell me about Luray?" Issa said to the roomful of women.

Jen, a middle-aged schoolteacher, raised her hand.

"I lived in Luray five or six years ago."

"Is it a city or a small town?"

"Definitely toward the small side of things. I suppose there were probably five thousand people living there back then. Now, I imagine it's much less."

"How big is it from one side to the other?"

"Maybe three miles east to west, and a mile or two north to south. The business route of Highway 211 runs right through the middle of town."

"Any idea where they might have set up a slave auction?"

She shook her head. "About the only thing Luray's famous for is its caverns."

"What caverns?"

"Luray Caverns. It's basically a big cave, filled with mud flows, mirrored pools, and stalactites. It's beautiful though. Or it was, anyway. Without electricity, it can't be much more than a dark hole."

"A dark hole might be exactly where they keep people who they think of as monsters. Which side of town are these caverns on?"

"They're to the far west. The highway runs right by the entrance."

Issa nodded. "Then that's where we'll start." When she looked around at the roomful of women, every set of eyes was on her. "Those of you who decide to come along should understand that we may all be dead in a few hours. Keeping that in mind, I'd like a show of hands to see who's coming."

The women looked around at one another. There were eleven in total, not nearly enough for what had to be done.

Dolly was the first to raise her hand.

"I'm comin'. Jerome and the Lord Jesus would 'spect nothin' less."

Other hands began to go up. When it was all said and done, five of the eleven women had agreed to go, including Theresa and Jen.

"All right," said Issa. "Counting me, that makes six." She looked to Dolly who had somehow become her de facto first officer. "What do we have in the way of weaponry?"

Dolly stepped aside so that everyone could see a small round table. A lever-action Winchester carbine and two semi-automatic handguns sat next to a box of ammunition and several loaded magazines. A large Bowie knife had also been stuck into the far side of the tabletop.

She picked up the Winchester and showed it to the group.

"First up is a rifle and a box of shiny bullets to go with it." She set the Winchester down and retrieved one of the handguns. "We also have a Beretta," she said, reading the inscription on the weapon's slide, "along with two magazines that look darn near full." Setting it down, she picked up the second pistol and read its inscription. "Next up is a Gold Cup National Match with two smaller magazines, also full. And finally," she said, motioning to the Bowie knife, "we have a big knife."

"Don't forget about Issa's rifle," said Theresa.

Dolly nodded. "That makes for a total of four guns and a knife."

"Four or fourteen probably wouldn't make much difference," said Issa. "Our goal should be to get in, free your loved ones, and get back out with as little fuss as possible."

"Makes sense, but who gets the guns?" said Jen.

"That depends. Who knows how to use them?"

None of the women's hands went up. Admitting that they knew how to shoot was the equivalent of volunteering for combat duty.

"All right then," said Issa. "We'll leave the guns here. Each of you get a rake or a shovel from the shed out back." She turned and started for the door.

"Wait a minute!" cried Theresa. "I can shoot... a little."

Issa paused and looked over her shoulder. "Oh?" She eyed the other five women who had agreed to come along. "Anyone else?"

Two other hands went up, a big-boned woman named Marcy and a petite chain-smoker who insisted that everyone call her Lulu.

"What do you know? Three volunteers. Three guns." She turned to Dolly and the other woman who had not raised her hand. "You two need to find a weapon, be it a stick or the Bowie knife."

They nodded, but neither of them reached for the knife. It took a special kind of person to welcome the thought of killing a man with a sharp blade.

One of the women who had not volunteered to come along said, "What are *we* supposed to do?"

Issa shrugged. "You can either stay here and wait for Dolly and the others to return, or you can go your own way. The choice is yours."

"Does that mean you're not coming back?"

Issa shook her head. "I'm going north after this is done."

The woman eyed Issa's rifle. "But shouldn't we stick together... like a family?"

Issa thought of Tanner's gruff voice and Samantha's innocent smile.

"You make your own family. I already have one."

CHAPTER 4

As the RV started north along Highway 17, Mason and Bowie settled into the trailer being pulled behind it. Most of the goods the junkers had collected were consumables: canned food, cigarettes, bottles of soda, toilet paper, boxes of nails, reading glasses. A few of the items were more valuable, including a pair of matching bolt-action hunting rifles, a mishmash of ammunition piled together into a large canvas sack, some cold-weather army jackets, a kerosene space heater, and a wooden crate filled with an assortment of hammers, wrenches, and screwdrivers.

Mason piled a few of the army jackets between two 55-gallon drums of water and settled back against them. Bowie lay at his feet, sniffing a bag of charcoal briquettes.

"You hungry, boy?"

The dog's head whipped around.

"Yeah, me too." Mason fished an MRE from his pack, and for the next ten miles, he and Bowie shared beef with black beans, chipotle tortillas, spiced apples, and pound cake. All in all, not too shabby for end-of-the-world cuisine.

When they finally arrived at the intersection of Cowpen Neck Road and Morris Farm Lane, the RV came to a stop. A sprawling cornfield lay to their right, last year's stalks dry and withered from never having been fully harvested.

Bartley opened his door and came around to stand beside the trailer with Hoss watching him through the RV's back window.

"You sure this is the place?" Bartley turned and studied the empty Virginia landscape. "Not much here."

Mason climbed from the trailer, and Bowie hopped down beside him.

"I guess I'll find out. Either way, I appreciate the lift."

Bartley glanced back at the RV.

"Hoss wants me to ask you again about the drugs. You sure you ain't willin' to make a trade? He said you can take your pick of anything on the trailer." He reached down and dusted off a case of Hormel Chili. "Got some good stuff in here."

Mason shook his head. "It's for the kids, remember?"

Bartley let out a frustrated sigh. "Yeah. Thing is, Hoss don't really care much for kids."

Mason slipped his pack over his shoulders.

"That's okay. I'm sure they don't care much for him either."

Bartley bit at his lip, obviously hunting for words that would close the deal.

Mason patted him on the shoulder.

"He'll get over it."

"I'm not so sure," he said in a low voice.

"Listen. You and Kyle don't seem like bad men. Maybe it'd be better if you made your way without Hoss."

He gently shook his head. "Nah. Last thing our mother ever said was that family's all we got."

"Hoss is family?"

"Half-brother. Same as Kyle, only different daddy." When he saw the puzzled look on Mason's face, he said, "My mother, well, some might say she got around a bit."

Mason chuckled. "At least you have family. That's something, I suppose."

"Now you understand why Kyle and I don't really have a choice."

"You always have a choice. No man gets a pass on that."

Bartley looked away. "Take care of yourself, Marshal." With his head hung low, he turned and trudged back to the RV.

Mason and Bowie stood, watching as the junkers wheeled the RV around and headed back along Cowpen Neck Road. When they were finally out of sight, Mason turned in a slow circle, surveying the farmland that stretched in every direction. The only house within sight lay a few hundred yards to the east.

He looked over at Bowie. "I guess we'll start there."

Mason kept to the road, hoping to avoid having to slog his way through soft dirt and overgrown fields. As they approached the home, he noticed that the farmland directly beside it was much better maintained. The ground had been recently tilled, and it looked like seedlings were beginning to push up through the rich soil. He couldn't tell what was being grown, but someone was obviously giving it attention.

Hoping to avoid startling the homeowner, Mason approached along a small paved walkway that led up to the house. The structure itself was nothing special, a single-story farmhouse painted a pale shade of gray.

There were, however, several banks of solar panels lining the roof, as well as an amateur radio tower and water tank stationed along the right side of the house. A weathered gray barn easily twice the size of the home sat to the rear of the property. Visible within was a faded yellow Air Tractor AT-501 crop-dusting airplane.

As Mason traversed the narrow walkway, he heard singing coming from around back. The voice was soft and warm, and the melody friendly.

Bowie looked up at him.

"Anything that pretty can't be too dangerous."

Together, they detoured around the side of the house only to find themselves staring at billowing white sheets blowing in the morning breeze. A long clothesline ran the length of the yard, and nearly every inch of it was being used. A young woman stood with her back to them, hanging the last few items as she sang to herself. She wore a white blouse and faded green skirt, both of which looked handmade. Her sandals and a Browning 20-gauge pump-action shotgun sat next to a wooden bench that overlooked a small herb garden.

Mason stood for a moment, listening to the young lady sing. For a moment, he was reminded of Connie West, a lover who had once invited him to stay with her and live the life of a farmer. He had declined the offer, not so much because of the lifestyle but rather the vengeful nature of the one doing the asking.

Feeling a bit like an uninvited voyeur, Mason cleared his throat.

The woman wheeled around, her eyes darting over to the shotgun.

He raised both hands, palms out.

"You won't need it."

She took a moment to study him, and he couldn't help but do the same. The woman was barely out of her teens, her sun-soaked skin slick with a glossy sheen of sweat. She had strawberry blonde hair pulled up into a simple bun, thin strands hanging down in front of one eye. The top two buttons of her blouse were undone, and bare breasts pressed against the thin fabric.

Before she could say a word, Bowie wandered closer, his tail wagging from side to side as if he was trying to squeegee a windshield. He pressed his wet nose against one of her hands, and she giggled.

"Well aren't you the friendliest thing," she said with a beautiful southern accent.

"Sorry," Mason said, walking toward her. "Bowie's not one for formal introductions."

She stroked the dog's enormous head.

"That's quite all right. We're not very formal around these parts."

He extended his hand. "I'm Mason."

The young woman quickly wiped her hand on her skirt and gave him a firm shake.

"Jessie."

"Nice to meet you, Jessie."

"Can I help you with something?"

"I hope so. I'm looking for Jack Atkins. I believe he may live around here."

The woman's eyes narrowed. "Why are you looking for Jack?"

"I guess you could say we're old friends."

"You and Jack are friends?" From her tone, she didn't seem to believe him.

"Okay, 'friends' might be stretching it a bit. Truth is, we've talked a few times on the radio."

She caught sight of the badge on his belt, and a tentative smile came to her lips.

"Wait a minute. Are you Marshal Raines?"

"In the flesh."

Her face lit up. "Oh my goodness, he'll never believe you're here!"

"You know Jack?"

"Of course, I do, silly! He's my father."

"Your father?"

"That's right. And he told me all about how you helped to save us from the likes of President Pike."

Mason shrugged off the compliment. "Honestly, I think all I did was make a mess of things."

"Brave *and* humble." She clapped her hands together with excitement. "I love it."

Jessie's smile was contagious, and Mason found himself beaming like a proud schoolboy.

"Really, it wasn't like I—" He stopped in mid-sentence. The shine in her eyes was not going to be dimmed by anything he said, and even if it could, he didn't want to be the one to do it.

Jessie suddenly seemed to realize that they were standing in front of her family's clothesline.

"Daddy would never forgive me for being so impolite. Come," she said, turning toward the house. "I'll get you something to drink." As they passed the small bench, she snatched up her shotgun, popped open the breech, and draped it across her shoulder the way experienced hunters often did. "We don't get many visitors out here," she explained. "And those we do aren't always welcome."

"I understand."

She pulled open the screen door and motioned for him to go inside.

"Make yourself at home. We don't have much, but the least I can do is offer you a place to rest your feet."

"Much appreciated," he said, setting down his pack and M4.

Bowie didn't make it through the door before it swung shut, and he stood, staring in through the screen.

"You and Jack live here alone?" Mason asked as he sat down at the small kitchen table.

Jessie never broke stride as she lifted two glasses from the cupboard.

"Ever since Momma passed, nearly five months ago."

"I'm sorry to hear that."

She returned to the table, carrying glasses of iced tea, minus the ice.

"She'd been battling cancer for the better part of two years. Once the hospitals closed, Momma never really stood a chance. Daddy and I did what we could for her, of course, but cancer is what it is. She made us promise not to cry for her when she was gone, and I'm doing my best to keep that promise."

"She sounds like a strong woman."

"Oh, you have no idea," she said, shaking her head. "Momma wouldn't back down from no one. I once saw her run off two coyotes in nothing but slippers and a bathrobe."

He grinned. "Do you have any brothers or sisters?"

"Nope. It's just me." There was a liveliness to Jessie's voice that filled the room like a warm campfire. "Momma was much younger than Daddy, and I suppose they were hoping to have a boy somewhere along the way. It didn't happen, and so they made do. What about you? Any siblings?"

Mason shook his head. "Single child. Same as you."

"And your parents, are they…?" She hunted for a delicate way of putting it.

"Both alive as far as I know. My mother's living with the Amish, up in New York, and my father's back at our cabin, in the Blue Ridge Mountains."

"I suppose your daddy's a marshal too?"

"No, he's… something else."

She offered an understanding smile. "Even so, the Good Lord put us all here for a reason, don't you think?"

Mason thought of all that Tanner had done for young Samantha.

"I suppose."

"When I was a little girl, Daddy used to tell me that I was put here to bring a little sunshine into the world. That was his nickname for me—Sunshine. Silly, right?"

"Fitting, I'd say."

She smiled. "I never figured you to be so sweet. Truth is, I imagined you being one of those hardnosed stuffy types, like Daddy and I used to watch in his old westerns."

Jessie picked up her glass and took a long drink of the tea. Mason took the opportunity to do the same. He was thirstier than he'd thought, and when he turned the glass down, it was half-empty.

Bowie let out a little whine.

"Now where are my manners?" Jessie said, hopping to her feet. She filled a bowl with water and carried it out to him. When she returned to sit at the table, they could hear the big dog slurping water like he had just hiked across the Mojave.

"Thank you."

"Not at all." She looked over at Bowie. "I imagine he's your best friend in this whole world."

The words surprised Mason. He couldn't remember a single person, not even Ava, ever saying something like that. Now, after having heard them aloud, he realized just how true they were.

"That he is."

"Me, I love animals—cats, dogs, pigs, you name it. Have, all my life."

"From what I can tell, they seem to love you back."

"I've always thought that animals can tell what's inside a person."

"Bowie's been a pretty good judge of character, even if I haven't always heeded his advice."

She looked out at the wolfhound. "Have you had him a long time?"

"Going on a year."

"And before that?"

"Before that, he was a military working dog."

"I believe it. His eyes are almost as serious as yours."

Mason cracked a smile. "I have serious eyes?"

Jessie leaned forward and rested her chin on her hands, studying his eyes. It made Mason's stomach tie into a strange little knot.

"Are you kidding?" she said. "It's like looking down the barrel of a gun."

Mason tried his best to avoid staring back into her rich brown eyes, reminding himself that she was probably fifteen years his junior, not to mention the daughter of the man whose help he was soliciting.

"In case that was meant as a compliment, thank you."

"Oh, it was." She batted her eyes playfully. "What about mine?"

"I'm pretty sure your eyes could melt frost on a windshield," he said with a chuckle.

She giggled and sat back up. "That's sweet. Momma always said that my eyes were my best attribute."

Glancing down at the firm breasts straining against her thin blouse, Mason wasn't sure he agreed.

"They *are* beautiful." He cleared his throat, hoping that it might help to clear his mind as well. "So, is Jack home? I had a favor to ask of him."

"No," she said, her face losing some of its cheer. "Daddy's not home at the moment."

Mason waited for her to say more.

"Truth is, he's been gone a couple of days." She wasn't quite able to hide the concern in her voice.

"Mind if I ask where he went?"

"Up to Grey's Point Camp."

Mason wrinkled his brow, unfamiliar with the name.

"It's a big RV campground where folks gather to trade supplies. To hear Daddy tell it, it's become something of a hub for preppers, survivalists, and anyone else who managed to find their way through the worst of it."

"Why didn't he take you with him?"

"He says it's no place for a lady, not that anyone's ever accused me of being any such thing."

"Did he go there for supplies?"

She nodded. "Lately, he's been going once a month, but this is the first time he's been gone for more than a single night." She waved it away, obviously putting on a brave face. "I'm sure he's fine. Just running a little late, right?"

"Could be."

She took a deep breath to collect herself.

"You said you needed a favor. Maybe I can help."

Mason wasn't at all sure about making himself at home in another man's space.

"Please," she said. "It would help to get my mind off all this worrying."

"All right," he said. "Does Jack still have his HAM radio?"

"Are you kidding? Daddy's radio is probably the one thing in this house he loves more than me."

"Is there enough power to run it?" Mason thought of the solar panels lining the roof.

"Oh sure. We've got a whole bank of car batteries that'll give you plenty of juice."

Bowie raised his head abruptly from the water bowl and gazed toward the side of the house. Both Jessie and Mason took notice.

"Are you expecting company?"

"It must be Daddy!" She hopped up and hurried out the back door.

Bowie bounded after her, equally as curious about who was approaching.

Mason chose to be a bit more cautious, stepping into the living room and pushing aside curtains that covered the front window. A familiar silver RV sat parked along the road, and three men approached along the walkway with shotguns in hand. Hoss was leading the way.

Shit!

Before Mason could decide on a course of action, Bowie and Jessie rounded the side of the house. The junkers swung their weapons up and began shouting commands. Bowie instinctively crossed in front of Jessie, the hair on his back growing stiff as he began barking ferociously.

Mason glanced back at his M4 lying next to his pack inside the back door. Even if he had it in hand, it wasn't going to solve the problem. His best chance at preventing bloodshed was to try a little diplomacy, even if it did put him in harm's way.

He pushed open the front door and stepped out. Hoss immediately shifted his aim to cover him.

"You should have made that trade when you had the chance, Marshal."

Mason shrugged. "A man should have the right to choose what he keeps and what he gives away. I would have thought you of all people understood that."

"What I think is that you're an asshole who didn't know what was good for him."

Mason turned to Bartley and Kyle.

"Is this how you two want to live? Taking what you want at the point of a gun?" Both men seemed unwilling to even look at him as they kept their weapons trained on Jessie and Bowie.

"They do as they're told," snarled Hoss. "And if you're smart, you'd better start doing the same."

Mason said nothing more. It was clear that the three men held a bond that wasn't going to be broken by a few choice words from a stranger.

"All right. How do you want to do this?"

"Start by tossing your pistol."

Mason took a moment to size up his chances of shooting all three men before one could get off a shot. Not good.

He lifted out the Supergrade with his thumb and index finger and gently lobbed it onto the grass a few feet away.

"What is it you want?" Jessie said, her voice more determined than afraid.

"He knows. Don't you, Marshal?"

"My pack's inside on the kitchen floor. Go on and take what you want."

"You're damn right I'm gonna take what I want. Now get!" He motioned with the muzzle of the shotgun for Mason to lead the way.

Mason glanced over and saw Jessie staring at him.

"It's going to be all right. I found some medicine that these men want. Once I give it to them, they'll go." He turned back to Hoss. "Isn't that right?"

"I'm not promising you a damn thing."

Bowie turned toward Hoss, his lips pulled back into a snarl.

"Bowie!" shouted Mason.

The dog quieted, studying his master.

Mason shook his head. "Not this time."

Confused, Bowie turned back to face Bartley and Kyle. Jessie squatted down and wrapped her arms around the giant dog. Her embrace seemed to calm him, and he reluctantly settled against her.

Hoss lifted the shotgun to his shoulder and growled, "I won't tell you again, Marshal. Move!"

Mason turned and led him into the house, moving carefully so as not to alarm the big man. They passed through the living room and into the kitchen.

He motioned toward his pack. "Do you want me to get them, or do you want to do it?"

Hoss eyed the M4 leaning next to the backpack.

"You just sit your ass down in one of those chairs and hope I don't get a wild hair to redecorate the walls."

Mason sat, his hands resting in his lap.

Keeping the shotgun trained on him, Hoss sidestepped over to the pack. He squatted down and flipped open the side pocket. The fentanyl lozenges were inside. Holding the shotgun with this right hand, he reached across to fish out the small plastic housings. Several fell from his grasp, and he glanced down to pick them up.

Mason flipped the table up to act as a shield and lunged forward. The tabletop crashed against the big man, knocking him onto his haunches and pinning the muzzle of the shotgun to the wall. With his shoulder pressing against the table's underside, Mason used his right hand to draw the thick Fällkniven blade that hung from his belt. He brought it overhead and drove it down as if chipping away at a block of ice. The tip of the 6.3-inch cobalt steel blade lopped off Hoss's left ear and opened a gash along his cheek.

Hoss screamed, dropping the shotgun to shove the table away.

As he was lifted into the air, Mason brought the blade down again. The knife pierced the side of the junker's neck, cutting through his carotid artery and larynx. Hoss let out a gurgled scream, and his arms buckled under the weight of the table. Mason reared back again, this time driving the heavy blade through the top of the man's skull.

Hoss collapsed and lay still as the table settled over him.

Mason gave the knife a tug. Stuck. He cranked it from side to side, cracking the skull to create enough of a gap to break the suction of the man's brain. Sliding the knife free, he wiped the bloody blade on the leg of Hoss's trousers and inserted it back into its sheath.

Mason moved the table aside. Hoss's eyes were open, and tiny rivers of blood raced down his face. Remarkably, he was still alive.

"Don't look at me like that," Mason muttered softly. "You knew it would eventually end this way. If not here, then somewhere else."

Hoss said nothing as his face slowly lost its color.

Mason reached down and picked up one of the fentanyl lozenges. He popped open the plastic sleeve and gently inserted the lollipop into Hoss's mouth. The big man made no move to stop him, nor did he offer thanks.

"That's all I can do to ease your suffering. I suspect it won't last long."

Mason picked up his M4 and turned to face the living room. No one came rushing through the front door. That was the good news. The bad news was that there remained two men with shotguns outside.

A couple of options came to mind. The first was to take another go at reasoning with them. They were, after all, seemingly of slightly better character than their older half-brother. The problem with that choice was that it put him, Jessie, and Bowie at their mercy. And while there were exceptions to the rule, Mason had found the old saying about blood being thicker than water to be poignantly true. Few men could easily move past seeing their brother lying in a pool of blood. Such images brought with them a desire for justice, and if not that, revenge.

That left Mason with but one way forward. He would have to kill Bartley and Kyle. It was unfortunate, but then again, killing always was.

With the decision made, he turned his attention to coming up with a viable plan. Even if he had his Supergrade in hand, there was simply no surefire way to put down both men before one squeezed off a shot. He would have to come at them in a way they didn't expect.

A thought came to mind. It was the kind of stunt that was probably best saved for the newest Jason Bourne movie, but at the moment it was all he had.

Mason reached down and dug through his pack, coming up with a single 5.56 mm cartridge whose only distinguishing mark was a dull black tip. He had commandeered a handful of the M995 armor-piercing rounds when intercepting a band of illegal arms traffickers some months earlier. While conventional M855 green tip ammunition typically did a better job on soft tissue, the tungsten core of the M995 was designed to offer better penetration, especially at long ranges. For what he had in mind, penetration would be paramount.

He ejected the magazine from his M4, cleared the chamber, and loaded the M995 round onto the top of the stack. There was no need to load more than one armor-piercing round, as this would be a one-shot, winner-takes-all kind of event.

Ammunition was only part of the equation. He also had to get into position, not to mention pull off the shot of a lifetime.

Mason pushed his way through the back door and headed around the far side of the house. He veered off, exiting the backyard and ducking into a grove of oak and pine trees. Once he was sure that he was far enough away not to be detected, he circled around until the junkers came into view. Bartley and Kyle stood side by side, perhaps six feet apart. Jessie knelt in front of them with her arms still wrapped around Bowie's neck. The dog had settled down and was now doing his best to give her the tongue bath that she was obviously requesting.

Bartley and Kyle were growing nervous. That much was clear from the way they shifted their feet around. For his part, Bartley was doing his best to lean around to see through the front door but apparently not having much luck. Kyle, meanwhile, was eyeing Jessie with an interest that went beyond passing curiosity. Perhaps he was weighing the merits of adopting his older brother's views on taking whatever he wanted. The one thing Mason could say for certain was that they weren't going to stay put much longer. Once they separated, his window of opportunity would be closed.

Mason thought that the best way to kill both men instantly would be a simultaneous headshot. Sure, there were other ways of killing two people with a single bullet, but aiming for the thoracic cavity with hopes of piercing both men's hearts felt more like a "close your eyes and cross your fingers" type of gamble.

He brought the M4 to his shoulder and checked the sight picture. Too far right. He took three wide steps to the left and checked it again. Almost there, but the height difference of the two men would cause one to take a bullet to the ear and the other to get away with a haircut. He took another half-step left and dropped to one knee. One more quick check of the sights, and he settled for it being good enough.

There wasn't a branch or rock nearby to rest the rifle on, so Mason pressed the stock against the nearest tree for support. Iron sights. Eighty yards. An easy shot. Easy if he wasn't trying to hit two volleyball-sized objects that were moving around like fishing bobbers.

He took in a breath, let out half, and watched as the muzzle slowly settled. His finger applied slow steady pressure to the trigger, knowing precisely where and when it would break.

Boom!

The gun bucked, and he forced it back down in case a second shot was needed.

It wasn't. Both men had fallen.

Mason scrambled to his feet and raced forward, the stock of the rifle pressed to his shoulder. Seeing him, Bowie pulled away from Jessie and bolted toward his master. They met halfway between the house and the trees, and together they advanced on the fallen men. Jessie had retreated to stand beside her front door, her hand resting on the handle.

Mason approached the two junkers. It was not a pretty sight. The bullet had entered Bartley's right temple and exited through the opposite brow, taking with it a three-inch chunk of skull. Together, bullet and bone fragments had torn through Kyle, leaving him looking like he had taken a shotgun blast to the face.

Bowie sniffed Bartley's leg and then looked back up at Mason.

"I know," he said with a heavy voice. "But I didn't see another way."

"Marshal?"

He turned to find Jessie cautiously approaching.

"Are you okay?" she asked.

"Me? You're the one I'm concerned about."

"I'm fine," she said with a quick shake of her head. "It's not the first time men have come to my home intent on taking things." Despite the tough talk, her voice trembled slightly.

Mason instinctively put an arm around her. She stiffened for a moment and then slowly settled against him. There were no words to make things right. All he could say was, "I'm sorry."

She lifted her head and looked into his eyes.

"Sorry? For what?"

"I brought armed men to your home. That's on me."

She reached up and placed a warm palm against his cheek.

"No. These men brought themselves here." She paused. "I do want to ask you something though."

"All right."

"Why didn't you just give them what they wanted?"

"In my experience, when a man realizes he can take anything you have, he won't stop at your belongings."

"What do you mean? What else is there to take?"

Mason said nothing as he stared into Jessie's sparkling brown eyes. She was young and desirable. Not only to him, but to any man, a prize that she probably didn't even fully understand at her age.

"Me?" she said.

"I couldn't take that chance."

Her eyes clouded with tears. "You, sir, are a good man."

He offered a slight smile. "Tell me that after you see what I've done to your kitchen."

CHAPTER 5

Tanner kept to his planned route, traveling east on Highway 421 before turning north onto Highway 11. Having a nun onboard made for a quiet ride, with Samantha occasionally humming a tune from the backseat and Sister Mary Margaret compulsively rubbing the silver crucifix that hung around her neck.

After nearly an hour of not speaking, Samantha couldn't hold it in any longer.

"Have you been a nun a long time?" she asked, leaning forward between the seats.

"Since I was twenty-eight years old," Sister Margaret said, not bothering to turn toward her. "I joined the monastery right after leaving the Army."

"The Army?" Samantha looked at her as if trying to ascertain how much muscle might be hidden beneath the nun's habit. "What did you do for them?"

"Believe it or not, I was a combat medic."

"Wow, that's so cool! Were you in World War II?"

Sister Margaret cut her eyes toward Samantha.

"I most certainly was not."

"Surely not World War I. You can't be *that* old."

The nun cleared her throat. "At the monastery, we have a policy that children are best seen and not heard."

"Really? That must be terribly boring. Tanner and I talk all the time, don't we, Tanner?"

"Yep," he said. "There's never a moment of peace."

She reached forward and patted his shoulder.

"He's kidding, of course. We talk about all kinds of stuff, everything from gypsies to the fights I get into at school."

Sister Margaret turned to Tanner. "Your daughter gets into fights at school?"

"On occasion."

"And you're okay with that?"

"As long as she wins."

Sister Margaret's eyes narrowed. "Children fighting is not something to be condoned."

"Oh, he doesn't condone it," offered Samantha. She thought for a moment. "Actually, I think he might. But at least I haven't had to pull my knife on anyone yet."

"Your knife!"

Samantha drew a fixed-blade knife from a sheath along the small of her back. Its razor-sharp edge glistened against the blade's black boron carbide coating.

"See?" she said, holding it up between the seats. "Tanner says everyone should carry a knife. Don't you carry one?"

"I most certainly do not."

"Why not? They're super handy. You can skin a piece of fruit, carve a spear, cut rope, and of course, slice someone, but only if you absolutely have to. Truthfully, if it comes to that, you're usually better off with a gun."

Sister Margaret turned to Tanner, frown lines forming on her already wrinkled face.

"This is no way to raise a child."

"You tend to your flock, Sister, and I'll tend to mine."

"Fine, but you do realize that you're not raising a sheep—you're raising a wolf."

"Not a wolf, a sheepdog."

"You're raising me to be a sheepdog?" Samantha said, not at all sure that she liked the thought of being transformed into a woolly animal with fleas.

"There are folks, like the good sister here, who depend on others to keep them safe," he said, trying to explain.

"They're the sheep?"

"Exactly. Then there are others who sit on the hill and watch for trouble."

"Ah, the sheepdogs."

"You got it."

"A sheepdog," she said, pursing her lips. "I guess I'm okay with that. They're kind of cute, right?"

"The cutest."

Sister Margaret shook her head, but said nothing more.

Sensing that the conversation wasn't quite as friendly as she first took it to be, Samantha put her knife away and moved to change the subject.

"What do you know about the children's asylum? Is it spooky? It sounds spooky."

Sister Margaret hesitated, obviously weighing the merits of continuing the conversation.

Samantha stared at her expectantly until she finally acquiesced.

"The DeJarnette Center has a troubled history, one that everyone living near Staunton knows well. It opened in 1932 as a sanitarium for wealthy people with substance addictions and serious mental afflictions. It was quite posh, with tennis courts and a golf course."

"That doesn't sound so bad."

"By itself, no. But there was a dark side to the center too."

"What kind of dark side?"

"Their doctors practiced something known as eugenics."

Samantha looked to Tanner for an explanation.

"Eugenics was a pseudo-science that promoted sterilizing the mentally ill and moral degenerates of the world."

"Sterilized? Like with alcohol?"

"No, dear," said Sister Margaret. "Sterilized as in making it so that they couldn't have children."

Samantha made a face. "How could they keep people from having children?"

"Dr. DeJarnette and those working under him forced such individuals to have surgery."

"Surgery? Like removing their baby-making parts?"

Sister Margaret nodded. "That's right."

"Who gave them the right to do that?"

"It might surprise you to learn that the Supreme Court did."

"The Supreme Court said that it was okay to operate on people who didn't want it? You're sure it was the *Supreme* Court?"

Tanner grinned. "You have no idea what the Supreme Court is, do you?"

"Of course, I do," she said, crossing her arms. "They were the court that decided the most supreme things, like who got to have babies."

"Clever beyond your years."

Sister Margaret said, "It was only after witnessing Hitler's extremism that Americans came to reject the idea of selective breeding for the creation of a superior race."

"Did they operate on kids too?"

"Not for that purpose, no. In fact, children didn't come to the center until the 1970s, when it transformed from a private institution to a state-managed healthcare system." She hesitated. "There were, however, rumors about experiments conducted on children as well."

"What kind of experiments?" Samantha asked, not sure that she wanted to hear the answer.

"Infecting them with horrible illnesses, starving them, confining them for weeks at a time, even shocking them with electricity to see if it might change their behavior."

Samantha looked over at Tanner, her face wrinkled up like she had just licked a lemon.

"It's like you say. People are awful."

"Always have been, always will be."

They drove for a while in silence, passing through the communities of Chilhowie, Marion, and Atkins. As they neared the town of Wytheville, they spotted a young man and woman walking along the side of the highway. Both carried backpacks and looked like they hadn't enjoyed a bath in quite some time. As soon as they saw the Power Wagon, they turned and stuck their thumbs out.

Tanner sped up.

Sister Margaret said, "A Christian lends a hand to those in need."

"Doesn't apply. I'm Buddhist."

"Even so. But for the grace of God, that could be you and your daughter."

Tanner wasn't biting, but Samantha took the nibble.

"Maybe she's right. They're probably tired of walking, and we're headed in the same direction anyway. What could it hurt?"

Tanner growled, slowly moving his foot onto the brake. By the time they came to a stop, the Power Wagon was thirty or forty yards past the hitchhikers. The man and woman hurried forward, approaching from the passenger side.

As they drew closer, Samantha started second-guessing her suggestion to stop. The man's face was covered in a scraggly beard, and a bright red scab circled his neck, like he had recently been the victim of a botched lynching. His face was pocked with acne scars, and his nose looked like it had been broken so many times that it no longer knew which way was up. The woman looked only slightly better, with greasy bleached-blonde hair, thick bags under her eyes, and a crusty cold sore on her upper lip.

"I thought we'd never get off this road," the man said, bellying up to Sister Margaret's half-open window. When he saw how she was dressed, he blurted, "Are you a real live nun?"

"I most certainly am," she said with a thin smile.

The man turned to his traveling companion.

"Look, Deb, a real live nun."

"A what?" The woman pressed closer. "Jesus, Billy, you're right!" She reached in through the window and touched Sister Margaret's habit. "I don't believe I've ever met a nun. I once knew a stripper who dressed like a nun, but that probably don't count."

Sister Margaret said, "We'd be happy to give you a ride if it might help to lighten your load."

"That'd be right neighborly of you," Billy said, taking a step back so she could open her door. As it swung open, he reached behind his back and pulled a Bersa Thunder 380 semi-automatic pistol from his waistband. "On the other hand, maybe we'll lighten *your* load a little."

"What are you doing?" she exclaimed, shrinking back.

A lopsided grin came over his face as he pushed the gun toward her.

"Ain't it obvious? I'm robbing you."

"She ain't the smartest nun, is she?" cackled Deb.

"Apparently not." Billy's face turned serious, and his hand steadied. "Now get out of my truck, all of you."

Tanner weighed his options. Going for his shotgun was a nonstarter. If he punched the gas, they would almost certainly get clear of the hitch-hikers, but not before Sister Margaret took a bullet. Given that she was the one who suggested that they stop, it seemed only fitting. Having such thoughts and acting on them, however, were two very different things.

"I ain't gonna say it again!"

"Get 'em, Billy. Get 'em good," Deb said, wringing her hands like a junkie in need of a fix.

Sister Margaret climbed out. "Would you really rob those who offered to lend a hand?"

"You bet your holy britches I would."

Deb snickered. "Holy britches. That's a good one, Billy."

Billy spun Sister Margaret around and pushed her against the hood, like a police officer preparing to frisk. He slapped her playfully on the butt.

"Stay put now, you hear?"

She said nothing.

Billy turned the gun toward Tanner.

"You next, Tarzan."

Tanner opened his door, leaving his shotgun resting on the floorboard. He caught Samantha looking toward her rifle leaning against the rear door. Tanner shook his head and pulled her door open as well.

"Out you go, kiddo."

Billy watched them carefully, holding the gun close to his mangled nose. As they came around to stand beside Sister Margaret, he motioned to Deb.

"Check 'em for anything valuable."

Deb inched forward and ran her hands up and down the nun. Her only find was a set of worn wooden rosary beads stuffed into Sister Margaret's pocket. She studied them for a moment before tossing them onto the hood.

"She ain't got—" Deb stopped as she noticed that Sister Margaret was clutching something at her neck. "What you got there?"

Sister Margaret opened her hand to reveal the silver crucifix.

"It's just a token of my faith. It's worth nothing to you."

Deb spun her around to face her, and slapped her hands away so that the cross hung freely from Sister Margaret's neck.

"It's purty, and I want it. Take it off."

"Please, a crucifix is not—"

"Billy," Deb said, turning to him. "She won't give me the cross."

He stepped forward and pressed the gun against Sister Margaret's stomach.

"Give her the damn necklace, or I'm gonna open a hole in that fat belly of yours."

Tears formed in the nun's eyes as she slowly pulled the crucifix over her head. Deb snatched it from her, giggling, as she moved on to search Samantha.

"What you got, little girl?"

Samantha leaned back against the truck, her hands behind her back.

"I don't have anything, but you should probably check to be sure."

Feeling a bit more confident with a twelve-year-old girl, Deb squatted down and began quickly frisking her, starting at the ankles and working her way up. In the blink of an eye, Samantha's knife appeared from behind her back. She grabbed the woman's hair with one hand and brought the knife against the back of her neck with the other. Billy swung the pistol toward her, but as he did, Tanner stepped forward and grabbed it. The gun discharged, a bullet ricocheting off the asphalt to strike the bottom of the truck. Tanner wrenched the pistol away and flung it behind him.

Billy rushed forward, driving a shoulder into Tanner's chest. At barely a hundred and fifty pounds, it wasn't even enough to make him take a step back. Instead, Tanner twisted at the waist and drove a forearm onto the smaller man's back. Legs buckled, and Billy went down to his knees. He frantically wrapped both arms around Tanner's legs. Perhaps he was hoping for a takedown, but it looked more like he was preparing to do something untoward.

Tanner reached down, grabbed a handful of hair, and pulled the man back to his feet. As soon as he was upright and dancing on his toes, Tanner turned to check on Samantha. Deb knelt before her, doing her best to remain still. A thin streak of blood was visible across the back of the woman's neck.

"You okay?"

Samantha's eyes were set with determination. "This is us being sheepdogs, right?"

"It most certainly is."

"So what does a sheepdog do with her?" She tilted the woman's head up slightly.

"Leave that to me."

Dragging Billy behind him, Tanner stepped over and grabbed Deb by the hair. She shrieked in pain as he yanked her to her feet. Samantha sheathed the knife and watched as Tanner steered the two would-be robbers over to where Sister Margaret stood.

"Give her back the necklace."

"Here! Take it!" Deb squealed, holding out her hand.

Sister Margaret slipped the crucifix back over her neck and said, "Please, there's no need for any more violence."

Tanner ignored her. Sister Margaret clearly didn't understand when the need for violence ended. Still holding Billy and Deb by their hair, he dragged them around to the rear of the truck.

"Sit," he commanded, shoving them to the ground next to the fender.

Both of them flopped down, rubbing their scalps.

"Do something, Billy!" she whined. "He hurt me."

"Whaddya want me to do? He took my damn gun!"

"I dunno. Hit him or something. You're a man, ain't you?"

"Damn right, I'm a man." He started to stand, but when Tanner turned with a glare, Billy settled back to the ground. "I'll get him if he touches you again. Promise."

Samantha squatted down to look under the truck. A steady trickle of fuel dripped onto the asphalt.

"They hit the gas tank."

Tanner bent over and took a quick peek.

"Crap," he muttered.

"What are we going to do?"

"With them or the truck?"

She shrugged. "Both."

"These two are easy. I'll put a boot to their heads and leave them for the buzzards."

Samantha tilted her head sideways as if to say, "Really?"

"What? They shot our truck."

"Still…"

"You better listen to her," started Billy, "'cause if you don't—"

Tanner stepped forward and kicked him in the thigh. It was hard and fast and no doubt would leave one hell of a bruise.

"Shut your pie hole."

Billy flopped over, clutching his leg and moaning like he had just been shot. Seeing her boyfriend hurt, Deb jumped to her feet, screaming like a wounded barn owl.

Tanner kicked her too, the toe of his boot catching her on the hip. She fell back to the ground, tears streaking down her face.

Sister Margaret rushed forward and pulled at Tanner's arm.

"What's wrong with you? A man doesn't kick a woman!"

"Says who?"

"Says anyone with a sense of decency. By dropping down to their level, you become nothing better."

He pulled his arm free. "Who ever said I was going for anything better?" He turned back to Billy and Deb. "I'm going to fetch my shotgun out of the cab. If you're still here when I get back, I'll put a load of buckshot in both your bellies." He turned and started around the truck, listening as they scrambled to their feet and ran down Highway 11. He didn't even bother returning with the shotgun. Instead, he stopped and dug through a small toolbox in the truck bed.

Samantha came over and stood beside him.

"That was nice of you."

"I've been telling you I'm nothing but sweet."

"You're a bully is what you are," chided Sister Margaret. "And frankly, I'm ashamed to be associated with you."

"Feel free to head off in search of better company at any time," he said, straightening up with a screwdriver and a small wrench in hand.

Sister Margaret's nose flared, but she said nothing more.

"What are you thinking?" Samantha said quietly.

Tanner reached in through his open window and popped the hood.

"Right now, I'm thinking we need to get some new wheels."

He stepped around and began removing the lugs that held the battery in place. When it was free, he lifted the battery out and set it on the ground. Next, he hoisted out two of the jerry cans from the bed.

"You two carry the gas, and I'll get the battery."

"Are we taking them with us?" Samantha asked, testing the weight of one of the cans. It was heavy but manageable, if swapped from hand to hand.

"Have to. No guarantee they'll be here when we get back." He brought a hand up to shield his eyes from the sun as he stared down the highway. There wasn't a single abandoned car in sight. "It might be a hike, but with a battery and fuel, we should eventually be able to get back on the road."

"Even if we manage to come back for the other gas cans," she said, passing him his shotgun and retrieving her rifle from the cab, "they won't be enough to get us to Mount Weather and back. Not with losing a tank full of gas."

"We'll manage. We always do."

Samantha picked up one of the cans and grunted.

"I hope it isn't too far."

"You and me both," he said, lifting the battery.

They turned and started down the highway, Sister Margaret reluctantly trudging along behind them. Tanner stopped and glanced back over his shoulder. The remaining can of gas sat untouched beside the truck.

He nodded toward it. "Believe me, Sister, it isn't going to get any lighter."

ॐ ॐ

The search for a new set of wheels led them to a small white house facing Highway 11. A lawn mower sat in the center of the yard, grass and weeds nearly swallowing it whole. A rusted white and brown 1976 Ford Country Squire sat parked in the gravel driveway.

Samantha set the gas can down and rolled her shoulders around as she peeked in through the station wagon's dingy windows. The headliner hung down, and insulation from one of the rear seats puffed out from a large split in the upholstery. Crumpled beer cans lined the floorboards, and there was a sealed glass jar of dark yellow liquid sitting beside the driver's seat.

"It's not much to look at."

"Maybe not," said Tanner. "But it's old enough to hotwire." He pulled a screwdriver from his back pocket and held it out to her. "You still remember how?"

She opened the driver-side door, and it made a noisy squeak.

"I think so."

"And how do you know this isn't someone's car?" Sister Margaret said, breathing heavily as she set the gas can down.

Tanner faced the house. "Good point. I certainly wouldn't want someone stealing my vintage station wagon. Come on, Sam. Let's go see if anyone's home."

"I'm assuming vintage is a nice word for junk," she said, following after him.

"You know the old saying: 'One man's junk is another man's vintage.'"

"Yeah," she said, nodding. "I think I've heard that one."

They left Sister Margaret standing beside the car as they stepped up onto the porch and gave the door a quick knock.

No answer.

Tanner tried the knob.

Unlocked.

He leaned his head inside and hollered, "Red Cross! Anyone home?"

Again, there was no answer. The house looked like a lonely bachelor's pad with a sunken recliner, a worn carpet trail leading between the chair and the kitchen, and a plate of half-eaten food sitting on a small TV stand.

Tanner stepped inside, swinging his shotgun up to waist level. Samantha followed behind him, her rifle also at the ready. She wandered over to the plate and used the muzzle of her rifle to nudge what looked like it might have been a pork chop in a previous life.

"How old do you think this is?"

Tanner didn't answer as he carefully moved into the kitchen. It too was empty. He pulled open a couple of cupboards. Cans of food lined the shelves.

"Found some food," he said over his shoulder.

Samantha hurried into the kitchen. "What kind?"

He scanned the labels. "Fruit cocktail. Refried beans. Chicken noodle soup. Tomato sauce."

"Tomato sauce isn't food."

"Tell that to the Italians."

Before he could stop her, Samantha pulled open the refrigerator. The inside was covered in a thick layer of slimy black mold. Red plastic bowls sat neatly stacked with labels stuck to the front. Monday: Chicken and black beans. Tuesday: Roast pork and potatoes. All of this she took in with a quick glance before immediately slamming the door closed.

Too late. The stench of mold and rotting food filled the kitchen.

"Whew," she said, wrinkling her nose. "That's awful."

Tanner waved his hand in front of his face and coughed.

"Let's go see what else is here."

They proceeded through the living room and down a narrow hallway. A bedroom sat to either side, with a bathroom between them. The corpse of a man, dried and withered, lay in front of the commode. From the looks of it, he had died while using the toilet, his pants pulled down and bunched around his ankles.

"What happened to him?" she asked.

"Fell off the pot."

She rolled her eyes. "I know that. But how do you die sitting on the toilet?"

"I'd rather not know."

Tanner pushed open one of the bedroom doors. Inside was a double bed, a nightstand, and a small dresser. A sliding closet door was slightly ajar. He walked over to the nightstand and picked up a set of keys. One was a house key, but the other was almost certainly for the old station wagon out front.

"These might make things a little easier," he said, jingling them in the air.

Samantha nodded as she eyed the closet with curiosity.

"Go on," he said. "Figure out why it's calling to you."

She stepped closer and slid the closet door the rest of the way open.

"Anything?" he said, rifling through the nightstand.

"Clothes."

"Imagine that."

"You might like these."

When he looked up, he saw that she was holding a pair of boots. They were big and black, and looked like they could kick in the side of a school bus.

"I might indeed."

She passed them to him. "They're heavy, but then again..."

"Then again what?"

She shook her head, smiling. "Nothing."

He growled as he sat on the edge of the bed and pulled off his boots. They had carried him hundreds of miles, not to mention going a couple of rounds with a Komodo dragon. An upgrade seemed long overdue.

Based on their nearly unblemished soles, the black boots looked to be basically new, perhaps worn for a few hours to break them in. A small

American flag was stitched into a flap hanging from the cuff. He checked the label inside. Danner Acadia, size 13 EE. Tanner slipped them on. The fit was about right, maybe just a bit snug in the toe box. He laced them up and got to his feet.

Samantha stood watching him. "Well?"

He jumped up and down a few times, and the lighting fixture overhead shook.

"I think they'll work."

"Assuming the house doesn't come down on us first," she said with a snicker.

"Anything else in there?" he said, looking past her.

She turned back to the closet. On the top shelf was a shoe box with a dingy orange rag poking out the top. Samantha lifted it down and set it on the bed. Inside, she discovered a box of .45 Colt ammunition, an empty crossdraw leather holster, and an oil-soaked rag wrapped loosely around something.

She carefully unfolded the cloth, revealing a stainless-steel derringer. It had two barrels, one sitting directly on top of the other, and a rosewood grip carved with an eagle overlaying an American flag. The word "Patriot" was etched below the flag.

"Tanner?"

"Yeah?" he said, still admiring his new boots.

"What's this?" She turned to him, holding up the pistol. It wasn't much bigger than her palm, but there was an undeniable heft to it.

He whistled softly. "That, darlin', is a Bond Arms derringer."

"A derringer?"

"You don't see them much anymore on account of all the newfangled polymer guns."

"Are they any good?"

"Nothing better, if you're up close and personal."

She held it out to him. "How's it work?"

"To load it, you push this lever and turn the gun over."

When he flipped the pistol, the barrel flopped open, rotating around a thick metal hinge. Both chambers were empty. He reached into the shoe box and retrieved one of the cartridges.

"Why's it silver?" she asked, staring at the cartridge curiously.

"Some folks believe silver flies straighter and hits a little harder than lead."

"Does it?"

"Let's just say I'd rather not be hit by either one." He inserted it along with a second cartridge into the pistol. When he flipped the weapon back over, there was an audible click as it latched shut. "Safety's here," he said, working a small pin that slid in front of the hammer. "If you can see red, it's ready to fire, just like a shotgun."

"Do both barrels shoot at the same time?"

He shook his head. "The gun automatically indexes between barrels when you cock the hammer."

"But you have to cock it before firing, right?"

"Yep. It's single action."

"At least it wouldn't go off accidentally."

"Exactly." He handed it back to her.

She held it up and aimed down the fixed sights machined into the steel.

"Do you think I could handle it?"

"What's to handle? Put it to someone's chest and pull the trigger. Worst case, the gun and the bad guy hit the ground at the same time."

Samantha lifted out one of the cartridges from the box. They were big and beautiful.

"Silver bullets," she murmured, holding it up to the light. "That's cool, right?"

"Nothing cooler."

Setting the cartridge back in the box, she let the gun rest on her palm and lifted it up and down as if weighing it.

"I think I'll keep it. That's okay, right?"

"I don't think John will mind."

"John?" Her lips turned up into a smile. "Oh, I get it." She glanced over at the bathroom door. "We should really do something for him."

"Like what?"

"I don't know. Bury him or something."

"Why?"

"You took his boots, and I'm taking his gun. The least we can do is not leave him lying beside the toilet."

"Sounds like a line from a country-western song."

"Huh?"

"Doesn't matter. What matters is I don't have a shovel, and even if I did, I don't feel like digging a hole deep enough for a body."

She looked around. "We could put him in the bed."

"What good would that do?"

"If you were dead, wouldn't you rather be left lying in your bed than on the floor of your bathroom, with your pants down?"

"Good point." Tanner reached over and pulled the bedspread off the bed. Dragging it behind him, he stepped over to the bathroom and draped it over the body. "Help me roll him up."

Samantha hurried over, and together, they rolled the body into the bedding. Once Tanner was sure that all the man's piece parts were accounted for, he scooped the bundle up and carried it over to the bed.

"Happy?" he said, flopping it down.

She touched the tightly rolled bundle.

"Thank you, sir, for your boots and pistol. We'll try to take good care of them."

Tanner twirled the keys around his finger.

"Don't forget the wagon."

"Oh yeah," she said. "And for the vintage car, too."

I t took nearly an hour for Mason to load the junkers' bodies onto their trailer and dump them in a nearby field. When he returned to the Atkins' family home, he found Jessie on her hands and knees, carefully scrubbing the kitchen floor. Despite her hard work, there remained a noticeable darkening where Hoss's blood had seeped between the boards.

Mason approached the screen door and gave it a soft rap with his knuckles.

"I'd understand if I were no longer welcome."

Jessie stood up and tossed the bloodstained rag into the sink.

"Don't be silly," she said, pushing open the door. "When people die, they leave a mess behind. That's no more your fault than it is theirs."

As he stepped inside, Mason looked back at Bowie and said, "Stand guard like you mean it this time."

Bowie yawned and flopped down on all fours, enjoying the midday sun on his face.

Jessie looked past Mason, studying the open field behind her home.

"Do you think anyone will come looking for them?"

"I doubt it. From what I could tell, it was just the three of them, all half-brothers."

"All of them?" she said, cracking a smile. "How exactly does that work?"

He shrugged. "Either way, I believe we've ended that particular family line."

She glanced at the rifle hanging across his back and then at the Supergrade on his hip.

"Did you learn to use those in the military?"

"There, and other places."

She nodded. "Daddy used to be a pilot in Southeast Asia. Did he ever tell you that?"

Mason shook his head.

"He flew F-4 Phantoms. Said they were the best fighter planes in the whole world at the time. Have you ever been in one?"

Phantoms had been replaced with Eagles, Tomcats, and Hornets by the time Mason had served.

"No," he said. "That was before my time."

"When I was little, he used to tell me stories about honey bears, snub-nosed monkeys, and golden jackals." She smiled, her eyes taking on a far-away look. "It sounded like a magical place."

Mason said nothing. He had been to Southeast Asia several times on military assignments, but his memories were quite a bit darker than chattering monkeys.

Jessie shook her head and smiled.

"I'm sorry. Sometimes I forget I'm not that little girl anymore."

"Don't be sorry. There's still a piece of her in you, and that's a good thing."

"Do you still want to use Daddy's radio?"

"If you don't think he'd mind."

"He wouldn't. Come on," she said, motioning for him to follow.

Jessie turned and led Mason into a small den connected to the living room. It smelled of cigar smoke, and there were empty coffee cups sitting on nearly every surface. Across the room was a long workman's bench, topped with all manner of amateur radio equipment, some old enough to contain vacuum tubes and others built around state-of-the-art digital circuitry.

Mason quickly surveyed the electronics. He pointed to a wire that disappeared into the ceiling.

"Does that connect to the antenna outside?"

"That's right." Jessie reached over and flipped a few switches, turning on the transceiver, tuner, and power supply. A low-pitched buzz sounded. "It should be ready to go. All you have to do is dial in a frequency and press the talk button on the microphone."

Mason sat on a rolling stool in front of the workbench and considered how best to proceed. Reaching out to General Carr was not going to be as easy as making a phone call. While it was true that the New Colony used radio broadcasts to relay important information, none of those channels were suited to his requesting a private call with their Chief of Security.

Given the time of day, Carr was likely onboard the USS John F. Kennedy, an aircraft carrier sitting in port at what used to be the Norfolk Naval Station. The decision to conduct government operations aboard an aircraft carrier was one made primarily with security in mind. It was not protection from a foreign enemy that was of concern but rather protection from the masses, should they grow hungry or desperate. Breaching such a vessel was all but impossible for an angry mob, and if worse came to worst, the ship could be put to sea, allowing the government to relocate en masse.

Not only was the carrier secure, it also had communications equipment, sleeping quarters, cafeterias, and other infrastructure. For many government workers, the Kennedy had become the equivalent of an enormous waterborne Winnebago.

The dilemma facing Mason was that reaching out via radio would be anything but private. Broadcasts were monitored and recorded, making anything that he and Carr said a matter of public record. Given the sensitive nature of the accusations against him, Mason preferred to explain himself in a more private radio setting, if at all possible. The only way to avoid government scrutiny, however, was to get Carr to agree to communicate using an unmonitored frequency. But even that required first making contact over official channels.

Mason tuned the transceiver to a frequency that he knew the New Colony used for emergency broadcasts.

Pressing the talk button, he said, "Is anyone listening, over?"

Within seconds, a firm female voice said, *"This channel is reserved for official communications. Be advised to immediately redirect to another channel or face criminal prosecution."*

Mason recognized the voice as that of Betsi Greene, a middle-aged, ex-Navy electronics technician with an affinity for two things, riding her Harley and training service animals. Thanks to her having fallen instantly in love with Bowie, she and Mason had developed a friendly, some would say flirty, relationship. While Betsi took her duties seriously, he wondered whether that coquettish interest might be enough to get her to bend the rules just this once.

"Sorry about that, Twidget," he said, using the nickname for sailors who worked with electronics. "Could you suggest a frequency open to public use?" There was no way that any random individual would have been familiar with her background, and he was certain that she now knew that it was him on the line.

There was a long pause, followed by, *"Suggest you switch to a more suitable amateur channel, such as 16.36 megahertz. Out."*

Mason knew full well that 16.36 megahertz was outside the recognized amateur bands. She was directing him to a frequency that wasn't actively monitored.

He quickly dialed in the new frequency and waited, listening to the static.

Looking over his shoulder, Jessie said, "I'm confused. What exactly are you doing?"

Before he could answer, a hushed voice sounded from the radio.

"Mason? Are you there?"

"I'm here, Betsi."

"Are you and Bowie okay?"

"We're both fine. Just laying low at the moment."

"Where are you?"

"It's better if I don't say."

After a long pause, she said, *"There's been chatter about you. None of it good."*

"What kind of chatter?"

"Members of your team claim that you turned on them, killed one, hurt three others. Plus, they said you..." She paused. *"They said you raped a woman."*

Mason glanced back in time to see a look of concern come over Jessie's face.

"It's not what it sounds like," he said with the quick shake of his head.

"Good, because what it sounds like is that I let the wrong man into my home."

"I'll explain everything when I'm done here."

She nodded. "I'm counting on it."

Mason turned back to the radio.

"Betsi, I can't explain it all right now, but I need for you to believe me. None of what you're hearing is true."

There was no reply.

"Betsi? Are you there?"

"I'm here."

"This is one of those times when you have to listen to your gut. Ask yourself if the man you've come to know these past few months is capable of those crimes."

There was another pause. *"No. He's not."*

"You're sure?"

"One hundred percent."

"All right then. Next time I'm onboard the Kennedy, we'll share a drink, and I'll explain the whole thing. But right now, I need a favor."

"What kind of favor?"

"I need to reach General Carr so I can explain things to him. Can you make that happen?"

"I can try."

"Ask him to contact me on this frequency as soon as he can."

"If I do, you're going to owe me more than a drink."

"What did you have in mind?" he said, grinning.

"That depends on how well you clean up."

He chuckled. "Fair enough."

"Stay put and await his broadcast."

"Roger. Out here."

Mason leaned back and crossed his arms, noticing for the first time that his shirt was spattered with stiff speckles of dried blood.

"She likes you," said Jessie.

"Betsi's good people."

"Is she pretty? She sounds pretty."

"I guess so. To be honest, I hadn't really noticed."

She raised an eyebrow. "You didn't notice if a woman was pretty?"

"Let's just say I've had my share of bad luck with women. The prettier they are, the worse the luck."

"Is that how you ended up in this predicament? A pretty woman?"

He tried to force a smile, but the image of Brooke's face made it impossible. She had betrayed him, and it still burned like a hot poker.

"I'm sorry," she said, touching his shoulder. "That isn't any of my business."

He shook his head. "It *is* your business, because I promised you an explanation."

Mason stood up and walked over to look out the window. What Locke had managed to pull off was difficult to explain without going through the entire elaborate story. And elaborate stories were almost universally viewed with skepticism. He needed to keep it simple but factual, both with Jessie and with General Carr.

"Let me start by saying that I didn't attack my own men, and I most certainly didn't rape anyone."

"Okay," she said, waiting for more.

"I discovered something terrible about The Farm. When I confronted its leader, he set things in motion to either discredit or kill me."

"The Farm? Isn't that where they make those disgusting food bars?"

"You have no idea just how disgusting they really are."

"But how did he make you look like a criminal?"

"He tricked my own team into coming after me. I had no choice but to defend myself."

"By killing them?"

"One died. The other three were injured."

She nodded. "And the woman? What happened with her?"

Mason let out a sigh. "I took her to be something that she wasn't. In the end, she helped to set me up."

"Why would she do that?"

"I'm pretty sure it's because all women are evil," he said with a slight chuckle.

She grinned. "Not all. Just most."

"I can go into great detail on everything if it'll make you feel better about my being here."

Jessie shook her head. "That's not necessary."

"Are you sure?"

"You saved my life not two hours ago. I think that earns you some credit."

"Thank you."

"Now," she said, "let's see about getting you out of those clothes."

Mason's eyes grew wide, and she giggled.

"So I can wash them, Romeo!"

"Oh, right."

"Follow me," she said, wheeling around. "I'm sure Daddy's got something in his closet that'll fit you."

৵ ৵

Mason sat in front of the radio, a large bowl of vegetable soup in one hand and a spoon in the other. Thick chunks of homegrown potatoes, carrots, tomatoes, and corn were all mixed into a savory beef broth. He could hear Jessie singing outside as she pulled bedding from the clothesline. There was a sense of peace in the air, a warm feeling of invitation and family that country life often captured.

He took a deep whiff of the soup.

It smelled absolutely delicious.

Mason began to eat, taking his time to enjoy the subtle flavors of the vegetables. Fresh food of any type was hard to come by, especially when living in the colony. Every bite took him back to a time when food was more plentiful, and the hardest decision someone had to make was whether to eat General Tso's Chicken or an Italian meatball sub.

As he was finishing, Jessie came back into the den, a sly grin on her face. She held something in her hands. When he realized what it was,

Mason sat up straight, his mouth hanging open as he searched for an explanation.

"I believe these are yours," she said, holding out the brightly colored prophylactics.

He squinted awkwardly as he tried to explain.

"They're, uh, survival gear."

"Oh, yes, I'm sure they are."

"No, you don't understand. They're for—"

The radio sounded. *"This is General Carr. Come in, over."*

Mason looked at the radio and then back at Jessie, uncertain about which warranted his attention more.

She motioned toward the radio and said, "Go on. I'm just funnin' with you." She wheeled about, shaking her head lightly as she left the room.

Still a bit red-faced, Mason leaned toward the microphone and pushed the talk button.

"Mason here."

"Good to hear your voice, Marshal."

"You too. I hope I didn't pull you away from anything too important."

"Bandits hitting convoys, dogs terrorizing neighborhoods—same as every other day." There was a pause. *"I need to know what happened out there."*

"I fell into a trap, one that won't be easy to pull myself out of."

"Go on."

"Locke offered me a job at The Farm."

"Not too surprising given your talents with a gun. Did you take it?"

"Before I could decide one way or the other, I discovered something awful."

"What's that?"

"They're killing infected people and using them in their food bars."

"Come again?"

"You heard me. Locke and his men are hunting the infected like animals, and processing them at the plant."

"Good God! Are you sure?"

"I saw it with my own eyes, General. When I confronted Locke, he claimed he didn't have a choice, that people would starve without the protein."

"And he let you leave without a fight?"

"I guess he figured that if he killed me, you and others would start asking questions. Instead, he turned my own team against me. How are they, by the way?"

"Red's dead, but I guess you already knew that."

Mason thought back to Red lying in the cargo ship's hold, pleading for him to carry him out. It had come down to a choice between Bowie and Red, and Mason had zero regrets about his decision.

"And the others?"

"The rest are alive, but injured to one degree or another. Dix was fished out of the James River with a broken arm. Cam announced that he's done working for the colony. And Beebie, well, Beebie's got a serious hard-on for you at the moment."

"It was them or me, and when those are the options, I'm gonna choose me every time."

"Even so, it's not going to set things right in their minds. Any one of them will kill you if given the chance."

"Understood." Mason paused, trying to decide how to word his next question. "General, I need a straight answer from you on something."

"Go ahead."

"Did you know what Locke was doing?"

"Hell no, I didn't know. I've eaten a few of those bars myself."

"What about Governor Stinson? Do you think he's aware of what's going on?"

"Stinson's not a bad man. Indecisive at times, but not rotten at the core like Pike was. I can't see him signing off on something like that."

"Then I think it's about time he knew what he's feeding to his citizens. I have a hunch it might be the source of the colony's unexplained illness."

"You think the food bars are causing the Craze?"

"I don't know for certain, but the timeline sure fits."

"I'll take care of letting Stinson know what's going on. But you need to get back here ricky-tick so we can sort things out."

"Before I come in, I have a favor I need to do for someone."

"A favor's important enough to risk being shot?"

"This one is."

"Okay, but you need to understand that I can't clear this alone. Until you come in and explain yourself, the colony's going to consider you a criminal. That means if they get wind of your location, they'll send a team out after you."

"Roger that."

"Watch yourself, Marshal. This thing may get a little muddy."

"You do the same, General. Mud has a way of getting everyone dirty."

❧ ☙

When Mason caught up with Jessie, she was standing in the kitchen, folding a basket of clothes.

"Did you get it all straightened out?" she asked, glancing over her shoulder.

"I made contact. That's a start."

"From what I could hear, it sounded like they want you to go in and explain yourself."

"I'll report back like a good soldier, but only after you and I do something first."

She set the clothes down and turned to face him.

"What do you mean?"

"You've been kind enough to feed Bowie and me." He glanced out the screen door to see the big dog lying on his side enjoying an afternoon siesta. "Not to mention letting me use the radio. I thought I might return the favor by helping to find your father."

Jessie eyes grew wide. "You mean it?"

He nodded.

"And I can come with you to Grey's Point?"

"I think you'll have to. I've never met Jack in person and would probably walk right by him."

"I won't be any trouble. I promise."

"I'm not worried about you being trouble, only about trouble finding you." He gestured toward her nearly see-through blouse. "You might want to put on something a little more, well, trail worthy."

Jessie glanced down, and for the first time seemed to realize that there wasn't a lot between her breasts and his gaze. What might have embarrassed another woman merely brought a smile to her lips.

"And here I thought you didn't notice things like that."

"I notice, believe me. The problem is, so will others."

"Give me a few minutes to change," she said, snatching up a handful of clothes and hurrying from the room.

While she was busy dressing, Mason pushed open the screen door and stepped outside.

Bowie sat up, his eyes struggling to stay open.

"Better wake up, boy. We're getting ready to move."

The dog yawned, letting out a high-pitched *yeeaww*.

Mason glanced back at the screen door.

"We're going to have company on this one, so I need you to be on your best behavior."

Bowie's head turned to follow his master's gaze.

"I know it's dangerous to bring her along, but we don't have a choice."

Bowie cocked his head sideways.

"This isn't like that. This is a good deed. Nothing more."

Bowie shook his head and let out a little snort.

"Yeah," said Mason. "I thought that's what you'd say."

By the time Tanner and Samantha jumped off the old Country Squire and put in some fresh fuel, it was getting near lunchtime. A quick trip back inside the home yielded six cans of chicken noodle soup, an unopened box of crackers, and a Costco-sized tub of fruit cocktail. After everything was opened, they hopped up onto the hood of the car to enjoy their afternoon feast.

Sister Mary Margaret seemed less than enthused by their culinary choices.

"Shouldn't we warm this in a pot with some water?" she said, eyeing the soup.

"No need," Samantha said with a noodle hanging out of her mouth. "All you gotta do is pour a little water in on top every few bites." She used her water bottle to demonstrate. "See?"

Sister Margaret took a quick whiff of the soup and set it aside.

"I think I'll wait to eat until I get back to the monastery."

"Suit yourself," said Tanner. "More for us, right, Sam?"

"Uh-huh," she said, her mouth full.

The nun checked her watch and let out a frustrated sigh.

"Believe me," said Samantha, "it's better to let him eat. Tanner turns into an ogre when he's hungry."

"I do not."

Samantha looked at Sister Margaret and mouthed, "He does."

The nun turned and stared down Highway 11 as if hoping to spot a taxi.

"How much further is it?" asked Samantha.

"At least two hours. Maybe three," she said, not hiding her frustration at their slow pace.

"You're worried about the nuns."

Sister Margaret said nothing.

"Can I ask you something?"

"I feel like you're going to ask either way, so go ahead."

"Why didn't you and the other nuns fight those men? Is it against your religion or something?"

"Defending oneself is not against our religion. Unlike your father, however, we don't prescribe to the idea that violence solves every problem."

"But you have to admit that it's needed sometimes, right?"

Sister Margaret was slow to answer, and when she did, her eyes were distant.

"During my time in the war, I saw enough violence to last a lifetime. Never once did I see it actually solve a problem. For every person who was killed, two more were convinced to take up arms because of his death." She shook her head. "Violence solves nothing."

"You know, Sister, you may be right," Tanner said, tipping the can up to pour the last bit of soup into his mouth.

Samantha wheeled around in disbelief. "Huh?"

"I'm just agreeing with her. Violence probably isn't the best way to solve problems. Unfortunately, your enemy often doesn't share this enlightened view and keeps coming with hatchet in hand." He wiped his mouth with a sleeve and let out a little burp. "That leaves you to either accept the moral shortcoming of putting a bullet in his eye or have him cleave your skull in two. Like it or not, that's the reality we face."

Sister Margaret frowned. "You're doing your daughter no favors by putting these notions into her head."

"You say that, but yet here she is—fed, safe, and of a mindset never to become a victim. All in all, I'd say she's doing just fine."

"Don't forget loved," Samantha said, brushing cracker crumbs from her shirt.

He leaned over and kissed her on the head.

"And loved."

"Yuck! You just got soup in my hair."

"Get used to it, darlin'. Ask anyone and they'll tell you—love's messy."

Sister Margaret seemed little amused, and walked to the rear of the car to sit on its bumper.

Tanner leaned over and whispered to Samantha.

"I don't think she gets us."

"Give her some time. She'll come around. We're pretty adorable." She paused. "Well, I am, anyway."

After retrieving the remaining fuel from the Power Wagon, Tanner turned the Country Squire north on Highway 11. For the next two hours, they passed through a handful of small communities, including Pulaski, Dublin, and Radford, without seeing a single soul.

As they neared Salem, Samantha said, "It's awfully quiet out here."

"Nothing wrong with quiet," answered Tanner.

"I guess."

"You don't like quiet?"

She shrugged. "It's sort of like the dark. You never know what's out there, hiding."

"You worry too much."

"I'm making up for you not worrying enough."

A series of gunshots sounded from up ahead. They were still some distance off, perhaps a half-mile or so. Even so, Tanner rolled to a stop.

Sister Margaret turned to look at him. "What are we doing?"

"Tanner and I have a strict rule about staying out of other people's troubles," explained Samantha. More gunshots sounded. "And *that* is definitely other people's troubles."

Sister Margaret pointed to an on-ramp.

"Maybe we can get on I-81 and avoid Salem all together."

Tanner glanced back at Samantha. "What's the map say?"

She studied the map lying beside her on the seat.

"Sister Margaret's right. The interstate goes right around Salem. We could get back on Highway 11 in Cloverdale."

"How far?"

She used her fingers to estimate the distance.

"Six miles or so."

Tanner looked from the highway to the on-ramp. Both had risks.

"What's the problem?" asked Sister Margaret.

"The problem is that interstates are dangerous," said Samantha.

The nun craned her head, attempting to see up the on-ramp.

"Dangerous how?"

"Bandits and wild dogs for sure. Who knows what else?"

"Bandits?"

"It means robbers."

"I know what it means. Are you saying they frequent the interstates?"

"Yep. One time, we got cornered by a gang of them on motorcycles. They even zapped Tanner with a cattle prod."

"Lovely, I'm sure," the nun said, cutting her eyes at him.

Samantha seemed puzzled. "I don't think you understand. It was a real cattle prod. You know, one of those things they poke cows with to get them to move. It wasn't lovely at all. Poor Tanner fell to the ground, twitching like a nervous cat."

"I think she was being facetious," said Tanner.

"Facetious? What's that mean?"

"Callous and snooty at the same time."

Samantha looked at Sister Margaret and furrowed her brow.

"Nuns shouldn't be allowed to be facetious."

The sincerity of Samantha's scolding put Sister Margaret on the defensive. She tipped her head. "My apologies."

"It's okay. I forgive things super easy."

Sister Margaret worked to strike a more conciliatory tone.

"I'm glad to hear that your father has at least taught you the importance of forgiveness."

"Tanner? Forgiveness?" She cracked up. "That's a good one."

"It's from your mother, then?"

"I guess so. She always said it's never good to go to bed angry."

Sister Margaret glanced over at Tanner.

"The woman must truly have the patience of a saint."

Samantha shook her head. "Not anymore. She's dead."

Sister Margaret's voice softened. "I'm sorry to hear that. I really am. Perhaps if she and your father had raised you together—"

"Oh, Mom and Tanner were never together."

Sister Margaret looked confused.

"He adopted me." Samantha looked over at Tanner. "That's okay to say now, isn't it?"

"In present company, I think it's fine."

"He rescued me from a burning building last year, and we've been together ever since."

A concerned look came over Sister Margaret's face.

"You're telling me that this man is not your father?"

"He is now. I decided to let him raise me."

"*You?* A twelve-year-old girl decided that?"

"Actually, I was eleven at the time."

"But he's a—"

"Criminal?"

"I don't know. Is he?" She looked at Tanner with a mixture of apprehension and dismay.

"Not anymore. I think he escaped. That's right, isn't it, Tanner?"

"Let out for good behavior," he said, relishing in her discomfort.

Sister Margaret was absolutely beside herself.

"Don't you have other family who could take you in? An aunt or a grandmother, perhaps?"

Samantha pursed her lips, thinking. "I don't really know. Maybe." She shrugged. "It doesn't really matter though. Tanner and Issa are my parents now."

"Who's Issa?"

"She's my new mom. I don't call her that though, because it feels kind of funny. We met her when we were down in the tunnels under Washington, D.C. Tanner fought for her hand in marriage. You should have seen it. It was *so* romantic."

"And where is she now?"

"Missing. That's why we're on the road. Issa went back to her colony to show them she could get pregnant."

"Her *colony?*"

Before she could answer, Tanner said, "I think you've said enough, Sam. We don't want to bore the good sister."

Samantha was confused for a moment, but then her face cleared.

"Oh, I get it," she said in a stage whisper. "We don't know if we can trust her yet." Samantha pretended to lock her mouth with a key. "Tick a lock."

"If only it were that easy," he muttered.

Another round of gunshots from the road ahead settled the decision, and Tanner steered the wagon onto the on-ramp.

"You watch behind us," he said over his shoulder.

"Right." Samantha spun in her seat to get a better view out the rear window.

Like every other interstate, I-81 was congested with abandoned cars, trucks, and tractor trailers. Most had been pilfered, leaving purses, clothes, plastic cups, and human bones strewn across miles of roadway. Trapped on the cold stretch of asphalt, people had slowly settled into their cars to die, like elephants into a dark cave spilling with ivory.

Sister Margaret began to whisper a prayer, and neither Tanner nor Samantha interrupted her. A little heavenly protection was welcome by convert and heathen alike.

Tanner steered the big car through a winding path that meandered its way around the wreckage. A pack of dogs dug through an abandoned bakery truck, pulling at blue plastic crates with their teeth. The animals were little more than skin and bones, their ribcages visible through their sparse fur. As the station wagon approached, a few scattered, but most stood and watched it pass, hoping for an opportunity to feast on something tastier than stale hamburger buns.

"Sister Margaret," Samantha said without taking her eyes off the road.

"Yes, dear."

"Why does God allow so much suffering?"

Sister Margaret seemed startled by the question.

"Tanner says that suffering's just part of the world, but he's a Buddhist. I wondered if you might see things differently since you're a nun."

"My faith teaches that suffering is a result of sin. When God first made the world, there was no sin, and thus no suffering. Once we began to sin, however, suffering forever became part of our existence."

"Are you saying that God is punishing us just because we made a few mistakes along the way? That doesn't sound very fair."

She offered an understanding smile. "No, dear. God isn't punishing us with suffering. We brought that upon ourselves. Even so, perhaps He does allow it to exist because of all the good that comes along with it."

Samantha looked out at the starving animals.

"What good could possibly come from those dogs dying of hunger?"

"The good, dear, is that you saw their suffering and felt compassion."

Samantha sat quietly for a few minutes, staring out the rear window as she mulled over Sister Margaret's words. In the end, she filed them away to sit alongside other tidbits of insight that Tanner and her parents had shared with her. One day, she thought, she would need to sort through them, deciding what to keep and what to throw out. For now, though, they could stay, each doing their part to make the world a bit less mysterious.

They drove on for several more minutes, and whether it was due to divine providence or simple dumb luck, they managed to travel the brief stretch of interstate without being accosted by man or beast.

Tanner took the off-ramp just past Cloverdale, and everyone breathed a collective sigh of relief at being free of the interstate. An immediate left turn put them back on Highway 11, a Hardee's to their right and a Pilot gas station a little beyond that. A school bus sat parked in the center of the four lanes, a steady cloud of pale gray smoke puffing from its tailpipe. Its windows were covered with newspaper, and a handful of bullet holes riddled the back door.

Tanner brought the station wagon to a stop twenty yards behind it. Going around the bus would put them at risk of taking passing fire from its windows, the equivalent of being broadsided by a pirate frigate.

"What do you think happened to them?" asked Samantha.

He slipped the car into park but left it running.

"Nothing good."

"Are we checking it out?"

"Have to," he said, climbing out with his shotgun in hand.

Samantha snatched her Savage .22 rifle from the seat and reached for the door handle.

"Where do you think you're going?" Sister Margaret said with a disapproving tone.

Samantha pushed open her door. "I go where he goes."

"But it might be dangerous."

"Exactly. That's why I'm going."

↞ ↟

As they approached the school bus, Tanner and Samantha heard sobbing coming from within. It was a deep emotional weeping that was uncomfortable to listen to. Together, they hugged the right side of the bus, ducking beneath its paper-covered windows as they shuffled forward like members of a SWAT team. When they arrived at the forward door, they found it partially ajar.

Tanner leaned around and peeked into the bus. The driver's seat was empty and the interior nearly dark. He motioned for Samantha to stay put as he leaned forward and pushed the door the rest of the way open.

Voices could be heard, someone pleading, "Please! We have to do something!"

Tanner crept up the stairs. The stench was so pungent that he had to force himself to breathe only through his mouth. When he reached the top step, he spun to the left with his shotgun raised.

Two dozen men, women, and children huddled together on green vinyl seats, each of them with the classic symptoms of having been infected— black glossy eyes, swollen joints, skin marred by blisters. A small group of people stood near the back of the bus, tending to a teenage girl lying on the floor. One man in particular seemed utterly heartbroken, sobbing uncontrollably as he held the young woman's hand.

When Tanner appeared, parents pulled their children close, draping arms protectively around them. Several men scrambled into the aisle and stood defensively, their hands raised in tight fists. One of the women who had been tending to the injured teen quickly pushed her way forward.

"Please!" she begged. "We don't mean anyone harm. There's no need for more bloodshed."

Tanner lowered his shotgun.

As the woman came closer, he saw that she was probably around his age, full-bodied in a hearty sort of way, with a head of short gray hair that looked like it had been cut with garden shears.

"We're travelers," she explained. "If we've inadvertently stopped on your property, we'll gladly move."

He shook his head. "I don't own this stretch of road any more than you do." He looked past her to the fallen girl. "What happened to her?"

"Shot in the stomach by men less understanding than you."

"She going to make it?"

The woman's face grew long. "She's lost a lot of blood. I don't suppose you happen to be a doctor."

"No," he said, rubbing his chin. "But I might just know one. Have a couple of your people bring her out the back." Tanner turned and clomped back down the steps.

Samantha looked at him expectantly.

"Well?"

"Go get the car. Hurry!"

Without hesitation, she wheeled around and raced for the car. Sixty seconds later, the Country Squire screeched to a stop as the back doors of the big orange bus swung open.

Sister Margaret climbed from the car.

"What's the big emergency?"

Her answer was quick in coming, as two men handed down the teenage girl. The woman Tanner had spoken with climbed out behind them.

"Where should we put her?"

"On the back of the wagon," Tanner said, hurrying around and folding down the car's tailgate. Several blankets lay wadded up in the back, and he quickly spread them over the door. He turned to Sister Margaret. "You said you were a combat medic. This girl could use your expertise."

"Are you kidding? That was nearly forty years ago! And besides," she said, looking around, "there's nothing here. No sterile compresses, no saline solution, nothing!"

Tanner leaned into the station wagon and dragged forward his pack. Flopping it open, he pulled out a small first-aid kit and pressed it against Sister Margaret's chest.

"This is what you have to save that girl's life."

She glanced down at the kit and then over to the unconscious girl being laid atop the tailgate. The entire front of the young woman's shirt was soaked with blood.

"What you're asking is impossible. Anything I do will probably only kill her that much faster."

"She's dead inside of ten minutes anyway. If you screw up and she dies in five, I don't think anyone's going to hold it against you."

Sister Margaret's eyes filled with tears.

"I'm sorry," she choked, handing him back the first-aid kit. "I gave up that life a long time ago."

Tanner's face turned red, and he seemed ready to give her the old "Time to cowboy up" speech when Samantha stepped forward.

"Sister Margaret," she said softly.

The nun looked at her, eyes still clouded with tears.

"I'm just a kid, so I don't know much. But have you ever thought that maybe God doesn't only allow suffering so that we can learn compassion?" She shrugged. "Maybe He lets it be here so we could feel the joy in relieving it."

Sister Margaret stared at Samantha for a long moment, blinking back tears. Finally, she took a deep breath and exhaled hard. Without a word, she moved to the young woman's side and placed her fingers on the radial side of her wrist. The pulse was surprisingly strong for someone who had lost so much blood.

"We need to get this shirt off so I can see the wound."

Samantha drew her knife and began carefully cutting away the cloth. As she peeled it back, a dark bloody hole became visible near the girl's navel. Samantha did her best to ignore it, focusing instead on the blade of her knife as she continued cutting through the sleeves and collar.

Once it was clear, she slid the shirt free and said, "What next?"

Sister Margaret turned to the two men who had carried the teenager out.

"Roll her onto her side. I need to see if there's an exit wound."

One man grabbed the girl by the shoulders, and the other took her by the hips as they rolled her toward the nun. Sister Margaret bent over and studied the girl's back. It was smeared with blood, but there were no signs of trauma.

"Okay. Roll her back over, nice and gentle."

They did as she instructed.

"Get me a bottle of clean water."

Samantha raced over to her pack and returned with a bottle of water in hand.

"The cap's not even broken on this one," she said with a note of pride.

Sister Margaret began pouring it over the wound, and a hole about the diameter of a pencil began to take shape. Blood continued to ooze out.

She turned to Tanner. "I need a sterilized wipe."

Tanner opened the first-aid kit and pulled out several small alcohol wipes.

"These are all I have."

"They'll do." Sister Margaret tore open two wipes and carefully scrubbed her hands. She used two more to wipe off the area around the wound.

Samantha held out her knife. "Here you go."

"What's that for?"

"To get the bullet out."

"Put that thing away. We're not cutting this girl open."

"But—"

"But nothing. Finding a bullet without imaging is nearly impossible. Besides, it might be the only thing preventing additional bleeding."

"But won't it kill her?"

"If she dies, it won't be because of a piece of lead sitting inside her. It'll be because of what the bullet destroyed on its way in." Sister Margaret turned back to one of the men. "Tilt her head back and monitor her breathing. We don't want her airway to become blocked by her tongue." She turned to the woman. "Go find something to put over her—coats, blankets, anything. We need to keep her as warm as possible to prevent shock."

The woman turned and hobbled back toward the bus, her swollen joints reminding everyone of her affliction. In less than a minute, she returned with two thick blankets, placing one over the girl's legs, and folding the other to cover her exposed breasts.

Sister Margaret wiped the wound again, studying it carefully.

"The blood's dark, and it's not pulsing."

"Is that good or bad?" said Samantha.

"It's good, because it means it's probably not coming from an artery. Of course, that doesn't mean she's not bleeding internally."

"And if she is?"

"If she is, she's going to die. There's nothing I can do to stop that." She turned to Tanner. "I need several clean compresses to stop the bleeding."

Tanner dug through the first-aid kit, coming up with a handful of thin white gauze bandages and a roll of surgical tape. Neither looked up to the task at hand.

Sister Margaret tore them open and placed them over the wound. Almost immediately, blood began to seep through.

"These aren't going to be enough."

Tanner looked through the bag for a trauma bandage. There wasn't one. He searched his pack and pulled out a white t-shirt that could have been mistaken for a small tent.

"What about this? It hasn't been worn since it was washed."

"It's not sterile, but it'll have to do."

Using the windshield as a cutting board, Tanner quickly sliced the shirt into pieces with his knife. Once the stack of cloth was thick enough, Sister Margaret laid it over the blood-soaked gauze and applied pressure with both hands. She stood there for ten long minutes, never once letting up. Once she was certain that the bleeding had stopped, she used the surgical tape to hold it in place.

When she was finished, she stepped back and used the last of the remaining water to clean the blood from her hands.

"Is she going to live?" asked the woman.

"If she doesn't die in the next thirty minutes, there's a good chance the injury itself isn't going to kill her. But if she doesn't get antibiotics in the next couple of days, the wound will likely become septic."

She nodded. "They may have medicine where we're going."

"Where exactly is that?" said Tanner. A bus load of infected people taking a roadside sabbatical was not something he encountered every day.

"We're going to Mount Weather. We were told that our kind is gathering there to rebuild."

Samantha turned to Tanner, her eyes wide.

"Who told you that?" he asked.

She shrugged. "Word has been spreading for the last few months. There's a community forming there, a community in which we can be safe from violence like this."

"Do you know who's heading it up?"

She shook her head. "I have only heard her referred to as 'Mother'." The woman turned to Sister Margaret. "Thank you for what you did."

"She might still die."

"She might, but at least you gave her a fighting chance." She turned to the two men. "Be gentle loading her back onto the bus."

Together, they lifted the girl through the rear door, careful not to disturb the bandage. As they pulled the door closed, the woman turned to face Tanner.

"Why would anyone do something like that?"

"People are always looking for a reason to kill."

She nodded and then reached out and placed her hand on his arm.

"Thank you."

He shrugged. "I didn't do anything."

"You did the most of all. You showed us that there are still some out there who can look past our marred skin and black eyes. There are those who can see us for what we used to be. We won't forget what you did for us."

With that, she offered one last nod and hurried back onto the bus.

CHAPTER
8

The drive from Gretna to Luray took nearly four hours. Issa led the way in her Prius, and Lulu followed, driving the slavers' flatbed truck. Dolly and Jen rode with Issa, while Marcy and Theresa rode with Lulu. They came in from the west, along Highway 211, passing the Schewel Furniture Company, a BB&T bank, and a Taco Bell, all of them dark and lifeless.

As was often the case around towns and cities, the closer they got to Luray, the more congested the road became. Tractor-trailers, cars, panel vans, and even a fully loaded logging truck were encased in the perpetual traffic jam. Many of the vehicles' doors remained open, a hint at the desperation people had faced when the outbreak first manifested. As nearly all of them had learned, however, the virus was not something that could be escaped.

Jen pointed to a long lazy curve up ahead.

"The caverns are just around that bend."

Issa steered the Prius into a McDonald's parking lot. The building was dark and the windows shattered. Two distinctive clumps of dried human remains lay beside the door. Bloodstained skulls sat atop yellow and black uniforms, embroidered golden arches still visible on their shirts. Unlike the adjacent roadway, the parking lot was relatively deserted. Apparently, a Big Mac was the last thing escapees had on their minds.

She brought the car to a stop at the far side of the lot and climbed out. Lulu pulled the flatbed truck in next to her, taking up several empty parking slots. A few seconds later everyone stood huddled together, staring at Issa as if they expected her to roll out charts and maps outlining some foolproof blitzkrieg.

She didn't. Instead, Issa bent down and checked the laces on her boots.

"We got a plan or what?" Lulu said, puffing on a cigarette she had scavenged from one of the dead slavers.

Issa pointed to a dense plot of trees to the east.

"Jen says the caverns are that way. The first thing we're going to do is see if we're even in the right place." She turned and started for the trees. "Spread out a little, and try to stay quiet."

Dolly followed a few steps behind Issa, and Jen a few behind her. The other three women ignored Issa's advice and clustered together, twenty or thirty yards back. When the trees finally broke, they did so into a sprawling parking lot, roughly the size of something found outside of a Wal Mart. A crowd of perhaps eighty people huddled in front of a wooden platform. A handful of men could be seen working on the structure, and the intermittent thwacking of hammers reverberated through the air.

Before Issa could really get a good look at things, a pickup truck turned onto the road leading into the parking lot. She quickly ducked back into the trees to avoid being seen, and motioned for Dolly and Jen to take a knee.

Once it had passed, they darted over to her.

"The entrance to the caverns is over there," Jen said, pointing to the left side of the lot.

Issa brought her hand up to her brow as she tried to cut the glare of the sun. The brightness of midday was causing her eyes to leak a thin mascara-like substance that slowly trickled down her cheeks.

The other three women approached from the rear, and Issa let everyone gather together before discussing what to do next.

"It looks like they're building something," said Marcy.

"A stage," offered Theresa.

"That ain't no stage," said Dolly. "It's an auction block."

"If that's true, where are the slaves?"

No one had an answer. Unfortunately, from their vantage point, much of the lot remained blocked from view.

"Let's move further around to get a better look," said Issa.

She turned and began walking northeast, careful to stay twenty or thirty feet inside the tree line. Dolly and the other women resumed their respective posts behind her. As they approached the north end of the field, the parking lot came into full view.

The stage was just that, a stage, likely from a local high school band department. Wooden stairs had been erected on either end to facilitate easier foot traffic. A pot-bellied man stood at the edge of the stage, smoking a pipe and giving directions to a handful of workers as they completed the final preparations.

Having cleared the trees, they could now see five flatbed trucks parked along the southern edge of the parking lot. Several dozen prisoners had already been unloaded and stood in a jagged line beside the trucks, armed men watching over them.

Lulu turned to Jen. "Looks like you were right. This is where it's happening."

She nodded. "How are we going to free them with all those guards watching?"

"It's not only them watching," added Marcy. "There's probably a hundred and fifty people out there now, with more arriving every minute. It's going to be hard to get close enough without being seen." She held up the Colt Gold Cup and looked down its sights. "I don't think I could hit any of them from here."

Issa gently pushed the gun down.

"The only thing we have is surprise. If we give that away, we're all dead."

"If you ask me, this whole thing's doomed from the start," said Lulu. "The guards have us outnumbered ten to one."

"Not if you count the prisoners," countered Issa.

Dolly said, "You're thinkin' if we set them free, they can help do some of the fightin'."

"No. I'm thinking that if fifty or sixty prisoners are running in different directions, it'll create enough confusion for quite a few of them to get away. Throw in a few well-placed gunshots, and we might just start a full stampede."

"That's a good idea, but it ain't gonna work unless they know they s'posed to run."

Issa nodded. "They also need to know that we have a truck ready to carry them away from here."

"But how are we possibly going to get word to them?" said Jen.

Issa pressed her lips together. "Simple. One of us is going out there to tell them."

She cringed. "Who?"

"The one who has the best chance of not being noticed."

Issa looked around the group. Each of the women had their own disfigurements from the pox. Marcy's joints were swollen, and she tended to hobble from side to side when she walked. Jen's face and hands were covered with scars from the blisters. Theresa hadn't been afflicted too badly, although patches of her red hair had fallen out, leaving her scalp bare in some spots. Lulu and Dolly were probably the two least affected, although like all the infected, their eyes were as black as obsidian.

"I'll go," said Dolly.

Everyone turned to her, surprised.

"But you're..." Jen searched for the right word.

"Old, I believe, is the word you're lookin' for? And that part's true enough. But the way I see it, ain't nobody gonna pay an old woman no mind." She lifted her flabby breasts. "What used to be in the attic is now hangin' in the cellar." She grinned. "I'll go, and I'll find my Jerome. Once I do, I'll tell him to pass the word on to the others. I can't shoot for nothin' anyhow, so this'll be my part in all this."

Issa nodded. Dolly was not only the first to volunteer, she was also the most logical choice.

"Assumin' I make it to Jerome, what exactly should I tell him?"

"Tell him everyone has to try to escape all at once," said Issa.

"But how they gonna know when's the right time?"

"They'll know because we're going to create a diversion to draw away some of the men. When that happens, it'll be their cue to move."

"What kind of diversion?" asked Lulu.

Issa studied the parking lot more closely. As people waited for the auction to begin, many were mingling outside a large brick building with a Luray Caverns Welcome Center sign out front. A little past it was an outdoor playground, and beyond that, a sprawling single-story structure.

She turned to Jen. "What's in that far building?"

"It's a museum filled with old cars."

Issa nodded. "That'll do nicely."

"Do for what?" said Theresa.

"For burning."

Her eyes opened wide. "You're going to start a fire?"

"No," she said, "*we're* going to start a fire. And a big one at that."

঵ ঵

Issa popped the hatch on the Prius. A five-gallon plastic jerry can full of gasoline rested in the back, with blankets wedged around it. She lifted out the canister and set it on the ground. It was heavy, maybe thirty pounds or more.

"This should be plenty to get things going."

Dolly seemed concerned. "But child, ain't you gonna need that to get back home?"

"I'll find another way."

"But yo' husband—"

"My husband's already out looking for me. Of that, I have no doubt. If I can make it to Mount Weather, he'll find me."

Dolly pressed her lips together and nodded.

"We sure owe you some kinda debt for what you're doin' here."

"Only if I don't get us all killed." Issa closed the hatch and picked up the gas can. "This thing's heavy, and I'm not planning on carrying it all by myself. So, stay close." She wheeled around and started back through the forest.

The walk back to the lookout position seemed to take forever, partly because they had to haul the gasoline, and partly because everyone knew the trouble they were heading toward. They arrived to find the parking lot teeming with people, easily three or four hundred now, and more arriving in a steady caravan of cars and trucks. Unlike pre-Civil War auctions, the slave buyers were not southern aristocrats in search of farm labor but, rather, families who had managed to survive the outbreak only to discover that hardship was now a way of life. The temptation to have a "lesser" person around to do the lowliest of chores was apparently strong enough to overpower any sense of moral decency.

Issa pulled off her sunglasses and held them out to Dolly.

"Put these on to hide your eyes."

When Dolly slipped on the large-framed glasses, she looked like an African American version of fashion icon Iris Apfel.

"I'll try to get 'em back to you when this is over."

"Don't worry about that. You and Jerome just keep running."

Dolly nodded. "I'll put my hand up in the air once I've gotten word to him." She leaned in and gave Issa a hug. "In case I don't see you again."

Issa softly patted the old woman's back.

"Just be careful."

Dolly said nothing more, releasing Issa and walking out into the parking lot like someone who had stepped away to use nature's facilities. Her gait was calm and slow, and no one seemed to take the least bit of notice.

Issa turned to the other women.

"The rest of us will circle around through the trees and slip in behind the car museum." She reached down and picked up the jerry can. "Let's move."

Their pace was quicker now, Issa leading them in a slow jog. For things to go off as planned, she needed to have the diversion ready before the auction got underway.

By the time they arrived at the back of the museum, Issa was breathing heavily, her arms crying for a rest. She set the fuel by her feet and studied the back of the building. While the face of the museum was a conglomeration of brick, wood, and stone, the rest of the structure was constructed of painted concrete block. A low-bay door was at the rear of the building, no doubt to allow cars to be brought in and out. A service entrance sat beside it.

Issa turned to Jen and Marcy.

"While we're getting things ready inside, you two go and get eyes on Dolly. Let me know once she raises her hand."

They nodded and hustled around the side of the building.

Issa, Theresa, and Lulu moved up to the back of the museum. The service entrance was a metal-clad security door without any kind of a handle, lever, or knob. Issa thumped it with her fist.

Solid core. No way to kick it in.

She stepped over to the low-bay door and gave the two small handles a tug.

It didn't budge.

She straightened up and studied the rear of the structure. Her eyes were drawn to three rectangular windows about eight feet off the ground. Used only for light, they had no way of being opened.

She turned to Lulu, who was by far the lightest of the group.

"We'll lift you up so you can climb through and open the door."

"And what exactly am I supposed to do about the window?"

"Smash it out with your pistol."

"That sounds like a good way to get myself all cut up."

"We have to get inside somehow. Given my condition, I'm not taking a chance on falling. So, unless you want to lift Theresa, you're the one."

Lulu eyed Theresa. While not fat, she had a soft layer of flab covering most of her body.

"I'll do it if you want," she offered.

Lulu shook her head. "Nah. I've got it. Just don't drop me."

Issa and Theresa stood beneath one of the windows, their hands cupped in front of them. Lulu stepped up, and they lifted her into the air. Teetering slightly, she tapped the butt of the Beretta against the glass until it shattered. She took her time, clearing the frame of any remaining shards.

"Okay, lift me higher so I can climb through."

Straining under her weight, Issa and Theresa hoisted her up another foot so that she could slip through the opening. Lulu belly-rolled through and dropped down into the museum. A few seconds later, the back door opened.

Theresa went in first, and Issa followed, carrying the jerry can. The museum was dark except for what sunlight filtered in through the windows.

To their immediate left was a baby-blue 1896 Peugeot. Two faded bench seats sat facing one another, a brass-tipped handle poking up from between the seats, allowing the rearmost rider to steer the vehicle. The front of the car was equipped with a single bulbous headlight that resembled a searchlight, and the sides were adorned with matching brass lanterns. Next to the Peugeot sat a mint-green 1903 Speedwell, and next to it a split-seat 1905 Riley. On the other side was an enormous open-air stagecoach with black leather seats and beautifully polished wood poles supporting the roof.

"Look at this place," Theresa said with awe. "It's like an old movie set."

She was right. The entire building was filled with antique cars, old-time carriages, and covered wagons. The women wandered for a moment, reading some of the signs standing in front of the carefully preserved vehicles.

There was a bright blue 1931 Morgan sports car that would have been at home on the set of *Chitty Chitty Bang Bang*, and a 1930 Cord that, with a few added bullet holes, could have passed for Bonnie and Clyde's getaway car. There were probably fifty vehicles in total, each as irreplaceable as the next. Issa didn't know if it was a private collection or gathered together for the sole purpose of selling tickets to connoisseurs of vintage automobiles. It didn't really matter either way because in a few minutes, all of them would be lost forever. Part of her regretted destroying such memorable pieces of history, but if it helped her and the others to survive, so be it. Casualties of war, as it were.

A desperate pounding sounded on the back door, and a voice hissed, "Issa, open up!"

Issa hurried over and pushed open the door. Jen stood on the other side, her face flushed, sweat beading along her forehead.

"What is it?"

"They got Dolly!" she panted.

"What? How?"

"They caught her talking to the slaves. They're beating her right now. It's bad, Issa, real bad. I think they're going to kill her."

"Where's Marcy?"

"She got scared and ran back to the truck. Said she'd have it waiting for us."

Issa's nostrils flared as she forced air out. The plan was going sideways. She looked over her shoulder. Theresa and Lulu stood staring at her, uncertain of what to do next. No doubt both were wondering if Marcy had had the right idea.

"You three get this fire started," she ordered. "Splash gas on as many vehicles as you can, start the fire, and then get back to the truck. Wait for everyone as long as you can, but when you have to go, go!"

Jen reached out and touched her arm.

"What are *you* going to do?"

Issa lifted the big Merkel. "Something stupid."

CHAPTER 9

Even after cleaning out the garbage, the cab of the junkers' RV stunk of body odor and spoiled fruit. The body odor was easy enough to explain, but it took Bowie's superhuman nose to find the remnants of a moldy peach under one of the seats.

The back of the RV, however, was in surprisingly good shape. The Plateau XLTD followed the traditional camper design with two long cushioned benches that doubled as beds, a laminate table between them, and a collection of storage cabinets, bellows, and cutouts. The camper also featured a refrigerator, a small range, a sink, and a bathroom closet that offered both commode and shower. Everything was high end, with solid maple cabinetry, white Corian countertops, and supple leather upholstery.

The live-in area was directly accessible from the driving compartment, giving the cab a roomy feel. The driver's and front passenger seats both faced forward, but the second row could swivel to face either the road or the camper's interior.

As Mason stepped from the RV, he found Jessie waiting for him. She had a daypack slung across one shoulder and was wearing a pair of knee-length hiking shorts, a tight-fitting black undershirt, and a lightweight flannel shirt with the sleeves rolled up. Around her hips hung an old-fashioned leather gun belt equipped with a stainless-steel Ruger Vaquero and a long line of .45 Colt cartridges.

"Better?" she said, extending her arms to either side.

"Much." He nodded toward the gun. "Do you know how to use that thing?"

She drew the Vaquero and used her opposite palm to slap back the hammer. An old clay pot near the corner of the yard exploded. Jessie gave the pistol a quick spin around her finger and pushed it back into the holster.

"Well enough," she said with a sly grin.

While Mason was not one who thought much of fancy gun tricks, the motion was fluid and the bullet on target, which suggested that she had spent the requisite time practicing.

"Shall we go?" he asked with a smile. "Or would you like to shoot a few silver dollars out of the air first?"

"Funny." She rubbed the handle of the Vaquero. "Daddy gave me this for my sixteenth birthday."

"Did he teach you to shoot it too?"

"We spent the whole summer shooting soup cans off the fence out back. By the time Halloween rolled around, I could hit 'em as fast as I could work the hammer."

"Beautiful *and* dangerous," he said with an approving nod. "Nice."

She beamed with delight. "I've had men describe me as one or the other, but never both." She turned and studied the junkers' trailer packed full of oddities. "Are we taking all that with us?"

"I thought it might help us to blend in. You did say that Grey's Point was a big swap meet."

"Makes sense to me." She walked around and opened the RV's passenger-side door.

Mason let Bowie into the backseat and then climbed in behind the wheel.

"I'm assuming you know the way."

"Oh sure," she said, settling against the leather. "I've lived here all my life." She looked out the side window as if considering half a dozen routes. "It's probably best if we go straight up Highway 14 to Fort Nonsense and then turn left onto Highway 3."

"Fort Nonsense? That's a real place?"

Jessie smiled. "Daddy said they named it that way on account of the military having built their fortifications facing the wrong direction during the Civil War."

He chuckled. "That would do it." Mason started the RV, put it into gear, and eased away from the curb. "About how far is it to the campground?"

"Maybe twenty miles. Even pulling a trailer, we should be there inside of an hour."

"Did you leave a note for your father in case we miss him?"

She nodded. "I told him I ran off with a tall, dark stranger."

He cut his eyes at her and she giggled.

"Lighten up, Marshal. This is going to be fun."

Bowie added his two cents by leaning forward and licking the back of his ear.

Mason forced a smile but said nothing. Having made a living out of finding people, he had come to one conclusion. When someone went missing, more often than not, fun was the last thing involved.

જે જી

The first half of the trip to Grey's Point Camp passed without incident. Highway 14 was empty of traffic, save for the occasional traveler or farming tractor. Those who did pass offered a wary wave, perhaps out of neighborliness, or perhaps as an attempt to keep altercations to a minimum.

Jessie proved to be a good traveling companion, never feeling the need to fill the cab with unnecessary chatter. Instead, she sat peacefully looking out the window as the world slowly rolled past.

Bowie, on the other hand, fidgeted in the backseat, moving from one side to the other, but never quite willing to go back into the main camper to lie down.

"Are you not comfortable back there, boy?"

Hearing his master's voice, the dog pressed his enormous head between Mason's and Jessie's seat and let it settle onto the center console.

Jessie reached down and stroked the soft fur on his nose.

"Poor thing. He looks lonely."

"I can't see how. He's got me 24/7."

"Maybe he needs the company of a female dog."

"A doggy girlfriend?"

"Exactly. It seems only fair. I'm sure you've had a few lady friends along the way."

"Don't get me started," he grumbled.

"Oh, come on. It couldn't have been all bad."

Mason thought of Ava lying next to him in the grass, of the warmth of Connie West in the cab of his truck as rain poured down outside, and of the passionate whispers of Leila Mizrahi in the darkness of his mountain cabin.

"No," he admitted softly, "not all bad."

"What were they like?"

"My girlfriends?"

"Yeah."

"I don't know. Women."

"*Really?* Women, you say?" She chuckled, and he couldn't help but join in.

"Sorry. I've never been good at talking about old flames."

"Why's that, do you suppose?"

"For one thing, I'm not sure they'd *want* me talking about them."

"Ah, I get it. You're not one who likes to kiss and tell."

"I suppose."

"Any other reason?"

He shrugged. "I guess I feel a sense of loss when I talk about people who are no longer part of my life, girlfriends or otherwise."

She studied him thoughtfully.

"What?"

"It just surprises me that you're such a sensitive man. It's no wonder women are drawn to you."

"You say that, and yet here I am spending my nights with this slobber monster." He reached over and ruffled Bowie's fur. "What about you? Lots of boyfriends over the years?"

"Oh sure. Let's see… there was Tom Doniphon, Will Kane, and oh yeah, can't forget Jason McCullough. All rugged, hardworking men. Just the way I like 'em."

Mason smiled. "I see."

Something caught Jessie's eye, and she turned and pointed up ahead.

"Look! There, beside the road."

Mason spotted an old man sitting along the edge of the asphalt, his face cupped in both hands. He wore dirty slacks, a pair of mud-soaked pants, and a thin white undershirt that was torn and smeared with blood. As the RV approached, he tried to stand but lost his balance and fell back to the ground.

"He's hurt," she said.

Mason brought the RV to a stop a few feet short of the man.

"Just be careful. We don't know—"

Without waiting for him to finish, Jessie swung open her door and hopped out.

Bowie squeezed his way into the front seat and turned to Mason, obviously seeking permission to go after her.

"Yeah, yeah, go on."

The dog scrambled out of the cab, quickly catching up to her.

Mason opened his door and climbed out, taking a moment to study the road. On one side sat a storage rental facility, and on the other, an overgrown field with a sign that read "Mobjack Nurseries." Neither of them looked like good hiding spots for would-be robbers.

While it wasn't particularly cold, Mason walked around and lifted out one of the green army jackets from the trailer. By the time he reached the old man, Jessie was helping him to his feet. The stranger was in his late sixties or early seventies and seemed confused, his eyes wandering from person to person as his mouth moved, even though no sound came out.

"Put this on," Mason said, slipping the jacket over his shoulders.

The man turned to him, leaning so far forward that he nearly fell.

"Johnny…? Is that you, boy?"

"No, not Johnny. Just a friend," Mason said, keeping him upright as he worked to get his arms into the sleeves of the jacket.

"Not Johnny?"

Mason spoke slowly. "I'm Mason. And that's Jessie and Bowie."

The man's eyes grew wide as he spotted the wolfhound.

"Reindeer!"

Mason chuckled. "Close enough. Can you tell us what happened to you?"

The man touched a bloody bump on his head.

"He hit me. Right here." He leaned forward, and once again, Mason and Jessie had to keep him from falling.

"Who hit you?" asked Jessie.

"Yellowbeard hit me."

She turned to Mason. "Yellowbeard?"

He shrugged. "Yellowbeard."

"Yes, yes! Yellowbeard hit me!" the man said, striking his head with his fist.

"Easy," Mason said, trying to calm him. "What's your name?"

"I'm Henry," he said proudly. "Henry," he repeated as if liking how it sounded the first time.

"All right, Henry. Do you live around here?"

The man gave him a big smile. "Yes I do." That, however, was the extent of his answer.

"And where *is* your home?" Jessie said, trying to coax it out of him.

"I live at the Brambles."

Mason and Jessie stood confused.

"Brambles!" the man said again, his voice rising.

She reached out to hold one of his hands.

"Can you show us how to get there?"

"To the Brambles?"

"Yes. Can you take us there?"

The man's eyes lit up. "Yes, yes, I'll take you." He began pulling her as he started down the highway.

Jessie looked back at Mason, uncertain if she should resist or go along.

"If he's walking, it must be close. I'll follow behind you in the RV." He motioned to Bowie. "Go with them."

The dog hurried after Jessie and Henry, occasionally leaning in to sniff the mud on the back of the old man's trousers.

Mason returned to the RV, started it up, and inched along behind them. The old man seemed confident of where he was going, leaving Mason reasonably sure they weren't being led to an empty cornfield somewhere.

Henry eventually turned down a narrow drive constructed of uneven slabs of concrete. Mason coasted along behind them, feeling the RV bump over each joint in the road. The sides of the drive were lined with saplings just beginning to get their leaves, too sparse for anyone to hide behind. After nearly a quarter-mile, the drive ended at a cul-de-sac with four houses.

The old man released Jessie's hand and hurried toward a light gray, two-story home. The sign out front read "The Brambles Day Support Center." Several people stood by the front door, but upon seeing the RV, they began pushing by one another to get inside. As soon as Henry came close enough, frightened hands reached out and pulled him into the home.

Jessie stood with Bowie at the end of the drive, and Mason exited the RV to join them.

They studied the building. A half-dozen men and women peeked out through various windows, swishing the curtains closed whenever they feared they had been discovered.

"What do you think it is?" she asked.

"Some kind of assisted living center, maybe."

She started for the door. "We should at least make sure Henry's going to be okay."

Mason didn't believe they were necessarily on the hook for ensuring the old man's wellbeing, but he didn't resist either. The willingness to show goodwill toward others was a trait that defined all men.

Bowie tagged along too, warily eyeing the faces peeking out at them.

Jessie stepped up to the door and gave it a firm knock.

No one answered, but they heard the distinct sound of people rushing around inside.

"I think they're afraid of us," said Mason.

She took a few steps back and looked toward one side of the house and then the other. The faint sound of voices could be heard coming from the backyard.

"Shall we?"

He shrugged. "Why not?"

Together, they followed a brick walkway leading around the house. The backyard consisted of a large courtyard shaded with several oversized umbrellas. Men and women ranging from teenagers to the elderly sat around outdoor tables, coloring pictures and playing children's card games. All of them seemed oblivious to their approach.

Jessie turned to Mason and whispered, "I think they're…" She hunted for the right word. "Impaired."

He nodded. The people before him were like children, completely disconnected from the dangers and horrors of the world around them. The question was, how were they still alive?

Jessie seemed to be wondering the same thing.

"Where are they getting food and water?"

"Someone must be taking care of them."

No sooner had he said the words than the back door opened. A man hobbled out. The flesh on his face and arms was disfigured from the pox, and he wore a dark pair of wraparound sunglasses, no doubt to shield his eyes from the sun. He dressed as if he were preparing for a spot of Sunday tea, with recently pressed slacks, a long-sleeved white shirt, and a button-up vest. His age was hard to discern, but his hair was gray and he walked with the help of a cane.

"I can assure you that we have nothing worth taking," he said in a gravelly voice. "But if you must take what little we have, please do so without hurting anyone."

"We're not here to steal anything," Jessie said, stepping closer. "We helped an injured man who told us this was his home."

"You brought Henry home?"

"He sort of brought *us* here. But yes, we walked him down from the highway."

The man moved toward them like a spider, slowly and deliberately, placing his feet with the greatest of care and using the cane to probe the ground before him. There was something unnerving about his motion, and Mason instinctively let his hand hang down ready at his side.

"My name is Porter. Franklin Porter."

"Nice to meet you, Mr. Porter. I'm Jessie. This is Mason." She glanced around to find Bowie licking the face of a middle-aged woman with Down syndrome who giggled with delight. "And that pile of fur is Bowie."

Porter noticed Mason's badge and recited, "Justice. Integrity. Service."

"You know something of the marshal service."

A thin smile touched the man's scarred face.

"Lately, it seems I know something about nearly everything."

Henry's bruised face appeared in the window behind Porter, and he waved enthusiastically.

Jessie smiled and waved back. "I'm afraid Henry got into a little trouble before we found him."

"That part," said Porter, "was Papa Doyle's doing. His or one of his boys."

"Who's Papa Doyle?" asked Mason.

He turned and pointed off to the northeast.

"A most unfriendly neighbor."

"Your neighbor assaulted Henry? Why?"

"Doyle would no doubt say that Henry was stealing some of his crops."

"Was he?"

Porter shrugged. "Probably. Strawberries have started to come in, and they can be pretty tempting. I'm afraid it will only get worse as summer approaches."

"Can't you talk with this Doyle fellow?" said Jessie. "Let him know about Henry's condition? Surely he—"

"No, dear. Papa Doyle is not a man of such sensibilities. To him, these people are nothing more than unwanted mouths to feed—weeds to be plucked from the field, as it were."

"And to you?" said Mason.

Porter slumped forward, letting his weight rest on the cane.

"To me? How could I even put it into words? They are family. Brothers and sisters, each and every one of them."

It was spoken with such heartfelt sincerity that Jessie felt her eyes cloud with tears.

"You must have cared for them for a very long time," she said.

"No, dear, not long at all."

"Oh," she said with surprise. "I thought that—"

"I know what you thought, but my story is not one of a caretaker growing old with his patients. Come. Let me show you something."

Porter began his careful advance toward the far corner of the property. Mason and Jessie followed, leaving Bowie behind to watch over those playing games.

Porter stopped in front of a row of eight identical wooden bins, each measuring roughly three feet in both width and length. The structures had been constructed with the greatest of care, the interiors painted black, and the tops sealed with large plates of glass set at a slight incline. Misty streaks of condensation covered the inside surfaces of the glass, water droplets slowly trickling down into a collection channel made from PVC pipe. From there, the water routed through a short length of yellow tubing, passing through a tight-fitting rubber stopper into a clear, gallon-sized jug.

"What are they?" asked Jessie.

Porter looked at Mason, pausing to see if he might be able to answer.

"They're solar distillers."

"That's correct."

Jessie leaned over one to look inside. A pool of cloudy water rested in the bottom.

"I get it. You fill them with polluted water and let the sun evaporate out the fresh. Is it pure enough to drink?"

"Oh yes, very much so."

"Pretty clever. Did *you* build them?"

"Oh heavens, no," he said. "I merely designed them. One of our residents, who was once a master carpenter, led their construction."

"How much water do they produce?" asked Mason.

"A unit provides approximately a gallon of fresh water each day. That accounts for a few milliliters being discarded to eliminate the hydrocarbons that evaporate first, of course."

Jessie nodded her approval. "Wow, they're lucky to have someone around that's so smart."

"That, my dear, is the remarkable part."

Sensing he had a story to tell, Jessie and Mason turned to face him.

"You see, six months ago, I lived here as a resident. My cognitive abilities were roughly that of a kindergartener."

"How's that possible?" said Jessie.

"How indeed?" Porter rubbed bony fingers over his scarred flesh. "I can only conclude that the virus somehow caused a mutation in my brain. I not only regained my intellect, I began to see things in ways that I could never have imagined. That new understanding enabled me to develop solutions to some of our many challenges."

She wrinkled her brow. "You're saying that the virus made you into a genius?"

He closed his eyes and nodded humbly.

"I believe that is accurate."

Jessie looked over at Mason. "Have you ever seen anything like that?"

"No, but I have seen mutations that were truly unbelievable." Images of the gluttonous *pishtacos* that lived in the JIF peanut butter plant came to mind. "The notion that the virus might affect cognitive abilities in a positive way isn't such a stretch."

She turned back to Porter. "Did any of the other residents see a similar improvement?"

"All of the others who became infected died, including our original caretakers. I was the lone survivor of the virus. The rest of the patients you see here were fortunate enough not to become infected."

"And now you're using your intellect to help them."

"That's correct."

"What are you doing for food?" asked Mason.

"We eat from many sources, including scavenging from abandoned homes. But one source that was particularly bountiful through the winter months was our deer traps. Come," he said. "I'll show you."

Porter led them into a grove of trees a short distance from the house. Within it sat a chest-high cage constructed from fencing, metal pipe, and a door screen. The screen had been drawn up like a set of blinds and suspended in place with a simple cotter pin, leaving one end of the cage open. A trip wire was tied to the pin and routed across the inside of the cage about three inches above the dirt. A thin trail of dried corn led to a larger pile at the far end of the cage.

"You've built a Clover trap," Mason said, eyeing the setup.

"Is that what it's called? Sometime in my life, I must have seen something similar. Its concept and construction became rather obvious when, well, when I began to think again."

Jessie poked her head in through the open door and studied the apparatus. It was all pretty simple. As the deer entered to eat the corn, it would bump the wire and cause the screen to fall, trapping it inside.

"I'm surprised the deer don't try to fight their way out." She had once seen a full-grown buck nearly kill a man and couldn't imagine the thin wire cage holding such an animal.

"Indeed, I supposed they could if they were so inclined. Fortunately, deer are surprisingly docile when trapped and will remain relatively motionless until they see people approaching. The cage can then be collapsed on top of the animal to hold it down for dispatching."

"How many traps do you have set up?" Mason said, looking around to see if he could spot another one.

"A handful. We leave the cage doors tied open until our food runs low. That way the deer come to trust them. It's rare that we must prepare a meal without meat. We also started a garden, but most of the crops won't be ready until summer. Hence, the reason for our problems with Papa Doyle."

Jessie looked over at Mason. "There must be something you can do."

"Anything I do would be short-lived. They'll be neighbors long after we're gone."

"He's right," said Porter. "Whatever treaty we agree to has to work for us in the long run. It can't rely on the interventions of an outsider."

"Still," she said, touching Mason's arm, "you could at least talk to him. Maybe see if you could convince him to soften his response a little."

"All right," Mason said reluctantly. "But don't expect a miracle. Men like Doyle don't change their ways with a good talking to."

"It's a good thing you were there to help," said Samantha. "Tanner and I wouldn't have known what to do with that poor girl."

Sister Margaret offered only a curt nod. Ever since treating the young woman, she didn't seem to be in the mood for talking.

Samantha turned to Tanner. "I should really learn some doctoring skills. You know, in case you get shot."

"Me? What about you?"

"Well, yeah, I guess that's possible too. I just figured you're more likely because of your…"

"My what?"

"You know. Your size."

"What about my size?" he said, sucking in his gut.

"You're what my mom would call 'well-upholstered.'"

He cracked a smile. "Well-upholstered. I like that one."

"I thought you might. Seriously though, I should take some formal medical training, maybe at the hospital in Boone. You and Mason both know the doctor there. I'm sure he'd be happy to teach me. Who knows? Maybe one day I could become a doctor myself."

"I figured you more for a chicken farmer."

She smiled. "I do love chickens."

"Me too," he said, licking his lips.

Sister Margaret watched their banter out of the corner of her eye, saying nothing.

For the next hour, their conversation ebbed and flowed as Samantha recounted tales of their many adventures. She seemed particularly pleased with herself whenever she could draw a concerned look from the good sister. In time, they quieted, each settling into their own rhythm of passing the time.

As they neared the town of Staunton, Sister Margaret began to guide them, pointing out the various turns to take. They circled a large shopping mall and carefully traversed a neighborhood populated with houses that had surely been built when Tanner was a child.

She pointed to an intersection ahead.

"We'll need to turn up there."

Tanner steered the station wagon onto Frontier Drive, passing two small banks that shared a common green space between them. Whether there was still money in their vaults had become irrelevant to even the most ardent treasure hunter when the New Colony had declared that the "greenback" was officially nothing more than funny money. The only currency that held any value in the post-pandemic America was the gold-backed credit, and even it was often looked upon with suspicion.

With the banks disappearing in his rearview mirror, Tanner noticed that the roadside attractions were becoming fewer and fewer.

"You sure this is the way?"

Sister Margaret nodded. "They built the hospital away from things to keep it out of the public eye."

He steered around a slow curve, and a large brick building came into view on their left side. The sign out front read "Coffman Funeral Home and Crematory."

"That's kind of gross," Samantha said, leaning her head out the window to get a better look.

"People must be prepared for burial," countered Sister Margaret.

"Well, yeah, but putting a funeral home in with an ice cream shop." She shook her head. "That just seems wrong."

Sister Margaret looked to Tanner to see if he would correct her. When he didn't, she said, "It's not that kind of cream, dear."

"No? What kind is it then? My mom liked cream in her coffee, but I really like whipped cream. Tanner does too, don't you?"

"Oh yes," he said with a grin.

"It's not any kind of cream," Sister Margaret said, her voice rising. "It's a crematory."

She turned to Tanner. "They don't make cream at a crematory?"

"Seems like they should."

Sister Margaret let out an exasperated sigh.

"A crematory is a place where bodies are burned."

Samantha looked surprised. "Bodies? Like human bodies?"

Sister Margaret nodded. "That's right."

"Then why don't they call it a burnatory or a meltatory? Even crispatory would be better than crematory."

"I suppose it's because—"

"I mean, really, why bring cream into it at all?"

Sister Margaret shook her head. "Young lady, you are impossible."

Samantha looked to Tanner and shrugged. "Did I say something?"

Before he could answer, Sister Margaret pointed toward a sign resembling a small gravestone. Faded blue letters spelled out the words "Frontier Culture Museum."

"That's it. That's our turn."

"The asylum is part of a museum?" said Tanner.

"Not officially, no. From what I understand, they acquired the center after it closed."

He slowed and turned onto the narrow drive. The trees had grown out over the road, creating a dimly lit tunnel. To the right was a dirt driveway that looked like it hadn't been traveled in many months.

Samantha leaned forward to rest on the back of Tanner's seat.

"It's kind of creepy, isn't it?"

"Don't start." Before he could even get the words out of his mouth, tips of the branches began scraping against the sides of the Country Squire.

She cringed. "It's like giant fingernails scratching to get in."

Tanner turned to Sister Margaret. "How much further?"

"It's still a little ways yet. We have to pass by the museum."

He continued on, breathing a sigh of relief when the road opened up into a large parking lot. Surprisingly, there were only three vehicles in sight: a black Crown Victoria, a Jeep Wrangler, and a white Chevrolet Astro Van.

"That's it!" exclaimed Sister Margaret. "That's the van they used."

"You're sure?"

"Positive."

"Well, that's good news, I suppose," he said, pulling the station wagon in next to it. "Maybe we won't have to search the old asylum after all." He glanced back at Samantha. "I know Sam will be disappointed though."

"Hardly."

Together, the three of them climbed from the car and took a long look around. Directly to the south was a handful of buildings with turquoise-colored roofs. The one furthest to their left had a huge sign out front that read "Homemade fudge—Buy 1 lb, Get 1/2 lb Free."

"Yum," said Samantha. "I wonder if they have any left."

"Never know," said Tanner. "We might find a block or two."

"Ooh, I hope they have jelly-donut flavor. I love that one best of all."

"Do you two ever stop with all the back and forth?" snapped Sister Margaret. "It's driving me crazy!" She turned and stormed off toward the buildings.

Samantha watched her go. "What's gotten into her?"

He shrugged. "Must not like fudge."

"Ah," she said, nodding. "Maybe nuns aren't supposed to enjoy sweet things."

"Either way. More for us."

Tanner lifted his shotgun from the car, and Samantha grabbed her rifle. Walking side by side, they took their time approaching the museum. The buildings turned out to be a gift shop, locked up tighter than a jewelry store, two administration buildings, also locked, and an Exhibits Center that served as a passage into the outdoor museum. The door to the Exhibits Center had been propped open with a bale of hay.

By the time they caught up to Sister Margaret, she was already inside the Exhibits Center, stepping around a life-sized statue of an American Indian that had toppled through a glass display case. To her left was a long counter with a sign hanging from it that read "Tickets purchased here."

"What kind of museum is this?" Samantha asked, kneeling to study the fallen statue.

Sister Margaret said, "It was built to show the different Old World influences on early America."

Samantha nudged the statue. "Like Indians?"

"To some degree, I suppose. Mostly, the museum looks at the influences of settlers from places like Germany, Ireland, and England."

"If you ladies are done with the history talk," said Tanner, "I wonder if we might get a move on."

Samantha stood up. "Just getting my education wherever I can."

Sister Margaret seemed to like that, a thin smile crossing her face. She turned and pointed to a half-open door on the other side of the Exhibits Center.

"I would think we should go that way."

Tanner took the lead, pushing open the door and stepping out into a small courtyard. On the opposite side, a rock-covered trail wound through a thin copse of trees. Three golf carts sat parked beside the trail, but based on the height of the grass surrounding them, none had been moved in several months. So much for riding.

"What's that?" Samantha said, pointing to a handful of ruddy-colored huts to the west.

"That, darlin', is our first clue."

Tanner led them through the trees and across a field of limp grass. As they drew closer, they saw that the huts were part of a meticulous recreation of a small African village, no doubt to commemorate the contribution of African slaves to the settling of America. A waist-high mud wall surrounded the village.

Tanner stopped behind a large cypress tree and motioned for Samantha and Sister Margaret to come up beside him.

"What are we doing?" asked the nun.

Before he could answer, two women stepped from one of the huts. While it was impossible to make out their faces at such a distance, there was no doubt that they were wearing nuns' habits.

"That's them!" she said, starting to push past him.

"Easy, Sister," he said, blocking her way. "I've found that it's usually not the best idea to go running up to trouble, unprepared."

"That's true," seconded Samantha. "He usually stomps up to it."

He threw her a grin. She knew him too well.

"Let's just watch for a moment and see what's what, shall we?"

Sister Margaret slowly settled behind the tree.

"Okay, but we need to get them out of there. Look at the poor things."

While the nuns appeared to be tired and their clothes a bit dirty, neither seemed injured or otherwise harmed.

"I think they'll survive another couple of minutes."

At his insistence, they stood quietly watching as the two nuns carried armloads of branches to a fire pit. It wasn't long before a man stepped out from behind one of the huts, zipping up his pants. Even at a distance, they could see that he was young and handsome, not to mention having both the hair and physique of Chris Hemsworth. A hunting rifle hung lazily from one shoulder.

"Oh my," whispered Samantha, her breath catching in her throat.

Tanner cut his eyes at her. "What was that?"

"I didn't say anything."

"Uh-huh."

"He's the one who shoved me to the ground," said Sister Margaret.

The gleam in Samantha's eyes faded, and she reluctantly swung her rifle up to rest on a limb.

"All right. Where do you want me to wing him?"

Tanner rested a hand on her shoulder.

"Before we go shooting anyone, let's see what they want."

She stared at him. "Who are you, and what have you done with Tanner?"

He grinned. "Just cover me while I go say hello."

"Snipers' rules apply?" she said, lowering her cheek onto the stock.

"You got it," he called back over his shoulder.

As Tanner marched off toward the camp, Sister Margaret leaned close to Samantha and whispered, "What exactly are snipers' rules?"

"They're pretty simple, really. First and foremost, don't shoot Tanner."

She nodded. "That one makes sense."

"Second, if you do shoot Tanner, don't shoot him anywhere important."

Sister Margaret waited, but Samantha said nothing more.

"That's it? All the rules have to do with shooting *him?*"

"Pretty much."

"It seems like you should have a rule about when to shoot someone else."

"Oh, that one's easy."

"It is?"

"Sure. If Tanner starts bleeding, I start shooting."

Sister Margaret quieted as she tried to make sense of her feelings about seeing a young girl aiming down the sights of a rifle.

Tanner wasn't a particularly quiet man. Fortunately, Hemsworth wasn't a particularly observant man either. If it hadn't been for the two nuns staring at Tanner with wide eyes, he might have been able to tap the young man on the shoulder and shout "Boo!" As it was, he made it to within twenty feet of the wall before Hemsworth turned to face him.

The man fumbled to pull the rifle off his shoulder.

Tanner leveled the shotgun at his belly.

"That would be a mistake." He motioned to the side. "Throw it away."

After a brief pause, Hemsworth tossed the rifle over the mud wall.

"Who are you?" he asked.

"Funny, I was about to ask you the same thing."

Tanner advanced through an opening in the wall. As he stepped into camp, a third nun exited one of the huts, folding a green wool blanket with the words "Official U.S. Property" printed on the side. When she saw what was happening, she hurried over to stand next to the other two.

"That's three," muttered Tanner. He sidestepped over to the women, careful not to take his eyes off Hemsworth. "Where's Sister Mary Number Four?"

"Who?" said one of the nuns.

"The fourth nun. Where is she?"

"Sister Mary Clare was giving them trouble, so they took her away yesterday evening."

Tanner nodded, turning his attention to Hemsworth.

"This is the part when you tell me where to find Sister Clare."

"Go screw yourself, old man."

The "old man" comment stung more than it probably should have, and Tanner considered blowing a knee out as a lesson in good manners. In the end, he let wisdom triumph over vanity, reminding himself that it was tough to get a screaming man to tell you much of anything.

He raised an arm, waving to Sister Margaret and Samantha. They stepped out from behind the tree and hurried over.

As soon as they arrived, he turned to Sister Margaret.

"Here. Hold this," he said, handing her the shotgun.

She stared at the sawed-off shotgun like it was the Lance of Longinus, damning her to an eternity of being mauled by hungry lions. She tried to pass it back to him, but Tanner had already turned to face Samantha.

"If he gets lucky and puts me down, shoot him."

Samantha raised her rifle. "Leg or body?"

"Dealer's choice."

Samantha nodded. "I'll go leg on account of… you know, his body."

"How is that at all fair?" Sister Margaret said as she lowered the shotgun to the ground.

"I live by the rule that the man who holds the gun decides what's fair." Tanner stepped toward Hemsworth and said, "Feel free to tell me when you've had enough."

Hemsworth raised his hands into tight fists.

"Maybe you were something back in your day, but—"

Tanner punched him. It was a quick left jab, nothing more, but it caught Hemsworth squarely in the mouth. The young man stumbled back and raised his hands to his face. When he pulled them away, they were slick with blood.

"You mother—"

Tanner hit him with another jab, this time to the nose. Again, Hemsworth stepped back, his nose now at an ugly sideways angle, blood trickling out. He started to say something else when Tanner drove a knee into his gut. Air was suddenly in short supply, and the young man doubled over, gasping.

"Stop it this instant!" shouted Sister Margaret. "You're hurting this man!"

Before Tanner could stop her, she rushed forward and started tending to Hemsworth.

"Let me see," she said softly, trying to pull his hands away from his face.

Hemsworth jerked upright and spun Sister Margaret around. He braced one arm against her throat and the other against the back of her neck. Sister Margaret's face burned bright red, and she gurgled something that sounded a lot like "Buggers."

Hemsworth turned to Samantha. "Put the rifle down, or I'll break her neck."

Samantha looked over at Tanner. "Well?"

"Shoot him in the eye."

The other three nuns all began to protest at once.

Tanner held up a hand. "Hush. We're negotiating."

Confused, they slowly quieted.

Samantha raised her rifle. "What if I miss and hit Sister Margaret?"

"It's all right. I never liked her that much anyway."

Sister Margaret's eyes widened, but she was incapable of speaking.

"What are you, crazy?" Hemsworth said, trying to duck behind the woman's narrow shoulders.

Samantha took a deep breath and rested her finger on the trigger.

"Wait!" he shouted, shoving Sister Margaret away and raising both hands in front of him.

Tanner nudged Sister Margaret out of the way and raised his fists like a boxer getting ready for the bell.

"Now, where were we?"

Hemsworth looked left and right.

"If you run, she'll shoot you," Tanner said calmly. "Your only way out of this is to tell me what happened to Sister Clare."

"Fine. What the hell do I care anyway? It wasn't like she was mine." Hemsworth bent over and spat blood from his mouth. "Last I saw of her she was over at the old dairy building." He pointed off to the northeast.

Unless there were maidens outside, milking cows, Tanner had no idea how to tell a dairy building from a lumber mill.

"What's it look like?"

"It's white and octagonal," he said, wiggling a tooth to see if it had come loose. "You can't miss it."

Tanner turned to the nuns, finding Sister Margaret standing over them like a mother hen.

"Did this man…" He searched for a delicate way of saying it. "Break any of your covenants?"

They seemed utterly baffled by the question.

He sighed. "Three nuns, one knucklehead with too much testosterone. Come on. You know what I'm getting at."

One of the women shook her head.

"Oh no, nothing like that. They wanted us to be pure for the weddings."

"The weddings?" exclaimed Sister Margaret. "Don't they know you serve God?"

"They knew, but I got the feeling that was why we were chosen. They wanted women who were pure, both morally and physically."

Tanner turned back to Hemsworth. "All in all, that's good news for you. It means no broken bones."

He stepped forward and fired a tremendous right cross to the man's jaw. Hemsworth went down hard, landing flat on his back with his arms splayed out to either side. Tanner raised his foot, preparing to add insult to injury. As he did, Sister Margaret gasped. Tanner stomped anyway, hard, like he was putting out a campfire. When he was finished, Hemsworth's face looked worse than Jess Willard's after going three rounds with Jack Dempsey.

Tanner bent over and used the man's t-shirt to wipe blood from his boots.

"Horrible," Sister Margaret cried, as she tried to shield the eyes of the other nuns.

"I know," he grumbled. "These are new boots."

꘠ ꘢

Tanner and Samantha took point, leading Sister Margaret and the other three nuns along the gravel trail. Their first stop was at a decrepit English cottage whose walls were a patchwork of dark pink panels framed by thick black beams. The roof had been constructed from overlapping clay tiles, and a tall brick chimney protruded high into the air. At the base of the chimney was a stone that read *EW 1692*.

"Wow," said Samantha, pausing to study the old home. "It's like the witch's house in *Hansel and Gretel*." She stuck her nose into the air and sniffed, as if hoping to smell gingerbread cooking.

A young woman appeared from a small patch of trees to the south, a wooden yoke balanced across her shoulders. A bucket dangled from each end, water sloshing with every step. When she saw Tanner and the others, she set the water down and hurried around to the rear of the house.

Samantha turned to Tanner. "Do you think she lives in this old house?"

"If she does, she's not alone." He nodded toward one of the windows on the second floor. A man could be seen staring out.

"Should we go check it out?"

Tanner shook his head. "They're leaving us alone. Let's do the same."

As they walked past the cottage, Samantha said, "Why do you think they chose to live in such an old home?"

"Not everyone wants the cushy life that we have."

She snickered. "You do realize that we live in a cabin."

"So?"

"So, I used to live in the White House."

"If you think about it, the only difference between our cabin and the White House is the color of the wallpaper."

She rolled her eyes. "When you say stuff like that, I know you're just trying to sound smart."

"Actually, I'm trying to get you to ask yourself what really defines happiness."

"There you go again," she said, shaking her head.

"Or better yet, whether happiness is something to be defined at all."

"Stop, you're killing me!"

He smiled. Samantha didn't like accepting his tidbits of wisdom, but he hoped that at least a few of them managed to wriggle their way into her nutty little brain.

They continued along the trail, eventually coming upon a small estate. According to the sign out front, it was an original construction from the 1700s, brought over from Ireland. The small farming spread consisted of a home and two secondary buildings, their roofs made from thick layers of stiff yellow straw.

A stone pen had been built in front of the home, and within the pen were a handful of well-fed pigs. Directly behind the pen was a garden with tiny green plants poking up through freshly tilled soil. The only thing that seemed out of place was a bright yellow poster hanging on the stone wall. On it, a burly man tossed seeds from a metal tray. At the bottom of the poster were the words "Only Healthy Seed Must Be Sown!"

A woman peeked out through an open window, a fretful expression on her face. She turned and spoke to someone, and a few seconds later, a man with thick arms and an even thicker body appeared in the open doorway. He cradled an over-and-under shotgun in both hands, but his relaxed posture suggested that he wasn't looking for a fight.

Tanner raised a hand, and the big man reluctantly wandered over, stopping on the far side of the stone pen. Sensing there wasn't any immediate danger, Samantha leaned over the short wall and began patting one of the pigs. The pig snorted and pressed its snout to her palm.

Startled, she pulled her hand away, but after carefully counting her fingers, went back to giving him a good petting.

"Nice looking pigs," Tanner said, hoping to start things off on a friendly note.

The man nodded. "Nearly fat enough for eatin'." He let his eyes wander to the four nuns. "All of them yours?"

"We most certainly are not!" exclaimed Sister Margaret. "I'll have you know we're devout servants from Our Lady of the Angels Monastery."

"Angels, you say?" He mulled on that while working a wad of chaw from one side of his mouth to the other. "What you folks doin' 'round here?"

"Rescuing prisoners," she said accusingly.

"I see." He pulled the pinch of tobacco from his mouth and flicked it down to the pigs. The fattest of the bunch hurried over and gobbled it down.

Sister Margaret looked past him at the woman peeking through the window.

"Are you keeping that woman against her will?"

"I s'pose you'd have to ask her that." He turned and hollered, "Hattie! Get out here so these folks can set you free."

The woman moved to stand in the doorway. Her condition was abundantly clear, pregnant, probably six months or a little more.

"Free from what?" she hollered back.

"Me, I reckon."

"A little late for that now," she said, stroking her swollen belly. "Where were they 'fore you got me like this?"

"You sure? Cause I don't want you kept against your will. Take anythin' you want 'cept for the pigs," he said, chuckling.

"Funny," she sneered. "Now get your sorry backside in here. We got work to do 'fore nightfall comes."

The man turned back to Sister Margaret.

"I don't s'pose that offer extends to me?"

Sister Margaret said nothing.

"Yep. That's what I thought." He turned and meandered back to the door, muttering, "Against her will. That's a good one, all right."

Tanner looked over at Sister Margaret and smiled.

"I'm thinking there might be a lesson in that somewhere."

"Oh?" Her voice was haughty. "And what might that be? That not everyone requires saving?"

"I couldn't have said it better myself." He turned and continued along the gravel path.

Sister Margaret and the other nuns followed. Samantha took a moment longer to give a few parting scrubs to the pigs before hurrying to catch up.

The trail took them around a large counterclockwise loop. At the far end, they came upon two long hangars with grain silos out front. A handful of low bay doors on one of the hangers stood open.

Tanner turned to Sister Margaret. "You and the ladies hold tight."

She nodded.

As Samantha headed off with Tanner, Sister Elizabeth could be heard saying, "Shouldn't she be staying with us too?"

Sister Margaret's response was as succinct as it was telling.

"Don't even get me started."

Tanner and Samantha walked to the closest of the bay doors. Inside were jumbled piles of antique furniture, some surely dating back two or three hundred years. Chairs, tables, cabinets, even doors and window frames lay about. The air was laced with the unmistakable odors of wood stain and sawdust.

"What's all this for?" she asked, stepping out from behind him.

"Must be for the exhibits. Either that or someone's a serious hoarder."

She traced her fingers along the arm of a rocking chair and carefully sat down. The wood creaked under her weight but held.

"It's probably better if you don't sit on any of this," she warned.

"I wouldn't dream of it. Stuff's probably eat up with termites."

She hopped to her feet. "Termites!"

"Oh yes. They're terribly dangerous." Tanner held up a hand and made a little pinching motion with his index finger and thumb. "The little devils crawl into your ears and chew right through your brain."

A flash of fear crossed her face, but it quickly melted away.

"Well then, I guess *you* wouldn't have anything to worry about," she said with a grin.

He ruffled her hair. "You're getting wise to my ways. Shame."

They exited the building and headed toward one of the silos. A rickety metal ladder ran up the side.

"Climb up and see if you can spot the old dairy farm," he said.

What would have been met with heated debate months earlier elicited only a resigned sigh.

"Fine. But next time you get to do it."

"Scout's honor," he said, holding up a hand.

She slipped the rifle over her head.

"Were you ever even a Boy Scout?"

"For a while."

"I suppose you got kicked out."

He made a pained face. "I'm hurt. I really am."

"Yep. That's what I thought."

Samantha turned and hopped up to grab the first rung. Her upper body strength had improved significantly, and she was able to pull herself up the first few rungs without the use of her legs. When she was about twenty feet off the ground, she stopped.

"Can you see it?" he called up.

Hanging by one arm, she leaned around to get a better look. In the distance, she could make out the parking lot and even the blur of the old station wagon. To the right of the lot was an oddly shaped building with a bright red roof.

She pointed. "That must be it over there."

Tanner tried to peer through the trees but couldn't get eyes on the building.

"Is it octagonal?"

Samantha studied the building. It could have been octagonal. Then again, it could have been round, square, or half a dozen other shapes. Hard to tell from a distance.

"I think so."

"You do know what an octagon is, right?"

"Of course I do," she said, starting back down the ladder. "It's the shape of the signs you ignore every chance you get."

As she neared the bottom of the ladder, he scooped her off and gave her a quick tickle before setting her on the ground.

"You're going to break a rib one of these days," she said, rubbing her side. "And then how are you going to feel?"

"I'll feel fine. You'll be the one with the broken rib."

She shook her head, but there remained a playful grin on her face.

"Brute."

"Sissy."

Together, they walked back to Sister Margaret and the nuns, Samantha giving Tanner a few good pushes to the shoulder to pay him back for the tickling.

"Well?" said Sister Margaret.

"That way," he said, pointing.

Without offering anything more, Tanner wheeled about and started walking. Sister Margaret hurried up next to him as Samantha stayed back and began talking to the nuns about how one joined "the nunnery."

"Did you find the dairy building?" asked Sister Margaret.

"We think so."

"You *think* so?"

"We're debating on Sam's knowledge of shapes."

Sister Margaret glanced back at Samantha. She was feeling of Sister Elizabeth's habit, like a tailor looking to make a suit.

"You and she have a… a different relationship. I see that now."

"Yeah, so?"

She offered a slight shrug of her shoulders.

"Perhaps it's not all bad."

Tanner cocked an eye in her direction.

"Careful, Sister. I might think you've decided we're not the dysfunctional heathens you first took us to be."

A thin smile came to her lips.

"I said no such thing."

Tanner wasn't sure if she was denying ever saying it, or denying having changed her mind. Either way, he figured it really didn't matter.

Staring at the trees ahead, she said, "Thank you for not abandoning Sister Clare."

"I don't quit in the middle of anything. Not my way."

She nodded. "Why do you think they separated her from the others?"

"You heard the man. She wasn't cooperating."

"With what?"

"Being their slave bride, I suppose."

She shook her head in disgust.

"What are you going to do if they won't let her go?"

"Whatever I have to."

"Might I at least ask—"

"No," he said gruffly. "You may not."

Her eyes tightened. "When I asked you to help me, I didn't know you were a walking wrecking ball!"

"Ooh, I like that!" Samantha said, hurrying up beside them. "Tanner Wrecking Ball Raines. It has a nice ring to it."

Tanner glanced over at Sister Margaret, who seemed to understand that their talk was over.

"Just remember," she said quietly, "God will hold you responsible for whatever you do."

He shrugged. "God can do what He wants, and I'll do the same."

They continued on, eventually abandoning the trail to cross through an Indian campsite, likely built in recognition of the many contributions Native Americans provided to early settlers. A handful of carefully constructed domed structures stood in the center of the campsite. All of them appeared to be empty.

As they passed by one of the domes, Samantha ducked inside for a quick look. The frame consisted of bent saplings lashed together, with bark and grass covering the walls. There was an earthy smell to the hut, reminding her of the night that she and Tanner had slept under the stars and feasted on rabbit and dandelions.

She smiled. It was a good memory, even if it did involve using socks to mop the water off plants.

She stepped back outside and found Tanner waiting for her. The nuns had continued ahead a short distance before stopping at the edge of the clearing.

"Why aren't these tipis pointy?"

"Because they're not tipis. They're wigwams."

She giggled. "Wigwams, really?"

"Call them wickiups or wetus if you like."

She shook her head and marched on, convinced that he was making up words again.

Tanner smiled and fell in step behind her, satisfied that one day while paging through some dusty old American history book, she would come across the word wigwam and giggle with surprised delight. He was absolutely convinced that in the not so distant future, Samantha would proclaim that he, Tanner Raines, was the smartest person she had ever known. Well... perhaps not *absolutely* convinced.

Once past the Indian campsite, they trudged through a heavily forested area filled with thorny vines that seemed especially drawn to the nuns' habits. By the time they stepped clear of the trees, Sister Margaret seemed close to taking Bernard of Menthon's name in vain. Only the sight of the white octagonal building in the distance seemed to calm her enough to remember that the Patron Saint of Hiking had little to do with the prickly vines.

"This way," Tanner said, skirting the tree line until they came up behind a long rectangular building. Based on its size and location, he thought it must have originally been built to house the dairy cows. The stench coming through small open-air windows at the top, however, confirmed that somewhere along the way it had been converted into a public latrine.

He peeked around the corner to study the octagonal building. It was quiet, no one going in or out. There was, however, a shiny gold Mercedes S550 parked in the driveway.

He turned to the nuns. "How many men have you seen?"

They looked to one another, unsure of who should answer.

Finally, Sister Josephine spoke up. "There were three men, all big and strong. The one guarding us at the huts was the smallest—"

"And the most handsome," added Sister Eunice. When Sister Margaret cast a disapproving look her way, she shrugged. "Not that I noticed."

"Don't forget about the old doctor," added Sister Elizabeth.

Sister Josephine cringed. "I wish I could."

"Tell me about him."

"They called him Dr. Langdon. He wore a white lab coat and talked a lot about the importance of good genes and sound moral values. He asked us questions to see how smart we were." She looked to her feet as if suddenly ashamed. "He also examined us."

"To make sure you were healthy?"

"It was more than that. It was… personal."

Sister Margaret placed a hand on her shoulder.

"He wanted to know if we were virgins," explained Sister Eunice.

"Why?"

"I suppose to see if we were worthy of marrying his men. He said we were to become like Adam and Eve, repopulating the world with people who were superior in every way."

A funny thought came to mind, and Tanner did his best to smother a grin.

Sister Margaret took notice. "Is there something amusing about all this?"

"No disrespect to the young ladies," he said with a polite nod, "but kidnapping nuns to start a superior race is like hotwiring a Yugo to enter the Indy 500."

"Oh really? And just who would *you* kidnap?"

"I don't know. Maybe some proud Viking shieldmaidens."

Her face twisted with confusion. "Viking shieldmaidens?"

"Women who would charge bare-breasted onto the battlefield, sword and shield in hand. Now *that's* what a master race is built on."

Sister Margaret's eyes grew wide, and she seemed at a complete loss for words.

Satisfied, Tanner turned to Samantha. "You ready to go do this?"

"As ready as a Viking princess."

"I'm pretty sure we weren't talking about princesses," he said, leading the way.

"Oh Tanner," she said with a smile. "Don't you know? We're always talking about princesses."

CHAPTER 11

Papa Doyle lived less than a half-mile away, through a thick forest of oak and shortleaf pine, and Mason decided to make the trek on foot. Bowie tagged along, occasionally stopping to uproot a mushroom or buried acorn. As he trudged his way through the bedding of dried leaves and broken branches, Mason was reminded of how therapeutic nature could be. There was something incredibly peaceful about walking through a forest with a dog at one's side, smelling the odor of pine and listening as squirrels flitted overhead.

According to Porter, Papa Doyle's property consisted of a little more than eighty acres, including farmland, grazing land for livestock, and land set aside to grow Christmas trees. Doyle's father had come over from Ireland, and to hear Porter tell it, Papa Doyle had become something of a cross between traditional Irish farmer and Virginia hillbilly.

Mason also learned that Papa Doyle had three grown sons and a young daughter, all of whom had managed to evade the pandemic thanks to rural living, a decent stockpile of necessities, and a bit of dumb luck. His wife, Olivia, however, had not been as fortunate, and what little bit of neighborliness the family once had, vanished with her passing.

As Mason stepped clear of the trees, he came upon a young man chopping firewood. The boy was in his late teens but thick-chested and as strong as a mule. He swung the axe like someone who had done it so many times before that it had become mindless rote—the *swish* of air followed by the inevitable *crack* of wood splitting in two. Each time he split a log, he tossed the pieces onto a pile sitting next to a makeshift stove.

The young man was either so focused on the task at hand or, more likely, had fallen into daydreaming, that he had yet to see Mason or Bowie standing twenty feet away.

Mason looked past him to study the Doyle family home. It was a two-story, A-frame structure, badly in need of a paint job but sturdy enough to weather a hurricane. Bed sheets hung from nearly every window, dangling down like deflated balloons.

As if coming out of a stupor, the young man spotted Mason and raised his axe defensively.

"Who are you?" he barked.

"I'm here to talk to your father."

His eyes cut over to the house.

"What about?"

Mason touched his badge. "My business is with him."

"You're the law?"

"More days than not, I am."

The boy tightened his grip on the axe.

Mason placed his hand on the Supergrade. It was hardly a fair fight, but he made no apologies for bringing the better weapon.

"I came here to talk, but if you insist on something else, I can oblige."

The young man seemed to lose his nerve, setting down the axe and hurrying toward the house. Seconds later, he emerged a bit more confidently with his father and two older brothers following close behind. To say that the Doyles were big men would be like saying that redwoods were big trees. Papa Doyle was particularly massive, with a hard, swollen belly and a blonde beard that was as thick as a lion's mane. He carried a pair of wireframe spectacles in one hand and a baseball bat in the other.

Bowie tucked his head and let out a warning growl.

"Easy, boy," said Mason. "We're uninvited guests on their land. Let's see if we can get this done without hurting anyone."

Papa Doyle stomped down the wooden porch steps, his three boys moving to stand behind him, their eyes and fists equally tight.

"What the hell are you doing on my property?" Doyle said, fumbling to don his glasses without whacking himself in the eye with the bat.

"I'm here on behalf of your neighbors."

"What neighbors?"

"The folks living over at The Brambles."

"The mentals?"

"Mentals?" Mason said with a disparaging look. "Really?"

"Better than what I wanted to say. What's this all about anyway?"

Mason had thought about what he was going to say on his way over, and the best he could come up with was to appeal to the man's better judgment. Neighbors had to learn to live together. It was a truism as old as mankind. Seeing Papa Doyle in the flesh, however, made him second-guess the effectiveness of any such argument.

"Are you a Bible-reading man, Mr. Doyle?"

"You came out here to sell me a Bible?"

Mason smiled. "No, not to sell you one, but to ask you if you've heard the verse, 'Love thy neighbor as thyself.'"

Papa Doyle shook his head. "You're wasting your time, Preacher. I quit believing that garbage when…" He trailed off.

"When your wife passed?"

His eyes narrowed. "What the hell do you know about that?"

Mason thought of Ava. "I know that losing a good woman can be hard to come back from."

Doyle shook his head angrily. "Then you must also know that there ain't no all-powerful being looking out for us hardworking folks. It's just us and the dirt."

"Daddy?" A girl appeared at the screen door behind Papa Doyle and his sons. She was ten or eleven, and looked weak and tired. Her eyes were dark and hollow, and the nightgown she wore was stained with speckles of dried vomit.

Doyle turned to his youngest son.

"Gavin, go take care of your sister."

"Pa, you know I hate dealing with that stuff."

Doyle's face grew tight. "You do it, boy! And clean her up some while you're at it."

Without further protest, Gavin turned and went into the house, ushering the girl away from the door.

"What's wrong with her?" asked Mason.

"None of your damn business. That's what."

"If I had to guess, I'd say she's suffering from dysentery and dehydration."

Papa Doyle said nothing.

"Is there something wrong with the food?"

"Ain't nothing wrong with the food. We been eating the same thing for more than ten years."

"The water then?"

Doyle shook his head. "Boiling it to make sure it's safe."

Mason stepped over to a large black pot sitting atop the outdoor stove. It was filled with murky water, obviously pulled from a lake or river.

"Boiling isn't always enough." He bent over and took a whiff. It stank so much that his eyes began to water. "Not if there are chemicals in it."

"Nothing's wrong with the water." Despite his assertion, Doyle seemed uncertain. "If there were, my boys and I would have come down with the sickness."

Mason straightened up. "I suspect you've all had your share of belly-aches, but you're bigger and stronger than she is."

Doyle said nothing, but he glanced back at the screen door.

"You must have sensed it was the water," said Mason. "Why else would you hang out the bedsheets, if not to collect rain water?"

The big man eyed the sheets hanging from the windows.

"For what good it's done. Hasn't come a rain in damn near two weeks."

Mason approached to within a few paces, watching as Doyle and his boys visibly stiffened. Bowie inched up beside Mason, ready to do his part.

"Mr. Doyle, I sense that you're a man who values an honest day's work. Am I right about that?"

"You are. And that's why I'm not giving anything to those… those people, no matter who they send over here to do their begging."

"What if they offered a trade?"

Doyle's eyes narrowed. "What kind of trade?"

"Let's say they give you a gallon of clean drinking water for a basket of strawberries, or whatever else you happen to have coming up at the time."

"Where would they get clean water?"

Mason saw no point in lying. "They're making it."

"Bullshit."

"I've seen it myself."

"They're making clean water?" Papa Doyle said it like he still couldn't quite get his mind around the idea.

"Only one way to find out." Mason turned and began to walk away.

"Where the hell are you going?"

"To fetch an olive branch."

∾ ∿

Mason returned just under an hour later, carrying a clear plastic jug filled with water. Bowie and Jessie were at his side. Porter, too, had come along, which made the pace of the walk significantly slower. Despite hobbling along with the help of a cane, he insisted in bringing a second jug of water as his own peace offering.

They arrived to find Papa Doyle and Gavin sitting on the porch. Doyle's daughter sat curled up in Gavin's lap, her eyes closed and hands clutching her abdomen. The other two sons could be heard working around the side of the house, hammering nails and generally make a manly ruckus.

Papa Doyle got to his feet. "What do you have there?"

Mason held up one of the jugs.

"Fresh, clean water."

The big man came closer, licking his dry lips as he stared at the water.

Mason held it out to him. "Go ahead. Give it a taste."

Papa Doyle twisted off the cap and took a long swig, water spilling out around the sides of his mouth. When he turned the jug back down, he used the back of his hand to wipe the water dripping from his chin.

"What do you want for it," he said, licking the water from his hand.

"That one's free." Mason glanced over at Porter. "A gift from your neighbors."

"Ain't nothing free."

Mason shrugged. "They have more than they need, and you have a sick child. A little goodwill seemed in order."

Porter hobbled forward and handed Doyle the second gallon.

"What's this one for?"

"For you and your boys," he said, still winded from the hike.

Papa Doyle stood there holding the two jugs of water, looking a bit dumbfounded. For a moment, Mason wasn't sure if he was going to accept the water or splash it back in their faces. Reluctantly, he turned and set them by Gavin's feet.

"Take Katie inside and get her to drink as much of this as she can keep down."

Standing up, Gavin draped the girl over one shoulder and grabbed both jugs of water with his free hand.

As he disappeared into the house, Doyle turned back to Porter.

"I don't feel right taking something for nothing. I'll have my boys get you some strawberries."

The old man nodded, knowing better than to refuse a payment in kind from a prideful man.

Papa Doyle grunted and started to turn away.

"Your family's going to need a steady supply of water," Porter said quickly.

"Yeah?" Doyle said, turning back around. "How you gonna help with that? By bringing me water every day like we're some kinda babies on the teat?"

Porter met his stare. "No, Mr. Doyle. I'm going to show you how to make your own."

Papa Doyle's eyes pressed together. "Now why the hell would you go and do a dumb thing like that? Once we have our own water, we won't be needing you anymore."

"I'll do it because our families will be living next to one another long after you and I are gone. It might be a good idea for us to learn to help one another from time to time."

"And what exactly would we do for you?"

Porter nodded toward a thick baseball bat leaning against the house.

"You and your boys strike me as men willing to put up a fight, if it comes to that."

"So?"

"So that might be helpful, should trouble come our way."

Doyle seemed amused. "You want us to protect you?"

Porter swept his hand out before him.

"These are Sparta's walls."

"Huh?"

"It's a famous quote from King Agesilaus. When people would ask why Sparta lacked fortifications, he would gesture toward his men and say, 'These are Sparta's walls.'"

Papa Doyle mulled over the proposition.

"You're suggesting that we act as a little muscle if unsavory folks come around."

"What knocks on my door is only a few minutes away from yours. Besides," he said, smiling to reveal stained teeth, "I thought you Irish loved a good roughhousing from time to time."

"Oh we do," Doyle said, grinning. "We definitely do. And in turn, you'll help us to set up and maintain this magical water system of yours?"

"We'll do more than that."

"What do you mean?"

Porter gestured toward a portable generator next to the house.

"I think we can help you to get that up and running as well."

Doyle shook his head. "Can't. Ain't no fuel."

Porter turned and pointed to the large outhouse.

"That, along with manure from your cattle, will be your fuel."

Doyle chuckled. "You're going to convert crap into gasoline? Now that, I gotta see."

"Organic waste can be converted into methane gas, which with a small modification, your generator can use for fuel."

Papa Doyle looked uncertain, wondering perhaps if he was the butt of some joke.

"You're serious?"

"I most certainly am. We've already started assembly of a digester, and we could help you to do the same." He looked up at the sky. "The weather's warming, which will help to shorten the digestion cycle. I would expect that we'll have serviceable fuel within a month."

"What are you, some kinda rocket scientist?"

"No, Mr. Doyle. I'm just a man trying to keep his family alive. Same as you."

Mason watched with a sense of satisfaction as Porter extended a hand and Papa Doyle did the same. The big Irishman's paw completely enveloped the old man's bony fingers, but the deal was sealed nonetheless.

The unlikeliest of alliances had just been formed.

"What's the plan?" Samantha whispered as she crouched in front of a large buttonbush.

Tanner studied the old dairy building. What was most noteworthy, of course, was its unusual octagonal shape. Based on its clean lines and heavy trim, he thought it likely to be of German construction. Americans tended to keep farm buildings simple and replaceable, whereas Germans had a reputation for building things that lasted a lifetime. The structure had been freshly painted a nondescript white, and glass double doors now replaced the original swing-out barn doors. So unless cows had put in a requisition for a better view, the building must have been recently repurposed.

The doors were propped open, as were the building's many windows. An elderly man in a white lab coat could be seen sitting at a desk on the second floor, busily writing.

Samantha pointed. "That must be Dr. Langdon."

"Yeah," said Tanner. "The question is where's the other—"

He was interrupted by the unmistakable click of a revolver's hammer being cocked back.

From behind them, a voice with a distinctively Eastern European accent said, "Hands up and turn around."

Tanner and Samantha turned, careful not to make any sudden movements.

A man the size of professional wrestler Blackjack Mulligan towered over them. Easily four inches taller and eighty pounds heavier than Tanner, Blackjack was an incredible specimen of a man. Thick muscle defined his arms, chest, and shoulders, and what little neck remained had been swallowed by taut cords of meat. The impressiveness of his body, however, was offset by his repugnant face. Nothing was in proportion. His eyes were set too close, his nose bulbous and bright red, and his lips cracked to the point of bleeding.

Blackjack waved a massive Smith & Wesson 500 in front of them. Chambered in .50, the five-shot revolver could down a full-grown wooly mammoth.

"Drop the hardware."

Tanner tossed his shotgun away, and Samantha gently placed her rifle on the ground. This was not a time to get cute.

Blackjack pointed behind them. "March."

They turned and began trudging toward the dairy building, Samantha muttering, "That sure didn't go as planned."

Tanner said nothing. Having been on the wrong side of a gun twice in one day wasn't sitting well with him.

They entered through the double doors, stepping into a space that was part office and part medical center. The front half of the room was filled with a handful of gray government desks, all of them wiped clean. Metal examination tables lined the far side of the room, each covered with a thin white sheet. A rolling cart equipped with an assortment of calipers and rulers sat between them.

Behind the tables were shelves lined with medical books and plastic anatomical aids, including models of a human heart, a woman's reproductive organs, and a life-size newborn baby with detachable abdomen and skull.

Posters hung along many of the eight walls. One showed a woman sitting on a stool as she pondered the question: "Are you fit to marry?" Another read "Some people are born to be a burden on the rest." And yet another read "We neuter our pets… why not our weird friends and relatives?" The most interesting of them all, however, was a red and black *Star Trek* movie poster with the face of Ricardo Montalbán as Khan, the genetically engineered superhuman. Someone had penned "Was he so wrong?" across the bottom.

Blackjack shouted, "Dr. Langdon! We have visitors."

A few seconds later, the elderly man they had seen sitting by the window descended from a spiral staircase at the center of the room.

"Visitors, you say?"

"I caught them hiding out back, with guns."

Dr. Langdon turned to Tanner, and when he spoke, he seemed more curious than angry.

"Might I ask your names?"

"I'm Tanner Raines, and this is my daughter Samantha."

The doctor studied Samantha, his eyes thoughtful.

"Such a lovely young lady," he said, and tipped up her chin up with his fingers. "Especially here, and around the eyes." He stroked her hair. "Yes, very nice."

If it hadn't been for the hand cannon pointed at the back of his head, Tanner would have killed Langdon right then and there. Instead, he clenched his fists, imagining squishing the old man's eyeballs between his fingers.

"Thank you," Samantha said, smiling uncomfortably. "People say I look like my mother."

Dr. Langdon studied Tanner's face. "You surely must. Better for you though, I suspect, eh, dear?" he said with a little chuckle.

She looked over at Tanner. "I don't know. He's not so bad. Big, sure, and smelly sometimes. But I've seen worse." She glanced over at Blackjack. "A lot worse."

Dr. Langdon patted her on the head.

"That's the spirit, dear. Always make the best of what you have." He turned to Tanner. "Why were you were hiding in the bushes? Are you robbers?"

Tanner hesitated, debating on what excuse to offer.

"We're here to rescue Sister Clare," said Samantha. She knew that it was a gamble to just come out with it, but anything else they dreamed up would surely be seen for the lie that it was.

"Ah," he said with a nod. "You're here for the young women we…" He hunted for the right word.

"I believe *kidnapped* is the word you're looking for."

Dr. Langdon smiled. "Witty, too. I like that very much." He turned to Blackjack. "We should check on the other three women."

"No need," said Samantha. "They're already gone."

Dr. Langdon seemed surprised, the softness in his eyes having been replaced with something more sinister.

"And how would you know that, my dear?"

"I know because we set them free."

Dr. Langdon looked over at Blackjack, perhaps for a denial, but the big man only shrugged.

"All right," he hissed. "Where did they go?"

She shrugged. "The last time I saw them they were heading toward the highway in a bright yellow car. A Toyota, I think. Or maybe it was a Honda. I always get those two mixed up."

The doctor's eyes narrowed. "If that were true, you would have gone with them."

"That's what I kept telling my dad." She glanced over at Tanner. "But he insisted that we stay behind and find Sister Clare. Father Paul says he's a Good Samaritan. That means that even though he despises people, he tries to help when they're in trouble."

Dr. Langdon turned to Tanner. "Is what she says true?"

"All but the Good Samaritan part." It was a reasonable story, and if believed, it might keep Sister Margaret and the others from being discovered.

After a moment, Dr. Langdon shrugged and offered a resigned smile.

"I've always said that things will be what they'll be. Accepting life's little setbacks is how we move forward. Am I right?"

Tanner thought that sounded a lot like Buddhism, but he said no such thing.

"I'm curious though," Dr. Langdon continued. "Do you even know what we're doing here?"

"Starting a cult, by the looks of it."

"A cult? Oh heavens no, nothing so crude. We're trying to build a better society, one in which good people can live good lives."

"By kidnapping nuns?"

"It's not as bad as you make it sound. We're finding women suitable for marriage, and matching them to hardworking men. History shows that arranged marriages of this type are much more likely to succeed."

"And if they don't want to get married?"

"It's my belief that nearly all women want to marry and have children. Even those who don't should understand that it's their responsibility to do so." He began to pace. "Do you know why we chose this place to build our special society?"

"I'm guessing it's because of the asylum nearby."

He turned, surprised. "You know of the DeJarnette Center?"

"I know they used to conduct forced sterilizations and other butchery there."

Dr. Langdon nodded. "Ah, yes. On the surface, it might indeed have seemed like barbarism. But before you pass judgment, let me ask you something. What do farmers do to ensure superior offspring from their livestock?"

Tanner didn't answer.

"I'll tell you. They match the best animals. Those with weak traits are not allowed to breed. Truthfully, they're doing the entire species a favor by employing selective breeding. The late Dr. DeJarnette understood that, just as I do. Rather than sterilize women, however, I choose only to bring together morally and physically pure individuals to build a healthier society. Is that really such a terrible thing?"

Tanner smiled. "It seems like I remember someone else selling that bill of goods. His bold ideas led to gas chambers and mass graves. Where do you think yours are headed?"

Dr. Langdon shook his head, clearly disappointed.

"I can see that we're not going to agree. Very well," he said, turning to study Samantha again. "We've lost three women, but we've gained one in return, and a very promising one at that."

"I want her," blurted Blackjack.

Dr. Langdon cast a disapproving look his way.

"You've already been promised Sister Clare. She's a much better match for you. Besides, what kind of message would that send to your new wife if you gave up on her so easily? A wife isn't like an old wallet. You don't trade her in every time you want something newer."

"But she's over at the asylum. I don't even know if she'll come back alive."

"Don't be ridiculous. Your comrade will return with her at any moment. And I'm sure that spending a night in that creepy old building will have calmed her feisty spirit. Believe me, she'll be most thankful to you for taking her in."

Blackjack started to say something, but Dr. Langdon shook his head.

"I'll hear no more about it. You and Clare have been carefully matched, and that's that." He turned back to Samantha, slipping an arm around her shoulder as he led her toward the back of the room. "I'm sorry about that, dear. Men will be men. Come now. A quick examination will tell us what we need to know."

Samantha threw Tanner a frightened look. Clearly, things were heading rapidly downhill. He glanced behind him, assessing the situation with Blackjack. The man's revolver was still trained on him, but his eyes lingered on Samantha. It was now or never.

Tanner shuffled toward him, hands already in motion. He parried the pistol to one side before reaching around to try and twist the gun from the man's oversized mitt. They wrestled for control of the weapon, neither willing to let it go. Accepting that he wasn't going to wrest the revolver from Blackjack, Tanner trapped the big man's arm under his own, the gun extended straight out in front of them.

A thunderous *boom* sounded, and splinters ripped free from one of the beams over Samantha's head.

"Sam! Get down!" he shouted, shifting to cup the big man's hand with both of his own.

She dropped, first to her knees, and then all the way down on her belly, as the big barrel swung back in her direction. Dr. Langdon chose only to bend at the waist and cover his ears.

With his hands gripping Blackjack's, Tanner began working the trigger, each shot reverberating through his chest. The first round sent a handful of papers flying off a desk, but the second caught Dr. Langdon in the chest. The impact threw him over a nearby chair to land across Samantha's legs and back, pinning her to the ground.

The gun fired twice more, both rounds ripping holes through the far wall. When the revolver finally clicked over to an empty cylinder, Tanner released the man's hand and stepped away.

Furious, Blackjack hurled the weapon at him. It missed by nearly a foot, knocking one of the framed posters off the wall.

"I'm going to break your neck," he wheezed, clenching both fists.

Tanner took a traditional boxer's stance, knees slightly bent, hands up and ready. The time for talk had long passed. He took a quick glance back at Samantha. She had managed to roll Dr. Langdon off and was getting back to her feet, knife drawn.

"Stay there. I've got this."

"But he's so… muscley."

Tanner studied Blackjack. He was big and strong, but that same muscle would act like saddlebags filled with sand once he got tired.

"He's what you call a twenty-second man."

"What the hell's that supposed to mean?" Blackjack growled as he advanced.

"It means I figure you're good for twenty seconds. After that, you'll be like a twelve-year-old schoolgirl."

"Hey!" exclaimed Samantha.

Tanner had no time to offer an apology. Blackjack cocked a fist and leaped forward with a Superman punch. Given the man's size and strength, the punch would likely have knocked Tanner out, had it connected. It didn't. As soon as he detected movement, Tanner bent to the left, bringing his right hand to his ear and letting his forearm and elbow deflect the blow. Before Blackjack could regain his balance, Tanner twisted and fired a short jab to his ribcage. It wasn't nearly enough to put the big man down, but it did elicit a painful groan.

Blackjack wheeled toward Tanner, firing four short rapid-fire punches. All four made contact, and Tanner nearly tripped as he backpedaled away. Blackjack rushed forward, firing a left hook followed by a much more powerful cross. Tanner's ear absorbed the full impact of the hook but he managed to slip the deadlier cross. Sensing an opening, he lunged forward, driving his head into Blackjack's chin. Teeth crunched together, and the big man howled with rage.

Blackjack grabbed Tanner's head with both hands and flung him sideways. Rather than fight the momentum, Tanner went with it, rolling across a long table to land on the other side. Blackjack advanced, flipping the heavy table out of his way. But his pace had slowed, and he huffed air like an overloaded steamship.

He charged forward, trying to grab Tanner in a bear hug. No good. Tanner ducked beneath his outstretched arms, avoiding the grab while raking an elbow across the big man's ribs. Blackjack continued his steady advance, throwing a series of wild haymakers as he desperately sought a one-hit knockout. None of them connected, and with each motion, he became slower, clumsier.

Tanner straightened and let out a breath.

"All right. That's twenty." He went after Blackjack with a combination of precision and power, strike after strike pummeling the big man's face and body. Blackjack tried to fend him off, but nearly every counterpunch found only empty air. Soon, his face was swollen and bleeding, his ribs aching and bruised. He made one last desperate lunge toward Tanner, hoping to pull him to the ground where he could better use his mass.

It was the opening Tanner had been waiting for. With Blackjack's weight shifting to his lead leg, he became vulnerable to one of the most vicious strikes in all of martial arts, the Muay Thai roundhouse. Tanner whipped his leg around, connecting just above the big man's knee. As he executed the strike, he focused on the fundamentals, body upright and hips thrust forward as he rose onto the ball of his rear foot for maximum rotation. With so much weight on his lead leg, Blackjack had no chance to block it with his shin, instead taking the full blow to the knee.

The effect was devastating. Tanner's shin smashed against Blackjack's femur, dislocating it from the patella with a muffled *pop*. The man's leg bent sideways at the knee, and he howled from pain as his lower leg dangled beneath him like a broken chicken wing. Desperate to steady himself, he reached for a nearby table.

Tanner was having none of it. He shot forward and side-kicked Blackjack's back leg out from under him. The big man went down with a crash, pulling the table down on top of him.

Despite the dislocated knee, Blackjack rolled over and tried to get to his feet. Tanner quickly stepped around behind him and straight-leg punted between his legs. It was a kick comparable to Matt Prater's sixty-four-yard field goal, rupturing both of Blackjack's testicles and lifting his weighty frame nearly a foot off the ground. When he came down, Blackjack collapsed onto his belly with a thud and a grunt. He lay there, unmoving.

Satisfied that he was out for the count, Tanner turned to check on Samantha. She stood next to Dr. Langdon's body. Having taken a .50 slug to the chest, the doctor's white coat had become little more than a poor excuse for a towel.

"You okay?"

She nodded. "You?"

"I'm fine," he growled, turning toward the door. "Let's go find our guns and finish this."

Samantha trailed after him, hiding a smile.

"What's so funny?"

"For a minute, I thought you said *nuns*."

CHAPTER 13

J essie hummed Faith Hill's "The Way You Love Me" as Mason steered the RV down Highway 3. It was a scenic drive, the road lined on either side with dark green fields now overgrown with peanuts left unharvested. A light rain had begun to fall, just enough to force Mason to cycle the windshield wipers on and off.

"That was some pretty smooth negotiating you did back there," she said, rotating in her seat to face him.

"Unlike my father, I don't believe that every nail needs a hammer."

"Do you think they'll be okay? I can't imagine any two people being more different than Porter and Papa Doyle."

"Sometimes different is okay, good even. The important part is that they learn to complement one another."

She hesitated and then said, "Is that why you're still alone? Because you haven't found someone who complements you?"

He glanced over at her. "You sure ask a lot of personal questions."

Rather than apologize, she smiled and said, "A woman likes to know about the man she's traveling with."

Mason couldn't fault her for that. Jessie was taking quite the chance going off with him.

"I've known four women since the virus hit. One used me to get revenge on men who had wronged her, another put her mission above all else, and the most recent tried to have me killed."

"Yikes! You *have* had bad luck with women."

"Told you."

"But you said four women. What happened with the other one?"

Mason shook his head, unable to bring himself to talk about how Ava had died.

"I'm sorry," Jessie said, reading his expression.

"Yeah. Me too."

"The woman who tried to have you killed, what was her name?"

"Brooke." Even as he said the name, Mason felt his gut clench. The wound hadn't yet had time to heal.

"Were you serious about her?"

"I suppose."

"And Bowie?" she said, glancing back at the sleeping dog. "Did he like her too?"

"Bowie?" It seemed like such a strange question.

"He *is* your best friend in the whole world. I figured his opinion mattered."

It was not something Mason had considered before.

"They sort of tolerated one another."

She shook her head lightly. "Not a good sign."

"No, I suppose not."

"Forgive me for asking, but why do you think you keep getting involved with those kinds of women?"

He shrugged. "Men are blind when it comes to—"

"Sex?"

"I was going to say love, but yeah, that works too."

"You loved them?" Jessie seemed surprised, maybe even a bit disappointed.

"I don't know. Some of them." It was a question that he didn't want to think about. "Let me ask *you* something."

"What?"

"Why did you lie to me earlier?"

Jessie shifted nervously in her seat.

"What are you talking about?"

"You told me that you'd had lots of boyfriends, even rattled off their names."

"Yeah. So?"

"So, they were made up."

"Why would you say something like that?" Her cheeks were becoming flushed.

Mason started counting them off on his fingers.

"Tom Doniphon, Will Kane, and Jason McCullough." He looked over at her and offered an understanding smile. "I know those names."

"You do?" she said sheepishly.

"You're not the only one who grew up watching Westerns." When she said nothing, he repeated, "So I ask again, why'd you lie?"

"I, um, I didn't want you to think I was some kind of wallflower—you know, inexperienced with men."

"And are you?"

"Am I what?"

"Inexperienced with men?"

She took a moment to collect herself, her face slowly returning to its natural color.

"I'm twenty-three years old."

"And?"

"And I've never... You know."

"That's nothing to be ashamed of. You're waiting for your Prince Charming. Good for you."

"I guess. Still, I felt a little embarrassed being around a man with your experience."

"My experience?" he said, chuckling. "You act like I'm some kind of post-apocalyptic Casanova."

"You sure look like one," she said under her breath.

Mason turned to find her staring at him. When their eyes met, she quickly looked away.

"To be honest," she said, "I'm beginning to wonder if my Prince Charming is even still out there. Maybe he died from the pox, and I'll have to settle for his ugly brother, Prince Boring."

Mason shook his head. "You're a gorgeous young woman, Jessie, and one day some lucky man is going to have the good fortune of sharing in that beauty. Don't give it away to someone unworthy of you."

That brought a huge smile to her face.

"You really think I'll find the right man?"

"I know you will. Now, can we quit talking about our love lives and get back to the task at hand?"

"Of course." Jessie turned her attention to the highway, but it was clear that she was still thinking about what he had said. After a moment, she leaned over and kissed him on the cheek.

"What was that for?"

"For making me feel special."

With that, Jessie let the talk of relationships, both real and imaginary, fade away. Even though Mason welcomed the newfound silence, he couldn't help but reflect on the soft press of her lips.

A few minutes later, she leaned forward in her seat and pointed out the window at a private airstrip to their left.

"We're getting close. Daddy used to mention that airfield. He said that the next time he came up, he might try to land there, just to get the old plane some air time."

"I saw the yellow Air Tractor in your barn. I'm assuming he bought it for crop dusting?"

"That's what he'd tell you. Momma and I knew better."

"Oh?"

"Daddy's always been happiest when he's in the air."

"I see."

"What about you? What are you happiest doing?"

He thought for a moment, finally saying, "I guess I like setting things right."

"Like with Porter and Papa Doyle?"

"That, and other times."

"Give me an example."

"All right. A good example is what happened with the marshals at Glynco. When I discovered that a group of mercenaries had poisoned them to steal weapons, I felt the need to get justice for those who had fallen."

"Mercenaries poisoned U.S. Marshals?" she said in disbelief.

He nodded. It had been more than six months, but Mason could still remember the bodies lying with pools of vomit beside their open mouths.

"What did you do?"

"I followed them and made sure they paid for their crimes."

"By killing them?"

"Some."

"You let the others go free?" She seemed surprised.

Mason envisioned the hacked-up remains on the overpass. They had suffered a fate far worse than dying by his hand.

"No," he said, calmly. "No one went free."

Jessie's voice softened. "You've had a lot of death around you this past year, haven't you?"

"I've had a lot of death around me for a very long time. First as a soldier, then as a lawman, and now as… whatever it is I am to this world."

She reached over and placed a hand on his.

"You're the man who sets things right."

"I suppose I am."

They continued on, passing the airfield to come upon a large self-storage complex. The contents of many of the lockers had been pulled out and sorted through, likely by junkers in search of trade-worthy goods. A little past the facility sat Eckkards, a steak and seafood restaurant that was surprisingly teeming with customers. Motorcycles, RVs, trucks, and cars filled the small parking lot. Many other vehicles were either making their way into the establishment or back out onto Highway 3. Across the street, the Pilot House Inn motel was also nearly filled to capacity, with most of its doors propped open to allow for a little air flow.

People of every size and shape moved about, walking between rooms with bottles of liquor in hand, or crossing the road between Eckkards and the motel. Nearly everyone carried a gun, whether it be a hunting rifle slung over one shoulder or a Glock holstered at the waist. It wouldn't have surprised Mason to see a banner hanging over the road that read "Proud Sponsors of the NRA."

Despite the congestion, he didn't see anything even remotely resembling a campground.

"Is this it?" he asked.

Jessie shrugged. "I'm not really sure. I expected something… different."

Bowie sat up, and upon seeing all the people outside, tried to squeeze his way into the front row of seats for a better look.

Jessie put her arm across to block him.

"Just hang in there, boy. You'll get your chance to make friends once we stop."

The dog reluctantly backed off, but the anxious look never left his eyes.

"I'm going to pull over and ask for directions," said Mason. "See if you can keep Bowie from going out a window when I do."

She reached over and began stroking the dog's head.

"Oh, he's not going anywhere," she said in a puppy-dog voice. "Are you, boy?"

Bowie flopped down onto the console to better enjoy her attention.

Mason spotted a middle-aged woman and her teenage son standing on the side of the highway, selling small paper sacks of boiled peanuts. He pulled up alongside and rolled down his window.

"Afternoon," he said with a friendly smile.

"It surely is," she said, revealing a missing front tooth. "Care for some peanuts?"

Mason figured the woman's tongue might be a little looser with a paying customer.

"Sure. See if there's anything on the trailer that might be worth a couple of bags."

The woman motioned to her son, and he hurried around to examine the trailer. When he returned, he was holding a fishing rod, complete with a reel of string and a bright yellow lure. It wasn't an even trade, but given that the rod wasn't Mason's to begin with, he quickly agreed.

As she passed the bags of peanuts through his open window, he asked, "Is this Grey's Point?"

She shook her head. "That's still another half a mile or so up the road. They don't have no room though. If you're lookin' for a place to settle for the night, you'll have to do it here."

The teen leaned past his mother and said, "Are you here for the tournament?"

"What tournament is that?"

"The gunfighting tournament!" He tugged at a leather gun belt that held up a Taurus 82S revolver. "Momma says I can compete when I get a little older."

"No," she quickly corrected. "I said you *might* get to compete. Right now, you couldn't hit a dog if he was wettin' on your leg."

The boy's face flushed. "You just wait and see. By this time next year, I'll be better than anyone."

"Yeah, yeah. Until then, you'd best get busy with them peanuts. You wanna eat tonight, don't you?"

Before the boy could say anything more, Mason offered a parting wave and eased back into traffic.

"What do you think that was about?" said Jessie.

"The tournament?"

"Yeah."

"Boys wanting to play cowboy, I guess."

"Or girls."

He smiled. "Or girls. Let's just find Jack and get out of here before the shooting starts."

"Right."

They continued ahead, quickly becoming part of a long procession of RVs, campers, and trucks. The turnoff to Grey's Point Camp was marked with a blue and gray sign adorned with the image of a large fish. A banner had been draped across the sign that read, "Gunfighting tournament begins at 4 PM today!"

Mason turned in behind the other vehicles, finally making his way to a security booth at the entrance to the camp. A handful of men holding AR-15s stood guard. Without so much as a word, the lead man gave the trailer a quick onceover before hurriedly waving him through.

Once past the gate, the road split in three directions. Mason took the first right and meandered around the camp to get a better feel for the lay of the land. The north and west sides of the camp were small communities of mobile homes, perhaps three or four hundred units in all. Narrow roads with names like Shady Lane and Placid Harbor wove through the collection of boxy metal houses. Every home appeared to be occupied, kids playing in the yards, women hanging clothes out to dry, and men cleaning siding, painting roofs, and mending fences. These people weren't squatters; they were homeowners.

The camp butted up against Meachim Creek, a shallow bed of water, bordering the much deeper Rappahannock River. As such, scores of people fished the banks, working to pull in their suppers. The docks along the western shore were equally as busy, with boats filling many of the slips.

"I had no idea," Jessie said, marveling at the activity. "It's like a little city in here."

Mason was equally surprised. While it was far smaller than the New Colony, Grey's Point had a sense of ambitious busyness to it. The residents showed a frontier-like fortitude, far different than the colonists who had become accustomed to feeding off the government dole.

He steered the RV down Oyster Point Road, a long straight stretch of asphalt with a handful of small aircraft parked at one end. While it was not quite up to the standards of the private airfield they had passed earlier, the makeshift runway looked long enough for a small plane to get airborne.

He followed a tight curve and ended up near a large clubhouse at the heart of Grey's Point. Behind it were dozens of long parking lanes designed for buses and watercraft. South of the parking area was a huge market, tents of every shape and color stretching between rows of neatly aligned trees. Hundreds of people pushed their way through the crowded bazaar, trading everything from bottles of water to hiking boots.

Jessie leaned forward. "There!" she said, pointing. "That's Daddy's truck."

A rusted 1976 Chevrolet Silverado sat in one of the long parking lanes between the clubhouse and the market. Mason pulled the RV in behind the truck and killed the engine. Bowie sat up and pressed his nose against the window.

"He's got to be here somewhere," said Jessie. She eyed the bed of the truck. The bright blue tarp looked odd, like it had been haphazardly put back in place.

They climbed out of the RV and slowly walked around the pickup. The windows were up and the doors locked. There was nothing to indicate that

Jack had fallen victim to foul play. Bowie seemed particularly interested in something in the bed, propping his feet on the bumper and nudging the tarp with his nose.

Mason motioned for Jessie to take a step back. In his experience, Bowie took notice of only two things: food and dead bodies.

Mason grabbed the edge of the tarp and carefully folded it back. Underneath was a case of sixteen-ounce mason jars. He lifted one out and discovered that it was filled with dark strips of dried meat. Mystery solved, at least as far as Bowie's interest.

"That's Daddy's homemade jerky," Jessie said, breathing a sigh of relief.

Even though the jars were sealed, Mason wasn't surprised that Bowie could smell the meat. A dog's nose was nothing short of miraculous.

"Think he'd mind if Bowie had a little?"

The dog's head whipped around, staring at Jessie as if awaiting word on some life and death medical procedure.

"Of course not. If anything, he'd insist that you both have some."

Mason opened the jar and gave it a quick sniff. Worcestershire, brown sugar, molasses, and some kind of smoke flavoring. He lifted out a piece and took a nibble. Sweet but good.

"Here you go, boy," he said, tossing the rest of it to Bowie.

The meat was gone in an instant. Mason fed him three more strips before putting the jar back under the tarp. Bowie stared at him, his tongue snaking out to lick around his mouth.

"Maybe later," he said, securing the tarp. "Right now, we have a job to do."

"How are we ever going to find him?" Jessie asked, slowly turning in place. "There must be a thousand people here."

Mason pointed to the clubhouse. "Whoever runs this place is probably operating out of that building. Let's start there."

Mason, Jessie, and Bowie made their way toward the clubhouse, weaving their way through a seemingly endless mass of people. There was a buzz of energy in the air as folks haggled over goods or shared stories of what was happening across the country. Women carried fish wrapped in old newspapers, and children ran through the crowd, playing tag.

Security was present too, men in traditional blue police uniforms, carrying riot shotguns. By the looks of it, they were serious men used to doing serious work. With nearly every adult armed, Mason suspected that the crowd was also self-policing. If someone got too far out of hand, mob justice was going to take over.

Jessie hooked an arm through Mason's, not wanting to lose him in the crowd. Bowie used the opportunity to dart from place to place, investigating every new sound and smell. Together, they wove their way through the bustle of people, drawing ever closer to the camp's clubhouse.

They arrived to see a man emerging onto the clubhouse's second-story balcony. A crowd had gathered out front as if the Pope were preparing to bless them. Given the throng of people blocking their way, Mason and Jessie had little choice but to stop and listen.

The man could have been Sam Elliot's double, tall and lean, with a thick gray mustache, a white ten-gallon hat, and clothes that would have been right at home on a ranch in Montana. A pistol hung at his side, and one hand rested on it as he spoke.

"Ladies and gentleman," he said into a microphone, "if I can have your attention, please."

The crowd slowly quieted.

"Before we discuss the upcoming festivities, I'd like to remind everyone of the rules of Grey's Point." He began counting them on his fingers. "First, if you can't afford it, keep your grubby paws off it. Second, if a woman says no, put your pecker away. And third, don't hurt anyone without due cause. If you break any of these rules, you know what'll happen."

Several people began to chant "Fallen! Fallen! Fallen!" Soon, the entire crowd had joined in.

The announcer waved his hands, shushing them.

"That's right. If you break the rules, you're in the tournament." He glanced at his watch. "In a little under two hours, we'll gather at the fairgrounds to witness the first brutal test of speed and accuracy. For those of you interested in a front row view, let me remind you that if a stray bullet should happen to find your backside, feel free to take it home as a souvenir."

The crowd shared a nervous chuckle.

"Since many of you are no doubt unfamiliar with the rules of the tournament, allow me to explain. There are four rounds to the competition. Each gunfighter must successfully complete each round to advance to the next. The gunfighters who successfully complete all four rounds will be declared victors of the competition. At that point, they will be given the choice to either take their cut of the purse or compete against one another for an even larger share. Additionally, the gunfighter who ends up being the crowd favorite will be awarded a no holds barred—or should I say no *holes* barred—night with Lolita and her two lovely sisters!"

He turned and motioned to the door behind him. Three beautiful Latinas dressed in sexy white lingerie hurried across the balcony, waving and blowing kisses to the crowd.

The audience cheered and whistled.

"This, my friends, is definitely a case in which the only way to enter is to win!"

Some of the men pretended to pull away from their wives as if they too wished to join in the contest. More laughter ensued, and the announcer wagged a playful finger at them.

"All right now. It's time now to introduce you to our brave gunfighters."

He turned once again, giving someone behind him the thumbs up. Almost immediately, five men marched into view. They reminded Mason of *American Gladiators*, each man's persona taken to the point of caricature.

There was "Muchado," a big-bellied Mexican with a colorful sombrero and twin six-shooters holstered on gun belts draped across his chest, "Ringo," a handsome cowboy with fringed leather gloves, vest, and chaps, "Liberty," a barrel-chested, special ops soldier decked out in all manner of tactical gear, "Bones," a gangbanger whose face and arms had been painted to resemble a skeleton, and "The Reverend," a tall somber man with thick leather boots, a black duster that hung down to his knees, and a Nighthawk VIP hanging at his side.

Upon seeing the gunfighters, the audience went from attentive to ecstatic, hooting and hollering, and waving their hands in the air like they were in the presence of movie stars. The gunfighters stood before them, each reacting to the hysteria in his own way. Muchado got into the spirit of things by vigorously waving his hat in the air. Ringo and Liberty took a few gracious bows, while Bones flipped everyone the collective bird. The only one who seemed unmoved by the cheering was The Reverend. He stood stoic and cold, as if the entire event were beneath him.

The announcer inched back up to the microphone.

"All right, that's enough," he said, motioning for the crowd to once again hush. "If you really want to show your support, I encourage you to place your bets on the gunfighters you believe will emerge victorious. The house will be taking bets at each stage of the competition, but the best payouts are for those bets placed early."

The announcer waited until the gunfighters were offstage before continuing.

"A contest isn't a contest without worthy opponents. In our case those challengers have a name." He wound up like he was about to deliver a pitch. "Join me in welcoming… the Fallen!"

A line of twenty prisoners paraded across the balcony. Some were old enough to be grandparents, others young enough to have pimples. Most looked like they hadn't bathed in a month, their clothes soiled and hair greasy. All in all, they were a sorry-looking lot, hardly fitting of the descriptor "worthy opponents."

The crowd booed, some throwing water bottles or what was left of their lunch.

Jessie gasped and gripped Mason's hand.

"What is it?" he asked, fearing that someone had decided to play grab-ass with her while he wasn't looking.

"There!" she said, pointing to one of the prisoners. "It's Daddy."

Jack Atkins was much like Mason had envisioned: average height, slender but not skinny, military haircut, and eyes set hard with determination. He was pushing into his early sixties, but by looks of it, had another thirty years left in him. Dried blood covered his nose and mouth, and he walked with a discernible limp as he made his way across the balcony.

"He's hurt!" Jessie cried, trying unsuccessfully to push her way forward through the crowd.

Mason slipped an arm around her waist and gently pulled her back.

"There's nothing you can do for him right now."

She stood motionless, her eyes unable to leave her father.

Once the last of the Fallen had passed, the announcer returned to the microphone.

"Remember, this is as much a competition for them as it is our fearless gunfighters. If one of the Fallen should manage to defeat a gunfighter, his crimes are immediately forgiven, thereby releasing him from the competition. Let no one say that we at Grey's Point are not fair and just."

The crowd offered a supportive round of applause, but it hardly reached the hysteria they had shown the gunfighters.

"All right, folks. I'll see you over at the parade grounds. Remember, you can't win if you don't bet." The announcer offered one final tip of his hat before turning to leave the makeshift stage.

"My God," whispered Jessie, "they're going to kill Daddy."

"Maybe not."

She turned to him, confused. "You saw him. He's in no condition to fight. Not against men like that."

Mason nodded toward the announcer as he disappeared into the clubhouse.

"Maybe he'll help to get your father out of this."

"Why would he do that?"

Mason rested a hand on his Supergrade.

"Because he and I have history together."

Her eyes grew wide. "You know him?"

"I should. I served with him for nearly three years in the marshal service."

"That man's a U.S. Marshal?"

"He was. I'm not sure what he is now."

蜴 蜴

Mason sat on an old yellow sofa, staring out the clubhouse window at a tarp-covered swimming pool. Security officers stood to either side of him with shotguns in hand. He had asked Jessie and Bowie to wait outside because of her outrage at Jack's treatment and the dog's temperament toward men with guns. This was a time for diplomacy, not war.

The clubhouse consisted of a sitting room, a game area with billiard and foosball tables, and a large kitchen that no doubt had been used to host kids' parties and homeowners' association meetings. Several small hallways also led off to private offices. The announcer from the balcony appeared from one such hallway, his big white hat in hand.

As soon as he saw Mason, his face came alive.

"Mason Raines in the flesh. How about that!"

Mason stood up nice and slow so as not to startle the guards.

"Hello, Leroy."

Leroy Tucker walked over and pulled him into a big hug.

"I swear to God, it feels like a long-lost brother's come back from the grave."

Mason patted him on the back. "You too, my old friend."

Leroy leaned away to get a better look at him, and his eyes were immediately drawn to the Supergrade.

"I see you've still got my gun. I hope it's served you well."

"I couldn't have asked for anything better." Mason drew the weapon slowly and flipped it around so that the grip extended toward Leroy. "I'm sure it'll tell you a few stories."

Leroy gently pushed the pistol away. "I wouldn't dream of taking it from you. A man doesn't break a bond like that. Besides," he said, resting his hand on his own firearm, "I've gone modern."

The pistol at his side was an FN Five-seven. Chambered in 5.7x28 mm, the Five-seven was notoriously accurate with a trajectory kept to within a couple of inches all the way out to two hundred meters. It was also lightweight, had a twenty-round magazine, and with the right ammunition, could penetrate NATO's CRISAT body armor.

Mason nodded his thanks and holstered the Supergrade. Even with the Five-seven's obvious benefits, he would never have chosen one over a good 1911. Some things just felt right in his hand, and no amount of technological whiz bang could change that.

Leroy motioned for him to retake his seat as he settled into a chair, crossing his legs like a southern gentleman.

"You look good, Mason. You really do."

"You look as ornery as ever, old timer."

The nickname brought a smile to Leroy's lips.

"God, that brings back memories. Do you remember that time we cornered those three hombres hoping to scoot across the border with that sweet little waitress?"

Mason pressed his lips together. "I remember."

"The big one with the droopy eye thought he had it all figured out." He cleared his throat, adopting a respectable Hispanic accent. "Go ahead, Marshal. Arrest us. It don't matter none. In three months, we'll be back in Mexico with a warm titty in one hand and a cold *cerveza* in the other. Who knows? Maybe next time we come over, we say hello to your madre." He dropped back out of the accent. "What was it you said?"

"I said there won't be a next time."

"And then *bam!*" Leroy slapped his hands together. "It was over. I hardly had time to get my pistol out of the holster before all three of them were face down." Leroy shook his head as if reliving the moment. "My question is what would you have done if they *hadn't* gone for their weapons?"

Mason didn't know how to answer that. He wanted to say that he would have calmly taken them into custody, but he also remembered the terrified young waitress tied to the bed, soaked in piss and semen. She had lived, but that was about the extent of her good fortune. Some crimes could not be righted. They could only be avenged. It was not the proper mindset for a lawman perhaps, but it was what had filled him that day.

"It doesn't matter," Leroy said, waving it away. "They got what they deserved, and I was honored to be standing beside you when they did."

Mason nodded. "You were a good partner, Leroy. I never doubted for a minute that you had my back."

Leroy swallowed hard as if touched by the words, and said, "How is it that you weren't killed at Glynco with the others?"

"I was away on leave when the virus hit. By the time I got back to Glynco, it was too late." Mason didn't share the fact that he had hunted down and punished those responsible for the attack. "What about you?"

"As folks were bubbling up with blisters, I was out rounding up a joker who'd been threatening a district court judge."

"Did you get him?"

"Can you believe that slippery bastard jumped out a three-story window to avoid going to jail?" He cracked a smile. "Only good thing about the outbreak was that it saved me a ton of paperwork."

Mason glanced around the clubhouse. "How'd you end up here?"

"That's sort of a long story. Let's just say that after I heard what happened at Glynco, I sort of wandered for a bit. To be honest, I was feeling pretty low. Thought maybe there wasn't much use in living anymore."

"What changed?"

Leroy pulled a thin cigar from his shirt pocket, wet the crown with his mouth, and bit a small hole in the cap.

"I had the good fortune of running across a real nice family," he said, spitting out the piece of wrapper. "They took me in for a time, fed me, made me feel like there was still a little good left in this world."

Mason nodded. "The kind touch of a stranger can do wonders."

"In this case, it not only raised my spirits, it helped me to find my way."

"What do you mean?"

"I discovered that they were hurting in a bad way. The husband was hobbling around on crutches, thanks to being winged by a gang of teenage hoodlums. That left the missus and her two daughters in constant fear that they'd be grabbed up by the young men."

"It's that kind of world out there. What did you do?"

"I'll tell you what I did," he said, lighting the cigar with the quick flick of a match. "I found those boys and explained to them the error of their ways."

"Did that help?"

"Not really, no." He stoked the cigar to life with a few puffs. "To be fair, I think they were too used to living in a world in which right and wrong had to play by different rules."

"What happened?" Mason was pretty sure he already knew the answer.

"I took it upon myself to make clear the severity of the situation."

"You killed them?"

Leroy puckered his lips and blew a smoke ring.

"Every last one of them."

Mason said nothing. He had killed plenty, trying to right the wrongs of the world. Even so, there was something a little disturbing about Leroy's prideful tone.

"You know, I never did go back and tell that family they were safe. I suppose they eventually figured it out."

"I'm sure they're grateful for not having to look over their shoulders anymore."

"I suppose." Leroy took another long puff of the cigar. After he exhaled most of the smoke, he closed his mouth and swallowed, forcing the last bit out through his nose. "Truth is, I don't even really care. I came to understand that it wasn't about preventing suffering or injustice that drove me."

"No? What then?"

"It was about cleaning the shit off my boots."

Despite Leroy's callous language, Mason couldn't argue the point. The junkers were just the latest reminder that much of mankind was reverting to their baser instincts.

"After putting those dogs down, I realized that I'd found a righteous purpose in this new world."

"You're out to make sure that no one gets a free pass."

"Spoken like a true lawman," he said with a nod. "Along the way, I met up with others interested in establishing a society in which right and wrong still meant something."

"Is that what this camp is? A place where right and wrong mean something?"

"You're damn straight it is. Don't get me wrong. I know it's not perfect. But it's a whole lot better than what's out there." He flicked ashes toward the clubhouse door. "The folks in Grey's Point work hard and play hard, but nearly everyone here has learned to respect the rules."

"And if they don't?"

"If they don't, their neighbors report them. I made sure of that by offering a modest reward to those turning in violators. I figure that way everyone's in this together."

"If you remember your history, you might recall that reward systems like that have a way of breeding their own criminals. Thief-takers, I believe they were called—folks who set up heists only to report the unsuspecting robbers."

He shook his head. "It's not like that here. I have a thorough investigation done of every reported infraction. Also, if we were to see someone reporting an unreasonable number of criminals, we'd take notice. Once we conclude that someone is indeed guilty, we make an example out of them. Instead of stockades or public hangings, we opted for a contest. Good versus evil. The righteous against the fallen."

"You're talking about your tournament."

He smiled. "You know I've always had a thing for a good old-fashioned showdown. The tournament lets me experience that without getting all shot up."

"Will this be the first?"

"Third, actually. It takes a month or two between each to put them together. Not only do we have to come up with some pretty fantastic challenges, we also have to ensure that we have enough competitors on both sides of the aisle." Leroy took another long puff on the cigar and blew smoke out into the room. "What about you? Where'd you hitch your wagon? I see you're still wearing the badge."

Mason reflexively touched the Marshal's badge on his waist. He had accepted that it would forever be a part of him.

"I'm working for the New Colony. Running down trouble. Gathering supplies. That sort of thing."

"I figured as much. You were always the Boy Scout of the bunch. Is that why you're here? We do something to piss off the colony?"

Mason shook his head. "I'm not here on official business."

"But you're not here just to catch up with an old friend either. You want something. I can see it in your eyes."

"Yes."

"And you're not leaving here without getting it. Do I have that about right?"

"I don't know if I'd put it that way."

"What I know is that you're a man who moves with dogged purpose. While that isn't something to be ashamed of, it can also be a royal pain in the ass." He looked at his cigar, wrinkled his nose, and flicked it out an open window. "Okay, so let's hear it."

"You have a prisoner, one of the men who marched across the stage. I'd like to secure his release."

"What's his name?"

"Jack Atkins."

"Atkins…" he said, chewing on the name. "Can't say as I—" Leroy suddenly snapped his fingers. "Yes, yes, I remember Jack. Older fellow, claimed to be a Navy bird."

Mason nodded. "That's him."

"It's like I've always said, desperation can make good men do bad things."

"What'd he do?"

"For starters, he stole someone's belongings. That by itself would've put him on my shit list."

"What else?"

"When the owner confronted him, he shot him dead."

"That doesn't sound like Jack. Did anyone see the killing?"

"Only a dozen people. Even with that, I had one of my men investigate the whole thing."

"And?"

"And he concluded that Jack was at fault."

"Who did the investigation?"

Leroy's eyes narrowed. "Are you saying you don't believe him, or me?"

"I'm only asking who decided that Jack was a murderer."

He took a moment to consider the request before finally answering.

"His name's Ramsey, but before you go getting all suspicious, I should tell you that he's been with me from the beginning."

"What's he like?"

"A little rough around the edges maybe. No different than you and I were at his age. Plus, he's got that face to contend with." When Leroy saw that Mason didn't understand, he said, "Poor bastard got hit by lightning when he was a teenager. Believe me. You've never seen anything like it."

"Even so, mind if I talk to him?"

Leroy shrugged. "I don't see why not. But it won't change anything. Jack's already in the tournament."

"Can't you put someone else in his place until I get to the bottom of this?"

"I could, but I won't. This whole camp is built on rules. If it were to get out that I'm willing to bend them for a friend, well, you can see how that might look."

Experience had taught Mason that Leroy was not a man who changed his mind easily. Still, he had to try.

"His daughter's here. She came up with me to search for him."

Leroy pressed his lips together. "I'm sorry to hear that. I really am." He looked as if he had more to say, and Mason waited until he found the words.

"There might be a way."

"Tell me."

"The rules allow for any man to take the place of another. We put that in so younger sons could step in for an aging or ill parent. No one wants to see an old woman shot dead." He settled back against the chair.

"You're saying that I could fight in his place."

"I am. But before you go raising your hand like some damn fool, you had better think this through. You wouldn't only be putting your life on the line, you'd be signing up to kill a man who hasn't committed any wrongdoing against you or yours."

Mason took a long moment to consider things. Killing was never to be taken lightly, neither was risking one's life.

"Are the gunfights fair?"

"Everything about Grey's Point is fair. Honestly though, I'd feel a whole lot better if you just took the little lady home and let things be how they're gonna be."

"If I take Jack's place, I'd only have to defeat one gunfighter to earn his freedom?"

"That's right." Leroy's eyes dropped to the Supergrade. "But it wouldn't be with that tack driver. Each challenge has its own assigned weapons."

That added an element of uncertainty to things. Even so, Mason didn't see how he could go back and tell Jessie that he had left her father to die.

"I'll do it."

"Are you sure? Because once you sign—"

"I said I'd do it."

"Yeah," he said with a resigned nod. "I thought you might."

Tanner coasted the old station wagon behind a thicket of trees before bringing it to a stop. An enormous brick building stood in the distance.

"Why are we stopping so far away?" asked Samantha.

"Figured we might want to take a look-see before we go charging in."

"Right," Sister Margaret muttered from the backseat, "because that worked so well with Dr. Langdon." She apparently hadn't quite gotten over Tanner making her sit scrunched together with the other three nuns in the back while Samantha got to ride shotgun.

"Come on, Sam. Let's go see what trouble we can get in."

Samantha opened the door and lifted out her rifle, giving it a quick once over.

"That building is no place for a child," chided Sister Margaret.

Neither Tanner nor Samantha replied. It had been asked and answered, as the saying goes.

They walked around to the rear of the station wagon and dropped the tailgate. Tanner dug through his backpack until he came up with a flashlight.

"Leave your pack if you like, but bring your flashlight." He clicked his on and off a few times. "It's bound to be dark in there."

"Oh great," she said, fishing it out. "Just what I always wanted to do, poke around a haunted insane asylum."

"No one ever said it was haunted."

"Like there's any other kind," she muttered, closing the hatch.

Leaving the good sisters behind to say prayers on their behalf, they headed off toward the DeJarnette Center. It was positioned atop a gradual hill, and between the razor wire grass and clumps of rotting garbage, it was nothing short of a miserable slog.

The structure consisted of two enormous brick buildings held together by a third one that looked like it might have been added to house an indoor swimming pool. Measured end to end, the center easily stretched five hundred feet. The windows and doors had all been boarded up, no doubt an attempt to keep out vandals and metal thieves.

A six-foot-high chain link fence blocked entrance to the stairs, a tattered yellow hazardous material sign plastered across it. The gate had been chained closed, but it didn't look very tight. Tanner pressed a shoulder against it, creating a gap large enough for him to slip through.

Samantha stopped short and studied the sign.

"You do see this, right?"

"They probably put that up to keep out looters. Worst case, there's a little asbestos floating around. I'm sure it's nothing to worry about."

She frowned, not at all convinced.

"You can go back and wait in the car with the ladies if you like." There was something about the way he said "ladies" that was anything but flattering.

She growled and pushed her way through the gap.

Once she was clear, Tanner veered toward a set of concrete steps that led to the asylum's main entrance. At the bottom of the stairs, they paused to stare up at the enormous structure. Cracked paint covered the once majestic colonnade of Ionic columns. Dirt, animal feces, and rotting wood stained nearly every square inch of the once white trim and cornice, and a thick web of dried vines coated the underside of the lower story's overhang.

Samantha slowly shook her head. "Not haunted, my foot."

"It's just an old boarded-up building."

"I've noticed that whenever you use the word 'just,' things end up getting really awful."

"Bah," he said, starting up the stairs. "That's just your imagination."

"See! You did it again!" she said, following after him. "Seriously, I have a bad feeling about this."

"Have you ever once had a good feeling about going into a spooky old building?"

"Of course not."

"Why do you suppose that is?"

"Oh, I don't know. Could it be because every time we go into one, something tries to eat us?"

"Correction," he said, stepping onto the landing. "Something tries to eat *me*. You apparently taste like day-old haggis."

"I don't know what that is, but I'm sure I don't taste like it."

They stopped picking at one another long enough to examine the double doors leading into the center. Both had been nailed shut and covered with thick sheets of plywood. An intricate web of vines had stitched itself to the face of the wood, daring anyone to pull it down.

Samantha reached for them, but Tanner gently pulled her back.

"Not a good idea, kiddo."

"Why not?"

"Count the leaves."

She stared at them a moment, finally understanding.

"Poison ivy."

"Which means we're not getting in that way."

"There must be a door around back that Dr. Langdon's men use," she offered.

"I'm sure that's true, but I'd rather come up from behind them if at all possible."

"So you can clobber them?"

He grinned. "Clobber—I like that."

"I thought you might." She let her eyes wander over the entrance. "What about that?" she said, pointing to one of the boarded-up windows. "No vines."

Tanner walked over and examined the window. The bottom corners of the plywood had been kicked loose from the inside, but nails still held the rest in place.

"I think we can make this work. Stand clear." He grabbed the bottom of the board and pried it backward. The lower half broke free, and he hurled the wood out into the grass.

"Go in and check things out," he said, squinting to see into the dark hole.

"*Me?*"

"No reason for me to squirm through that little hole if it doesn't go anywhere."

Samantha peered in. A thick dusty curtain hung down, blocking her view. She used her rifle to push it aside, but the room beyond remained dark and eerie.

"Did I mention that I have a bad feeling about this?"

He clasped his hands and held them out for her to stand on.

"Up you go."

"You do realize that sending a twelve-year-old girl into a haunted house probably qualifies as child abuse?"

"You're stalling."

Samantha reluctantly slung her rifle across her back and climbed through the broken window. She pushed past the curtains and stood for a moment, letting her eyes slowly adjust to the darkness.

"Well?" he said.

"It's dark."

"Yeah? And?"

"Scary too."

He let out a frustrated sigh. "Is there a way to get into the rest of the building? I don't want to squeeze through this tiny hole without good reason."

"Maybe the size of the hole isn't the problem," Samantha muttered, as she pulled the flashlight from her back pocket and clicked it on.

The room was roughly square and about the size of a typical bedroom. The walls were painted a sickly shade of yellow, and the paint had peeled off in bite-size strips that resembled hundreds of Post-it notes ready for the taking. Tile covered the floor, but many of the squares were cracked or missing to reveal a wet subfloor beneath. Even the old metal bedsprings couldn't hide the true purpose of the room.

This was a prison cell.

She turned her flashlight toward the door on the opposite wall. It looked sturdy, and there were window bars to allow staff to see that the prisoner hadn't managed to hang himself with a bed sheet.

"There's a door," she called. "But I can't tell if it's locked."

"You want me to come in?"

Samantha knew that he would if she said yes, but she also knew that he would be a little disappointed. Tanner expected her to pull her own weight, even if it was considerably less than his own.

"I've got it."

She picked her way across the room, broken bits of tile crunching under her shoes like twigs in a forest. She reached out and touched the door. It was cold and heavy, and a steel plate surrounded the doorknob to prevent the lock from being jimmied from the inside. Using her thumb and two fingers, she gently tried the knob. It turned with a slight squeak. She gave the door a light tug, and it swung inward a few inches. Okay, mission accomplished. She didn't dare go any further without Tanner at her side.

Tiptoeing back to the window, she leaned toward it and said, "The door's open."

"All right. Stand clear." A leg as thick as a telephone pole swung through the window frame. The hole wasn't wide enough for Tanner's thick chest and back, and by the time he was inside, another big chunk of the board had broken free.

"I don't know why they have to make everything so darn small," he said, brushing splinters from his shirt.

Samantha bit her tongue, saying only, "It's a mystery all right."

Coming from the sunlight, Tanner could barely make out his own hands. He turned and gave the curtains a sharp tug. The rod overhead broke, and the curtains fell in a heap, sending a cloud of dust billowing into the air.

"Better," he said with a satisfied nod.

Samantha coughed lightly, but said nothing.

Even with the infusion of sunlight, there remained a pronounced look of despair to the room. Too many people had suffered for laughter to ever again be heard within its space. The light did, however, reveal dozens of small black handprints adorning one of the walls.

Samantha walked over and gently placed her hand over one of the prints. It was nearly a perfect match. When she pulled away, flecks of dried black paint stuck to her palm.

"Kids did this," she said, her voice solemn.

"Yep."

"Why do you think they put their handprints here?"

"Same reason prisoners scratch their initials on things."

"So they won't be forgotten."

"Exactly."

"I bet those kids never thought someone would find them after all these years."

"Probably not." Tanner walked over to the door and pulled it open. A dark hallway went left and right. A matching room sat directly across from him, the door hanging by a single hinge. He glanced back at Samantha. "You coming?"

"Yeah," she said, turning away from the prints.

Together, they stepped into the hallway. Samantha pointed her flashlight first in one direction and then the other. In addition to the broken tile, papers, x-rays, and old medical records littered the floor.

"You feel that?" she said.

"What?"

"The air. It's wet, like someone just turned off a shower."

"Just air."

"Evil air, like in a dungeon."

He glanced over at her. "Been in lots of dungeons, have you?"

"No, but I'm pretty sure this is how they'd feel." She paused. "I do have one question though."

"Don't ask me if I think there are ghosts living here."

She pressed her lips together, saying nothing.

"Well?"

"You said not to ask you."

He growled. "Stay close, and use your light to show the way, Kolchak."

"I don't know who that is, but I'm sure he had every right to believe in ghosts."

"That he did."

She inched closer and shined her flashlight down the hallway. The darkness seemed to push at the edges of the beam, as if threatening to reduce it to nothing but a pinpoint of light.

"Just so you know," she said as they began their careful advance down the hallway, "ghosts can turn your hair white."

"That's all right. I like white hair."

"Well, sure, at your age it's fine. Past due, even."

"Watch it."

"Seriously. Name one girl with white hair who's pretty. Just one."

Tanner thought for a moment. "How about that hot chick on *Game of Thrones.*"

"Who?"

"You know. The one with all the dragons."

"Dragons?" she said with a spark of childish joy.

He smiled. "See. White hair might not be so bad after all. Might land you a couple of dragons."

They continued down the hall, passing several identical cells, all of them empty.

Samantha pointed to something on the floor.

"What's that?" she said, squinting. "A dead rat?"

Tanner walked over and picked it up. It wasn't a rat. It was a thick padded mitt.

"It's a glove," he said, handing it to her.

She took a moment to examine it. The outside was made of cloth, but there was a thick layer of cotton batting sewn inside. A cord had been tied around the wrist to hold it in place.

"What do you think they used it for?"

"Don't know. Maybe to keep the kids from hurting themselves. Or maybe to give them a good whipping without leaving a mark."

"That's terrible," she said, carefully setting it back on the floor where they had found it. For some reason, she had a strange feeling that they shouldn't disturb anything in the old building at the risk of angering the spirits that lived within.

They continued ahead until they came to a tall decorative arch that passed from one part of the building to another. There were children's paintings along its frame—a robot that looked like a cross between Iron Man and Optimus Prime, a mermaid with rays of sunlight coming from her hair, and a smiling blue fish with teeth as sharp as any great white's. All were faded and cracked.

Samantha scanned the floor, spotting a handful of shotgun shells and some bloody gauze. She touched Tanner's arm and nodded toward her find.

"There was a fight here."

He used his flashlight to study the walls. They were peppered with small holes from the buckshot. The wall closest to Samantha also had deep dents from where something had struck it. She made a fist and set it against one of the crushed indentations. If someone had hit it, they had hands twice the size of Tanner's.

"What could do this?" she said nervously.

"These walls are old. Probably wouldn't take much to knock them out."

A metallic clang sounded from behind them, and Tanner and Samantha spun around.

A metal bowl wobbled on the floor, some twenty feet away.

"I'm pretty sure that wasn't there when we walked by," she whispered. "And even if it was…" She left the rest unsaid.

They stood for nearly a full minute, watching the hallway with weapons firmly in hand. Nothing came for them, and the only sound was that of their breathing.

"Let's keep going," he said, wheeling around.

Samantha gave the bowl one final look before turning to follow.

At the end of the hallway was a set of double doors. Faint traces of light shone from underneath. Tanner cautiously tried the doorknob.

Locked.

Samantha leaned forward and placed an ear to one of the doors.

"I hear something. It sounds like someone crying."

"Sister Clare?"

She shrugged. "You listen."

Tanner placed his ear to the door. It was cold and quiet.

"Hear it?" she said.

"Uh—yeah. Real faint."

She shook her head. "You're an awful liar."

"I'll have you know I'm a fabulous liar." He motioned for her to scoot out of the way. "Stand clear."

She hurried around behind him as he lined up for the kick.

"They're not going to like this."

"Who's not?"

"The ghosts."

"That's their problem." Tanner lunged forward, thrust-kicking the doors with the flat of his foot. The lock broke, and both doors swung open.

Samantha leaned around him with her rifle ready.

The room consisted of a large open reception area on one end and something resembling a school cafeteria on the other. Row after row of long metal tables with built-in benches filled most of the space, and a doorway in the far wall opened into a commercial kitchen.

"Smell that?" she said.

He took a sniff. There was a pungent smoky odor, acrid and sweet at the same time.

"What is it?" she said, her face wrinkled.

Tanner wasn't entirely sure. Not decomposing bodies. That was an odor they both knew all too well.

"Burnt food maybe?"

"And the sound? You hear it now, right?"

He stood still and listened. There was indeed a gentle whimpering emanating from the kitchen.

"I hear it." He cut off his flashlight and stepped into the cafeteria. Thanks to a door along the back wall, the room was lit enough to make out all four corners. No one was lying in wait.

Samantha drifted toward the kitchen. "I think it's coming from in there."

She passed through the open doorway, discovering that the dishwashers and sinks had been removed, leaving bare plumbing sticking up through the floor. The only appliance that vandals had not managed to steal was a brick kiln set into the wall. A waist-high pile of wood sat next to it, and something smoldered within.

Samantha listened for a moment. The whimpering had ceased, but she noticed a slick trail of blood leading off to a set of accordion-style pantry doors. Hearing Tanner approaching from behind her, she crossed the room and peered into the open forge. It was hot and fiery, and she drew back to shine her flashlight into the oven.

"Look," she said, turning to Tanner. "There's something sparkly in there."

Tanner reached down and grabbed one of the boards from the pile. Using it like a fire poker, he slowly dragged out a small chunk of the flaming mass. Even though it was charred to the point where the bones had started pulling apart, there was no mistaking it for anything but a human hand. A large jeweled ring still clung to one finger, the gold so hot that it seemed to glow.

"Gross," she said, drawing back even further. It was far from the most disgusting thing Samantha had ever seen, but when combined with the smell of burning flesh, it was pretty rank. "Do you think it's Sister Clare?"

"I doubt it. That's a pretty fancy bauble for a nun."

"But why would they burn someone?"

"My guess is she probably died here in the building, and they wanted to get rid of the body."

Tanner used the board to push the hand back into the fire. He turned abruptly when a moan sounded from behind the pantry door.

"Someone's in there. And they're hurt," she said, pointing to the blood on the floor.

Tanner walked over and pulled open the doors, shotgun at the ready. A man sat wedged between two giant bags of dog food, clutching his abdomen. His trousers were soaked in blood, and the foul stench of human waste surrounded him. In addition to the gut wound, his face looked like he had been beaten with a baseball bat, large red hematomas on his cheekbones, forehead, and jaw. He was as big as Tanner, but lean like an athlete—no doubt another of Dr. Langdon's chosen specimens. Between the bushy mustache and hard set eyes, he reminded Tanner of Stacy Keach, back when he played private detective Mike Hammer.

"Help me, please," he croaked.

Tanner studied the man's stomach. The wound was uneven with deep jagged bite marks along its periphery. Something had gnawed his belly open, and intestines now bulged out from between his fingers.

"What happened to you?"

Keach didn't seem to hear him, instead continuing his incessant pleading.

"Listen to me," Tanner said, lifting the man's chin. "I'll get you out of here, but first you need to tell me where you took the nun."

"The nun?"

"That's right. Where is she?"

"You'll help me?"

Tanner nodded. "Tell me where she is, and I'll carry you out to Dr. Langdon. He'll get you patched up in no time."

Keach looked down at his belly.

"I'll… be okay?"

"Are you kidding? A few stitches and you'll be right as rain."

Keach swallowed, gagging on something that had bubbled up from his gut.

"Peery Building, second floor," he gasped. "You'll need…" He swallowed again, finding it harder to keep down the bile. "Keys." He twisted sideways so that Tanner could see the ring of keys hanging from his belt loop.

Tanner pulled the ring free. There were a dozen keys, but even so, it was a manageable problem.

He stood up. "Come on, Sam."

Bloody fingers reached for him. "You promised!"

Tanner leaned over so that his face was directly in front of Keach's.

"If I were a better man, I'd put a bullet in your head. But I'm not. So you'll sit here smelling that woman you burned, hoping that whatever did this to you doesn't come back for a late-night snack."

Tanner straightened up and headed toward the set of double doors leading into the Peery Building. Samantha followed after him, taking one final look back at Keach. The big man sat with his eyes closed, face twisted with agony and hopelessness.

"You were right," she said, her voice subdued.

"About what?"

"You *are* a fabulous liar."

CHAPTER
15

Jessie stood beside the RV, wringing her hands.

"I can't let you do this. It's not right."

"I don't see any other way to get Jack out of this mess," countered Mason. "Do you?"

Her eyes widened as an idea formed. "*I'll* do it. I'll compete in his place."

Mason shook his head. "No, Jessie. This isn't for you."

"Why not? I can—"

"You're not a killer. That's why not. You said so yourself."

"But I'm his daughter. I should be the one to stand in his place."

"Jack would never allow it. You know that."

She pressed her eyes shut. "This whole thing is just so unfair. There's no way Daddy could have murdered anyone, and whoever's saying that he did is a liar."

"That may well be, but it's an injustice we're going to have to live with."

"But what if…" She swallowed hard. "What if something happens to you?"

"If it does, I'll need you to do me a favor."

"What?"

Mason looked down at Bowie. The big dog lay on his side, occasionally raising his head as if someone in the distance were calling his name.

"Take care of Bowie for me."

Jessie squatted down and gently scrubbed Bowie's belly. In response, he rolled onto his back, hoping for something a bit more vigorous.

"Of course, I'd take care of him." She stopped and looked up at Mason. "You don't have to do this."

"I know that."

"Then why are you? You don't even know Daddy, not really."

He smiled. "No, but I know you."

She nodded, her eyes clouding.

Mason looked off toward the parade grounds to the south. A large crowd was gathering. The tournament would be getting underway soon.

"We'd better get over there before this thing starts."

Jessie stood up and wiped her eyes. Bowie took notice and rolled to his feet. As they started toward the open field, Jessie reached out and took Mason's hand. It surprised him, but he said nothing, content to feel her fingers pressing against his. Bowie trudged along behind them, pausing only to smell the occasional passerby.

After nudging their way through the thick crowd of spectators, they arrived at the edge of the parade grounds. Chest-high steel barriers had been erected along both sides for spectators to duck behind them, should the need arise. Tractor-trailers had also been parked at either end to act as backstops. In the center of the field were two rows of old cars, spaced about twenty yards apart. Mason suspected they were likely put there to act as cover for the upcoming challenge.

Like opposing football teams, the Fallen stood to one side, and the gunfighters to the other, the difference being that the Fallen also had a contingent of armed guards to act as cheerleaders.

"Come on," he said, leading Jessie by the hand. "Let's go find out how this thing works."

They hurried across the open field to find Leroy standing in front of a makeshift wooden scoreboard.

"Ma'am," he said, tipping his hat.

She nodded, a coldness in her eyes.

"Believe me," he said, "I understand your sentiments completely." His voice softened. "Have you had a chance to speak with your father?"

"No," she said, turning to face the prisoners. "Is he here?"

"I had him pulled from the line." Leroy pointed, and she spotted two guards standing next to her father at the far end of the field.

"Is it all right if I go to him?"

"Of course."

She looked to Mason, and he nodded.

"Go on. Explain things to him."

Jessie turned and headed across the field, her pace quickening.

Bowie watched her go, whining softly.

Eyeing the wolfhound, Leroy said, "I believe that's the biggest dog I've ever seen."

"His name's Bowie."

Leroy leaned over to give him a pat, but when Bowie pulled his lips back, he thought better of the decision.

"He suits you. Mean as all sin."

Mason eyed the scoreboard. The names of the five gunfighters were listed along the left side, and numbers one through four were shown across the top.

"It's a simple tally showing which gunfighters win each round," explained Leroy.

"Five gunfighters, four rounds. That means twenty of the Fallen could be killed."

"Possible, I suppose. But I don't expect that to happen. Competitions like these are unpredictable. Someone fumbles a draw or trips over their own shoelaces. You know what I always say."

"Shit happens."

Leroy grinned. "Exactly. Someone will fall short along the way. That's what makes this kind of thing interesting."

"You said those who manage to complete all four rounds will have the option to face off at the end."

"That's right. The final phase of voluntary showdowns between the winners lets greed decide who goes home with a larger share of the purse, and who gets buried at the hands of his comrades."

"How are the gunfighters and prisoners matched?"

"The order of the gunfighters is determined by a simple card draw. In this case, Muchado came up with the low card, so he's going first. The Fallen were chosen by Ramsey." Leroy pointed to a man standing near the prisoners. He was young, perhaps in his late twenties, and had a wiry, dangerous look to him.

"He and I still need to talk."

"The tournament will be over tomorrow. You can talk to him then."

Mason looked off toward Jessie and her father. He seemed to be arguing with her, no doubt about Mason standing in for him.

"Was Jack selected to fight in this challenge?"

Leroy nodded. "He's up last. Or should I say, you are."

"Did you arrange that?" By going last, Mason would have the best opportunity to come up with a plan. It was as much as any competitor could ask.

Leroy offered a thin smile but said nothing.

"Who will I be going up against?"

"You'll face Bones. He's particularly effective up close, and I know first-hand that you're faster than rattlesnake spit on the draw. Since neither of those skills will come into play during this particular challenge, it should be a pretty fair match."

Mason studied the field. "What exactly is the challenge?"

Leroy pointed to the two lines of cars.

"The gunfighter stands behind one set of cars, the Fallen behind the other. Both men are given an identical unloaded handgun. One cartridge is placed atop each of the cars. The challenge is to see who can retrieve the ammunition, load their weapon, and dispatch their enemy the fastest. It's the ultimate test of operating under pressure."

"Any rules?"

"Only that the fight goes on until a contestant is unable to continue."

"It doesn't have to be to the death?"

"No, but most end up that way."

"What happens if a Fallen should win?"

"If that happens, the gunfighter is removed from the board and the Fallen goes free." Leroy motioned toward the prisoners. "It's easy to feel sorry for them, but you have to remember that they're serious criminals. This competition gives them a chance to wipe the slate clean, maybe even come out as something of a folk hero."

Mason studied the line of prisoners. Many were trembling so violently that their legs could barely hold them up.

"Funny," he said. "They don't look like heroes."

⇠ ⇢

Jack, Jessie, Mason, and Bowie stood clustered together on one side of the field along with hundreds of others, watching as Leroy used a bullhorn to announce the start of the first round. When his name was called out, Muchado marched onto the field, waving to the crowd as he took his place behind the first row of cars.

His opponent was simply called "Prisoner 11," a man in his late forties with the build and complexion of someone who had spent much of his adult life sitting behind a desk. When he refused to step forward, two guards grabbed him by the arms and dragged him out onto the field.

"Listen!" he screamed. "There's been some kind of mistake. I didn't do anything wrong. Please, you've got to believe me!"

The crowd appeared deaf to his pleas, and the guards never slowed as they moved him into position behind the second row of cars.

Ramsey walked onto the field and delivered an unloaded Colt Trooper to each of the men. Chambered in .357 Magnum, the Trooper was a common service revolver back in the 1970s and 80s. Both weapons were well worn, but equally operable. Ramsey called their attention to the cartridges placed across the tops of the old cars. He also pointed to a man standing ready with a rifle, should one of them break the rules and go for the ammunition before the match had officially started.

With the rules clearly explained, Ramsey hurried from the field as Leroy once again brought the bullhorn to his mouth.

"Shooters ready?"

The big Mexican waved his hat in the air. Prisoner 11 just stared at the gun in his hands.

Leroy raised his pistol into the air and fired. The match had begun!

Muchado strode toward the closest car, calm like he was getting ready to put down a lame horse.

Realizing he had only one chance to survive, Prisoner 11 rushed forward, stumbling and falling before he could even reach the cars. He scrambled back to his feet and lunged for the first cartridge. His panic caused him to knock it over, sending it rolling off the other side of the car. Frantic, he looked over at Muchado. The big Mexican had arrived at his car and was calmly retrieving the cartridge. He held it up in his opponent's direction and offered a toothy smile.

Prisoner 11 looked left and right, trying to decide which way to go. Both remaining cartridges were roughly the same distance away. He ducked down and waddled his way over to the next car. Terrified to even look in Muchado's direction, he stood up and dove across the roof of the second car, landing on the hood with the cartridge clutched firmly in his hand.

Lying on his back, he fumbled to open the revolver. His hands were shaking so violently that it took five long seconds to figure out how to release the cylinder. It was only as the weapon finally opened that he realized he was no longer alone.

Muchado stood ten feet away, the revolver hanging loosely at his side. Without saying a word, the big Mexican brought the weapon up and fired. Traveling along a downward trajectory, the bullet pierced the man's left eye, exited through his mandible, and tunneled into the car's engine compartment. Prisoner 11 rolled off the hood, leaving behind a bright wet stripe of blood.

Muchado came closer and bent down to pick up the unused cartridge that had fallen from Prisoner 11's hand. He blew it clean and carefully loaded it into his own revolver. Once he had the cylinder lined up, he bent over, placed the muzzle of the gun to the back of the man's head and pulled the trigger.

The concussion from the blast sent blood and brains spraying out to either side.

The big Mexican straightened and offered another flamboyant wave of his sombrero to the crowd. A thunderous cheer erupted. Like spectators at a cage match, it took only the scent of blood to bring out their most primal urges. They whistled and cheered, some even calling for him to retrieve another cartridge and shoot Prisoner 11 again. Before Muchado could decide whether to comply with their bloodthirsty request, Ramsey and another man hurried onto the field to remove the body.

Jessie stood beside her father, watching in horror. When she spoke, her voice trembled.

"How could anyone do that?"

Jack put his arm around her shoulder and turned her away from the field.

"Men who have lost their humanity can do anything to one another. I know that from my time in the war." He looked over at Mason. "Marshal Raines, I can't let you go in my place. If this is to be my final hour, I'll face it with my head held high."

"I'm sure you would, Jack, but that isn't something you want your daughter to witness."

Before he could reply, Jessie turned to Mason, her voice pleading.

"You said that your friend was a marshal. Surely, he must know this is wrong. Talk to him. Make him stop."

Mason watched as Ramsey and the other man lifted Prisoner 11's body into a wheelbarrow. This wasn't about right and wrong. It was about entertainment in its most primitive form.

"I'm afraid this thing has taken on a life of its own. The only way forward is straight down the middle."

Jessie's face tightened. "I can't watch someone do that to you. I just can't."

Mason offered an understanding smile. "Why don't you take Bowie back to the RV and wait for us. Jack and I will be along as soon as it's over."

She hesitated.

"Please, Jessie," urged her father. "Go on."

She looked into Mason's eyes. "Tell me it's going to be okay."

When he spoke, his voice was calm and reassuring.

"It's going to be okay."

Jessie pressed her lips together and nodded. She leaned in and gave Mason a long kiss to his cheek. With her lips to his ear, she whispered, "Be careful."

She released him and turned to Bowie. "Come on, boy," she said, trying to adopt a happier voice. "What do you say we go back and have some more of that jerky?"

Bowie looked up at his master, uncertain if he should go or stay.

Mason gave him a quick nod. "Go on. Keep her safe."

How much the wolfhound really understood was anyone's guess, but he followed Jessie into the crowd, licking his lips as he went.

As soon as they were out of earshot, Jack turned to Mason.

"I'm not going to allow you to compete in my place."

Mason had expected as much. When he spoke, his words were slow and deliberate.

"Yes, Jack, you are. Because when you stop and think about it, you'll come to the same conclusion that I did."

"What conclusion?"

"That some things are best left to professionals."

☙ ❧

The next three rounds went by as quickly as the first, Ringo, Liberty, and The Reverend all dispatching their opponents with little difficulty. Each man had his own particular persona, Ringo playing the wholesome gunslinger set on vanquishing outlaws, Liberty, the patriotic soldier carrying out a sanctioned seek-and-destroy mission, and The Reverend, the mysterious, cold-blooded preacher who rode into town determined to deliver final penance. All proved themselves not only capable of keeping their nerve under pressure, but also of killing without hesitation or remorse. The Reverend, in particular, moved with a precision rivaling that of any professional assassin.

When the fourth round was complete, Ramsey approached with guards at his side to escort Jack onto the field. It was the first time Mason had seen Ramsey up close, and he was struck by his disfigurement. The left side of his face was stippled with a strange branch-like pattern of scars. It looked like the limb of a tree, complete with offshoots ending in leafy-like protrusions. By itself it was not particularly repulsive. Some might even say it was intriguing. The right side, however, was something else entirely. His face had melted from the eyebrow all the way down to his chin. The ball of the eye remained intact, but the whiskered skin along his cheek and chin looked like lumpy vanilla pudding sprinkled with coffee grounds.

Ramsey faced Jack and said, "Are we going to have to drag you out, old timer, or are you man enough to walk?"

Before he could reply, Mason stepped forward.

"I'll be fighting in his place."

Ramsey sized him up. "You're the one who came to see Leroy."

"That's right."

"You two know one another?"

There was a cockiness to the man's voice that didn't sit well with Mason, so instead of answering, he said, "When things calm down a bit, I'd like to have a word with you."

Ramsey's eyes opened wide, and he turned to one of the guards with a grin.

"Can you believe the stones on this one?" He turned back to Mason. "What the hell do you want with me?"

Mason nodded toward Jack. "I'd like to hear your version of what happened."

"My version? Who the hell do you think you are?"

Mason straightened to his full height, his hand hanging down by his Supergrade.

"I'm a Deputy Marshal inquiring about the commission of a crime."

"No, hotshot. Right now, you're nothing but a walk-on." He held out his hand as he eyed the Supergrade. "Hand it over."

Mason slowly pulled the pistol free, but instead of handing it to Ramsey, he passed it to Jack. The guards stiffened, but they made no attempt to take it from him.

"Hold this until I get back."

Mason's bravado seemed to irritate Ramsey, and he turned to Jack and said, "My bet is you're going to get to keep it."

Mason followed Ramsey and the two guards out onto the field. Bones was already in place behind the opposite set of cars. He wore blue jeans but no shirt or shoes. His face, chest, arms, and feet had all been recently painted white, making him look like Baron Samedi.

Once Mason was in place, Leroy raised the bullhorn and said, "Shooters ready?"

Bones responded by blowing him a kiss. Mason just offered a quick nod.

Leroy stuck his pistol in the air and squeezed the trigger.

Watching four matches before his own had given Mason perspective on what worked and what didn't. The challenge was not so much a test of shooting skill as it was steady hands. The competitor who could load and fire first was likely to win the event. The problem was there were no guarantees that the firearm was accurate or the cartridge reliable. A bent sight or a bad round could turn victory into failure. With a single shot, there were no second chances. That line of thinking led Mason to formulate an entirely different strategy.

As soon as the crack of Leroy's pistol sounded, Mason broke into a dead run. Instead of stopping at the first row of cars, he slid across the hood and continued across the open gap. Bones was also in motion, rushing forward with his hands outstretched. It took him three full seconds to realize what was happening, but by then it was too late.

Bones struggled to mentally change gears as he frantically grabbed for the closest cartridge. He had it in hand and was in the process of opening the revolver's cylinder when Mason slammed into him.

It wasn't pretty, but it was effective.

Bones found himself lying flat on his back with Mason scrambling atop him. He swung the empty revolver up, hoping to clock Mason on the side of the head. Fighting from one's back, however, was rarely a winning proposition, and Mason managed to quickly hook his left arm around the man's elbow, locking it in place.

"Get the hell off me!" Bones shouted as he tried to buck him off.

Mason's answer was to smash his revolver into the man's face. The Trooper was the equivalent of a forty-three-ounce metal mallet, crushing the man's nose and opening a gash along his cheekbone. Blood leaked out, and he fought frantically to get out from underneath him.

Wriggling on his back, Bones squirmed away a few inches, but it wasn't enough to escape a second blow, this one to his mouth. Teeth broke and gums tore, and he began gagging as his mouth filled with blood.

He bucked again, this time managing to free his trapped arm and roll onto his belly. Exposing his back was the last thing he should have done. Mason brought the pistol down to the base of his skull. Much like a rabbit punch, the blow brought both pain and disorientation. Confused and desperate, Bones pushed up and began scrambling forward, spit and blood dripping from his mouth.

Not wanting to kill the man, Mason released the pistol and slipped an arm around his neck. He hooked it back against his other arm and set the choke. With his forearm and bicep cutting off the flow of blood to the man's brain, Bones was unconscious before he could recite N.W.A.'s timeless line, "You are now about to witness the strength of street knowledge."

Mason held him for another ten seconds to be sure that he was out cold before he got back to his feet and retrieved both pistols. An uncomfortable hush had settled over the crowd. No one was expecting the violent gang-banger to be bested by some unknown challenger. Worse yet, no shots had been fired. What kind of gunfighting competition didn't involve the shooting of guns? Boos rose from the crowd, accompanied by fists waving angrily in the air.

Leroy hurried onto the field and brought the bullhorn to his mouth.

"Everyone shut the hell up!" He nudged Bones with his boot. The man didn't so much as moan. "One competitor is unable to continue, and the other remains standing. He is, therefore, the winner." He lifted Mason's hand into the air to officially bring the match to a close.

More boos and jeers sounded, but they eventually tapered off as the losers reluctantly accepted their bad luck.

Looking down at Bones, Leroy said, "That's one way to get it done."

"So, that's it then," said Mason. "Jack's free to go?"

"As promised." He looked off toward the setting sun. "You might want to get him and his daughter out of the camp before nightfall to avoid any undue fuss with people who lost bets."

"And tomorrow? The killings continue?"

"The tournament will go on, if that's what you're asking."

Mason shook his head. "This isn't right. You know that, Leroy."

Leroy's eyes tightened. "Mason, you and I have seen what bad men can do. This tournament is a way to send the message that no one is above the law. Now," he said, letting out a frustrated breath, "I really do think it's best if you take your leave."

An idea scratched its way to the forefront of Mason's mind. It bordered on the crazy, but there was a simplicity to it that felt undeniably right.

"Is there anything to prevent me from fighting in another round?"

Startled, Leroy sputtered, "Well, technically no, but—"

"How would I go about it?"

"You'd have to fight in place of a different Fallen. But why the hell would you do something like that?"

Mason looked out at the crowd.

"I'd do it so that these people might come away from this tournament with a very different message."

"What kind of message would you possibly be giving them? That it's okay to break the law?"

"No," he said with a quick shake of his head. "That all men, even criminals, should be treated with some measure of respect." He turned and pointed to the long line of prisoners being marched off to a holding area for the night. "Those men are no different than slaves being tossed into an arena for Roman gladiators to butcher."

"And what? You're planning to be their Spartacus?"

"That's right."

"You can only fight one match each round. Even if you win, many of them are still going to die."

"Just because I can't save all of them doesn't mean I shouldn't save some. Besides," he said, setting his jaw, "if I remove a gunfighter every round, this thing's going to get smaller in a hurry."

Leroy shook his head. "Don't do this, Mason. These men will kill you."

"Ask yourself something, Leroy. Is it really my safety you're worried about?"

He bit at his lip. "Okay, fine. I admit it. If you were to win, it wouldn't be good for the tournament. Gunfighters would be a lot less likely to sign up if they thought there was a real chance they might be killed."

"Right now, I don't give a damn what's good for your tournament or your gunfighters." He met the man's stare. "You brought people together to see men slaughtered. I'm going to show them something else."

"What?"

"I'm going to show them that a hero isn't measured by the shine of his pistols or the speed of his draw. He's measured by when and where he decides to make his stand."

CHAPTER 16

Tanner studied the double doors leading from the cafeteria into the Peery Building. They were identical in every respect to the ones he had kicked in on the other side of the room, the only difference being that these were already ajar.

He grabbed the handles and pulled the doors the rest of the way open. A dark hallway similar to the one they had just traveled lay ahead.

Samantha glanced nervously back at the kitchen.

"What do you think attacked that man?"

"Can't really say." Tanner clicked on his flashlight and shined it down the hallway. There was quite a bit more junk lying about than in the other building—broken chests of drawers, smelly stained mattresses, and shattered fluorescent lights, all lying atop a bed of medical records.

"A wild animal though, right?"

"Could be."

She turned to him. "You're not being very encouraging."

"I wasn't trying to be." She looked a bit rattled, so he quickly added, "Look, whatever got hold of him is probably long gone. And if it does come back…" He patted the shotgun. "We'll teach it why man is still king of the jungle. Now, are you ready to go find Sister Clare?"

"I guess so."

Tanner started down the hall, and Samantha fell in beside him, muttering, "But I'm pretty sure that lions are still king of the jungle. A man wouldn't stand a chance against something that big."

He smiled. Tanner knew that if he could get Samantha's mind on something else, she could usually shake the fear.

Proving him right, she said, "How many kids do you think stayed here?"

"I don't know. Four or five hundred."

"Were there really that many crazy children?"

"Maybe. Or maybe it was just folks locking up what they didn't understand."

She wondered if he was still talking about the kids. Tanner had never forgiven the justice system for his incarceration.

"I wonder what kind of experiments they—"

Something dark crossed the hallway in front of them, and Tanner instinctively placed an arm in front of Samantha.

"What is it?" She swung her flashlight from one side of the hall to the other. Other than an old bedframe and a tipped-over filing cabinet, it appeared empty.

"I thought I saw something."

"You *thought* you saw something or you *did* see something?" she said, her voice wavering.

"Probably just the flashlight playing tricks on me." Tanner continued forward, but instead of being quiet and careful, he began to kick things out of his way.

"What are you doing!" she exclaimed.

"Making sure there are no ninjas hiding."

"Ninjas?"

"Little samurai dudes in black clothes."

She scoffed. "I know what a ninja is."

"Then why'd you ask?" He smiled. It was always satisfying to get her at her own game.

Something crossed the hallway behind them, briefly dimming the light coming from the cafeteria. Tanner and Samantha both spun, weapons and flashlights raised.

Nothing.

"Ninjas…," she repeated, this time slowly, as if genuinely considering the possibility.

Tanner shone his flashlight all the way to the end of the hall. There was a stairway. Unfortunately, it was at least fifty yards away.

"Put your back to mine. I'll watch the front, and you watch the rear."

"Right," she said, moving into position.

"If you see something, shoot first, apologize later. Understood?"

"Got it."

They advanced down the hall, moving at a steady but controlled pace. Samantha walked backwards, and Tanner dragged his feet so that they didn't accidentally trip over one another. Unlike in the original building, the doors to most of the dormitory rooms were closed. Tanner thought that both a blessing and a curse. While they could easily be walking past a threat, only to have it sneak up behind them later, having the doors closed also meant that someone couldn't simply lunge out from an open doorway.

When they were about halfway down the hall, the door to the cafeteria slammed shut. Samantha immediately fired a shot, more as a reflex than from actually seeing a target.

"Go, go, go!" Tanner said, picking up the pace.

They arrived at the end of the hall to find that the stairwell door had been propped open with a decorative floor mirror. The words "come play with me" had been written on the glass in something red and sticky.

"In here, Sam!" he said, ushering her into the stairwell as he watched the hallway.

"Up or down?" she asked, looking at stairs.

"Hold tight a minute." Tanner swept the hallway with his flashlight beam. Mattresses. Furniture. An old fan. His thoughts came out as words. "No way to follow us without being seen. Unless…"

"Unless what?" she said.

"The rooms. They must be interconnected."

"What does that mean?"

Instead of answering, he said, "What was it you saw back there?"

"Nothing more than a blur. Something big, darting from one side of the hall to the other." She stared out into the darkness. "What do you think it is?"

"I don't know, but whatever it is, it seems to be stalking us."

"Stalking? Why?"

"I told you, I'm quite delicious," he said, hoping to lighten the mood. It didn't work.

She shivered. "I'm scared."

"Come on." Tanner turned and began climbing the stairs with a sense of purpose.

Samantha followed close behind, taking them two at a time. They reached the second-floor landing and stopped to do a quick inspection of the hallway. Like the floor below, there was a hodgepodge of furniture, including several small student desks, a chest of drawers, and a bedframe. An assortment of children's clothes was also strewn about, like the crankiest of toddlers had thrown a temper tantrum at not finding their favorite pajamas.

"Sister Clare!" he shouted.

Fists began pounding on one of the doors.

"In here!" a muffled voice called.

Tanner and Samantha hurried forward, using their flashlights like light-sabers to navigate the almost impenetrable darkness. They found Sister

Clare in the fourth room on the right, peering out through a barred windowless frame.

"Help me, please!" she said, pressing her face to the bars.

"Hold tight. We'll get you out of there." Tanner began rifling through the keys, trying them one at a time.

"Who are you?" she asked, her voice calming.

"Friends of Sister Margaret." Even saying the word "friends" in the same sentence with the grumpy old nun's name felt like an unforgivable sin.

"Sister Mary Margaret? She's here?"

"Outside, waiting for you."

Samantha pressed her shoulder against Tanner's back as she watched the stairs behind them.

"Hurry!"

"I'm trying." He fumbled the keys, and they fell to the floor. "Crap!"

A dark mass appeared at the end of the hallway, and Samantha brought the rifle to her shoulder.

"Something's coming." She squeezed off a shot, and a piece of plaster fell from the wall next to the stairwell.

With the keys and flashlight in one hand and his shotgun in the other, Tanner turned, ready to cut down whatever was coming their way.

There was nothing but darkness.

"I don't see it!"

"It was there a second ago."

Tanner turned back and tried another key in the lock. No luck. He moved onto yet another. And then another. On the sixth key, he felt the lock move. He twisted harder. There was resistance but also a little rotation of the cylinder. He leaned into it.

Snap!

"Son-of-a—"

Samantha fired another shot. Tanner didn't even bother to look. His focus had to be on getting Sister Clare out of the room.

"Stand back! I'm going to blow the lock."

Sister Clare hurried out of sight. "Okay!" she shouted. "I'm clear!"

Tanner stepped to one side of the door and aimed just above the lock. He turned the shotgun so that the muzzle was at forty-five degrees, ensuring that the blast would go into the locking mechanism and door jamb rather than the room. While the double-aught buckshot wasn't the right load for the task, the lock wasn't a Sargent and Greenleaf either. This was about destroying the wooden frame as much as it was shredding the lock housing.

"Fire in the hole!" He squeezed the trigger.

Boom!

The mangled lock tore free of the frame. He bumped the door with his boot, and it swung open.

Samantha fired another shot down the hallway.

"It's too fast!" she cried. "I can't hit it!"

Tanner leaned in through the open door to find Sister Clare standing in the corner, hands clamped over her ears.

"Let's go, let's go!"

Rushing over, she said, "There's something living in this building."

"What is it?" Samantha asked, refusing to take her eyes from the hall-way.

"I don't know, but it was scratching and banging on my door last night."

"To get in?"

"No," she said hesitantly. "I think it was playing with me."

"Chitchat later," said Tanner. "Right now, we need to find a way out of here."

"I wouldn't suggest going back that way," Samantha said as she quickly reloaded.

"Then we go deeper." He turned and faced the hallway. "Like before, Sam, only with the good sister sandwiched between us."

"Like grape jelly?"

He smiled, relieved that her usual perkiness seemed to be returning.

"Yeah," he said. "Like grape jelly."

Tanner positioned himself in front again, and Samantha took up the rear. Even with his flashlight lighting the way, the old building held a hundred places to hide. All they could do was push forward.

As they shuffled down the hallway, Tanner spotted rays of light coming from one of the rooms up ahead. He hurried closer, relieved to find the door unlocked. Pushing it open, he discovered a room whose outside wall had been damaged, the plaster, wood, and brick all having given way. A thick mound of black manure had been piled up from the outside to seal the hole, but a six-inch gap along the top allowed rays of sunshine to stream into the room.

"In here," he said, ushering them in and slamming the door closed. "You two see if you can dig us a way out through the dirt while I cover the door."

Samantha and Sister Clare hurried over to the mound and began digging. It didn't take long for Samantha to figure it out.

"Eww!" she said, turning to him with hands covered in black muck. "This isn't dirt!"

"Really?" he said, doing his best to sound innocent. "What is it?"

She squinted. "You know exactly what it is."

He couldn't quite hide the grin, and she flung a handful in his direction. "It's cow poop!"

"Good. That means it's soft. Now hurry up."

She growled and turned back to the pile.

"I'm going to get you for this. And when I do, it's going to be sooo sweet."

A face appeared in the door's barred window. It was only there for an instant, and Tanner wasn't entirely sure of what he had seen. It was human-like, two eyes, two ears, and a mouth, but the entire head was covered with thick black fur. Its nose resembled a pig-like snout, and its forehead was swollen like that of early humans. Its eyes were equally strange—luminous and set within deep cavities. What concerned Tanner most, however, were the thick fangs that protruded from its lipless mouth.

By the time he swung the shotgun up, it was gone. He fired anyway, a fist-sized hole appearing in the door as the deafening blast shook the room.

Sister Clare screamed, but both she and Samantha continued their frantic digging. Light poured into the room as the hole grew bigger.

Tanner glanced over his shoulder. The gap was easily big enough for Samantha to squeeze through, and perhaps barely so for Sister Clare.

"Up and out, both of you. Now! Hurry!"

"It's not big enough," cried Samantha.

"It is for you. I'll dig my way out after you two are safe. Now go!"

She shook her head. "No way. If one stays, we all stay. Right, Sister Clare?"

The nun's wide eyes showed anything but a willingness to fight.

The door to the room slowly swung inward, and Tanner turned to face it, his shotgun held at waist level. Nothing came through. Whoever, or whatever, had pushed it open had ducked back out of sight.

"Sam!" he shouted without turning around. "You've got to get her out of here. We promised Sister Margaret."

Samantha turned to Sister Clare. "Go on. If you crawl on your belly, you'll make it through."

Not needing to be told twice, Sister Clare squirmed through the narrow hole. Once she was clear, Samantha turned and stepped up next to Tanner, her flashlight and rifle trained on the doorway.

"Okay, what's the plan?"

"The plan was to get you to safety."

She placed the edge of her boot against his.

"I feel pretty safe."

He let his eyes cut over to her. She stood tall and proud, her chin raised.

"All right. Let's put our backs against the wall. That way—"

What happened next occurred with such speed that neither Tanner nor Samantha had time to react. The beast was huge but also incredibly fast, knocking Samantha to one side and driving Tanner back against the wall. Before he could recover, it began to beat him with its enormous fists.

Tanner tried to bring the shotgun up, but the creature ripped it from his grasp and flung it out into the hallway.

With the monster's mouth closing in for the kill, Tanner lunged forward, driving his head under the beast's chin. The blow was tremendous, setting the creature back on its heels. Hoping to turn the tide, Tanner swung a wide haymaker that would have put Rocky Marciano on the mat. But the creature was too quick, not only avoiding the punch but once again driving him back against the battered wall.

Samantha groaned as she struggled to get to her feet. One cheekbone felt swollen and sore from where her face had struck the floor. She turned to find what looked like a massive grizzly bear attacking Tanner. It smashed him against the wall, and the old framework shuddered with the impact. The beast began striking him over and over, pounding its huge fists against his head.

She snatched her rifle off the floor and rotated the flashlight with her foot to point in the creature's general direction. She brought the weapon to her shoulder but hesitated. There was no clean shot. Tanner and the beast were so entangled that the bullet was as likely to hit one as it was the other.

She had to get closer.

As Samantha formulated a plan, Tanner was fighting for his life. The hairy beast was stronger and faster, but it lacked any real skill in hand-to-hand combat. Instead, it pummeled him like an ape, determined to pound him into blood sausage. Tanner did his best to counterattack, but he found himself having to use his forearms to shield the sides of his head, like a boxer caught against the ropes.

The beast lunged forward, jagged teeth snapping at his face. Pivoting at the waist, Tanner fired a short right hook. The blow caught the creature on its snout, and blood erupted from both nostrils. It squealed and snorted in pain, quickly returning to smashing him with its powerful fists.

Samantha crept closer, her rifle extended like an infantryman's brandistock. When the muzzle touched the creature's hairy back, she pulled the trigger. A muted pop sounded, and the beast whirled around, howling with rage. It slapped away the rifle and barreled into her, lifting Samantha off the floor to send her flying into the corner of the room.

It took Tanner a moment to get his bearings after the creature turned. His ear and cheek were on fire, and one eye was nearly swollen shut. He let out three quick breaths and forced his head to clear.

Samantha! The thought hit him like a bolt of thunder.

The beast advanced toward her, snarling, with its huge hands outstretched.

Tanner took two large steps and leaped onto the creature's back, snaking one arm around its neck, while the other attempted to secure some kind of choke.

No luck.

The girth of its neck was simply too big to completely lock his arms. Desperate, he resorted to yanking the creature's head back, anything to keep it from biting Samantha.

Even with his strength, Tanner was no match for the beast. Samantha knew that if she didn't do something fast, they were both going to die. Her first thought was to use her trusty knife. It was a good blade, certainly capable of cutting the monster's flesh. But instinctively, she knew that it would not be enough. And then it came to her.

The silver bullet.

Samantha reached across her waist and slid the Patriot free. It looked insignificant, a pea shooter against a beast as powerful as Goliath. But it was her one and only hope. She sat up and shoved it against the creature's belly while thumbing back the hammer. The trigger pull was harder than she had anticipated, and for a moment she thought she might have accidentally left on the safety.

Suddenly, the gun bucked and a loud *boom* sounded. Blood splashed over her hand, dripping from her fingers like warm maple syrup. She cocked the hammer and squeezed the trigger a second time. Another thunderous *boom*, only this time the gun flipped sideways, twisting out of her slick hands. She held her breath, uncertain what effect, if any, the bullets might have had.

And then… everything went dark.

CHAPTER 17

I ssa ran along the back of the museum, skirting an intricate maze constructed from eight-foot-high evergreen hedges. What were once perfectly manicured bushes now had spindly green shoots reaching into the air. As she rounded the far corner of the maze, she took a knee and stared out into the parking lot.

It didn't take long to find Dolly. The old black woman lay on the asphalt, cupping her face. A teenage boy stood over her, hands outstretched as he pleaded with four armed men. Based on their angry shouting, they appeared to be in no mood for mercy.

One of the men stepped forward and drove the butt of his rifle into the boy's gut. He doubled over and dropped to his knees, nearly gagging from the pain. The man kicked him in the face with the flat of his boot, sending the teen to the pavement.

Issa glanced back at the museum. A thin trail of black smoke had begun to rise from the rear of the building. She looked around and cursed under her breath. No one had yet to notice the fire. Nearly everyone was fixed either on the stage in anticipation of the coming auctions, or on the vicious beatings of Dolly and her grandson Jerome.

Bells began to toll, a rich musical tune filling the air. The crowd cheered and turned to face a large stone tower to the south. Sensing that it was their chance to escape, Jerome helped Dolly to her feet, and together, they pushed past the men.

But it was not to be. The same man who had hit Jerome brought his rifle up and took aim at their backs.

Issa was in motion before she even had a chance to think about what she was doing. Still kneeling, she swung the Merkel up and fired. The recoil sent her tumbling onto her backside, but the shot was true, and the man with the rifle stumbled forward and collapsed to the ground.

The crack of the rifle sent people ducking in place, their eyes searching for the shooter. Fingers pointed and shouts sounded as people spotted her.

Issa rolled to her feet, watching as Dolly and Jerome ran southeast past a small service station. It seemed unlikely that they would escape, but at least they had cleared the crowd.

She quickly replaced the spent cartridge and searched for a place to hide. The tall hedge maze struck her as the perfect spot, until she realized that it would be like a rat running into a trap. Distance was her only hope.

Issa began to run, racing across Cave Hill Road and veering southeast to follow Dolly and Jerome. Several men pushed their way through the crowd. One took a potshot at her that missed by mere feet, shattering a car window. As she gained ground, she heard faint shouts from the crowd.

"Fire!"

Bright yellow flames now licked out through the museum's cracked windows.

Still standing on the stage, the potbellied man waved his arms and shouted for people to remain calm. It didn't work. The more he yelled, the more people panicked. Soon, scores of people pushed against one another, trying desperately to reach their cars without being trampled. As chaos ensued, the slaves seized their opportunity. Some ran. Others turned on their captors. Gunshots rang out as men fired on the slaves, often missing to hit bystanders. What started as a fearful retreat quickly turned into a terror-driven stampede.

Issa stayed her course, sprinting along the far side of Cave Hill Road. Dolly and Jerome were dead ahead, the old woman hobbling as fast as she could while dragging an injured leg behind her. Issa caught up to them as they crossed beneath the Lee Highway overpass.

"Hurry up, old woman," she said, slipping an arm around Dolly's other shoulder and nodding to Jerome.

Dolly looked over and smiled, blood covering her teeth.

Picking up the pace, they practically dragged Dolly along the ground. As they passed a small manmade lake filled with dark blue water, shouts sounded from behind them. Issa glanced back and saw six men running in their direction. Cars and trucks also began to spill from the parking lot, some escaping the chaos, others giving chase.

She accepted that there was no way they were going to outrun their pursuers, certainly not with Dolly in tow. Issa had a choice to make. She either had to abandon the old woman and her grandson, or risk sharing their fate.

She could hear Tanner saying, *"They're dead weight and you know it."*

"Even so," she whispered, "I can't leave them."

"Then you'd better find someplace to hole up, and fast."

Issa spotted two women coming out of the bell tower up ahead.

"There!" she huffed, pointing to the stone tower that rose more than a hundred feet over their heads.

They made it to the doors just as the women were preparing to lock up. Issa waved the Merkel at them, and they quickly abandoned any sense of duty to race off across the open field. Together, she and Jerome carried Dolly into the tower and closed the doors behind them. The wood was heavy, perhaps Australian Buloke or some other form of ironwood. That was the good news. The bad news was that the deadbolt was keyed on both sides, and they didn't have the key.

Issa turned and surveyed the tower's interior. Everything was painted a dingy beige, and water stains ran down the walls. The lowest level had been set up for remote viewing of the carillon player sitting several stories up. A dusty large-screen television was mounted to a wooden table with a "Do Not Cross" fabric barrier roping it off. Several heavy wooden chairs sat stacked in one corner. Resting beside them was a toolbox and a fire extinguisher.

Metal steps wound around the inside walls of the square tower all the way up to the belfry. The stairs themselves seemed quite defendable. Unfortunately, there was a long narrow window directly opposite the doors that looked just big enough for someone to squeeze through. Two entrances, one gun. They weren't going to hold out for very long.

Issa turned to Jerome. The teen was wearing a long-sleeve flannel shirt and filthy blue jeans held up by a leather belt two sizes too big.

"Give me your belt," she said, holding out her hand.

"What?" He brought his hands in front of the buckle protectively. "Why?"

She slapped his hands aside and pulled the belt free. Hurrying back to the doors, she slipped it through the two handles and cinched the leather tight. It was a start, but it wasn't nearly enough. She rushed over to the toolbox, hoping that someone might have stashed a spare key. No luck. She did, however, find two large flathead screwdrivers and a hammer. Racing back to the doors, she hammered the screwdrivers between them and the surrounding frame.

She turned to Jerome. "Get your grandmother upstairs and find a place to hide."

"But she's hurt!" he said, his voice shaking.

"I'll be all right," Dolly wheezed. But she didn't look all right. A small gash above her eye seeped blood, and she clutched one wrist close to her body.

"But, Grandma—"

"No buts. Do what she says." She slipped an arm over his shoulder, and he reluctantly pulled her to her feet. Together, they staggered up the stairs.

Issa retrieved the fire extinguisher and followed after them, stopping when she reached the first landing. Shouts were coming from outside, and someone jerked on the door handle. When the door refused to open, they bumped it with their shoulder.

The belt and screwdrivers held.

Knowing that it wouldn't be long, Issa pulled the pin on the fire extinguisher and sprayed the lower level and metal steps below her. A cloud of white vapor filled the air, the monoammonium phosphate settling to provide a slick residue on the surfaces.

Something heavy smashed against the doors. They shuddered but once again held.

Issa brought the Merkel up and fired a single shot through the center of one of the doors. Ironwood or not, the door was no match for the 500-grain bullet, and an inch-diameter hole appeared in the door. Screams sounded from outside, followed by a series of wild gunshots. More holes appeared, but they did little to break the doors free.

As Issa reloaded, she moved to a nearby window and peered out. A crowd was gathering, perhaps twenty people, nearly all of them brandishing weapons. This was not a fight she could win. If they were smart, they would simply force her to retreat up the stairs and start a fire on the lowest level, either suffocating her with smoke or burning her alive.

Another blow hit the door, and this time the frame began to give way.

The enemy was coming, and Issa had no way to stop them.

To say that Issa was afraid would have been an oversimplification. Certainly, she felt fear clawing at her gut, but mostly there was a sense of regret. It wasn't so much from having chosen to help the enslaved women, as it was knowing that she would never again feel Tanner's strong embrace or hear Samantha's amusing quips. She also felt profound sadness for her unborn child who would be robbed of the chance to smell a flower or chase a butterfly. She was consoled only by the knowledge that it would die in the comfort of her womb, the bond between mother and child unbroken.

Her nostrils flared as she drew in a breath. Death may be galloping ever closer, but he wouldn't be departing with only her and her baby. She would see to that.

The door burst from its frame and crashed onto the floor as one giant block of wood. Men were stacked one behind the other, and she fired directly into their midst. The huge slug hammered into the first man's chest, shredding his heart and blowing an enormous hole through his back. It continued on, ripping through a second's man stomach and kidney, before finally coming to rest against a third man's hip. All three men collapsed to the ground.

Two others leaped over them to land on the stone floor coated in foam. Both men skated briefly before one flopped onto his back and the other slid into the flat-screen television.

Still recovering from the recoil of the shot, Issa swung her rifle toward the man lying on his back and fired a second time. The bullet grazed the side of his head, taking with it a chunk of the man's skull.

Two more men dashed into the tower, more careful of their footing as they sought cover. Issa wheeled around and raced up the stairs. Rather than try to fight from the stairway, she continued on all the way up to the highest level.

It housed an office of sorts, complete with table, chairs, and a wooden cubbyhole for papers. At the center of the space sat an antique carillon. The clavier was similar in appearance to a conventional organ except that in place of keys there were wooden handles. Dozens of metal turnbuckles rose from the carillon to connect into the open-air belfry overhead. The bells themselves were not visible thanks to a low-hanging ceiling, but a ladder at the back of the space granted access.

Dolly and Jerome sat huddled beside the instrument. Both looked completely spent from their climb up the stairs.

Seeing the frantic look in Issa's eyes, Dolly shook her head and said, "You should have left us, child."

"Yes," Issa puffed, trying to catch her breath. "I should have."

"Then why didn't you?"

Issa didn't have an answer. Part of her had wanted to leave them, but another part knew that she couldn't. Perhaps there was still too much humanity left in her.

"Would you have left *me*?" she countered.

Dolly seemed surprised. "Course not."

"There. You have your answer."

Issa reloaded the Merkel, a radiating pain in her shoulder reminding her that the big gun punished both shooter and target alike. Assuming the slavers didn't just decide to burn them out, they would have to come up the narrow staircase no more than two abreast, and even that would be awkward. Issa figured she could take at least a few of them before they overran her.

She readied the gun and waited for the stomp of men's boots on the heavy metal stairs.

They didn't come. Instead, she heard a commotion coming from the ground floor. Maybe they were drawing straws to see who would go first, or worse yet, maybe they were gathering firewood.

Another thirty seconds passed. A minute. Two. Her hands trembled slightly. What the hell were they waiting for?

Dolly sat forward, tilting her head to listen.

"Why ain't they comin' for us?"

As if in answer to her question, the staircase began to shake as men pounded their way higher. Too loud for one man or even five. They were coming all at once. Better that way, thought Issa. Like Tanner, she preferred to die in the fire of battle, not be picked apart by cowardly carrions.

Large figures rounded the corner and pushed their way into the belfry. They halted at the sight of Issa kneeling beside Dolly and Jerome, gun aloft, her finger on the first of the Merkel's two triggers. Her finger twitched reflexively, but instead of squeezing, she lowered the gun and stared in disbelief.

A mass of infected men stood before her, armed with hatchets, clubs, and rifles. A giant with thick muscular limbs and a skull like that of a Klingon stood before her, looking pleased with himself.

"Korn?" she breathed.

He crossed his massive arms and grinned.

"Issa!"

Korn covered the space between them with two giant steps and extended his hand. She took it and rose to her feet. His eyes were drawn to the swell of her stomach, and his face became pale.

"You're with baby."

She nodded. "Yes."

"But how?"

"Things are not as we thought. Our women are not barren." She left the rest unsaid. No man wanted to hear that he was sterile.

"Does Mother know?"

She shook her head. "I was on my way to see her when…" Issa looked back at Dolly and Jerome. Both stared with wide eyes, uncertain if doom or salvation had arrived. "It's okay," she said. "They're friends."

Korn motioned to them. "Go. You're free."

Jerome helped his grandmother to her feet, and together, they hobbled toward the staircase. As Dolly passed, she brushed a hand across Issa's back.

"Thank you, child. Perhaps the Lord will see fit for us to return the favor one day." And with that she was gone, gently nudging her way through the throng of fighters lining the staircase.

Feeling Korn's eyes on her belly, Issa gently rubbed a hand over the tight skin.

"I suppose I must look very different to you."

"Different," he said, nodding, "and the same." There was a sadness in his voice that even his gruffness couldn't hide.

"You've changed too." There remained a savage fire in Korn's eyes, but he was better spoken. He also carried an AR-15 over one shoulder. Six months earlier, he couldn't have fathomed the mechanics of operating such a weapon. She looked past him at the infected warriors starting back down the stairs. Many of them, too, seemed calmer and more rational.

As if sensing her thoughts, he said, "Mother says we're beginning to think again."

Their eyes met, and he seemed ready to say something that she didn't want to hear.

"How is it that you came to be in this town? This tower?" she asked.

He walked to a window that looked out onto the grassy field below. His army of nearly five hundred fighters was mopping up the last of the slavers.

"Mother sent us to end this. To end *them*."

"Mother is reaching out beyond Mount Weather?"

He nodded.

Issa wasn't sure if that was a good thing. Where Mother's army went, butchered bodies were invariably left in its wake.

"She knew of the slavery?"

"She knows many things."

Issa gently rubbed her stomach. "She doesn't know this."

"No. And perhaps she shouldn't." Korn stepped closer, and Issa tightened her grip on the Merkel hanging at her side. He struggled to speak. "You and I, we were almost one."

"Yes," she said. "But now I'm another's."

"Even so, no good will come of you going to Mother like this."

"How can you say that? The women deserve to know." Her words came out stronger than she intended, and she attempted to soften them by saying, "Don't they?"

He shrugged. "You have always made your own choices." There was something about the way he said "choices" that suggested he was not merely talking about going to Mount Weather.

"Come," he said, turning toward the doorway. "We will see if you are as wise as you are headstrong."

CHAPTER 18

J essie sat next to her father on one of the RV's long benches, the engine and air conditioner both running. The cool air felt particularly wonderful to Bowie who hovered over a vent with his mouth open and eyes closed. Mason leaned against one of the storage closets, his arms crossed in front of him.

"I don't understand this at all," Jessie said, clearly frustrated. "Why would you continue to put your life at risk? Daddy's free. We can leave this wretched place."

"He's doing it out of a sense of duty," explained Jack.

She stared at her father. "But even if he miraculously won all of his matches, most of those poor souls still won't go free."

"My goal isn't to set them free. It's to help people lose their taste for this tournament." When Mason saw her about to protest further, he said, "Do you remember that boy selling peanuts on the side of the road?"

She nodded.

"I don't want him following in these men's footsteps."

"I understand that. I really do. But you're taking too much on yourself."

"Maybe. But right now I'm the only one standing in their way."

"That's... that's—"

"Noble?" he said, cracking a smile.

She snorted. "I was going to say *nuts!*"

Their eyes met, and her gaze softened.

"Isn't there something I can say that will change your mind?"

He gently shook his head. "I've been told I'm very stubborn. I think I got that from my father."

She offered a resigned sigh. "Just know for the record, I'm one hundred percent against this."

"Duly noted." With the matter as settled as it was likely to get, Mason turned to Jack. "Maybe it's time you tell us what happened."

Jack leaned back and took a deep breath.

"There's not a whole lot to tell. A man approached me yesterday afternoon and asked if I'd come in from out of town to trade. I told him I had, and that I was looking for a few dresses for my daughter." He glanced over at Jessie.

"Daddy, you didn't need to buy me dresses."

"I wanted to do something nice for you. I know it's been hard since your mother passed."

"What did this man look like?" Mason pictured Ramsey's scarred face, wondering if he might have been involved.

"He was small and wiry, like a jockey. Blonde hair, blue eyes. Said his name was Jeremy Wilde, and spoke with a slight accent, English or Australian, maybe."

None of that lined up with Ramsey.

"Go on."

"He said he could find the dresses for me in exchange for an antique clock that I'd brought to trade."

"Then what happened?"

"A couple of hours later he showed up with three of the nicest little dresses you've ever seen. We exchanged items and that was that. I didn't see him again."

"But something went wrong."

Jack nodded. "Later, when I was packing up to go home, a man and a woman approached me, mad as hornets. Said I'd been spotted stealing their stuff and demanded I let them search my truck."

"Did you?"

"No, not at first. I figured it was some kind of scam, so I told them to go to hell. We had words, and people started taking notice. If I've learned one thing in my life, it's that getting noticed is never a good thing. Not wanting to draw too much attention, I finally gave in."

"And?"

"And as soon as the woman laid eyes on the dresses, she started hollering about how they belonged to her daughter." He glanced at Jessie. "I tried to talk some sense into them. I really did. But the more I said, the madder they got. Finally, I told them to just take the dresses, that I didn't want any trouble."

"Did that calm them down?" asked Mason.

"It did the man. Unfortunately, his wife kept pressing him to make an example out of me."

"And did he?"

"He tried." Jack rubbed his swollen nose. "While I may not look like much, I've been in a few fights over the years. When it was all said and done, he was the one on the ground. I started to leave, but his wife still wouldn't let it go. She kept on until her husband got up and came at me with a knife." He swallowed.

"You shot him?"

"I didn't have a choice."

"But it was self-defense," Jessie argued, reaching over to hold her father's hand. "You shouldn't have been arrested for that."

He shrugged. "A few of the local law enforcement types held me until they could investigate. Once they did, they claimed that I was a thief and a murderer."

"Were the items really hers?" asked Mason.

"Probably. I figure the little guy stole them in order to make the trade. Honestly, the whole thing doesn't make sense. Why would someone go to all that trouble just to get an old clock?"

Mason shook his head. "It wasn't about the clock."

"What do you mean?"

"It was about you, Jack."

"Me? I'm nobody."

"Exactly. You're an outsider, without anyone to vouch for you."

"True, but no one has reason to wish me harm either."

"That's not the point. It wasn't personal—it was business. They needed to pad the ranks for the tournament."

Jack sat up straight. "You think they set me up?"

"I do."

"That's one more reason to get out of here," exclaimed Jessie.

Mason nodded. "I agree. You and Jack should take his truck and head home. I'll be along shortly."

Bowie let out a loud yawn and everyone turned his direction.

"Correction. Bowie and I will be along shortly."

"But we can't just leave you here," she said. "Not after what you've done for us."

"I'm afraid you don't have much of a choice."

"What do you mean?"

Mason looked over at Jack. "Your father's been cleared of the charges, but it doesn't mean that the man's family or friends aren't going to come looking for their own justice. I know I would."

"He's right," said Jack. "If I stay here, it's going to put all of us in danger." He turned to Jessie. "We need to leave. Now."

"But—"

"No buts. Not only might the man's family come for me, the organizers of this little tournament might as well. If I really was set up, they may see me as a loose end." Jack got to his feet, and Jessie held an arm to help steady him.

Mason straightened, and when he did, Bowie raised his head.

"It's settled then. You two will head home while Bowie and I get a few answers."

"How are you planning to do that?" asked Jessie.

"Simple. I'm going to ask Jeremy Wilde where he got those dresses."

శ్రీ ఈ

It was approaching dusk by the time Mason walked Jessie and Jack to their pickup truck. He offered the appropriate farewells, a firm handshake for Jack and a warm hug for Jessie. She seemed to want to say something more to him, but settled for a quiet squeeze of his hand.

As they drove away, Mason and Bowie stood next to the RV, watching as the truck disappeared in the distance. Bowie turned to him and whimpered. Mason couldn't be sure whether the dog was thinking of Jessie or the beef jerky, but he knew which was on his mind.

"Maybe we'll see them again one day," he said softly.

Bowie cocked his head as if he didn't understand.

"Besides, it's better this way. A girl that nice didn't need to be hanging around with the likes of us."

Bowie turned back to the road, perhaps hoping to catch one final glimpse of the truck. He didn't. Jessie and her father were gone.

Mason turned and walked north, toward the clubhouse. Bowie calmly trotted beside him, doing his part as the steadfast companion. They wandered past a large crowd settling bets. None were particularly happy to see Mason.

"You cost me a lot of money," one man shouted.

Mason continued on, saying nothing. Engaging in a shouting match with a crowd that had lost money was a good way to wind up face down behind a dumpster.

As he circled the clubhouse, a woman in her sixties hurried toward him. Her grown son clopped along behind her, as if wearing shoes three sizes too big. Physically, he was every bit a man, but there was a vacant look in his eyes that suggested he didn't have all of his faculties. Neither of them seemed intent on congratulating Mason on his industrious win, and he stopped and squared himself as they approached.

"Where is he?" the woman demanded.

"Who?"

"That murderer you saved. The man who killed my husband!"

"He's gone."

She spat on his shirt. "You bastard."

Bowie didn't like the tenor of the conversation and brushed past Mason with a growl. The woman's son reached behind his back, and when he did, Mason placed a hand on the Supergrade.

"You'd better be reaching for a dog biscuit."

The young man turned to his mother, and she gave a quick shake of her head. He shrugged and let his hand fall back by his side.

Mason turned to the woman. Even though he could understand her rage, he would not permit unchecked violence. Neither did he bother saying the meaningless "I'm sorry for your loss." In all his years, he had never once seen those five words make a damn bit of difference.

Instead, he said, "It wasn't my intent to rob you of your justice."

"Your intentions don't mean a damn thing," she snarled. "Only what you've done."

She was right, of course. The old saying about good intentions paving the way to Hell was spot on.

"Let me ask you something."

"What?"

"How did you and your husband learn that Jack stole your dresses?"

"What's that matter?"

"I'm guessing that a short man with blonde hair tipped you off."

Her eyes narrowed. "How'd you know that?"

"I know because he's the one who *gave* the items to Jack."

"You're a liar!"

He shrugged. "Believe what you want. But if I'm right, that man is the one truly responsible for your husband's death."

She looked over at her son. "Lucas, you ever seen him around before?"

He thought for a moment. "Yes, Momma, a few times."

"Where?"

He pointed to the throng of trading stalls to the south.

"Near that booth that sells the maple candy."

The old woman turned back to Mason.

"Why would he steal our things, give them to someone else, and then tell us he had them? That don't make no sense."

"Maybe you should ask him. It could be that your anger is misplaced."

"Or it could be you're full of donkey shit."

Mason chuckled. "Could be."

She stared at him a bit longer before turning to her son.

"Come on, Lucas. Let's go see if we can find him before it gets dark."

They took a wide circle around Bowie as they marched toward the open-air market. Mason followed for a time but eventually lost them in the crowd. The smell of food was thick in the air, as many of the booths had switched over to selling supper. There was everything from rabbit stew to goat kabobs, and despite reminding himself that hygiene was no doubt lacking, Mason found himself walking ever closer to the stalls.

Bowie pressed the point by tipping his nose into the air and taking deep whiffs of the food.

"Fine," he said. "But if I get sick, I'm blaming you."

Mason stopped at the nearest stall and exchanged a few credits for several thick slices of pork and an enormous yeast roll soaked in butter. He made his way out of the market and sat with his back pressed to an oak tree to enjoy his supper. The bread proved a bit chewy, but the pork was delicious. Bowie seemed to agree with his assessment, wolfing down the meat as fast as Mason could toss it to him.

As they were eating, Mason kept a watchful eye on the market, hoping that he might catch a glimpse of Jeremy Wilde. Dozens of people moved in and out, making it impossible to watch them all, and he eventually settled against the tree to enjoy the coming sunset.

Bowie lay beside him, the big dog doing his best to extract a twig that had gotten tangled in his fur. Mason reached over and pulled it free, holding it out for him to inspect.

"Thumbs, my friend. They make all the difference."

Bowie sniffed the twig and gently pulled it from his fingers to chew on.

Mason smiled. "Fair enough. You've got your ways, and we've got ours."

A shadow came over them, and Mason wheeled around, drawing his pistol as he rose to one knee. The old widow stood alone, looking down at him.

"What do you want?" he said, holstering the weapon.

"I know where he is."

"Who?"

"The man you claim stole my dresses."

"Okay. Where is he?"

"Come with me, and I'll show you."

Mason stood, and Bowie did the same.

"Why didn't you and your son just deal with him?"

"I'm an old woman, in case you didn't notice. And Lucas, well, he ain't quite right. Even if he was, I wouldn't want him getting caught up in something like this. Next thing you know, they'd put him in with the Fallen."

"Better me than him, is that it?"

"Hell yes, better you than him. Besides, you owe me."

"How do you figure that?"

"You freed the man who killed my husband. The least you can do is help avenge his death."

The woman turned, and against his better judgment, Mason followed. They walked north, passing the clubhouse to enter the housing district. Neat rows of mobile homes lined both sides of the street. A few people still milled about, preparing for nightfall, but most had retreated to the safety of their homes. There were no streetlights or electric lighting, and the only light shining through windows was the soft glow of candles.

When they arrived at the end of the street, the woman walked over and ducked behind a car. Lucas was already kneeling behind it, his eyes fixed on the nearest mobile home. He cradled a Bushmaster AR-15 in both hands.

"Is he still in there?" she asked.

He nodded vigorously. "I've been watching the whole time, just like you said, Momma."

She turned to Mason. "We found him. Now you go do the rest."

All in all, it seemed like a fair request. Even so, he said, "I'm not here to kill him. I'm here to question him."

"If you don't do what's right, we will."

There seemed no point in discussing it any further, so Mason turned to Bowie and said, "Come on, boy. Let's go see if anyone's home."

Mason approached at an angle, doing his best to stay out of the front window's line of sight. He paused at the end of the home and hopped onto the metal trailer that protruded from underneath. A small window allowed him to peek inside, but he could only make out a bed and an antique dresser. Violin music sounded from further within, but with the bedroom door closed, he couldn't determine whether it was live or from a battery-operated player.

He paused to consider his options. If he had been trying to breach the home, or simply lay siege to it, a whole assortment of tactics could be employed. Given the uncertainty of the situation, however, Mason decided to keep it simple.

He continued around the front of the home, climbed the concrete steps, and rapped on the door.

The music stopped. Definitely live, not a music player.

He knocked again, this time stepping out from in front of the door. Old habits die hard.

After a few seconds, the door inched open. A man peered out, short, with blonde hair and bright blue eyes. When he spoke, there was a slight English accent.

"Can I help you?"

"I'd like to have a word with you, Mr. Wilde."

"Sorry," he said, closing the door. "I'm quite busy at the moment."

Mason stepped forward and placed his boot in the way of the door. "Make time."

"Do I know you?"

"Let's just say that we have a mutual acquaintance." Mason peered past him into the mobile home. A museum-quality M1 Garand leaned against the couch. It was a big weapon for such a small man, and he wondered if it was as much for show as it was self-defense. "Mind if Bowie and I come in?"

Wilde glanced at Mason's badge and then over at Bowie.

"Do I have a choice?"

"Not so much, no."

He stepped aside. "Then by all means, come in."

Bowie went in first, sniffing his way around the man's living room like someone had hidden a box of Bil-Jacs.

Wilde motioned toward a violin leaning against an open case.

"While it's not quite a Stradivarius, it is my most precious belonging. If you don't mind, I'd like to put it away."

"Go ahead," Mason said, resting his hand on the Supergrade. "Just don't make me nervous."

"Of course." Wilde picked up the violin and gently placed it into the case.

"How long have you been playing?"

"Almost four years," he said, snapping the case shut. "As I'm sure you heard, I'm still quite the beginner."

"It sounded pretty good to me."

He offered a gracious smile. "You're too kind. But, alas, like so many things, I'm afraid it's a dying art."

Once the violin was safely stowed, Wilde walked over and took a seat on the couch. The M1 Garand remained within reach.

"I'd appreciate you keeping clear of that rifle."

Wilde smiled. "Says the man with his hand on a gun."

"A necessary evil of my profession, I'm afraid."

Wilde slid to the other end of the couch.

"Better?"

Mason nodded, turning to look around the mobile home. There was a couch, a couple of chairs, a coffee table, and a small dinette set. Everything looked old but expensive, like they had been procured from a wealthy estate.

"Do you live here alone?"

"Indeed," he said with a smile.

"Don't take offense, but I'll need to check." Keeping Wilde in his peripheral vision, Mason started down the narrow hallway that led to three doors. Two were sitting open, one leading to a small bathroom and the other to a bedroom. He ducked his head inside each and saw nothing out of the ordinary.

The third door was not only closed, it had a small padlock across the jamb.

"What's in here?" he said, jiggling the lock.

"Just junk I've collected over the years."

"Come open it."

"I really don't think that's necessary."

"You can either open it, or I'll kick it in. These little homes aren't particularly sturdy, so there's a good chance I'd take part of the wall with it."

Wilde reluctantly got to his feet and came over to the door, Bowie on his heels. He pulled a small key from his pocket and opened the padlock.

Mason nodded toward the door. "After you."

He sighed and pushed open the door.

"I can explain."

Mason seriously doubted that. Before him was a workshop worthy of Thomas Crown. A long wooden workbench sat along one wall, its top littered with necklaces, rings, and watches. A jeweler's loupe and several small calipers lay beside them. To one side of the bench was a pegboard filled with an assortment of locks, and to the other a coatrack with several neat bundles of rope.

"Why, Mr. Wilde, you're a thief," Mason said, stating the obvious.

"I can assure you that I came by all of this quite legitimately."

"Oh I'm sure," he said, shaking his head. "The truth is I don't care what you've stolen. I'm here for another reason."

The words "don't care what you've stolen," seemed to cheer the man up.

"Oh? And what might that be?"

"Yesterday, you acquired some dresses for a man. Shortly afterward, you told the owners that he had stolen them. Why?"

Wilde's eyes flickered. "I have no idea what you're talking about."

Mason grabbed him by the arm. "Fine. We'll go see the old woman outside. Did I mention that her son has a rifle?"

"Wait," Wilde said, planting his feet.

"Why? Is your memory coming back?"

Wilde's face twisted with worry. "You have to understand. No one was supposed to get hurt, at least not there on the street."

"Go on."

"A few months ago, I was accused—quite wrongly I might add—of helping myself to a few worthless trinkets. It was nothing more than a harmless misunderstanding, really."

"I'm sure."

"Even so, I found myself in a bit of a predicament. My captor gave me a choice. I could either be arrested and forced to participate in that barbaric shooting competition, or I could help him to find criminals and other ne'er-do-wells living within the camp."

"You became his inside man."

"If that means a victim of his blackmail, then yes."

"Who'd you make the deal with?"

Wilde hesitated. "If I tell you that, I'm quite dead. And despite these miserable conditions," he said, looking around the home, "I still place some small modicum of value on life."

Mason decided not to press the point, at least not until he had all the facts. Once he did, he was confident that Bowie could help to loosen the man's tongue.

"This nameless person who unfairly blackmailed you, did he do it to have participants for the tournament?"

"Only in part. He truly was trying to clean up the camp. The fact that the offenders end up in the tournament was, in his words, 'a fortunate side effect.'"

"Then why'd you frame Jack? He doesn't live here, and he certainly wasn't a criminal."

"Well that's just it, now, isn't it? When you clean up, you eventually run out of dirt. And for a man in my predicament, running out of dirt is tantamount to announcing that I'm no longer useful."

Mason felt his anger rising, and he squeezed the man's shoulder.

"You do realize that you sent a stranger to die to protect your own hide."

"Easy," he said, grimacing. "Remember, I was just a pawn in all this. I'm not the one you should be mad at."

"You're saying that your blackmailer knew what you were doing?"

"Of course he knew."

"Then I ask again, who—"

The living room window suddenly shattered, glass spraying into the home. It was followed by a steady *thump, thump, thump* as bullets punched through the thin sheet-metal walls.

Mason shoved Wilde into the small workshop and dove in after him. As they fell to the floor, Bowie raced over.

"Lie down, boy," he said, pulling the dog down beside him.

They listened as bullets ripped through the living room, knocking pictures from the wall and shattering an oil-filled lamp that fortunately had yet to be lit.

Wilde pushed up on all fours and began crawling for the door.

Mason lunged for him, barely missing the man's ankle.

"Stay down! You're going to get yourself shot!"

Wilde never slowed as he disappeared around the corner.

More gunshots sounded, but this time the bullets began walking their way down the length of the home. So much for trying to stay out of the line of fire.

Mason slipped an arm around Bowie and dragged him out into the hallway, the goal being to put as many walls between them and the approaching shooter as possible. Items disintegrated all around them. Crosses fell from walls, light fixtures exploded, and puffs of sheetrock filled the air.

He looked left and right for a way out. Exiting through the back door would require going through the shooting gallery that was once the living room. The only window along the rear of the home was in the bathroom, and it was too small for a 140-pound wolfhound. Mason used his knuckles to tap on the floor, wondering whether he could tunnel his way out. No good. The joists were too closely spaced.

The mobile home was a perfect kill box, easily penetrated by a rifle round and nearly impossible to return fire from with any degree of accuracy.

"Wilde!" he shouted. "We need to get out of here!"

The Englishman appeared at the end of the hall, awkwardly crawling on his hands and knees, the violin case clutched to his chest. The wall beside him exploded in a white dusty puff as a bullet ripped through the sheetrock. He shrieked and toppled sideways, a fine spray of blood filling the air around him.

Mason laid his hand on Bowie's back.

"Stay!"

The dog flattened himself against the floor, his head whipping from side to side as he watched the home being torn up around them.

Mason high-crawled over to Wilde, bullets whizzing overhead. The man was alive, but based on the profuse bleeding, the bullet had hit the aorta or one of its coronary arteries. He had maybe thirty seconds before losing consciousness, and twice that before dying.

Wilde pressed a hand against the entrance wound, but that did nothing to stem the flow of blood coming out the other side.

"I'm hurt," he choked.

No, thought Mason, you're dead.

"Who are you working for?"

Wilde stared at him, his face slowly turning white.

"I told you," he breathed. "He'll... kill... me." His eyes drooped and then closed.

Dead man or not, he wasn't getting away that easy. Mason grabbed his shoulders and shook him.

"Wake up!"

Wilde's eyes slowly reopened, but they were glossy and distant.

"Come on, man. Tell me! Who was it?"

A thin smile came to his lips.

"It's beautiful, isn't it?"

"What's beautiful?"

"The music." Wilde's head tilted to one side, and his mouth fell open. He was gone.

Mason sighed as he reached forward and closed the man's bright blue eyes. Death was the ultimate escape, and not even a determined marshal could take justice beyond the grave.

He looked back at Bowie. The dog was confused and frightened by what was happening around him. Mason recalled a mantra that he and other rangers had adopted.

When in doubt, move.

He grabbed the violin case and hurled it through the front window like a grenade into an enemy encampment. A hail of bullets hammered the window frame and surrounding wall as the shooter tried to zero in on his target.

"Bowie!" he shouted, scrambling for the back door. "Let's go!"

Bowie hopped up and raced down the hall, nearly climbing over Mason as they pushed their way out the back door. Together, they crashed through a small bannister and landed atop one another in a thick pile of leaves.

Mason drew the Supergrade and scanned left and right. It was clear. He rolled Bowie off and rose to a crouch. Bullets continued pelting the home, some of them passing all the way through both sides. Hoping to get clear of it, he bent at the waist and raced toward the front of the mobile home.

As the street came into view, the old woman stepped out from behind the car with a semi-automatic pistol in her hands.

"You're as guilty as he is!" she shouted, wildly squeezing the trigger.

A bullet ricocheted off the mobile home's trailer, and the next two snapped branches on a nearby bush.

Mason had no desire to kill the old woman, but even less to be killed by her. Seeing no other choice, he dropped to one knee and fired the Supergrade. At nearly thirty yards, trying to wound was simply not an option. The bullet ended up going higher than he had intended, striking her in the bridge of the nose. Her head whipped back, and she toppled lifelessly to the ground.

Bowie rushed ahead and disappeared around the front of the mobile home. As soon as the wolfhound cleared the corner, he spotted Lucas. The man was running toward his mother with the Bushmaster cradled in both arms, shouting "Momma!"

Bowie went straight for him, leaping up at the last moment to latch onto his upper arm. The collision sent them both toppling to the ground.

Lucas screamed as he tried to push away the massive dog.

Bowie snapped and snarled, ripping off two of the man's fingers.

Blood streaming from the nubs, Lucas reached forward and grabbed Bowie by the mouth, desperately trying to hold him off. But Bowie was simply too powerful. He shook his head free and lunged for the man's face. One of his lower canines went up Lucas's left nostril as his upper teeth punctured the top of his scalp. Lucas let out a horrific screech, which ended abruptly when Bowie shook his head from side to side, breaking the man's neck.

By the time Mason reached them, Bowie was standing over the dead man, growling as if he wasn't entirely sure that Lucas was dead.

Mason looked left and right. A bullet-ridden home and bodies lying in the street confirmed what he already knew. It was time to go.

"Come on, boy," he said, wheeling around.

Together, they raced behind the row of homes, scrambled up a small hill, and disappeared into the night.

❧ ❧

Mason was covered in a cold layer of sweat by the time he opened the door to the RV. To his surprise, Jessie was there, waiting for him.

"What are you doing here?" he said, ushering Bowie inside.

"Well, hello to you too."

He looked both ways before ducking inside and closing the door.

"I didn't mean it that way. But I thought we agreed that you and Jack would head home."

"We did. But as we got to the front gate, I realized I couldn't leave."

"Why not?"

"I'd made a promise."

"What promise?"

"To take care of Bowie if something happened to you. How could I possibly do that if I wasn't here?"

He stared at her. What she said made sense. Unfortunately, it also put her right back in harm's way.

"What about Jack? Where's he at?"

"I made him leave." Before Mason could ask how she had managed that, she added, "If he stayed, he knew he'd be putting us all in danger. He's waiting for us at the motel we passed on the way in."

"I'm betting he wasn't happy about that."

"No, but Daddy knows when he can win a fight and when he can't."

"And he wasn't going to win this one, is that it?"

She smiled. "He complains that I have too much of my mother in me, even though we both know that's a good thing. But," she said with a shrug, "if you'd rather I leave…"

"No," he said, more quickly than he had intended.

She moved closer, her eyes probing his.

"No? Why not?"

That was a question Mason didn't want to think too hard about, so he said only, "Let's just say that everything seems a little less dreary when you're around."

A smile spread across her face, and they stared at one another long enough for butterflies to find their way down to his stomach.

"Now," she said, breaking the spell, "let's get you two something to drink." She lifted a bottle of water out from one of the cabinets and poured part of it in a bowl for Bowie, handing the rest to Mason. "What were you doing out there, anyway?"

"Trying to figure out what happened with your father."

"And did you?"

"It was Wilde, just like we thought. He was being blackmailed to find criminals for the tournament."

"Do you think…"

"What?"

She shrugged. "I was just going to ask if you thought your marshal friend might have been behind it."

Mason had given that question considerable thought while ducking between bushes. With Wilde's passing, there was really no way to know for certain. Leroy's self-proclaimed mission was to bring justice to people who thought they could escape it, not fabricate crimes for purposes of drawing a crowd. Even so, it was possible that what had started as a way to root out evil had become something else.

"I don't know for sure," he said. "But I plan to ask him."

"He might not appreciate your directness."

"Leroy knows what he gets when it comes to me."

"Even so, you should be careful."

Mason nodded thoughtfully.

"If he's not involved," she said, "maybe he'll cancel the tournament."

"Maybe." Mason tried to sound reassuring, but if anything, Jessie seemed more worried.

"He's not going to do that, is he?"

"I doubt it."

"That means you're going to have to face those terrible men."

There seemed no point in denying it.

"Yes."

She stared at him, unable to put words to her concern.

"I'll be all right," he said softly.

"I sure hope so."

"It's sweet of you to worry about me."

Jessie put on a bright smile. "Who says I'm worried?" She reached down and gave Bowie a good pat. "I was just thinking this monster would eat us out of house and home."

❧ ❧

Mason stripped off his shirt and sank into the camper's foam mattress. He closed his eyes, wondering what the next day would bring. Not only would he be fighting for his life, he might very well have to kill for sport—something that didn't sit well with him at all. Add to that the need to question Leroy and Ramsey and his day was sure to be the very definition of the word "dangerous."

A warm hand touched his shoulder, and he opened his eyes with a start. Jessie knelt on the floor beside his bed. Thanks to the moonlight shining through the camper windows, he could see that she was wearing a light pink sleep shirt with nothing underneath.

"Jessie, what—"

She touched a finger to his lips.

"Do you remember saying that someday someone would have the good fortune of sharing in my beauty?"

The camper suddenly felt as if the air had been sucked from it.

"I remember," he breathed.

She leaned forward and brushed her lips against his.

"I think you could use some good luck about now."

Mason put his hands on her shoulders and gently pressed her away. It was the hardest thing he had done all day, and that included escaping from the mobile home of certain death.

"Jessie…"

"Mason." Her mouth turned up into a seductive smile.

"I'm sorry," he said, shaking his head. "This isn't right."

"It isn't? Are you sure?" She kissed him again, this time tickling his lips with her tongue. "I mean really, *really* sure?"

He pushed her away again. "It's not that I don't want to. Believe me, I do. But you're so—"

"Beautiful?"

"I was going to say young."

"I'm not a child." She slid his hand down to her breast. "I'm not."

"I know that," he said, swallowing. He willed his fingers to pull away, but for some reason, they didn't seem to hear him.

"You're afraid you'd be taking advantage of me."

"That's part of it."

"Well, you wouldn't be."

"I wouldn't?"

"Of course not." She ran her hand down his chest, unhooked his belt, and slid it free. "I'm going to be taking advantage of you." She slid a leg over and straddled him.

Everything about her was warm and inviting, and Mason's voice failed him.

"So, it's settled then," she said. It didn't sound like a question.

"It's not just that," he confessed.

"What else?"

"I'm not ready for, you know, something serious. There was Brooke and—"

"I'm not Brooke."

"I know you're not."

"Besides, it's not like I'm asking for a proposal." She leaned down and kissed him again, long and hard this time. When she spoke, he could feel her warm, sweet breath on his face. "This is about something else."

"What?"

"It's about a girl getting her own real live cowboy. You wouldn't deny me that, now, would you?"

He said nothing. Really, what was there to say?

Jessie pulled her nightshirt over her head and tossed it aside.

Mason let out a sigh. "Ah hell."

"A little help here," Samantha groaned, her voice muffled as she forced one leg out from underneath the weighty beast.

With his arms still wrapped around the vile creature's neck, Tanner rolled him to one side.

"You okay?" he asked, helping her to her feet.

"Shaken, but not stirred."

He raised an eyebrow. "I'll take that as a yes."

"Another of my dad's sayings," she said, testing the tenderness of her jaw.

Once he was sure that Samantha was okay, Tanner retrieved his shotgun. She did the same, recovering her Savage .22 rifle as well as the Bond Arms derringer.

Together, they stood, staring down at the beast.

"What was it you were saying about monsters?"

Tanner shook his head. "To be honest, I don't know what that thing is."

She seemed surprised. "You don't?"

"I suppose you do?"

"Of course, I do. It's a were-pig."

He chuckled. "A what?"

"A were-pig. They're like werewolves, only pigs."

"And how exactly do you figure that?"

"Let's start with Exhibit A, the fur." She bent over and pointed to the thick black hair covering its chest. "Next, we have the flat snout and enlarged night-seeing eyes. And finally, there's the fact that only a silver bullet was able to kill it."

Tanner started to say how ridiculous her argument was, but as he stared down at the creature, words failed him. Perhaps the idea of lycanthropes transforming under a full moon were not as farfetched as he liked to believe.

"I think it's time we got out of this dump." He turned and inspected the pile of manure. It would be a dirty job digging a hole large enough for him to fit through. "So, which is it? Dig out through a pile of poo, or take our chances running into another of these beauties?" He nudged the beast with the toe of his boot.

Samantha opened the Patriot, dumped out the two spent shell casings, and inserted fresh cartridges.

"I don't know about you," she said, "but I'm walking."

ॐ ॐ

Tanner expected Sister Margaret to be absolutely gushing with gratitude at his having recovered all four of her missing nuns.

She wasn't.

Instead, she seemed hell-bent on blaming him for one sister being smeared head to toe in manure and the other three having so easily acquiesced to establishing a master race. Between her open disappointment and the stench of Sister Clare, the drive back to the octagonal dairy building was excruciating for everyone involved.

Tanner pulled up next to Dr. Langdon's Mercedes and jerked the station wagon to a stop.

"Out!" he shouted, loud enough that the windows vibrated.

No one had to be told twice, the nuns piling out of the car like it was on fire. Only Samantha seemed to find the humor in it all.

"What are you smiling at?" he said, doing his best to maintain his disgruntled demeanor.

"Oh nothing," she said, covering a smile.

The brightness in her eyes was enough to not only douse the fuse but turn the dynamite into a party favor.

He leaned in close. "Too much?"

"Nope," she whispered. "You're nailing it."

Sister Margaret straightened her habit and tipped her nose in the air.

"Mr. Raines, I believe our time together has come to an end." Her eyes cut over to the Mercedes. "We can find our way back to the monastery from here."

"You sure?" he said.

"It's barely thirty miles. I'm sure we'll be fine."

"All right then." Tanner walked around to the back of the old station wagon and lifted out his and Samantha's backpacks, followed by the cans of spare gasoline.

Sister Margaret looked at him, confused.

"What are you doing?"

"Just making sure you have wheels. I'm a gentleman, after all." He popped open the trunk of the Mercedes and began loading their supplies. "We know how nuns are all about the simple life, and we wouldn't dream of putting you in a situation that compromised your austere values, would we, Sam?"

Samantha eyed the shiny Mercedes. "Nope."

Sister Margaret huffed and motioned for the nuns to load back into the old wagon. After everyone had settled into the car, she rolled down her window and said, "You, sir, are anything but a gentleman."

Tanner met her stare. "That part's true enough. But if it was a gentleman you needed, you'd have ridden over here with Father Paul. Think about that on your drive home."

Her squint of contempt dissolved into something closer to mild disapproval. It was as good as he was going to get.

Sister Mary Margaret offered one final *hmpff* before driving away.

Samantha came over and stood beside Tanner, and together, they watched the car turn down the narrow drive and disappear from view.

"Are all nuns so cranky?"

"No," he said slowly. "Just the really good ones."

৯৵ ৵৬

The Mercedes S550 was as nice as any vehicle they had ever driven. With its soft leather interior, piano lacquer wood trim, and Bang & Olufsen sound system, it put new meaning to the phrase "riding in style."

Samantha settled back against the supple leather.

"Good call on the car. I mean it's only fair, right? We have further to go."

"Absolutely."

"How far is it anyway?"

"A hundred miles, give or take."

"What do you think Mother will say when we just show up out of the blue?"

"I don't know. Hello, maybe."

"I think she'll want to know how Issa got pregnant."

"Believe me, she knows how that works."

"You know what I mean. Issa will be the first woman from their colony to have a child. That has to make Mother happy because she won't need to have all the babies herself."

Tanner nodded noncommittally, but the more he thought about what Samantha had said, the more concerned he became. He put a little more foot on the gas pedal.

"Are we suddenly going to a fire?"

"We need to hurry."

"Well, yeah, but we don't want to miss Issa along the way either. What happened with being slow and careful?"

He shook his head. "I don't think she stopped anywhere. She'd know better. I think she's already at Mount Weather."

"That doesn't make any sense. Issa would know that we were worried about her. I can't imagine her staying longer than she needed to."

"Maybe she wasn't given a choice."

Samantha thought about that for a moment.

"You think Mother's holding her prisoner?"

"I think it's possible."

"What makes you say that?"

"Think about it. Mother's role in the colony is the giver of life. If others could also perform that function, her position of authority would be compromised. She might feel threatened by Issa."

"I don't know... Mother didn't seem like she was threatened by much of anything."

"I don't know either. But my gut is telling me that Issa may not have read this correctly."

Samantha didn't argue about it. Both of them relied on their gut to keep them out of trouble, and neither tended to unnecessarily question the other's intuition. If the universe went out of its way to whisper a warning, it was a good idea to cup an ear and listen.

They continued north, passing through the small communities of Lacey Spring and Tenth Legion. As they entered the town of New Market, subdivisions and small businesses began to pop up on either side of Highway 11. Neighborhoods eventually gave way to a quaint strip of small town restaurants, craft stores, and barbershops, many of which had their windows and doors smashed. At first, Tanner assumed it was just residual destruction from the outbreak, looters rising up to take what they wanted. It wasn't until he began to see fresh bodies dangling across broken window frames that he became anxious.

Samantha noticed it too. "Something happened here, recently."

"Yes, but it's not our concern."

She didn't argue about it. As far as Samantha was concerned, they had done enough righting of the world for one day.

As they continued on, a series of churches appeared on either side of the street. Methodist, Baptist, Lutheran—all denominations were present and all were equally in ruins. Buildings had been gutted from the inside out, with pews, cushions, and religious artifacts tossed onto their lawns as if by an act of religious defiance. More troubling still were the dozens of bodies lying in front of the Lutheran church.

Tanner swung the car over to the curb and stopped.

"What are you doing?" she asked. "You said it wasn't our concern."

"A few merchants killed in their stores isn't, but a whole congregation butchered on the front lawn of their church might be." He opened the door but left the car idling. "We don't want to be driving up on whoever did this."

Samantha sighed and pushed open her door.

"Can't we ever catch a break?"

"You're kidding, right?" he said as they climbed out. "We caught the biggest break of them all. We survived when most of the world didn't."

She nodded solemnly. "True. Plus, don't forget that we found each other."

"Uh, yeah, that too."

They strode onto the church's lawn, eyeing the bodies warily as if expecting them to stand up and give chase. None did. The dead remained dead, and hopefully that would never change.

Tanner knelt beside the body of a middle-aged woman. Samantha stood behind him, peering over his shoulder. The woman had been hacked with something sharp, a machete maybe.

"Can you tell how long she's been dead?"

He placed the back of his fingers against the woman's neck.

"A body might cool down a couple of degrees an hour, depending on the temperature around it. This one's still pretty warm." He lifted her arm and it moved freely. "Also, there's no rigor mortis. My guess is she's been dead for less than three or four hours."

Samantha turned and looked out at the sea of bodies littering the lawn.

"What could have killed so many people?"

Tanner found himself wondering the same thing. Except for the lack of scalping, the scene was akin to settlers having been massacred by bloodthirsty savages.

He moved over to the next body, hunting for more clues. The corpse was that of a young man, fit and strong. He was covered with dozens of deep puncture wounds on his chest, neck, and face.

"Are those dog bites?" she said, eyeing the wounds.

Tanner stood up, a deeply troubled look on his face.

"What is it?" she said.

"I know who did this."

"Who?"

"Mother."

"Huh?"

"This boy's wounds are from a nail board, the same kind her soldiers used down in the tunnels."

"But why would they be here in this little town?"

Tanner motioned for her to quiet as he tipped his head slightly. They heard the sound of vehicles approaching. Lots of vehicles.

"Someone's coming." She pointed toward an intersection a few hundred feet to the north. "From that way."

Tanner did a quick three-sixty, searching for a place to hide.

"Inside the church. Hurry!"

They raced up the steps and darted inside the old building. The double doors had been smashed in, but Tanner managed to push them partially closed. Many more bodies, men, women, and children, lay strewn all throughout the church. Whether they had been worshipping or seeking refuge was impossible to say. All that was certain was that the enemy had no appreciation for the word "mercy."

Tanner did a quick survey of the church to make sure that no one was in hiding. They weren't. Not a single soul had escaped judgment.

He hurried back to Samantha, who stood peering out through the broken doors.

"See anything?"

"Not yet," she said. "But the engines are getting louder."

Tanner checked his shotgun. Four, plus one in the pipe.

"Are we going to have to fight?" she said, slipping her rifle off her shoulder.

"I sure hope not."

Movement caught her eye, and she leaned around the door for a better look.

"They're coming."

Tanner stuck his head out. Rounding the corner was a fleet of vehicles—cars, trucks, motorcycles, even a few tractor-trailers. If they had been painted OD green, they could have easily passed for a military convoy.

"They shouldn't come this way, right?" said Samantha. "Mount Weather is the other direction."

Tanner said nothing. They both held their breath, watching as the lead vehicle came to a stop at the intersection. When it turned north, away from them, Samantha's shoulders sagged and she let out a sigh of relief.

"Thank goodness."

They crouched in the doorway, watching as vehicle after vehicle turned north. Tanner smiled. It looked like their luck might actually hold for once.

Until it didn't.

A pickup truck with two infected men up front and two in the back, abandoned the convoy and turned south, speeding toward the church.

"What are they doing?" she said.

Tanner pulled her back behind the door.

"Keeping us honest."

The pickup rolled to a stop next to the idling Mercedes, and all but the driver dismounted.

"Keep an eye on them while I look for a way out." Tanner spun around, and ran along a small hallway that led past several offices. At the end of the hall, he found a second exit, but it had been blocked with chairs, a large podium, and several pews stacked together. Digging out would take time they didn't have. Their only choice was to hide in plain sight.

He hurried back to Samantha.

"We need to pretend to be dead. Smear some blood on you and lie on the floor."

"Are you kidding?"

"Go on. It's not the first time you've hidden with the dead."

"No, and that might say something about your parenting skills," she muttered as she headed toward a pile of bodies at the back of the church. "You need to hide too."

"I will."

Tanner found a large man with his throat slashed not far from the front doors. A pool of dark crimson blood surrounded him. Tanner lay down directly against the man, his body turned sideways so that he could still see the doorway through squinted eyes. He kept his shotgun pressed between them.

No sooner had he and Samantha gotten into place than the door burst open. Two of the infected stood in the doorway, one holding a hatchet and the other a large-caliber revolver. The man with the revolver held it clumsily before him with his wrist bent.

Tanner felt his gut seize. When the hell did the infected start using guns? For that matter, when did they start driving cars?

One of the men entered the church as the other stood guard in the doorway. He advanced toward the front of the room, carefully looking down each row of pews. When he got to the front, he shouted to his partner.

"No one here," he said in a gruff voice.

The man in the doorway studied the bodies closest to him. He was still ten feet from Tanner, but it was clear that the gig was up. Better to keep the element of surprise.

Tanner rolled onto his back, swung the shotgun up, and fired. Momentum from the blast sent the man toppling down the stairs as buck-shot peppered his chest. Tanner sat up and spun around to see if he could get a clear shot at the other man.

No good.

Knowing that the third man would surely be coming up the stairs, Tanner dove toward the doors of the church, landing just in time to see him leaping up the steps with a heavy pipe in hand. He stuck the shotgun out in front of him and fired. The blast caught the man under the chin, folding his head back as a fountain of blood erupted.

Footsteps sounded from behind Tanner, and he whipped around.

Too late! The hatchet was already poised overhead, preparing to hack into his flesh.

Pop!

The infected man jerked as a .22 slug pierced his back. He staggered and wheeled around as Samantha cycled the bolt of her rifle.

It was the delay Tanner needed. He brought the shotgun up and fired twice. Two fist-size holes opened in the man's back, and he fell, his blood mixing with those of the churchgoers.

"What now?" she shouted.

"Over here!" he said, waving her closer.

She hurried back to him, carefully hurdling bodies and slippery pools of blood.

Tanner turned back toward the door, ready for the last of the infected to burst in at any moment. With four shells fired and no way to reload, he had but one left. As long as he didn't miss, it should be enough.

Nothing. No sounds of footsteps. No ugly face peeking in.

Tanner stepped closer and peered out. The pickup sat empty, its driver nowhere to be seen.

Samantha inched up next to him, her breathing labored.

"That could have gone better."

"They're dead. We're not. I count that as a win."

"Maybe," she said, peeking around the door. "But where's the last one?"

"How many rounds do you have on you?"

"Just the four in my rifle. If I'd have known you were going to start a war, I would have brought my backpack."

Tanner nodded. "Grab me that pistol, will you?" he said, motioning toward the revolver that the infected man had dropped.

She went over and retrieved the weapon. It was a stainless-steel Rossi, chambered in .38 Special.

"When did they start using guns?" she said, handing it to him.

He checked the cylinder. All six rounds had already been fired.

"What kind of idiot goes around with an empty pistol?" he said, tossing it away.

She took another peek out through the door, and when she spoke, her voice was little more than a whisper.

"Oh no."

"What is it?" he said, leaning around.

A handful of cars and trucks were speeding toward the church. Either they had heard the gunshots, or the driver of the pickup truck had managed to get word to them.

"Crap! We've got to get out of here." He eyed the Mercedes. The driver's side door was sitting open, but he couldn't recall if he had left it that way. "Back to the car, quick!"

They bolted from the church, Samantha leading the way. When they were halfway down the stairs, the driver of the pickup darted out from behind a bush and tackled Tanner. They tumbled a few steps before finally coming to rest.

Samantha stopped, but Tanner waved her on.

"Go! Get the car ready!"

The infected man who had tackled Tanner tore into him, biting and scratching like a wild animal. Tanner flung him off and got back to his feet. Out of the corner of his eye, he saw the vehicles racing toward them. He had to finish this quick.

As the man scrambled back to his feet, Tanner stepped forward and hit him with a powerful cross. Tanner weighed a good two hundred and fifty pounds, but he hit like a man who weight a hundred pounds more than that. The blow caught the infected man along the base of his left mandible, dislocating his jaw and cracking two of his back molars. The punch sent him whirling sideways, the man's legs threatening to take the easy way out. To his credit, he managed to convince them to do otherwise.

As he turned back to face Tanner, an uppercut was waiting for him. The strike rocked his head back, blood shooting from his mouth and nose. He teetered for a moment and then collapsed.

Tanner hopped down the remaining stairs, making a beeline for the Mercedes. Samantha was already climbing into the driver's seat. Tanner did a less than graceful belly roll across the hood, leaving a deep dent to mark his passing.

"Go, go, go!" he shouted, scrambling into the passenger seat.

Samantha looked at him with cold dread in her eyes.

"No keys."

He checked the ignition and then the floorboard. She was right. The keys were gone. One of the infected men must have taken them when they checked the vehicle. Frustrated, Tanner slammed his palm against the dash.

A handful of cars and trucks swerved onto the sidewalk and grass, quickly encircling the Mercedes. The infected began to pile out, each one armed and set on blood.

Tanner frantically looked left and right. Think, damn it! There had to be a way out.

If there was, he didn't see it. The shotgun shells were in his pack, and there wasn't time to retrieve them before being overrun. Even if there was, a few extra shells weren't going to win this fight.

He turned to Samantha. "I'll distract them while you run for it."

She shook her head softly. "It's okay."

Tears filled his eyes. "I mean it. Get out of here!"

She pulled her rifle close. "Let's make sure they remember us."

Tanner rubbed his face, rage filling his very soul. He let out a guttural scream and climbed out of the car. Samantha slid across the seat and stepped out behind him. She pressed her rifle to one shoulder, ready to make her last stand as bravely as any twelve-year-old ever had.

The infected slowly gathered, circling them like a pack of hungry jackals. Some held knives, others nail boards. A few even carried rifles, although they seemed perfectly content to use them as clubs for this particular skirmish.

Tanner looked down at Sam. There were no words to express how he felt.

She smiled, her eyes filled with tears.

"Yeah. Me too."

The infected advanced toward them, their eyes filled with an insatiable lust for violence. Tanner had but one shell left, but that didn't mean that he was finished. There was a power flowing through his veins unlike any he had felt before. He would pull joints from sockets, rupture organs, and break bones. By God, blood would surely flow in the streets this day.

"Come on!" he shouted, pounding a fist against his chest.

Before they could reach him, a figure shoved her way through the crowd, hissing and screaming. When she finally stepped into view, Tanner's heart nearly stopped.

Issa.

CHAPTER 20

M ason awoke to Jessie nuzzling his neck, her bare leg draped across his stomach. Rays of early morning sunlight poured in through the camper's windows, lighting her flesh like luscious honey. Where Brooke had exuded an intoxicating sexual energy, Jessie radiated a wholesome purity that made a man want to make her his, forever and ever.

Sharing a bed with a woman more than ten years his junior bordered on being morally questionable, but Mason's reservations about sleeping with her had vanished as quickly as her nightshirt. What happened, happened, and he was only the better for it.

Stirring, she kissed his neck. "Morning."

"It is that," he said, using his fingertips to gently trace the triangle of soft flesh along her lower back.

"Next time, let's find a bigger bed." She scooted closer, pressing warm breasts against his chest. "Or not."

"Next time?"

"I'm assuming you're still interested."

"Oh, I am, I am."

She smiled and kissed him again.

Bowie let out a high-pitched whine, and they turned to find him anxiously performing the pee-pee dance in front of the RVs side door.

"Sorry, boy," she said, hopping up to let him out.

Mason watched the way her naked body moved as she opened the door and let Bowie slip out into the morning light.

"I'm guessing you're not the shy type," he said, grinning.

She turned and faced him, her nude body tanned and firm.

"What can I say? I'm a country girl. We tend to accept nature the way it is." She put her hands on her hips, letting him get an eyeful. "I hope you're not too disappointed."

Mason wet his lips. "Believe me, disappointment is the furthest thing from my mind."

She sauntered over to the sink and began filling the basin.

"We'd better get cleaned up."

Mason checked his watch. It was a little past eight in the morning. He would need to get ready soon if he was going to reach the field before the competition started.

He sat up and tossed aside the thin sheet, his eyes refusing to completely turn away from Jessie as she dipped a rag into the sink and began washing her body.

"What do you think it's going to be like?" she said, running the wet rag over her neck and arms.

"Brutal and bloody. Same as yesterday."

"But you're going to win." It was less question than statement of fact.

"Of course."

"Because you're better than they are?" Once again, she was clearly fishing for reassurance. Perhaps it was to relieve her worry, or maybe she was just hoping to assess the likelihood of her first real lover returning to her in one piece.

"'Better' may be beside the point. I suspect today will be more about adapting than it is conventional gun handling."

"Why do you say that?"

"This is a show, not a gunfight. If it wasn't, they'd simply have us draw against one another to see who has the steadiest hand."

"Like in the Wild West."

"Exactly." He pulled on his trousers and hunted for a pair of socks.

Jessie moved on to gently scrubbing her stomach, letting the water run down the length of her thigh. Mason stopped with one sock on and one off, his mouth hanging open.

"You okay?" she said, looking back at him with feigned innocence. "You seem to have lost your concentration."

Mason tossed aside the sock and started toward her.

"You, young lady, are what's known as a vixen."

A seductive smile came over her face, and when she spoke, it was with a rich southern accent.

"Why, sir, I have no idea to what you are referring."

He slipped an arm around her naked waist and pulled her close.

"Well, hang on to your petticoat, miss, because you're about to."

Thanks to Jessie's sponge bath, they were nearly late to the parade grounds. A crowd of several hundred people had already gathered along both sides of the field. Leroy was standing next to the scoreboard, and Ramsey was out in the center of the field inspecting two large wooden trusses.

"What do you think those are for?" she asked.

Mason shrugged. "They must be part of the challenge."

They stood for a moment, Jessie awkwardly shifting from one foot to the other.

Mason said, "I hate to ask, but would you mind taking Bowie away from here? I'm afraid he'll run out onto the field."

She looked at him for a long moment, knowing full well that his request wasn't just for Bowie's sake.

"Of course," she said, leaning in and kissing his cheek. "Are you sure you're okay?"

"I'm fine," he said, uncertain of her meaning.

"I didn't distract you with my—my bath."

He cracked a smile. "Truth be told, my knees are still a little shaky. Even so, I think I'll manage."

She threw her arms around his neck and kissed him, this time on the lips. When she pulled away, there was a fierceness burning in her eyes.

"Give 'em hell."

His eyes narrowed as he looked off toward the four remaining gunfighters. Hell was exactly what he intended to bring.

With a last lingering look at Mason, Jessie whistled for Bowie, and together, they headed back to the RV.

As they disappeared into the crowd, Mason turned and walked over to Leroy. The old marshal stood tall and proud, watching as his field was readied for battle.

"I was kind of hoping you wouldn't show," he said, extending a hand.

"You know that's not me," Mason said as he shook it.

"No, I suppose not. You were never one to back down from a fight."

"I don't suppose there's any chance you'd just call this whole thing off?"

"I couldn't even if I wanted to." He turned and motioned toward the crowd. "Look at them. They'd lynch me if I tried."

Together, they turned and watched Ramsey directing several men as they put the final touches on the wooden trusses. Mason hadn't expected Leroy to have a change of heart overnight, but he still had one card left to play.

"I found the man who set up Jack Atkins."

"Oh?"

"He admitted to working for someone here in the camp."

"Doing what?"

"At first, he was helping to root out wrongdoers. When those became in short supply, it turned into something else."

Leroy grunted but said nothing.

"Was it you, Leroy?"

"Hell no, it wasn't me."

"Then it was Ramsey, or one of your other men. Someone in your organization is responsible for innocent people being shot dead. In my book, that amounts to murder."

"I'd like to have a word with this man, see if his story holds water."

"That'd be hard to do."

"Why? Did you kill him?"

Mason shook his head. "We found ourselves the targets of a vengeful widow. I got out. He didn't."

"Shame. With him gone, there's no way to know what's what."

Mason decided to press harder. If he could get Leroy to see the light, perhaps no one had to die today.

"This tournament's become something different than the rough justice you envisioned. It's become a crime in itself."

"Says the dead man?"

Mason's tone turned serious. "No. I'm saying so."

Leroy cut his eyes at him. "Careful. Old friendships only go so far."

"Funny. I was about to say the same thing."

"Meaning?"

"Meaning that I can't stand by and watch innocent men die, not by any man's hand."

Leroy turned and stepped closer, their faces only inches apart.

"For a minute, that almost sounded like a threat."

"There was a time when I wouldn't need to threaten. Not about something as wrong as this. Let the prisoners go, Leroy. You can banish them from the camp if you like, but set them free."

"Even if what that man said is true, it doesn't mean that most of the Fallen aren't guilty."

"Justice doesn't work that way, and you know it. Your system has been compromised. That means everyone gets a second chance."

"And if I don't set them free?"

Mason met his stare. "Either you'll clean this up, or I will."

Leroy's eyes narrowed, and he placed a hand on his Five-seven. Mason knew that drawing on someone standing so close was a skill in its own right. It required creating a small gap while keeping the firearm tight against the hip. He didn't know if Leroy had developed such skills, but he certainly had. Mason was confident that he could put three rounds in Leroy's gut before his gun ever cleared its holster.

Leroy relaxed and took a step back, an idea forming.

"I tell you what. I'll make you a proposition."

"Go on."

"I'll pit you against the gunfighters, one at a time." He snapped his fingers four times in rapid succession. "If you win, I'll take it as a sign from Lady Justice that you were right."

"The Fallen won't have to compete?"

"Not until this matter is settled. If you win, they go free. If you lose, the tournament gets back underway. We might be shy of a gunfighter or two, but we can always find someone willing to step in." He extended his hand. "What do you say... old friend?"

Mason weighed the offer. It was as good as any he was likely to get.

He reached out and shook Leroy's hand.

"Agreed."

Ramsey hurried over, his face tight with concern.

"Is there some kind of trouble here?" he said, glaring at Mason.

"Not at all," said Leroy. "Mason and I were just discussing a new development."

"What kind of development?"

"He's concerned that our selection process might have been flawed. Says someone was creating an environment that inadvertently put innocent men into the ranks of the Fallen." He glanced over at Ramsey. "You wouldn't know anything about that, would you?"

Ramsey's expression hardened.

"It doesn't matter," Leroy said, shaking his head. "Marshal Raines has volunteered to be the hand of justice. We've agreed to pit him against the gunfighters, one at a time. If he wins all four rounds, we'll release the Fallen."

"Why the hell would we do that? Do you know how long it took me—"

"We're doing it," he said, raising his voice, "because ever since I've known this S.O.B., he's been a man who knows right from wrong. The least we can do is give him a chance to drag us poor sinners down the righteous road of justice."

Ramsey exhaled and looked out at the crowd.

"It'll mean canceling a lot of bets."

"That's all right. Folks can place new bets, either on Mason or the gun-fighters. Besides," he said, slapping him on the shoulder, "you're missing the opportunity here. What's better than a stranger coming out of no-where to challenge our best? People are going to dig deep to put wagers on these fights."

Despite the pep talk, Ramsey was clearly not a fan of the new plan.

"I'll need a couple of hours to get everything sorted out."

"That's fine." He looked back at Mason. "Tell folks that old Leroy guar-antees they're in for one hell of a show."

స్వా ప్ర

While Leroy and Ramsey worked to restructure the tournament, Mason used the time to return to the RV and visit with Jessie and Bowie. Together, the three took a long walk around Grey's Point. Much of the camp was quiet and deserted due to folks gathering at the parade grounds, but there was still the occasional old woman hanging clothes, or children playing kickball in the street. It was a peaceful prelude to a day that portended all manner of violence.

"I'm curious about something," Jessie said, holding Mason's hand as they walked.

"What's that?"

"How do you do it?"

"I thought I showed you that last night," he said with a grin.

She squealed, turning and punching him playfully.

They both laughed, enjoying not only the frisky nature of their blos-soming relationship but also the comfort of having someone by their side.

"I meant," she said, her expression more curious than somber, "how do you stand in front of a man intent on killing you and not freeze up?"

"Admittedly, that can be a problem, especially for first-time shooters. The stress of a life-and-death situation can cause the loss of fine motor skills, some to the point where they can't work a safety or squeeze a trigger. Others have trouble with their vision, things becoming so blurry that they can't even see their sights."

"But not you?"

He shook his head lightly. "No. Not me."

She waited for more.

"I believe there are different kinds of people in this world. The vast majority have an inner flame that keeps them moving forward to do things like seek a better job, or ask a beautiful woman to dance." He squeezed her hand gently.

"That's a good thing, right?"

"Sure it is. Without it, they're doomed to spend the rest of their life in their mother's basement, sucking down two-liter bottles of Mountain Dew while playing endless rounds of Call of Duty."

She wrinkled her nose. "Thank you for that vivid scene of utter failure!"

"My point is that while most people have an inner flame, it never burns quite hot enough to function well in real do-or-die situations."

"But yours does?"

"I like to think so."

"Does that mean you don't feel afraid?"

He shrugged. "My pulse quickens, like everyone's, I suppose. The difference is that I'm able to use the adrenalin as fuel. Instead of my reactions becoming slower, they speed up. And instead of things becoming cloudy and muddled, everything suddenly comes into sharp focus."

Jessie stopped and stared into his eyes, as if searching for something.

"What?" he asked.

She shook her head. "Nothing. I just haven't met anyone quite like you before."

"Is that good or bad?"

She hooked an arm through his and resumed walking.

"Ask me tomorrow."

"Why tomorrow?"

"Because it will mean that you lived through today."

੭ ൏

It took closer to three hours for the betting to be sorted out. The crowd was none too happy with the sudden change in plans, but there was also a palpable excitement growing in the air. Who was this stranger? Why did he believe he could stand against the camp's most notorious and skilled gunslingers? Was he brave, or simply stupid? Skilled, or a buffoon with a death wish? He had managed to defeat Bones, but only by skirting the intent of the challenge. Did he even know how to shoot a gun? Most bet that he would be out in the first round, but a few were willing to accept longer odds on what they now saw as the competition's dark horse.

Leroy, Ramsey, and Mason stood in the center of the field as they prepared for the upcoming match. Mason studied the trusses. They were perhaps fifteen feet tall and set about fifty feet apart, with ropes hanging beneath them.

Ramsey turned to Leroy. "Ready when you are."

Leroy brought the bullhorn to his mouth and announced that Ringo would be the first gunfighter to face the man they were now calling "The Marshal."

Ringo strolled out onto the field, waving to the crowd. Despite his outwardly confident demeanor, there was a twitchiness to his smile. The tournament had clearly changed, and what had been billed as little more than target practice had turned into something arguably more dangerous.

Leroy motioned for Ringo and Mason to face each other while he explained the rules.

"Every skilled gunfighter needs to be able to fight from unconventional positions. For that reason, you will be hung by your feet and sent swinging through the air. The first one to kill or incapacitate the other wins the challenge."

Ramsey stepped closer and handed each man a Cimarron Model P. The single-action revolver was a recreation of the ones carried by gunfighters in the late 1800s. Ringo smiled from ear to ear as he twirled the pistol around his finger to the delight of the crowd. The Model P was perhaps the perfect weapon for a man so accustomed to playing cowboy.

Mason showed no such flair. Instead, he carefully dropped the cylinder to inspect the ammunition. All six of the .45 Colt cartridges remained unfired. He clicked the cylinder closed and weighed the weapon in his hands. Two and a half pounds, give or take a few ounces. The revolver sported a five-and-a-half-inch barrel, smooth walnut grips, and a simple fixed front sight blade. Compared to modern semi-automatic firearms, it was lacking in nearly every respect but one: it could still kill with the squeeze of a trigger.

"The pistol goes in the front of your waistband," Ramsey said, waiting until both men had stowed it accordingly. "If either of you draws before the round starts, I'll shoot you myself." He turned to Mason. "You, I'll shoot twice."

Mason said nothing.

"Ringo, you're with me," Leroy said, leading him toward the far truss.

Ramsey turned to Mason. "That means I get the pleasure of stringing you up."

Not liking the way that sounded, Mason reluctantly followed Ramsey to stand beneath the other truss.

"On your back with your feet together."

Mason did as instructed.

As Ramsey snugged the rope around his ankles, he leaned close and said, "If Ringo should happen to kill you, I want you to know that I'm planning to take care of that little sweetheart of yours. I wouldn't want her going without."

Again, Mason said nothing. Trading barbs with a man hoisting you up by a rope was a good way to get a boot in the face.

Once he was in the air, Mason was sent swinging from side to side, like the pendulum on a grandfather clock. Worse yet, with each movement, he began to rotate ever so slightly. Between the lateral movement and the slow rotation, Mason realized it would be difficult enough to see his opponent, let alone hit him with an antique revolver.

The crowd began to cheer and stomp their feet. Things were about to begin.

Leroy waited until everyone was clear of the trusses before turning to the shooters with the bullhorn pressed to his mouth.

"Shooters ready?"

Mason and Ringo each stuck a hand out to one side.

Leroy lifted his pistol into the air and fired a single shot.

The round was underway.

To hit a man-sized target at fifty feet was trivial, but to do so while hanging upside down, swinging from side to side, would be far more challenging. There were two possible approaches. The first was to try to track the opponent by following his movement with the muzzle of the firearm. And the second was to attempt to trap him, basically holding the gun out straight and waiting for the enemy to come into the line of fire.

Ringo opted for tracking, sweeping the gun from side to side as he tried to line up a shot. He was the first to fire, but his bullet missed by more than a yard, thudding into the heavy truss.

Mason took an entirely different tactic, drawing the pistol with his right hand while extending his left palm toward the ground. The drag of his hand quickly stopped his swinging, but he was still twisted at an odd angle, making a clear shot difficult.

Instead of trying to square his body with Ringo's, he looked up at his feet, took aim, and shot the rope. Shooting a rope is not as hard as some might believe, especially not at a range of only a couple of yards.

The trick was to ensure that the rope was taut and the bullet of a large enough caliber to sever most of the strands. The 250-grain, .45 Colt slug was up to the task, snapping the rope and sending Mason tumbling to the ground.

Ringo saw what he was doing and frantically squeezed off three more shots. One hit the dirt in front of Mason. The other two never came close, whizzing past him to smash into a truck full of wood that had been parked behind the truss. Unfortunately for Ringo, firing in such rapid succession increased his rate of spin, making it nearly impossible for him to regain his bearings.

Mason took aim and squeezed the trigger. The bullet hammered into Ringo's right shoulder, and he screamed in pain. To his credit, he managed to pass the pistol to his other hand before his injured arm gave way and flopped uselessly over his head.

Mason fired again, this time striking his left shoulder blade.

The gun fell from Ringo's grip as he momentarily lost consciousness. When he came too, both hands were brushing the ground, blood dripping over his leather gloves.

Mason untied the rope and walked toward Ringo with the Model P raised.

Ringo flopped his sagging right hand in the direction of his weapon, the desperate act of a desperate man.

"If you touch it, I'll put one in your chest," Mason said, cocking the hammer back.

Ringo went limp, every ounce of fight now gone.

Mason moved closer and kicked the weapon away.

Leroy hurried onto the field and declared Mason the winner. Surprisingly, the crowd didn't jeer or boo. While many had lost money or property, there was no questioning that they had witnessed a true test of skill and nerves.

One man stepped forward and held up several bills.

"Fifty credits on The Marshal!"

Another man quickly took his bet. Before long, dozens of people were shouting, some placing bets for Mason, others against. With Ringo's defeat, things had suddenly become more interesting.

Mason said nothing as he followed Leroy off the field.

"Pretty clever," Leroy said with an approving nod.

"Never fight by another man's rules. You know that."

"Even so, knowing's one thing, doing's another. I had often heard it said that you were a hard man to kill. I'm beginning to see why."

Despite it being offered as a compliment, Mason felt his temper rising. A man was being carried off the field, bleeding from two bullet wounds inflicted by his hand. The whole event reeked of glorified violence. To shoot a man was one thing, but to do so for a crowd's pleasure was something else.

"How long until the next challenge?"

"They'll need to set it up. I'd say be back in an hour."

Mason turned and began walking toward the RV. When he was halfway across the field, he saw Liberty approaching. The big man's gait was not one of someone looking for a fight. Even so, Mason stopped and placed a hand on his Supergrade.

Liberty came to within a few yards and stopped. He stood nearly a head taller than Mason and easily outweighed him by a hundred pounds or more.

"Can I help you with something?" Mason said, watching the man's hands.

"That was some fine shooting you did there. Merciful too."

"You came out here to compliment me on my compassion?"

"No," he said with a quick shake of his head. "I came out here to ask you something."

"All right," Mason said, taking his hand from his weapon. "Ask away."

"Why are you standing against us? Against the side of law and order? It seems contrary to the badge you're wearing."

"There's nothing lawful about what's happening here."

"But the Fallen are all violent criminals. If we don't deal with them, others will surely suffer at their hands."

"Some are criminals. Others may not be."

Liberty cocked his head. "Explain yourself."

"I met a man who helped to frame some of the prisoners. Truth is, there's no way to know how many are innocent."

"You know this for a fact?"

"I wouldn't be putting my life on the line if I didn't."

"Does Leroy know?"

Mason shrugged. "He's operating under plausible deniability."

Liberty turned and studied the Fallen. Even though they were no longer having to compete, Ramsey had made sure they were present to witness what their future might hold.

"Tell me one more thing."

"What's that?"

"How does a man know if he's standing on the right side of things?"

There was a sincerity to his question that surprised Mason.

"Every man has to make that decision for himself. But the fact that you're asking the question should be answer enough."

Liberty nodded and extended a gloved hand.

"You're not a man I'm willing to kill."

Mason shook his enormous hand, thinking that it reminded him of his father's oversized mitts.

"Good to hear that."

"Stay frosty, Marshal. The world needs men with a conscience, now more than ever."

☙ ❧

The third round looked to be more subdued than the previous ones. White circles had been spray-painted on the dirt about fifty yards apart for the shooters to stand inside. Two of the men who had set up the trusses were huddled behind a thick makeshift barrier to one side of the field. Both were wearing reflective yellow vests, no doubt hoping that the bright colors might reduce their chances of being accidentally shot.

Leroy stood between Muchado and Mason like a referee at a prizefight. Ramsey was off to one side, holding two matching long-barrel shotguns. Belted ammo pouches hung over each shoulder.

Leroy looked to Mason and then to Muchado, ensuring he had their undivided attention.

"This challenge will resemble classical skeet shooting, with targets being lobbed toward both men simultaneously."

Mason leaned around, trying to get a better view of the setup.

"Are they using catapults?"

"That's right."

"And must we hit every target?"

"No. A miss won't disqualify you. As with all the matches, it ends only when one of the competitors is either unwilling or unable to continue. In effect, you will be competing side by side in this round."

"We're not shooting at each other?" Muchado said in his thick Hispanic accent.

Leroy held up a finger. "Coming to that. The circles are your personal zones of protection. If you stay inside, your competitor may not fire upon you. If he does, he will have violated the rules." Leroy nodded toward Ramsey. "I think you know what happens at that point."

"And if we should step outside the circle?" asked Mason.

"If you do that, your competitor is free to shoot you, but you are not free to return fire. My advice," he said with a smile, "is don't step outside the circle."

"What exactly will they be throwing at us?" Muchado said, scratching his belly.

Leroy looked over at Ramsey, who said only, "Not knowing's part of the fun."

"You white devil, you," Muchado said with a laugh.

Leroy continued, "The weapon for this round will be a Winchester Super X3."

Ramsey stepped forward and handed a shotgun and shell bag to each competitor.

As Mason secured the canvas pouch around his waist, he counted at least twenty bright red number-9 shot shells inside. Birdshot of that type made it easier to hit targets, but it also did less damage.

"All right then," Muchado said, slapping Mason on the shoulder. "Let's see what kind of trouble they have in store for us, eh, amigo?"

Before Mason could remind him that they were anything but amigos, the big Mexican turned and marched onto the field, waving his sombrero like a bullfighter entering the Plaza de Toros.

Mason took his time getting into position, feeding shells into the weapon until there were three in the magazine tube and one in the pipe. This particular model of X3 was chambered in twelve-gauge, had a twenty-six-inch barrel, and was finished in a natural green camouflage color. Mason was by no means an expert with a shotgun, but he had shot clay pigeons numerous times and had even carried a pump-action M590A1 into combat on a few occasions.

Once safely inside the white circle, Mason spread his feet to a comfortable width, pointing them toward the men preparing to throw targets. He practiced swinging the gun up a few times. The weapon felt long and unwieldy. He reminded himself to focus on the targets, not the front bead. Shooting moving targets with a shotgun tended to be a point and squeeze operation. The fact that the targets would be coming directly toward him would make things that much more interesting.

Leroy stood to the side of the field, bullhorn in hand.

"Shooters ready?"

Both Mason and Muchado signaled that they were.

Another loud gunshot, and the match was officially underway.

Mason waited, his heart pounding. A metallic *kertwang* sounded, and objects sailed through the air. He swung the shotgun up, tracking the one coming toward him. Muchado's shotgun sounded first, and in Mason's peripheral vision, he saw the man's target explode into small wet chunks. Despite the temptation to fire, Mason waited to squeeze the trigger until he could identify the target.

It was nothing more than a rotten cantaloupe.

He relaxed, letting the fruit fall harmlessly to one side. No need to waste a shell.

The crowd offered a quick clap at Muchado's excellent shooting.

Mason began a silent count, anticipating that each target might be equally spaced in time. When he got to five, another target appeared. It was a glass bottle, a small strip of flaming cloth dangling from one end. Mason tracked the Molotov cocktail until it was at the apex of its flight before firing. The bottle exploded, sending shards of glass and fiery liquid raining down onto the field.

Muchado hit his target as well, and the crowd clapped with greater enthusiasm as two small fires now burned in the grass.

Mason began his count again. When he got to five, the familiar *kertwang* sounded. The cloud of residual black smoke from the Molotov cocktail made it hard to see the target. When he could finally make it out, he saw that the object was long and thin, and there was a bright spark at one end.

Dynamite!

He immediately swung the muzzle up and fired three quick shots, peppering the sky with a sea of metal pellets. Thunderous *booms* shook the air as Muchado followed suit. Unlike C4, dynamite was more likely than not to explode when shot, and both sticks did just that, rocking the air with two deafening blasts.

This time the crowd cheered and waved their hands. Everyone loved a good explosion.

Mason's ears rang as he quickly retrieved shells from the bag and loaded them into the shotgun. As he was inserting the last shell, the catapult sounded again. Perhaps fearing another stick of dynamite, Muchado fired almost immediately. His target vanished, turning into nothing but a pink mist. Resisting the urge to fire, Mason rested his finger on the trigger, waiting until he could be certain of his target.

"God, no," he muttered, his stomach knotting.

A fuzzy grey kitten sailed through the air, its tiny legs outstretched in pure terror. Mason lowered the shotgun and leaned out, hoping to catch the animal. He managed to break its fall, but it bounced off his hand and landed on the ground near his feet. He couldn't afford to check on it, instead turning his attention back to the sky.

Seeing what had happened, the crowd cringed and shrank back as an uneasy murmur spread throughout. Muchado, however, seemed merely amused, laughing loudly at their squeamish reaction.

Mason's face tightened. This was Ramsey's doing, and he would be held accountable. Now, however, was not the time to become angry or distracted, as that could very well have been Ramsey's intention from the beginning.

Mason returned to his slow count, skipping one and two because of his brief interaction with the kitten. *Three... four... five.* Another object sailed through the sky. It was small and olive drab in color, with a distinctive yellow band circling the top.

An M67 grenade.

Muchado's gun sounded, winging the grenade. Unlike the dynamite, it didn't explode. Instead, it tumbled from the sky to land about ten yards away from him.

Mason probably knew as much about M67s as any man alive, having carried them into combat on countless missions. He knew, for example, that they were filled with 6.5 ounces of composition B explosive, and equipped with an M213 pyrotechnic delay fuze. Detonation typically occurred four to five seconds after the spoon was released, allowing them to hit the ground prior to exploding. Fatality radius was five meters, and injury radius was three times that, with some fragments capable of traveling a hundred meters or more.

Most important of all, he knew what set them off and what didn't. As Muchado had just discovered, a load of birdshot would not detonate an M67. It would, however, destroy the grenade if fired from a close enough range. Mason ran through his options as the grenade flew toward him. Shooting it from a distance would leave the grenade viable, very likely injuring or killing him. But waiting with the hopes of destroying it was an all-or-nothing gamble. If he missed, or if it failed to be demolished by the birdshot, he was dead, simple as that.

He let out half a breath and watched as the grenade closed in—fifteen yards, ten, five, three.

Blam!

The shotgun bucked, and nearly all of the six hundred tiny lead pellets ripped into the grenade, obliterating it.

Mason immediately dropped prone, unconsciously holding his breath. No sooner had he hit the ground, than an explosion sounded. But it wasn't from *his* grenade. It was from Muchado's.

A split second later, the big Mexican howled in agony. Mason cautiously raised his head to see him lying on his back, screaming, while clutching his face with both hands. One of his knees had also folded backwards, the femur bone protruding through a bloody flap of skin. Despite his injuries, he had been lucky. The shock wave and shrapnel from the grenade could have just as easily killed him.

As Mason sat up, something soft brushed the back of his hand. He turned to find the grey kitten curling up against him, still dazed from its aerial adventure. Despite the rough landing, it seemed no worse for wear.

He gently scooped up the kitten and set it in his shotgun pouch.

"Look at you," he said, giving it a gentle rub under the chin. "You're not even eight weeks old, and you've already lost one of your lives."

It gave a soft, squeaky *meow*.

Mason stood up, letting the shotgun settle into the crook of his arm. As he walked toward the scoreboard to mark the winner's box, he heard the unmistakable sound of muted applause from the crowd. He wasn't sure what to make of it. Had they suddenly realized that the brutal murder of petty criminals and fuzzy felines was horribly unjust? More likely, they were shifting their allegiances, and bets, to the contestant they thought might bring home the prize.

He did his best to ignore them. Three of the five scheduled gunfighters had fallen, and one had voluntarily withdrawn. That meant there was only one more to go. Unfortunately, there was no doubt in Mason's mind that The Reverend wouldn't go down easily.

෴ ෴

"I think I'll call him Gunsmoke," Jessie said, stroking the kitten. She turned to Mason. "You're sure you don't want to keep him?"

Mason reached down and gave Bowie a hearty pat on the side.

"I'm afraid Bowie might have him for a late-night snack."

"Nah. Bowie wouldn't hurt a fly, would you, boy?"

Bowie licked his lips, and they both laughed.

"Okay, fine," she said. "Maybe it is better if he stays with me." Jessie kissed the kitten on the nose. The little fellow was nearly asleep, and she gently placed him on the hood of the RV while they talked.

Bowie propped up on the bumper with his front feet and sniffed the kitten. It purred and slowly closed its eyes. The big wolfhound nudged it, but the kitten refused to stir. Losing interest, he hopped back down and settled onto the dirt next to the RV's front tire.

Jessie moved closer to Mason, reaching out and taking his hands in hers.

"Only one more to go." Despite her words, she sounded nervous.

"I'll be all right."

"You say that, but The Reverend seems more dangerous than the others. Ruthless and cold, like something that crawled out of a graveyard."

"He's just a man."

"Maybe." She stared off toward the parade grounds. Ramsey and his men were busy clearing the field. "Do you know what the challenge is?"

"Leroy said it's going to be a simple showdown, one man facing the other. I even get to use my Supergrade."

"That's gives you an advantage, right?"

Mason thought of The Reverend's Nighthawk VIP. It was on par with his Supergrade, and he suspected that its handler was as well.

Jessie searched his face. "You're worried that he's faster than you. I can see it in your eyes."

"You're not much for pep talks, are you?"

"I'm sorry," she said, squeezing his hand.

"It's all right. But you need to remember that speed isn't all that matters."

"It's not?"

"Wyatt Earp once said that 'Fast is fine, but accuracy is everything. In a gun fight, you need to take your time in a hurry.'"

"Take your time in a hurry? What's that supposed to mean?"

"It means that you can't only worry about speed. You also have to hit your target when your heart's pounding and your hand's shaking."

"That fire in your belly that you were telling me about. You think it will help you."

"It has so far. Besides, The Reverend is afflicted by the same vices as every other man."

"What vices?"

"Arrogance, impatience, stubbornness, and greed, to name but a few."

"Okay. But how does that help you?"

"The difference in speed between two great gunfighters might be a hundredth of a second. If you can cause the one who's faster to think a little harder than normal, that hundredth of a second can easily change hands."

"So you *do* think he's faster."

Mason shrugged. "Maybe, maybe not. We've never seen him face off against an equal."

"If he were a hair faster," she said, pinching two fingers together as if measuring a small distance, "what could you do to slow him down?"

"Cause a little doubt, or anger. Anything to get his mind off the draw."

"Okay,…" she said, thinking. "So how are you going to do that?"

"I'm not sure yet."

"But you need —"

"Jessie," he said, cutting her off, "no amount of worry is going to change what happens. Trust that I'll get it done."

She pressed her lips together and nodded.

His voice softened. "I learned a long time ago that when two men face one another, whether it's across a judo mat or holding knives in a dark alley, the winner is often determined not by who has the greatest skill, but by who brought the most heart to the fight."

She rested her palms on his chest and looked up at him.

"Then I know everything's going to be okay, because you have the heart of a hundred lions."

Mason kissed her on the forehead.

"Now *that's* more like it."

⇴ ⇲

The crowd had grown to well over a thousand, nearly every adult in the camp coming out to see the big finale. Money would be won, and money would be lost. But what was perhaps most alluring was the prospect that a previously obscure U.S. Marshal might actually defeat all of the gunfighters through true mano-a-mano competitions. It was the stuff of legends, and everyone wanted to be able to say they were there when it happened. *If* it happened.

Mason stood a few paces from The Reverend, quietly studying him. The man's black suit was meticulous, and his straight brimmed preacher-style hat sat level on a head of wispy silver hair. He had a dark brooding presence and wickedly fast hands, but other than that, Mason knew very little about him.

The craftsmanship of his rig looked superb, probably made by Gary Brommeland, Milt Sparks, Don Hering, or one of the other great holster makers. There was a notch in the front to allow the muzzle to clear the holster that much faster. As for his weapon, the Nighthawk VIP was as fine as any 1911 ever made. Where Mason's Supergrade had been built with function in mind, the VIP added a sense of flair, with its hand-engraved nickel finish, 14-karat gold bead, and giraffe bone grips.

Jane Austen had once suggested that the difference between pride and vanity is that those who are proud are concerned with how they see themselves, whereas those who are vain are consumed by what others think of them.

Mason smiled. Before him was a man whose worth was determined by what others said it was worth. And that, he thought, might well be his weakness.

"Find something amusing?" the Reverend said in a hollow voice.

"I was just admiring your getup. Really nice. Sort of a Doc Holliday meets Father Lankester Merrin." Mason raised his hands, palms out. "But hey, no offense intended. It works for a man of your age."

The Reverend's brow furrowed.

"I'm sorry. That came out wrong. Truth is, you remind me of an old firearms instructor I once had. You should have seen that guy, fast as a rattlesnake. Well, until the arthritis started up, that is. Poor guy couldn't hold a spoon the last time I saw him. Lovely fellow, though."

"I've killed twenty-seven men with these hands." The Reverend held out his hands to show how steady they were. Unfortunately, his annoyance had introduced the slightest of tremors, and both men saw it. He quickly lowered them back to his side.

Mason turned to Leroy. "You should probably announce that to the crowd. Twenty-seven is a very impressive number."

Leroy cracked a smile, obviously enjoying the show.

The Reverend clenched his jaw. "You must think you're pretty funny."

"Me? Funny? Nah. Now my father, he's a hoot. If he were here, he'd probably say something like 'What does a Christmas tree and a reverend have in common?'"

The Reverend pressed his lips together, saying nothing.

"Don't know? The answer is that their balls are just for decoration." Mason offered him a prize-winning smile.

Leroy snickered, but based on The Reverend's scowl, he saw nothing funny about it.

"I'm going to put a bullet through your eye."

"This one?" Mason winked his right eye. "Or this one?" He blinked the other eye.

The Reverend seemed at a loss for words. What should have had Mason shaking in his boots was bringing only a playful grin.

Ramsey hurried over and said, "We're ready, boss."

"All right, gentlemen," said Leroy. "It's show time."

Leroy turned and escorted them onto the field. The distance had been carefully marked off in five-yard increments with stripes of white paint, like a Little League football field. Facing the crowd, he brought the bullhorn to his mouth.

"This challenge will be a test of both speed and accuracy. The contestants will start at a distance of fifty yards. Each man must wait for the sound of my pistol before drawing his weapon. If either competitor draws early, he will be shot." Leroy pointed to Ramsey, who proudly slapped the stock of his rifle. "Each competitor will have but a single cartridge in their weapon. If both competitors miss or fail to drop their opponent, they will move ten yards closer, reload, and repeat the draw. Like previous matches, it ends when one man is unable or unwilling to continue."

He brought the bullhorn down and turned to Mason and The Reverend. "Any questions?"

Mason raised a hand.

"Go ahead."

Mason spoke in a loud voice so that much of the crowd could hear.

"I was wondering if we could make it a little closer on account of The Reverend's eyesight."

People began to chuckle, and it slowly spread through the crowd.

The Reverend lunged toward Mason, and Leroy quickly stepped between them.

"You'll get your chance soon enough."

Nostrils flaring, The Reverend slowly took a step back.

Leroy turned to Mason and pointed further down the field.

"You're on that end, Rickles. The Reverend stays put."

Mason followed Ramsey out to his respective position. It was the longest fifty yards he could ever remember walking.

Once Mason was standing on the designated mark, Ramsey leaned in and said, "Vodka or whisky?"

"Excuse me?"

His melted face twisted into an unsightly grin.

"I plan on pissing on your grave tonight. I was just wondering if you preferred I drink vodka or whisky."

Mason slowly shook his head. "I've never been a betting man, but if I were, I'd wager that I'm going to be there when you take your last breath."

Ramsey's eyes tightened, but he said nothing more as he strode off the field.

With his hand resting on his Supergrade, Mason turned and faced The Reverend. The dark stranger stood in the distance, looking more like an undertaker than a man of God. A hundred things tried to push their way into his mind. Was Jessie watching? What would Bowie do if he saw his master shot? Had he unnerved The Reverend enough to cause a mistake? Did he even need to?

He let out a calming breath and felt his heart slow.

None of it mattered.

The only thing that mattered was the draw.

The *crack* of Leroy's pistol sounded.

Mason had heard it said that time slows down when people face a high-stress situation. For him, that had never been true. Instead, reflexes took over, his body moving on its own volition while his mind stood idly by to witness the motion.

The gunshot hadn't even finished echoing before Mason's gun cleared the holster. Trying to hip shoot at fifty yards was all but asking for a miss. Instead, he used both hands to push the pistol out in front of him as he took a giant step to the left.

He saw the muzzle flash from The Reverend's weapon at the exact moment he felt the Supergrade buck in his hands. Both men stood completely still, the crowd whisper-quiet as they waited to see who would fall.

And then it happened.

The Reverend slowly dropped to his knees, his gun wavering in his hand.

Mason released the slide and pushed the Supergrade back into its holster as he walked slowly toward the man. Leroy and Ramsey were also coming onto the field.

As he drew closer, Mason saw that the bullet had struck him in the center of his sternum. Blobs of blood burped onto the man's white shirt with each pulse of his heart. The Reverend teetered for a moment and then fell back across his legs. His eyes remained open, but spittle and blood sprayed with every breath.

The Nighthawk VIP lay beside his open hand, its slide also locked to the rear.

Mason knelt beside him and picked up the weapon. The only thing he could compare it to was the soft flesh of a woman's breast. It was that beautiful. He leaned over and placed the pistol atop the dark stranger's chest. With his last bit of strength, The Reverend lifted his hands and rested them on it as if determined to take it with him into whatever afterlife awaited.

They stared at one another, one gunfighter to another, saying nothing. The crowd stood absolutely mesmerized, watching as the victor paid his final respects to his enemy.

The Reverend let out a deep breath and closed his eyes.

Mason stood and turned to Leroy. His old friend lifted the bullhorn up to his mouth, and when he spoke, his tone was one of reverence.

"Ladies and gentlemen, I believe we have our winner."

CHAPTER 21

Tanner and Samantha could hardly believe their eyes. Issa stood before them, the heavy Merkel clutched tightly in both hands. A dark purple bruise covered one side of her face, and the corner of her lower lip was split. Before either of them could say a word, she wheeled around and swept the crowd with the big rifle's muzzle.

"Leave them be!" she hissed.

The infected suddenly seemed uncertain. Many began to take small steps backward. Whether it was the Merkel making them rethink their attack or simply the fury in her eyes, something gave them pause.

Issa slowly backed toward Tanner and Samantha. When she was within a few feet, she said over her shoulder, "What are you two doing here?"

"We could ask you the same thing," Tanner said, still trying to mentally piece together a story that made any sense whatsoever that would involve her being part of an infected raiding party.

"We were out looking for you," Samantha said, piping in.

"You shouldn't have come after me. I'm fine."

"You say that," said Tanner, "but you look like you ran into the same lamppost we did. What happened?"

Before Issa could answer, General Korn pushed his way through the crowd. He was unlike the others, not only in his size, but because the midline of his skull was striped with a thick sagittal crest, like that of a great ape. An M16 hung across one shoulder, but against the man's size, the weapon looked more like a child's toy than an actual assault rifle.

Tanner recognized Mother's most trusted general immediately. Not only had they fought for Issa's hand, they had also co-led the assault on Mount Weather. But that was when Tanner had been infected with Dr. Jarvis's blood. Now, he had no idea what to expect.

Issa swung the Merkel toward him.

"Tell them to back off."

Korn said nothing, instead taking a moment to study Tanner.

Tanner wondered if he even remembered him. The worst of the infected tended to be simpleminded. The fact that he was carrying a rifle was surprising enough. During their assault on Mount Weather, Korn's army had resorted to such primitive weaponry as the nail boards, and Tanner had assumed that they were incapable of fully understanding more sophisticated armament.

Korn stepped closer, walking past Issa as if thoroughly unimpressed by the big rifle. He came to within a few feet of Tanner and stopped. Tanner straightened, meeting the man's stare even as he towered over him. He had defeated Korn in hand-to-hand combat once before, but a rematch was not on his must-do list.

"Tanner is a friend," Korn said in his deep voice. He stepped closer and wrapped his thick arms around him. "Friend," he repeated, pounding Tanner on the back hard enough to leave a bruise.

"Yeah, yeah, good to see you too, big guy," he muttered, making a half-hearted attempt to return the brute's awkward hug.

One of the infected men in the crowd shouted angrily. Tanner couldn't understand what he had said, but Korn apparently didn't appreciate his tone. He marched over and rapped him sharply on the head with a thick gauntleted hand. The man's legs buckled, but Korn caught him by the throat. Holding him upright, he began reciting the story of how he and Tanner had led Mother's army into Mount Weather. Korn's English was at times broken, and he often seemed to leave out words that he felt were unimportant. Even so, it was a stirring, if not somewhat embellished, account of heroism and victory.

As he spoke, Samantha inched closer to Issa and reached out to touch the back of her arm.

"Hi Issa."

Issa turned to her, knowing full well that for a girl who rarely showed affection, Samantha's gentle touch was the equivalent of a tear-filled embrace.

"Hi Sam," she said, smiling.

"What happened to your face?"

"What? Am I not beautiful anymore?"

Samantha smiled. "No, you're still pretty. By the way, thanks for stepping in when you did. I think Tanner was about to go berserk on them."

"Of course." Issa turned to Tanner. "Still getting our daughter into trouble, I see."

He leaned closer and kissed her. What was meant to be a quick peck turned into more as Issa handed the big rifle off to Samantha and wrapped both arms around his neck. When they finally broke, they turned to find Samantha staring at them with an amused look on her face.

"What are you looking at?" he said.

"I was remembering when she first kissed you at the reservoir. It seems like you two can't get enough of each other."

"That bother you?"

She shrugged. "It's a little yucky, but kind of sweet too."

"Good, because we're likely to keep on doing it."

Korn finished his story and turned back to face them.

"All of you will come to Mother." From the way he said it, it was somewhere between a request and a command.

"Do you think we'll be safe without Jarvis's blood?" whispered Samantha.

Tanner turned to Issa for the answer.

"They're different now," she explained. "More able to deal with their rage."

Tanner looked past her to the church lawn filled with bodies. Some things may have changed, but others had not.

"How did you end up with them?" he asked.

"It's a long story, one that I'm sure you won't be happy to hear."

Tanner crossed his arms. "Go on."

"I met some women who needed help. It ended up being more trouble than we could handle. Fortunately, Korn and his army showed up in time to lend a hand."

"You shouldn't have gone off by yourself."

"No. I shouldn't have." She pressed up against him. "Forgive me?"

The heat of her body melted his anger like butter in a hot skillet.

"You're going to have to earn your way back into my good graces."

She grinned. "Oh, am I now?"

"There you go again," muttered Samantha.

Korn interrupted by pointing to the Mercedes.

"You follow to Mother."

Accepting that they weren't going to be able to simply shake hands and walk away, Tanner said, "We'll need the keys."

Before Korn could ask, the man that Tanner had knocked down the stairs stumbled forward. His cheek and mouth were both bleeding, but he said nothing as he handed over the keys.

Twirling them around his finger, Tanner said, "All right, lead the way."

Korn said something to two of the infected before turning and marching back to a burnt-orange Jeep Wrangler. His throng of fighters followed him back to their vehicles, all except the two who had been given orders. To Tanner's dismay, one of the men climbed into the backseat of the Mercedes, and the second held out a pipe, sharpened to a point on one end.

"Looks like we've got babysitters," he muttered.

"Yeah," Samantha said, squeezing in next to Issa. "The kind with pointy sticks."

"Let's just hope that Mother's glad to see us."

"Why wouldn't she be?" asked Issa.

He glanced over at the bulge of their unborn baby.

"Something tells me that throwing you a shower might be the last thing on her mind."

಄ ⫷

As Tanner approached Mount Weather, he couldn't help but recall the history of the compound. After the outbreak, it had been converted from one of FEMA's operation centers to an emergency retreat for the highest levels of government. With its rural 434-acre complex, as well as a 600,000-square-foot underground bunker, it had promised to be the ideal safe house for the President, the few remaining members of Congress, and a contingency of military personnel.

After a concentrated effort to seal the tunnels under Washington, D.C., however, the infected had risen up and overrun the center. Many of the soldiers and civilians had managed to escape to the New Colony in Norfolk, Virginia. Those who didn't were butchered by the infected as they poured in through an underground entrance. Tanner couldn't help but feel a sense of responsibility for those deaths, knowing full well that he had enabled the uprising with his incessant search for President Pike.

With the urging of their two unwanted passengers, Tanner turned right onto Blueridge Mountain Road. Directly ahead lay a large security building, the awning reaching out over the road. Four infected men in military uniforms stood guard with M4 rifles in hand. Tanner pulled in behind Korn and the rest of the convoy as the guards checked each car before waving it through.

As he inched the Mercedes closer, one of the men came alongside the vehicle. The guard's skin was pocked, and his eyes as black as soot, but his disfigurement wasn't as serious as the worst afflicted. He motioned for Tanner to roll down the window.

"You are to follow General Korn to our headquarters. If you do anything other than that, you will be considered hostile. Do you understand?" Given his condition, the man's speech was remarkably clear.

"Loud and clear."

The guard motioned for him to go ahead, and Tanner eased in behind Korn's Jeep. Other members of the convoy broke off, heading to different parts of the compound. By the time they pulled in front of a three-story metal and stone building, the procession had pared down to a handful of vehicles.

Samantha looked out her window as soldiers marched by in small formations. In the distance, she could see a grass-covered airfield with a dozen neatly parked helicopters.

"They've got an army, a *real* army."

"I told you," said Issa. "They're changing, becoming more human again."

One of the infected men grunted from the back seat, motioning for everyone to get out.

Tanner glanced back at their unwanted passengers.

"Smiley here apparently didn't get that memo."

They unloaded from the Mercedes and were escorted into the building. It was stuffy, and the air reeked of body odor. Thankfully, the temperature was still mild enough not to make it unbearable. A stairwell off to the right led both upstairs and down.

Korn turned to them. "You stay. I speak with Mother."

Without waiting for a reply, he turned and headed for the stairwell. The two men he had appointed earlier remained behind. It took nearly twenty minutes for Korn to return, and when he did, he marched directly up to Issa.

"Issa come. Tanner and girl stay."

Tanner studied his face, hoping to determine whether something had gone wrong. It proved impossible. Korn only ever wore two expressions. The first said, *I'm going to kill you,* and the second, *I'm not going to kill you right now, but I might kill you later.*

"Just so you know," muttered Samantha, "I do have a name."

Korn ignored her. "Issa come," he repeated, this time motioning with his hand.

Issa turned and gave Tanner a quick kiss on the cheek.

"No matter what happens, keep your cool," she whispered. "They're looking for a reason to surrender to their baser instincts."

"Aren't we all?"

She squeezed his hand and turned to follow Korn down the stairs.

"Where do you think that leads?" Samantha said, eyeing the staircase.

"Down," he answered.

She rolled her eyes. "Sometimes, I wonder why I even bother asking you things."

"You and me both."

They stood waiting for another ten long minutes with a whole lot of nothing happening. As the minutes passed, Samantha grew increasingly bored.

She turned and studied their two infected guardians. One was almost Tanner's height, but lacked thirty or forty pounds. His face was disfigured, jaw and cheekbones so prominent that they looked like they had been built up with plumber's putty. The other man was short and thick and had a face as flat as a bulldog's.

"I'm Samantha. What're your names?"

Neither man spoke.

She pursed her lips. "I think I'll call you Musketeer, because of your pointy chin. And you," she said, gesturing to the other man, "you can be Tillman on account of reminding me of a bulldog I once saw that could ride a skateboard? Crazy, right?"

Again, they said nothing.

"How do you two like it here?" She looked around. "It looks nice. Better than down in the tunnels, that's for sure. Do you guys ever get back down there?"

They stared at her with passionless black eyes.

She thought for a moment. "Hey, I know. Let's have a joke to liven things up. Knock, knock." She waited expectantly.

Musketeer and Tillman looked to one other but neither answered.

"Oh come on," she said. "Knock, knock."

Tillman's lips parted like he might speak.

"Ye-e-es," she coaxed, "go on."

He closed his mouth defiantly.

She shook her head. "Believe me, I can do this all day. Knock, knock."

Musketeer growled and said, "Who's there?"

She smiled. "Broken pencil."

He looked to Tillman, who only offered a slight shrug.

"Broken pencil who?"

"Never mind. It's pointless."

Both men took a moment and then made noises that sounded somewhere between a chortle and a gag.

"Good, right? You can use it later if you want." She turned to Tanner. "They like my jokes."

"They might be the only ones."

"Funny."

Korn reappeared from the stairwell, but there was no sign of Issa.

Tanner took a step toward him.

"Where is she?"

Musketeer and Tillman both puffed up as if readying for a fight.

Korn waved them back as he motioned to Tanner.

"You and girl come. See Mother."

Tanner thought about pushing the point of Issa's whereabouts but recalled her words of warning.

"Come on, Sam. Let's go see what Mother has to say."

"Okay," she said. "But you should know that if things get dicey, I've already used my best joke."

๛ ๛

Korn, Musketeer, and Tillman escorted Tanner and Samantha down a long flight of stairs. At the bottom, they followed a series of corridors to a thick steel blast door, sitting open. As they passed through the doorway, Samantha rubbed her palm across the shiny metal.

"It's like we're going inside a bank vault."

"More like a bunker."

"Is it the one you went into with Korn?"

"Same bunker. Different door."

"So it leads down to the tunnels?"

"It must."

They continued on, weaving through corridors lit by dim incandescent bulbs. Along the way, they passed small groups of infected. All of them wore military uniforms, and many carried notebooks or rolled-up maps.

Samantha leaned closer to Tanner and whispered, "They're planning something."

He nodded.

They followed Korn to a large double door at the end of the corridor. Two of Mother's troglodytes stood guard. Like Korn, they were larger than normal men, tall and thick with muscle. But unlike him, their hair had fallen out, their faces now a patchwork of boils and blistered flesh. The last time Tanner and Samantha had seen troglodytes, the fearsome creatures had been armed with nail boards. These two carried M870 pump shotguns. Times were a changing.

Korn turned to Tanner and Samantha and held out his hands.

"Guns."

There seemed no point in arguing about it, so they handed over their shotgun and rifle. Samantha did, however, keep the derringer tucked neatly away. Once their weapons were taken, Korn led them into the room, while Musketeer and Tillman remained outside.

When Tanner and Samantha had last seen Mother, she was a corpulent blob lying on a pile of blankets, babies suckling her six flabby breasts. Now, they stared at a woman whose face was unblemished, beautiful even, with long, perfectly brushed black hair and skin rich with color. She remained a behemoth, easily eight feet tall and topping five hundred pounds, but clothes once consisting of stitched-together bed sheets had been replaced with a handmade dress woven from a patchwork of brightly colored silk. She sat on a thick stack of cushions, straight and tall, and there was an air of elegance that made her seem every bit the queen.

Mother studied Tanner and Samantha as if reading their thoughts. When she finally spoke, her voice was silky smooth, almost to the point of harmony.

"How interesting that we should meet again. It seems that fate is never above reminding us that everything is possible."

As Samantha had done with their first meeting, she stepped forward and did a little curtsy.

"Your Highness."

Mother acknowledged her with a smile before turning her attention to Tanner.

"The last time you stood before me, you promised a new world for my people. At the time, I couldn't fully appreciate your words. But now, now I see."

There was something about her words that hinted of trouble in paradise.

"I promised to help your people escape the tunnels, and that's what I did."

"After which, you vanished without giving me so much as a chance to offer thanks."

"I thought it better if we moved on. Sam and I have a hard time staying put, don't we, Sam?"

She shrugged. "Lately, we've been doing okay."

He cut his eyes at her.

"What I meant to say was that we've been traveling a bit less than normal. But we did just get back from flooding a nuclear plant, if that helps." She looked over at Tanner for his approval.

He closed his eyes.

"Worst of all," said Mother, "you took our beloved Issa." She turned her glassy black eyes toward Korn. "Even my most trusted general felt her loss."

"Issa and I wed through your colony's claiming ceremony. Korn knows that better than anyone."

Mother nodded. "True, but what a man knows and what he feels are often not the same."

Korn shifted his feet around, obviously uncomfortable about the direction in which the conversation had turned.

"No matter," Mother said, waving a hand. "You and Issa have both returned. And her with child, no less." She paused. "My question is why?"

"I'm sure Issa explained that she wanted to share the good news with you. She was certain you'd be delighted."

"Delighted, you say?"

He nodded. "While a lesser woman might feel threatened, she knew that you, as the colony's beloved matron, would surely feel only happiness at seeing others experience the joy of childbirth." Tanner knew that he was laying it on thick, but the dance was underway with all its flourishes.

Mother smiled. "Of course I'm delighted. It does, however, pose a challenge."

"What kind of challenge?"

"How do you think our women will react to the revelation that they can only become pregnant by outsiders? It would create an unhealthy dependency, don't you think?"

Tanner considered pointing out a very different unhealthy dependency but decided it was not in his or Samantha's best interest. Instead, he said, "I suppose. Perhaps it's best then if only you and a handful of your trusted advisors know of her condition."

She smiled. "On that we find ourselves in agreement. Perhaps it will make things easier going forward."

"What does that mean?"

"Only that I haven't yet decided how best to handle this. Perhaps when the baby is born, it will become clearer."

Tanner didn't like the sound of that at all. They sure as hell weren't sticking around Mount Weather until Issa gave birth.

"We'll be sure to send word."

Mother took a deep breath and slowly let it out.

"You used to be like us. Now," she waved her hand, "now, you are not. Can you explain that?"

Samantha jumped in. "We had blood in our veins from the first person ever infected. It eventually wore off, so now we're back to normal. Uh, I mean now we're back to looking more like regular people." She puckered her lips, still not quite liking the way that it sounded. "What I mean to say—"

"I think she's got it, Sam," Tanner said, cutting her off.

"Interesting," Mother said with a nod. "You of all of the outsiders were able to experience our way of life when we struggled so dearly. Perhaps that makes you different than the others."

Tanner remained quiet, sensing that she was finally getting to the point.

Mother made a pained expression. "Not a day passes that I don't hear of horrors being inflicted on my people."

"I'm confused," Samantha said, raising her hand as if she were in school. "I thought your people were all here in Mount Weather."

"No, dear. My people stretch across this wicked land. All who are infected need someone to love and nurture them."

"Wow. That sounds like a big job." She found herself staring at Mother's enormous midsection. "No offense… Your Highness."

Mother turned back to Tanner. "Do you know what Korn was doing when he found Issa?"

Tanner thought of the dead bodies in front of the church.

"Waging war, by the looks of it."

"You're more right than you know. I sent him to destroy a community that was selling my children into slavery."

She waited to see Tanner's reaction. There wasn't much. He had seen his fair share of injustices in the world, and the idea that folks were selling one another into bondage didn't even raise an eyebrow.

Mother continued. "Women and children were chained up like animals and forced to serve their would-be masters."

Tanner glanced at Korn. "I'm confident he showed the slavers the error of their ways."

She smiled. "Of that you can be sure. But it points to a larger problem."

"What's that?"

"Those of us who were infected are no longer considered human. At best, we're treated as outcasts. And at worst…" Her jaw tightened. "At worst, we're treated as food. Tell me, Tanner Raines, what would you do if someone hunted your family to slaughter them like livestock?"

"Simple," he said. "I'd kill every last one of them."

She nodded with satisfaction. "Yes, I believe you would. Like slavery, cannibalism is not a sin that can be forgiven. That is why my armies will soon put an end to it." She seemed to lose herself in thought, but when her eyes refocused, they were clear. "Do you believe in destiny?"

Tanner looked at Samantha. They had come together under the unlikeliest of circumstances, and through nothing short of a string of miracles, they had survived long enough to become a family. Destiny, while making no sense whatsoever, seemed to describe their relationship perfectly.

"She asked you a question," whispered Samantha.

"I know she asked me a question," he grumbled. "I'm trying to decide how to answer it."

"Ah," she said, nodding. "I thought maybe you'd tuned out. You do that sometimes."

He turned back to Mother. "I think there are times when things occur for a reason. If you want to call that destiny, fine."

Mother nodded thoughtfully. "I do as well, which leads me to believe that your arrival here is not mere coincidence. You came to us once when we were in need. And now you arrive again at a time when we struggle to make sense of the dark world around us. I think our fates are intertwined."

"I'm here for Issa. Nothing more."

"That may be why you came here, but it's not to say that something else didn't guide your steps."

Samantha leaned close to him. "Is she talking about Sister Margaret?"

"Shh," he said, waiting for Mother to continue.

"You once led my army into battle. Perhaps that is to be your place again."

"Against who? The cannibals?"

"No. General Korn will leave tomorrow to dispatch them."

Korn nodded proudly.

"I'm speaking of our greatest enemy of all, the government that threatens to subjugate my people under the guise of law."

It took Tanner a moment to understand what she was proposing.

"You're going to attack the New Colony?" He shook his head. "That's suicide."

"You think we're too weak?"

Tanner knew better than to take that bait.

"I think you have too much love for your soldiers to engage in such a dangerous war."

"There is simply no other way. If we do not kill them, they will kill us."

"Even so, a direct attack on the colony would almost certainly fail."

"Many said those same words about this place when we cowered in the tunnels. You showed us that all things are possible. Perhaps you will do so again."

Tanner found himself caring more for the infected than he probably should have. Perhaps it was his relationship with Issa. Or perhaps it was some long-lasting side effect of Dr. Jarvis's tainted blood.

"There has to be another way."

"If there is, I don't see it."

Tanner didn't see it either, but an attack on the New Colony was not something he could support, let alone lead.

"If I can find a way to save your people without you having to send them to war, will you release Issa to return home with us?"

Mother thought for a moment before answering.

"Yes. I would do that, on the condition that you tell no one else in the colony of her pregnancy."

"All right. Give me until morning to come up with a plan."

Mother studied him. "Why do you believe that you can resolve this so quickly when we have spent months considering every option?"

"Maybe I think differently."

"That's true," seconded Samantha. "*Very* differently. Some might say it's almost like he doesn't think at all."

Tanner nudged her with his shoulder.

"Very well," said Mother. "But when we next meet, General Korn will already be marching on the butcher who feeds on my people. If you and I can come to an agreement, he will return home after that battle. If we cannot, his army will move on to destroy the New Colony, with or without your help."

Mother called for Musketeer and Tillman to be brought into the room. When they stood before her, she said, "Take them to be with Issa, and in the morning, return them to me. No one is to see or speak to them. Do you understand?"

Both men nodded and motioned for Tanner and Samantha to leave the room. As he exited, Tanner overheard Mother issuing instructions to Korn.

"General, give your troops the night to rest and enjoy the company of their wives, for tomorrow, they will march on the butcher of Smithfield."

CHAPTER 22

With the tournament over, the crowd disbanded to settle debts and take care of daily activities. Many came to pat Mason on the back and offer words of congratulations. He endured it only because, short of shooting them, he really didn't have a choice in the matter. When the field was finally clearing, Jessie appeared with Bowie at her side. Before Mason could even say hello, she rushed over and hugged him, laying her head against his chest.

Without looking up, she said, "I don't pray very often. Not because I don't believe. I just always figured He had better things to do than listen to a nobody cowgirl from Virginia. But today... today I prayed." She leaned back and looked into his eyes. "And here you are, alive and well. I guess He had time for me after all."

Mason smiled. "I guess He did."

Bowie bumped against his leg, and Mason leaned over to give the dog a quick pat.

"Good to see you too, boy." He looked back up at Jessie. "Where's Gunsmoke?"

She gestured toward the RV. "I have a feeling he's going to be one of those sleepy cats."

"Is there any other kind?"

Their attention was drawn to Ramsey and another man who were carrying The Reverend's body from the field.

"I didn't watch the gunfight," she said. "I couldn't."

Mason nodded. "It's all right."

She reached out and hooked an arm through his.

"Folks are talking about you like you're some kind of hero."

Mason didn't feel like a hero. He had set out to change peoples' minds about the tournament. In the end, he feared that he might only have given them a stronger taste for blood. Rather than allow that to ruin the moment, he reminded himself that wars were won one battle at a time. Every victory was to be celebrated.

Leroy wandered over, a smile on his lips. Even though his gunfighters were finished, the camp's tournament had turned into a story for the ages.

"I always knew you were wily," he said, patting Mason on the shoulder, "but working on The Reverend the way you did. That, my friend, was pure genius."

Mason offered a token nod. "I'm assuming you'll honor our deal."

"My word is my bond. I'll have security escort the prisoners out within the hour. Not sure where they're gonna go, but that's for them to worry about."

Mason turned and gestured toward Ramsey.

"What he did wasn't right."

"If, in fact, he did anything at all."

Leroy was right. There was no real proof that Ramsey had been working with Wilde. It could have just as easily been one of his men. Hell, it could have been Leroy for that matter. It was an injustice he would have to let go.

Mason extended his hand. "In case I don't see you again."

Leroy shook it. "Take care of my Supergrade."

"Count on it." He turned to Jessie. "What do you say we go find your father?"

"I was hoping you'd say that."

With Jessie and Bowie at his side, Mason returned to the RV. He went around to the trailer and began picking through the junkers' belongings. Most of it he decided to leave behind, but he did move the food, ammunition, some bandages, and a box of batteries to the RV. When he had finished, he unhooked the trailer, confident that someone would discover it before the day was through.

He was about to load up when Jessie nudged him and said, "Look. They're coming this way."

Mason turned to see Ramsey and two men armed with riot guns approaching.

Bowie moved forward to stand protectively in front of them, his tail tucked and hair standing on end.

Ramsey and his men came to within about ten feet before stopping.

"Better pull in that mangy dog, or I'm liable to shoot it," he threatened.

"It'd be the last thing you ever did," said Mason. "What is it you want?"

Ramsey let his eyes settle on Jessie.

"Oh, there's a whole lot of things I want. But right now, I'm here to tell you it's time to go. Your welcome permit is hereby revoked."

Mason didn't bother to question his authority. This wasn't coming from Leroy. Even so, it wasn't worth a fight.

"We were just about to leave."

"I didn't say that your little filly had to go." He turned to Jessie and ran his fingers over the melted side of his face. "I realize this can be a little off-putting at first, but believe me, once the lights are turned down, you'll never know the difference." He let his tongue snake out to lick the edge of the scar. "You might even come to like it."

Ramsey was obviously trying to initiate a fight that had been a long time coming.

Mason squared himself, letting his hand settle on the butt of his Supergrade.

"I'm game if you are."

Jessie reached forward and gently touched his arm.

"It's okay. Let's just go."

As they started to back away, one of Ramsey's thugs kicked at Bowie, perhaps thinking he could scare the dog off. What he got in return was a mouthful of teeth latched onto his foot. The man shook his leg from side to side, shrieking as blood dripped down the side of his boot.

"Bowie!" Mason shouted, reaching down to pull him off.

The dog released his bite, but as he did, Ramsey drew his pistol. Before he could bring it up, a gunshot rang out, and a dime-sized hole appeared at the base of his throat. He stumbled back, twisting as he fell to land face down in the dirt.

Mason looked over to find Jessie standing with her Vaquero drawn, one hand holding the weapon, the other lying ready on the hammer. A thin trail of smoke rose from the end of the barrel.

He turned and faced the two guards. One was balancing on one foot, and the other had eyes the size of silver dollars. Both were a hair away from making a mistake that would cost them their lives, either by his hand or Jessie's.

"This is the moment when you choose whether you have a long life or a short one. Choose wisely," he said, ready to draw the Supergrade.

Both men clutched their shotguns, looking at Ramsey's body and then back to one another. Bowie stood in front of them, growling with blood-stained teeth. This was not a fight they were going to win, and they seemed to know it. The only part they seemed uncertain about was how to get out of it alive.

Mason answered that by saying, "Put your shotguns on the ground, and go tell Leroy what happened. Keep in mind that if you lie to him, you'll answer to me."

They carefully set their shotguns on the ground and hurried away, one man helping the other as he hobbled across the parking lot.

∿ ∿

It wasn't until they were clear of Grey's Point that Mason finally began to relax. The past twenty-four hours had been filled with all manner of conflict. But with Jessie sitting beside him and Bowie snoring in the back-seat, the world seemed as right as it had been in a long time.

Jessie stared out the window, humming softly to herself. She hadn't said a word since the shooting. Mason had found that people reacted very differently to killing someone. Some became overwhelmed with guilt or shame. Others felt sick. Still others felt exhilarated, as if they had just climbed a mountain. He couldn't tell which of those, if any, Jessie was feeling.

"Are you okay?"

"I'm fine," she said, turning to face him. "And that's what worries me. I just killed a man, and I'm not shaking or anything."

"You didn't have a choice."

"I know," she said, glancing back at Bowie. "But shouldn't I feel some-thing? Sadness? Anger? Something?"

"There's no right way about these things."

"He was a bad man. I guess I know that deep down. Maybe it's helping me to cope with it."

Mason nodded. "Maybe."

"Do me a favor, will you?"

"Anything."

"Don't tell Daddy about my shooting that man."

"All right. But I'm sure he'd understand."

"I know, but he'd also go out of his way to try and make me feel better. I don't want that." She shrugged. "I don't need it."

Mason turned to her. "You're a strong woman, Jessie. Like your mother, I suspect."

Her face lit up with what was perhaps the most beautiful smile he had ever seen.

"Thank you. You don't know how much that means to me." Her eyes became distant as she envisioned her mother's face. "She was more than just my mother. She made me into who I am. Maybe there was someone in your life like that too?"

Mason thought of his father. Despite all his flaws, Tanner was probably more responsible than anyone for the man Mason had become. His lessons were never in words, but rather through actions, some to be admired, and some to be denounced. Throughout it all, though, he had managed to instill a deep-rooted sense of justice. That guiding principle had led Mason to fight for his country and serve as a marshal, doling out retribution to men who believed they were above judgment.

"Yeah," he said softly. "Maybe there was."

Both of them saw the Pilot House Inn approaching on the right. Jack's truck was parked out front, and he stood beside the road, one hand shielding his eyes from the sun.

Jessie leaned over and kissed Mason's cheek, her hand sliding down to rest on his leg.

"Could I ask for one other teensy little favor?"

"What's that?"

"Could we keep last night to ourselves? Daddy might *not* understand that."

"Oh Lord," he said, cracking a smile. "What have I gotten myself into?"

Tanner and Samantha were escorted to one of several large white hangars on the eastern edge of the compound. Windows along both sides of the building were open to allow for airflow, and bed linens had been hung in front of the windows to provide a modicum of privacy for its inhabitants.

Musketeer pushed open the door and motioned for them to enter.

Samantha leaned her head inside. "Pee-ew, it stinks in there."

"Go," he said, nudging her inside.

Tanner quickly stepped in behind her, hoping to avoid an unnecessary pipe to the back. As soon as they were inside, the door slammed shut. They could hear Musketeer and Tillman discussing who would guard the front door and who the back. It was going to be a long night for both.

Tanner and Samantha turned to study the military-style dormitory. Dozens of bunks and tall metal lockers spanned the length of the building. While it looked like it could house forty or fifty people, only Issa stood inside, nervously pacing in front of one of the windows.

As soon as they entered, she raced over and jumped into Tanner's arms.

"Thank heavens!" she breathed.

Tanner held Issa for nearly a minute before setting her down. Ever since her disappearance, a small part of him had feared that their time as a family had forever been cut short. Holding her in his arms brought not only a profound sense of relief but also a feeling that life could once again return to normal.

"Where are we?" Samantha asked, swinging open one of the lockers. Inside were military uniforms, toiletries, and boots, no doubt left behind by fleeing soldiers.

Issa couldn't hide her anger. "We're in a prison, that's where."

"But why?"

"Because Mother wants to keep this baby a secret," she said, rubbing her stomach.

"But what about Korn and the others? They already saw you."

"The only ones who saw me were loyal soldiers, not to mention *men*. They would have every reason to keep my pregnancy a secret."

"Ah, because they don't want their wives finding out?" she said, catching on.

"Exactly."

Samantha looked over at Tanner. "I sure hope you figure something out."

Issa turned to him. "What's she talking about?"

Before Tanner could explain, Samantha said, "Tanner has until morning to come up with a plan. Otherwise, we'll probably have to live here forever."

"A plan for what?"

"To save everyone so they don't have to go to war with the New Colony."

"What! They're going to war?"

"They are if we don't come up with something better," said Tanner. "Apparently, Mother's had enough of her people being treated as second-class citizens."

"But she can't win against the colony."

"That's what I told her."

"And?"

"And she thinks I'm some kind of divine sign that things might go her way."

"What does she—" Issa stopped as things suddenly became clear. "She wants you to lead her army again, with Korn."

He nodded. "I guess she figures if it worked once, it might work again."

"You're not going to do it." Issa crossed her arms defiantly. "I won't allow it."

"I won't allow it either," he said, hoping to soften her mood. "Which is why I told her I'd find another way."

"What other way?"

"Haven't come up with that just yet." He yawned. "Just need a little shut-eye to get the old creative juices flowing." Tanner flopped down on the closest bunk, the entire structure nearly collapsing under his weight. "Now, ladies, if you don't mind…"

Taking her cue, Samantha started down the long row of bunks, carefully patting each to determine its softness.

"Are these things assigned, or do we just pick one?"

ॐ ॐ

Tanner awoke to the sound of whispering. He sat up and looked around the barracks. Darkness was starting to take hold, but there remained enough light for him to see Issa standing beside a large open window, the makeshift curtain pulled to one side.

He slid off the bunk and walked over. To his surprise, nearly a dozen infected women huddled outside.

"Is this a jailbreak?" he said quietly.

Issa smiled. "No, nothing like that. These women are all widows, staying in the adjacent hangar. Prisoners in their own right as they await new husbands." She grabbed Tanner's hand and pulled him closer. "Come on. They won't bite."

"You say that, but I know otherwise," he muttered.

Issa pulled him to the window so that the women could see him better. Some stared with wary eyes. Most, however, seemed more interested than afraid.

"Sisters, this is the man I was telling you about. My husband Tanner."

An attractive woman with red hair reached through the open window and slapped his beefy shoulder. Satisfied, she nodded to the other women, many of whom cooed excitedly.

Tanner turned to Issa. "That some kind of welcoming ritual?"

"Something like that," she said with a smile.

"Am I good to get a bit more shut-eye?" he asked, stifling a yawn.

Issa nodded. "Get some rest." She looked off toward Samantha, who had chosen a bunk at the opposite end of the hangar. "Check on her too, will you?"

"Of course," he said, trudging off.

When he reached Samantha, she was just putting away her toothbrush.

"What are you doing all the way down here?"

"I figured you two might want your privacy. You know, to kiss and all."

There was something about the way she said it that didn't quite sound on the up and up.

"Uh-huh. What's the real reason?"

"What? Can't a girl do a good deed?"

"In my experience, no," he said, staring her down.

"Fine. A person who wasn't as nice as I am might point out that you snore like Godzilla."

He chuckled and reached out to ruffle her hair.

"Get some sleep, kiddo. I have a feeling tomorrow's going to be a busy day."

She stepped closer and awkwardly wrapped both arms around his waist. It was part of their nightly ritual, but every time she hugged him, he couldn't help but feel a lump in his throat.

"Goodnight, Tanner," she said softly.

"Night, Sam," he said, kissing the top of her head.

As Samantha crawled into bed, Tanner went back to his own bunk and sprawled out. He lay for nearly an hour, sliding in and out of consciousness as he waited for Issa to join him.

When she finally came over and sat on the edge of the mattress, she said, "I don't like this."

He scooted over. "Darlin', there's always room for two."

She patted his hand. "I'm talking about what Mother's doing."

"Give me a little time. I'll come up with something."

"You don't understand. Even if you find a way to avoid the war, I'm not sure she has any intention of letting me leave."

"She promised me that she would." He glanced back at the open window, remembering that Mother's offer had been contingent on them not telling anyone about the baby. So much for that little caveat.

"Even so," she said, "I'm worried. When Mother saw that I was pregnant, she seemed troubled."

"She should be. If the other women decide to start having kids with uninfected men, she'll lose some of her leverage."

"It's more than that. Mother's worried that it could cause humans and our kind to intermingle."

"Maybe that would be a good thing."

"Of course, it would. But right now she's so filled with anger that she needs there to be a defining line between good and evil, us and them. This," she said, rubbing her stomach, "blurs that line."

"I'll get us out of here," he said confidently. "One way or another."

"I believe you. I do." She reached out and placed his hand on her stomach. "But *this* will never be known, and that saddens me in a way I can't even begin to describe."

"Darlin', you just paraded that little Butterball in front of a dozen women. Word's going to get out."

"Yes. But without proof, it won't be enough."

Issa lowered herself next to him, resting her head on his arm. They lay like that for a while, her occasionally twisting to look at his wristwatch.

After the third time, he said, "Okay, let's hear it."

Issa slowly sat up. "It occurs to me that we have an opportunity, one that Mother may not have considered."

Tanner scooted up and propped his back against the end of the bunk.

"If you're thinking about us going out a window—"

"No, no, nothing like that."

"All right then. What's on your mind?"

"I'm going to ask you to do something, something that you're going to insist on saying no to. But I need for you to do it anyway." Issa clearly wasn't asking for just any old favor.

"There's nothing you could ask me to do that I wouldn't do. Not unless it meant hurting Sam in some way."

Issa shook her head softly. "It's not about Samantha. In fact, it's important that she know nothing about it." She took a deep breath but seemed to have trouble letting it back out. "You and I… we're great together, right?"

He nodded. "The best."

She brought her hands to her stomach.

"And when this baby came along, it was like a miracle from God."

"I'd like to think I had a little something to do with it."

She grinned, but there was a worry in her eyes that she couldn't hide.

"You most certainly did. And that's precisely what I need to ask of you."

Tanner furrowed his brow. "I'm not following."

Issa sat up straight and looked over at the open window.

"I want you to give those women what you gave me."

Tanner wasn't sure he had heard her correctly. Did Issa just ask him to sleep with a roomful of other women? He shook his head, trying to shake the madness loose.

"Are you asking me to—"

"Yes," she breathed.

He reached for her hand. "Issa, I'm yours. I don't need any other women. Lord knows, most nights you're more than I can handle."

"That part's true," she said, smiling. "But this isn't about me. Or you." She turned back to the window and glimpsed faces peeking in. "It's about them."

Tanner saw them too. Women huddling in the dark, waiting on some kind of cue to climb through the open window. To what? Him?

"Believe me, those women want nothing to do with me."

"You're wrong about that. I've spoken with them. Many see it the same way."

"What way?"

"They believe that you're special. You were one of us for a while. And even though you've changed back, they still sense a little of the blood flowing in your veins." She looked down at her stomach. "They want children, but they're terrified of the outside world. Mother has made certain of that."

"But I'm married. To you."

"Don't you think I know that?" Her voice rose, and tears pooled in the corners of her eyes.

"Hey," he said, pulling her to him. "Don't be sad."

"I'm not sad," she said, driving a fist against his chest. "I'm angry!"

"At me?"

"No, of course not. I'm angry at Mother. Her selfishness is forcing us to do this. And believe me, I don't like it any more than you." She took a breath, and her eyes softened. "You must think I'm the lowliest of women for even asking this of you."

"Are you kidding? I could never see you as anything but the proud warrior I fell in love with down in those tunnels."

They sat for a moment, holding one another while they let what had been said slowly settle over them.

Tanner was the first to speak.

"If you ask me to sleep with those women, I will, because I know that asking me is the hardest thing you could ever do. But you should know that if our places were reversed, I'd let the whole world rot in hell before I shared you with another man."

She let her head fall to his shoulder, as tears rolled down her cheeks.

"That's the kindest thing you've ever said to me. Truly." She lifted her head and gently kissed him on the lips. "And I love you for it."

"You're sure about this?"

"As sure as I've ever been about anything. But I want you to remember something." Her eyes tightened.

"Okay…"

"This isn't about sex, Tanner Raines. And you'd better not forget that."

"Not about sex. Got it."

"Think of it like donating at one of those doctor's offices."

Tanner looked over at the faces of eager women peering in through the window. They didn't look like any doctor he had ever known.

"You might want to tell them to tailor their expectations. I'm not Superman, you know."

Her lips turned up. "We both know that's not true."

❧ ❧

The first woman to visit Tanner was a tall brunette, thin to the point of being bony, with skin so white that it seemed to glow in the moonlight. She was hungry, and it wasn't for food. Their encounter was brief and violent, and it left Tanner with scratches across his chest and neck, not to mention the feeling of having just been violated.

The second and third women came as a pair, perhaps fearing that if they didn't share, there would be little left for the other. One had shoulder-length blonde hair and a body as voluptuous as Salma Hayek's, and the other was a redhead with small breasts but legs that went all the way to the floor. Fortunately, both women seemed to appreciate that the situation was incredibly awkward for everyone involved, and thus did their best to make it as enjoyable as possible. When they had finished, each kissed Tanner on opposite cheeks and used their clothes to quickly cover and slip away into the night.

With two sets of women more or less satisfied, Tanner felt drained and exhausted. There seemed little point in continuing. Unfortunately, the women didn't seem to agree. They came to him over and over, without apology, or even understanding. They had been promised a prize, and by Pothos, they intended to see that it was delivered in full.

❧ ❧

Lying in the dark hangar, Tanner listened as Issa slept beside him. He was completely spent, sweat and bodily fluid slowly drying on his naked body. He lay with his eyes open, Issa nestled against him, her warm body caressing his in ways that the other women couldn't begin to understand.

She seemed immensely grateful, relieved even. Tanner was relieved too. It was over, and he might never be the same. Eight women. Two long hours. Every one of them taking a little part of him with them. Issa had assured him that it would not be about sex, but she couldn't have been more wrong. Sex was all it was about. Raw and powerful, and devoid of any feeling whatsoever.

He let out a sigh. *Sex with a roomful of strange women. Poor, pitiful me.*

If Tanner were being honest, he could admit that he had enjoyed the sexual novelty of it all. Of course, he could never utter those words in Issa's presence or risk losing a testicle. No, he thought. This would forever be remembered as the ultimate sacrifice made only for the greater good. Safer that way.

Sleep came for him like a leopard creeping ever closer. He fought it off a little longer to give the night's rich memories time to take root. He let his mind wander one final time, recalling his and Samantha's journey to Mount Weather. Characters flashed through his mind like actors on a stage—the violent hitchhikers who capitalized on the goodwill of others, the poor infected girl who had fallen victim to a sniper's bullet, Sister Margaret and her wayward nuns, Dr. Langdon and his twisted plans for a better society. All of it was behind him, and for that he was thankful.

Issa's soft snores and gentle stirring seemed a stark contrast to the cold, lifeless DeJarnette Center that he and Samantha had explored. His mind's eye slowly settled on the image of the woman's hand he had dragged from the fire, the bright shine of her once precious ring contrasting with the charred bloodstained bone that it was wrapped around. There was a time when such a bauble would have cost a man his entire fortune. Now, it was worth only the weight of its gold.

The word played in his mind like it had some unappreciated importance. *Gold.* The famous bouncer-turned-actor Mr. T. had once said, "I believe in the Golden Rule—The Man with the Gold… Rules."

Tanner let his eyes drift closed. He had Mother's answer.

Gold would give her both power and influence, not only with the New Colony but with warlords, militia leaders, and everyone else who sought to rebuild in the apocalyptic wasteland. And Tanner knew of the one place in the world to find enough gold to turn her community of outcasts into one of the world's wealthiest city-states.

His mouth turned up into a smile as he imagined Samantha's bewildered face when he told her his plan, a plan that involved the plundering of the most famous gold reserve in the entire world.

Fort Knox.

The Survivalist
adventure continues with
National Treasure...

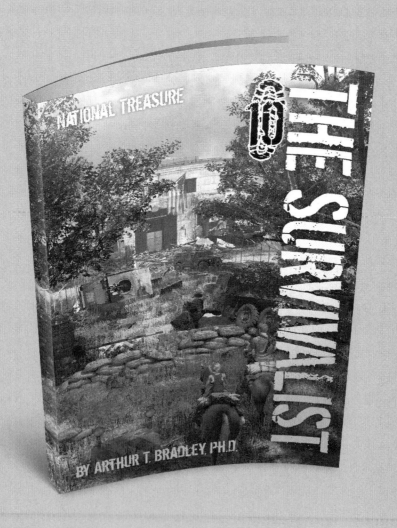

ONLINE INFO

For information on my books and practical disaster preparedness, see:

http://disasterpreparer.com

CONTACT ME

If you enjoyed this book and are looking forward to the sequel, send me a short note (*arthur@disasterpreparer.com*). Like most authors, I enjoy hearing from my readers. Also, if you have time, perhaps you would be kind enough to post a positive review on Amazon.com.

I frequently travel the world giving disaster preparedness seminars. If you are a member of a church, business, or civic organization and would like to sponsor a disaster preparedness event, please keep me in mind.

Best wishes to you and your family!

FREE NEWSLETTER

To sign up for the *Practical Prepper Newsletter*, send an email to:

newsletter@disasterpreparer.com

Do you have a Plan?

Ninety-nine percent of the time the world spins like a top, the skies are clear, and your refrigerator is full of milk and cheese. But know with certainty that the world is a dangerous place. Storms rage, fires burn, and diseases spread. No one is ever completely safe. We all live as part of a very complex ecosystem that is unpredictable and willing to kill us without remorse or pause.

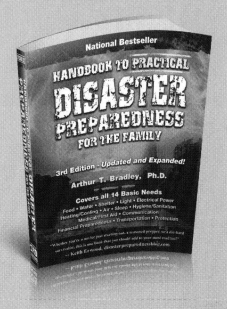

This handbook will help you to establish a practical disaster preparedness plan for your entire family. The 3rd Edition has been expanded to cover every important topic, including food storage, water purification, electricity generation, backup heating, firearms, communication systems, disaster preparedness networks, evacuations, life-saving first aid, and much more. Working through the steps identified in this book will prepare your family for nearly any disaster, whether it be natural disasters making the news daily (e.g., earthquakes, tornadoes, hurricanes, floods, and tsunamis), or high-impact global events, such as electromagnetic pulse attacks, radiological emergencies, solar storms, or our country's impending financial collapse. The new larger 8" x 10" format includes easy-to-copy worksheets to help organize your family's preparedness plans.

Available at Disasterpreparer.com and online retailers

Learn to Become a PREPPER

If your community were hit with a major disaster, such as an earthquake, flood, hurricane, or radiological release, how would you handle it? Would you be forced to fall into line with hundreds of thousands of others who are so woefully unprepared? Or do you possess the knowledge and supplies to adapt and survive? Do you have a carefully stocked pantry, a method to retrieve and purify water, a source for generating electricity, and the means to protect your family from desperate criminals? In short, are you a *prepper*?

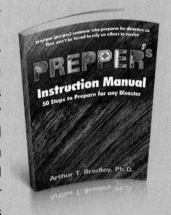

This book comprises fifty of the most important steps that any individual or family can take to prepare for a wide range of disasters. Every step is complete, clearly described, and actionable. They cover every aspect of disaster preparedness, including assessing the threats, making a plan, storing food, shoring up your home, administering first aid, creating a safe room, gathering important papers, learning to shoot, generating electricity, burying the dead, tying knots, keeping warm, and much more.

Recent events have reminded us that our world is a dangerous place, whether it is a deadly tsunami, a nuclear meltdown, or a stock market collapse. Our lifestyle, and even our very existence, is forever uncertain. Join the quickly growing community of individuals and families determined to stand ready.

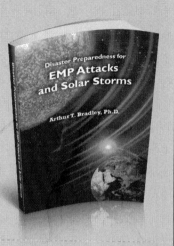